SO
MUCH
OF LIFE
AHEAD

HEARTS
OF THE
CHILDREN

VOL. 5

SO MUCH OF LIFE AHEAD

A NOVEL BY

DEAN HUGHES

DESERET
BOOK
SALT LAKE CITY, UTAH

First printing in hardbound 2005.
First printing in paperbound 2009.

Library of Congress Cataloging-in-Publication Data

Hughes, Dean, 1943–
   So much of life ahead / Dean Hughes.
     p. cm. — (Hearts of the children; v. 5)
   ISBN-10: 1-59038-472-5 (hardbound: alk. paper)
   ISBN-13: 978-1-60641-176-6 (paperbound)
   1. Mormon families—Fiction. 2. Salt Lake City (Utah)—Fiction.
I. Title. II. Series.
   PS3558.U3 6S67   2005
   813'.54—dc22   2005012227

Printed in the United States of America
R. R. Donnelley and Sons, Crawfordsville, IN

10 9 8 7 6 5 4 3 2 1

For Jack M. Lyon

D. ALEXANDER AND BEATRICE (BEA) THOMAS FAMILY
(1968)

Alexander (Alex) [b. 1916] [m. Anna Stoltz, 1944]
    Eugene (Gene) [b. 1945] [m. Emily Osborne, 1968]
      Daniel [b. 1969]
    Joseph (Joey) [b. 1947] [m. Janette, 1970]
    Sharon [b. 1949]
    Kurt [b. 1951]
    Kenneth (Kenny) [b. 1956]
    Pamela (Pammy) [b. 1958]

Barbara (Bobbi) [b. 1919] [m. Richard Hammond, 1946]
    Diane [b. 1948]
      Jennifer [b. 1969]
    Margaret (Maggie) [b. 1953]
    Richard, Jr. (Ricky) [b. 1963]

Walter (Wally) [b. 1921] [m. Lorraine Gardner, 1946]
    Kathleen (Kathy) [b. 1946]
    Wayne [b. 1948] [m. Dixie, 1970]
    Douglas [b. 1951]
    Glenda [b. 1955]
    Shauna [b. 1959]

Eugene (Gene) [1925–1944]

LaRue [b. 1929]

Beverly [b. 1931] [m. Roger Larsen, 1953]
    Victoria (Vickie) [b. 1954]
    Julia [b. 1955]
    Alexander (Zan) [b. 1957]
    Suzanne [b. 1959]
    Beatrice [b. 1966]
    Michael [b. 1970]

CHAPTER 1

Gene Thomas was glaring at his son. Danny was two-and-a-half, and he was relentless when he wanted something. "That's enough, Danny," Gene said, his hands on his hips and his voice raised enough to leave no doubt that he was serious.

Danny could look innocent, with his dark blue eyes, his hair as stiff and yellow as dried June grass, and that funny gap between his two front teeth, but he had a shrill voice. *"Shwings!"* he shouted for at least the tenth time, and he matched his father's stare even though his big eyes were wet and ready to spill over. He had climbed down from his high chair himself, and he was standing next to it now, his stout legs set firm. He had pulled his bib off before he had even begun to eat his breakfast— "because I don't *wike* it"—and then he had spilled his cereal down the front of him, wetting his shirt and leaving two little Cheerios stuck to his neck.

"We'll go to the swings in a little while. I told you that. But not right now. Daddy has some things he has to do first."

"Shwings!"

Gene tried to keep his control, but his voice was rasping toward rage when he said, "Danny, if you say that one more time, you're going to get a spanking."

"Shwings!"

Gene reached for Danny, not entirely sure what he was going to do if he got hold of him, but Danny was too quick. He spun out of Gene's grasp and ran away. He made it to the door of the kitchen, then seemed to realize that Gene wasn't chasing him. He turned back, shaking with anger, his face contorted and flushed, and he screamed, "*Shwiiiiiiiinnnnnngs!*"

Emily had told Gene to ignore Danny at times like this—to explain once and then pay no attention to his tantrums. But Danny had been pushing Gene harder all the time lately, as though he sensed that he could rile his dad more easily than he could his mother.

Gene knew he was overreacting—and playing into Danny's hands—but the screams were shattering to his nerves. He could feel his heart pounding, setting off tremors in his chest and shoulders. He turned back toward the sink, where he had begun to wash the breakfast dishes. He ran a little more hot water, rejuvenating the suds. He swished a dish cloth over a couple of plates and then looked out through the window into the backyard, searching for something to focus on, something to calm him.

The fall morning was bright but breezy; showers of brown leaves were falling from two tall red oaks in a neighbor's yard. The leaves had been piling up for days, and Gene knew he needed to rake them before rain came, or snow. Maybe he should do that today and let Danny jump in the stacks of leaves, but even the thought of it—the work and the patience—was exhausting, and Gene had promised himself, absolutely, that he would scrub the kitchen floor. The linoleum was patterned in browns and pale yellows, which hid the dirt pretty well, but Gene could feel the stickiness in places, even see the grime. Emily had mentioned the night before that she wanted to scrub the kitchen and bathrooms on Saturday, but he knew how busy she was, and he had heard what she really meant in the hesitant way she brought up the subject: she thought *he* should have gotten the job done by now. Emily had gone back to college at the University of Utah in September, and now it was late October, 1971. She could finish her degree in two quarters if she took a fairly heavy load, and that's what she hoped to do. Gene hadn't been pleased by her decision, but Emily had told him that if he couldn't go back to school yet, she might as well take the opportunity while Gene could be home with Danny. But she hadn't really consulted him so much as told him that's what she was going to do—and that still bothered him, even though the plan probably made sense.

Gene had gone through his final surgery toward the end of summer. A surgeon had reconnected his intestines and eliminated the colostomy sack he had lived with for a few months. In theory, Gene should have begun to feel much better now, but for over a year, since being wounded in the abdomen in Vietnam, he had gone through one surgery after another, and he was far from having his strength back. When he looked in the mirror as he shaved, he still wondered whose face he was seeing. His cheekbones had no flesh over them. His eyes looked recessed and tired—old. He wondered whether he would ever build back the muscle he had lost while lying in bed so many months. He hadn't known what a gift his body was, back when he had been an athlete, but he missed all that energy, felt as though he had lost part of himself.

Gene was trying to do his job, but he didn't like housework, and watching Danny had turned out to be much harder than he had ever imagined. The boy was fine as long as Gene gave him lots of attention, but he wanted stories all day, or he wanted Daddy to get down and play with him, running cars across the floor or making cabins with Gene's old Lincoln Logs. It was something that Gene had idealized at one time—the chance to be with his son, to play with him and finally build a relationship—but even getting up and down from the floor took something out of him. Even more, playing with Danny demanded his interest, and after reading the same books over and over, or building another cabin, which Danny would only knock down again, Gene was alarmed at how indifferent to everything he had become.

Emily was usually home in the mornings to make breakfast, but she left the dishes, and once she was gone, the daily routine would start all over. There were always diapers to rinse out and wash, always the mess that Danny created. Gene knew he should teach Danny to pick up after himself, but it was more work to do that than pick it all up himself—and he did want things to look decent when Emily came home. The trouble was, she had to study every night, and since Gene had no such regimen to hold to, he ended up watching Danny during the evenings, too. And the boy hated to go to bed. Every evening turned into a battle to get him to go down and then stay down.

Gene would finally try to relax once Danny was asleep. He would read the newspaper or turn on the TV, but his thought was that he had made it through another day and all he had to look forward to was a day like the one he had just survived. He kept telling himself he would feel stronger in time, and once he did, his patience would increase, but right now he found Danny's demands almost more than he could take. There had been times when he had given Danny a pretty good swat even though Emily didn't believe in doing that, but what scared him was the temptation he felt to spank him much harder, even a smoldering impulse to hurt him. Gene didn't do it, and didn't think he ever would, but his anger had been so wild a couple of times, he wondered what it would take for him to cross the line.

"*Shwings!*" Danny continued to shout.

Gene washed the utensils and placed them in the draining rack, fished around in the water for anything still left, then lifted the little metal basket that plugged the sink. By then Danny was not just screaming but crying, and Gene's hands were quivering, his lips shaking. He knew he couldn't take this much longer. He wanted to spank the kid as long as it took to shut him up, but he knew that was an outrageous idea. His other choice was to give up. "All right, Danny. We'll go. In just a minute."

"*Shwings!*"

Suddenly Gene rushed toward Danny, who tried to dash away, but this time Gene got hold of his arm and spun him around. "*All right!* You win! We'll go to the swings. Just shut up, will you?"

Danny dropped to the floor and tried to cover himself, like a little animal under attack. Gene was shocked with himself and, in a few seconds, disgusted. He took a couple of deep breaths and then lifted Danny—still folded up—into his arms. Danny was shaking as much as Gene was. "Daddy won't hurt you. We'll go to the swings now. But Danny's been a bad boy."

"Good boy." And now Danny began to sob, not in anger but sadness.

"I know. I know. You're a good boy. But you were naughty."

"Good boy."

Gene sat down on the floor, still holding Danny. "Are you so sure about that?" he asked, and he laughed a little. "Good boys don't yell at their daddies."

Danny twisted and grabbed Gene around the neck, stopped crying, and in the logic of a two-year-old, said, "Shwings," as though his desire to go was enough explanation for all the fuss he had made.

"I know I'm spoiling you, kid. Your mother would handle this better. But let's go to the park."

Danny released his hold and scrambled off Gene's lap, ready to go. Gene saw that gapped-tooth smile, and he realized once again how much he loved this little boy, but he also wondered whether the two of them could get through a whole winter together.

Gene got Danny's Keds on, which Danny had pulled off earlier for no explainable reason, and changed his wet shirt while Danny squirmed with impatience. Then Gene found Danny's hooded red sweatshirt on the bedroom floor, his own tan jacket in the hall closet, and he led Danny out to the car. He drove to Sugar House Park, several blocks south of his parents' home on Harvard Avenue, with Danny sitting in the seat next to his dad, chattering now, still about the swings. Gene hoped that before long he and Emily could afford to rent or even buy a home. His parents liked to have him and his family in their house, and they charged no rent, so it worked out well, but Gene wanted to be on his own. He especially found it hard when his parents or any of his siblings came and went with little warning. When Mom was home, she was good about doing the cooking, but she also assumed control, and Gene and Emily were suddenly guests again. When Dad came alone, he was always running around to take care of political matters, and he added another level of demand. He wasn't one to eat a bowl of cereal and call it breakfast. Emily had to do more in the morning, and Gene had more to clean up.

Gene wanted his life to start again, but his doctor had told him—and he could feel it inside himself—it would take a year or more from this point to feel somewhat like the man he had once been. Gene had planned for the war to take a year of his life, the army two, but it was going to end up taking much more. He had a hard time believing he would ever be entirely whole; he remembered that tight, clear focus he had once known. He couldn't imagine ever seeing that sharply again, moving that easily, knowing that surely. The loss angered Gene. Sometimes he felt a simmering resentment that he could talk himself out of, but at other times it would break out of him when he didn't expect it. He would overreact to some minor upset and shout at Emily or Danny, or he would suddenly be furious about a story on the news or a comment some person, usually a friend or family member, would make about the war. He had never been like that. He had had his opinions, but he hadn't reacted much to what others said. He felt booby-trapped now, as though his nerves were made of detonator cord.

In the car, as Danny babbled, Gene talked to himself. He had to calm down, be patient, take things as they came, and right now, make this time at the park nice for Danny. The poor little boy needed to get out of the house too, and he needed a daddy who wasn't cranky all the time. So when they got to the park, Gene ran with Danny to the swings, told him they were racing, and even though Gene was breathing hard as he picked up Danny and put him on the swing, he pushed for as long as Danny wanted to keep going—which was not easy to do. Danny's attention span could be short, but not when he was swinging. The only way Gene could ever get him off a swing without a fuss was to let him continue until he asked to get off himself. So Gene stood and pushed over and over, as Danny giggled. "High, high," he would yell, and when Gene pushed him harder, he would squeal with joy. The kid had no fear.

In time, however, Danny did see something else that interested him. He spotted two little girls playing in a sandbox not far away. Gene hadn't brought any toys along, and he feared that if Danny headed to the sandbox he might try to take the shovels away from the girls, but when Danny said he wanted out of the swing, Gene was glad to oblige. As soon as Gene set him down, Danny dashed to the sand, but then he stopped and looked at the girls. They were both a little older, Gene thought, if not much bigger. One of them was delicate and black-haired, the other sturdier, with lighter skin and hair. Danny hadn't had a lot of chance to play with other kids. He wasn't shy once he got started, but he was awkward about approaching. He watched the girls for a few seconds, and then one of them, the dark-haired girl, said to him, "Do you want to play with my bucket?"

She couldn't have been more than three. Gene was surprised by the motherly instinct, which he hadn't seen in many kids that age. Danny nodded his head, clearly delighted, but he didn't do anything. The little girl motioned for him to come closer, and then she said, "Watch me." She used a little shovel to scoop up some sand, then she let it slide into the bucket. She smiled when she looked up, her brown eyes as rich as stained walnut. Gene wondered whether Danny knew how pretty she was. Whether he did or not, when she extended the shovel toward him, he stepped closer, took hold of it, and crouched in the sand.

Gene walked closer to the kids. "Can you tell the little girl 'thank you,' Danny?" he asked, but Danny was too busy trying to balance sand on the flat shovel. He spilled most of it before he could pour it into the bucket. The little girl was watching him. "That's good," she said, again like a little mother.

Gene looked over at the two moms sitting on a bench near the sand. It wasn't hard to see who belonged to whom. The dark-haired woman was as thin as her daughter—a little too thin, but pretty, with the same eyes. She looked younger than Gene; both women did. They were wearing heavy sweaters—ski sweaters—as though they had expected the day to be colder than it actually was now that the wind was dying down, but also hinting to Gene that they were young women from the east side, probably pretty well off. "What a nice thing for her to do," Gene said to them.

"Mandy can be that way," the mother said. "But she might pick up the bucket and dump all the sand on his head, too. I never know what to expect from her."

"Yeah, I know the feeling. Kids are hard to figure out." Gene walked over to their bench and stood next to them.

The other young woman was a little heavy, with rounded cheeks, and with light hair that had been "frosted" into multiple tones. "What a good dad you are," she said. "We couldn't believe how long you kept swinging your little boy."

Gene unzipped his jacket. He was actually sweating from all that pushing. "I didn't dare stop," he said, and he laughed. "I don't like to deal with Danny's tantrums—and he knows how to throw one."

"Really? He looks *sooo* sweet."

"It's all a disguise. He's got me completely trained. I do whatever he tells me."

The women laughed, and they talked for a time about the stubbornness of little kids. Mandy's mother had a theory that girls were worse at three and boys at two. Gene admitted that he had no idea.

"Do you have other children?" she asked.

"No. He's our first one. My wife's going to school, and I'm playing Mom for a while. It's a harder job than I bargained for."

8

"You're a brave man. I admire you. My husband wouldn't make it through a single day with Erin."

Gene hadn't thought much about that. He rather liked the idea. Maybe he wasn't so abnormally impatient after all. "What I can't believe," he said, "is how much time Danny takes. I thought maybe I could get a few things done, but he wants my attention every minute—and he gets mad if I don't give it to him."

Both women laughed hard. Erin's mother, the one with the lighter hair, said, "Could you come over to my house and tell my husband that? He wonders what I do all day." And then she added, "By the way, my name's Becky, and this is Leanne."

"Nice to meet you. My name's Gene." He thought of shaking their hands, but that seemed a little too formal. Besides, he wasn't sure what else he could think of to say to them. He looked up at Mount Olympus in order to break eye contact, and he was struck by the beauty of the gray rock jutting against the soft sky. He also liked the smell of dry leaves in the air, the call of birds in the nearby trees, the calm he finally felt. He needed to do this more often—take Danny outside, breathe a little himself.

"As long as the weather holds out, we try to come here almost every day," Becky said.

"We let the girls play together for a while. It's a nice break for us, too. You might want to bring your Danny at the same time. I think he's got a crush on Mandy already."

"I can understand that. Those are two cute little girls." But Gene didn't commit to anything more than that. It was a little embarrassing to think of joining some sort of play group and becoming "one of the mothers."

"We came early today, but we usually come over for an hour at about eleven, take them home for lunch, and then try to get them down for a nap."

Again, Gene avoided any promises. "Do you have as hard a time getting them to go down as I do?" he asked.

"I do," Leanne said. "Erin goes down pretty well for Becky, but Mandy fights me. Then she gets worn out and cranky—and of course, so do I."

"Sounds like my house."

"Hey, but tell us your wife's secret," Becky said. "How did she talk you into staying home while *she* goes to school? Do you work nights or something?"

"No." Gene hesitated, and then he said as little as he could get away with. "I had to have a surgery. So I was home for a while anyway."

"Wait a minute. Your name's Gene Thomas, isn't it?" Leanne said. "I read about you in the *Deseret News*."

Gene had feared that this was coming. "Yes, it is."

"I've been trying to think where I knew you. You were at East High when I was still in junior high. My big sister had a crush on you."

Gene wanted to leave now. A little burst of wind rolled a catalpa leaf past his feet. He watched it and didn't look at Leanne when he said, "There's no explaining taste, I guess."

"You were the big sports star back then. And then you went to Vietnam and got wounded, didn't you? Is that why you had to have surgery?"

Before Gene could answer, Becky said, "Oh, my gosh. You're the congressman's son. You're the war hero. I read that article too. You were wounded really bad, weren't you?"

"Well, yeah. It's taken a long time to get everything straightened out, but I'm doing quite well now—even if I still look like a skeleton." He tried to smile. Danny had started to pick up handfuls of sand and toss them—not at the girls so far, but that might be his next idea. "Don't, Danny," Gene said. "Just play with the bucket." But that seemed to remind Mandy of the bucket Danny was ignoring now. When she picked it up, he suddenly decided he wanted it after all, and a little tug-of-war began. Gene hurried to stop him. "Danny, *no*. Let Mandy have her bucket back. Do you want to swing some more?"

Danny let the shovel go and stood up straight, reaching high toward Gene. "Shwings," he said. Gene was relieved.

"Weren't you in the Green Berets or something like that?" Becky asked.

Gene picked up Danny. He looked back at the women. He saw in their faces a kind of excitement, as though he were a celebrity. It was what he hated more than almost anything—reflected glory from his dad and from that newspaper article that had gotten almost everything wrong. "No," he said. "Nothing like that."

"But you were out on these really dangerous missions."

"They played that up too much," Gene said. "Anyone in combat in Vietnam is in danger."

"I guess that's true. I appreciate so much what you guys are willing to do over there. It just makes me sick when I see all these protesters burning the flag when you guys are willing to sacrifice so much for the rest of us."

Gene decided not to say anything. He was going to go back to the swings and push Danny for as long as he wanted. But Leanne said, "We owe our freedom to guys like you."

Gene looked at her for several seconds, standing stiff, holding Danny tight. He knew better than to disagree, but he couldn't resist asking, "What freedom did you get from Vietnam?"

Leanne looked at Gene, her eyes curious, obviously unable to think what to say.

"We *claimed* we were fighting to keep South Vietnam free. All we really did was destroy the country." His voice had gotten tight, even a little too loud. He took a breath and tried to speak more calmly as he added, "The only ones who still want us over there are the people who've gotten rich off drugs and prostitution and black-market sales. So honestly, don't thank me for saving your freedom. This whole war hasn't accomplished one thing."

Leanne was recovering a little. Her long, dark eyelashes lowered as she said, quietly, "I guess I know what you mean. But I think our soldiers did their best—and people shouldn't blame them for what went wrong."

Gene agreed with that, of course, but it was all so simplistic. No one back home seemed to have the slightest idea what had gone on and what was still going on in Vietnam. And so he let himself make one more point. "The truth is, we had no business going over there. I think we meant well, but there came a time when we knew we had made a mistake, and that's when we should have pulled out. Those protesters you don't like—and I don't like either—were actually right about that. Now, Nixon wants to take credit for bringing the troops home, when all he's done is get thousands more killed by taking so long to do it."

"But if we'd left in the middle," Becky said, "there would have been a bloodbath in South Vietnam."

"Bloodbath? What do you think this whole war is?" Gene heard his voice fraying again, rising, so he tried to slow down and soften his intensity, but the words kept coming, sounding too strong. "Do you have any idea how much blood we've shed over there? We've killed *millions* of people in Vietnam—lots of them women and kids. We've obliterated their villages, created *masses* of refugees, and backed a government that's completely corrupt. It's going to take *generations* to undo the harm we've done. Doesn't anyone in Utah ever stop to think about any of that? All I ever hear is this automatic response. Any time we send soldiers into battle *anywhere*, everyone has to spout all the old clichés about *fighting for freedom*. I'm sick of hearing it."

"I didn't mean to say—"

"No. It's okay. I didn't mean to react like that." He took a couple of steps closer to the women, and then he said, as calmly as he could, "But these holes they shot in me were for *nothing*. No one got any *freedom* from them. I've accepted that. It just drives me crazy that people keep justifying a pointless war." He started away, carrying Danny, who was grasping Gene tight around the neck now, as though the sound of his daddy's voice had scared him again. Gene slowed after a few strides, turned around and said, "I'm sorry. Really, I'm sorry. I didn't mean to . . . I don't know. I shouldn't have gotten into all that." Both women were staring at him, and so were the little girls. Danny had begun to whimper. Gene turned back toward the swings again, but then he knew he couldn't do it. He headed for his car. "Shwings," Danny said pitifully, but Gene kept going.

～∽～

By the time Emily got home late that afternoon, Gene was humiliated by what he had done. He thought maybe he would go over again the next day, at eleven, and just tell the women how sorry he was, and then maybe try to explain, quietly, how he felt about the war. He practiced things he could say, but even in his mind, his voice would fire like bullets, and he knew he could never do it. But why didn't anyone even *try* to think about what had actually happened in Vietnam? The troops were mostly withdrawn now, and within a year the last of the forces were supposed to come home. The Communists would take over sooner or later, Gene was almost sure, and maybe there really would be a bloodbath, but the point was, *nothing* was better in Vietnam for his having been there— or for all the other hundreds of thousands of Americans who had done their hitches.

What he developed more clearly in his mind was what he wanted to say to Emily, but he knew he had to speak carefully. He waited until she had told him about her classes and about the paper that was due next week—the one she needed to start working on that night. When she asked about his day, he didn't mention the park or any trouble with Danny. He continued to wait until Emily had retrieved a leftover casserole from the refrigerator and was putting it into the oven to reheat. Gene, by then, was washing a head of lettuce. He started in a calm voice. "You know, Em, I've been thinking that it might be a good idea if I start to work for Uncle Wally again. We could find a babysitter for Danny. I think it would be good for me to get back in the habit of working. I feel like I've got to start acting like the head of our household again—you know, producing some income and getting back into the work force."

"It's harder than you thought it was going to be, isn't it?"

"Being home?" He considered denying it, but he was willing to admit anything to change the way he'd been living for the last month. "Yeah. A lot harder. And the truth is, I'm not very good at it. I'm not patient enough with Danny. He keeps the pressure on all the time."

"But it's better for Danny to be with his daddy than to be with a babysitter. This quarter will be over in no time, and then it's just one more. I don't like leaving Danny as it is, but I'd feel *really* guilty if he weren't with you."

"Wouldn't that depend on the babysitter? We could maybe find an older woman in the ward—you know, someone who would love him like a grandma. Maybe my grandma would even take him. I'm afraid if I have to put up with his tantrums much longer I could end up busting his head open one of these days."

Emily was getting out utensils from a cabinet drawer. She looked up and turned toward him. "Gene! What a thing to say."

Gene didn't look at her directly. He was tearing leaves off the head of lettuce. "You know I don't mean that," he said. "But I worry sometimes, Emily. He really gets to me." He felt the tension in his voice again, stopped himself, held back for a moment, and then added, "To tell the truth, Em, he seems spoiled to me. He wants what he wants, and he wants it that second. I don't know how to deal with that."

"He's *two*, Gene. And don't start accusing me of raising him wrong. I haven't had a lot of help these last two years, in case you haven't noticed."

Gene glanced at Emily and saw the little swelling by her ear, the muscle that tightened when she set her jaw. He knew he had to back off and start over. He waited for a few seconds before he said, "I'm not saying anything like that. Maybe all two-year-olds are like Danny. But I don't think I have enough energy—or control of my nerves. I think he would be better off with someone else and I could start acting like a normal father. I want to work for a while, and then I want to get back into school."

"To study what, Gene? You haven't even applied. When I ask you what you want to do, you can't tell me. For all I know, you're never going to be able to make a living. I want to get my degree, but it's not for the self-satisfaction. It's so someone around here can make a living—in case you can't."

Gene's brain was suddenly full of red, of flashes. He stepped toward her and for an instant thought he was going to hit her. But he didn't. He stood before her quivering. "I'm trying to do better, Emily," he said. "I want to do better. But this last surgery—"

"I don't want to hear it anymore, Gene. I know you've been through a lot. But so have I. And I'm tired of your self-pity. You're not *Gene* anymore, and I don't know whether Gene is ever going to return to this marriage, but if he doesn't—and soon—maybe we don't have a marriage. If you can't take being home with your son, maybe you belong in a hospital. Maybe you need a shrink to help you work through some things. But don't tell me you're going to bust Danny's head open."

Evil words were in Gene's head, evil ideas. He wanted to drive his fist into her face. His rage was blazing, filling up his vision, everything the color of blood. And so he got out. He broke from the kitchen, strode to the front door, and then rushed out onto the street. He ran down Harvard Avenue, beneath the trees, leaves falling around him—flashes of color— past an old couple in his ward who said something to him. But he was running, tiring quickly but wanting to run until no colors were left in his head.

He didn't run long, couldn't. But he cut through the little triangle of grass that divided the street at the junction with Thirteenth East, then walked north until he was exhausted and, above all, sick with himself.

What was wrong with him that he wanted to scream at people, could even think of hurting his tiny boy and his wife? Maybe Emily was right. Maybe he was a psych case. Maybe he was dangerous. But he couldn't accept that, and so he told himself he hadn't actually done it and never could. And then he walked back up the street, said hello to the Halvorsons this time, and walked into the house, where he found Danny in the family room watching "his shows." He knelt by him, patted his head, and then hugged him while Danny paid no attention. Then Gene looked for Emily. She was sitting at the kitchen table with her face in her hands. He sat down in the chair next to her and put his arm around her back. "I'm sorry, Em. I'm sorry. I'll take care of Danny. I had a bad day, but I'll get myself together. I'll be all right."

Emily let him pull her closer. "Gene, I'm sorry. I'm the one with no patience. But you aren't well. You must know that. You need to start seeing someone."

"Maybe so. Maybe I will."

"It's what you always say, but you won't do it."

"I'm working my way back, Emily. I really am. I'm Gene. Honest. And I'll be the man you married one of these days. Now that the surgeries are finished and—"

"It's not the surgeries. It's your head, Gene. You've got to get some things straightened out inside your head."

"I know. But I'm doing better, even though you might not see it yet. Every day I get a little better."

Gene knew that wasn't true, and certainly Emily did, but he wasn't going to talk to a shrink. He wasn't going to rehash all the things he had experienced in Vietnam and revisit all his memories. The only answer was to push everything out of his head forever, and no one could do that for him. He just had to act like a man—like a father and a husband. He had to remember who he had been before Vietnam, and he had to forget everything else.

CHAPTER 2

Diane Hammond was happy to be finished with her eleven o'clock class, the last one of the day. She had left too many education classes to the end of her program, so this quarter she was taking two, and neither one was all that interesting. She was also taking a chemistry class to fill a science requirement, and she was discovering that she had forgotten most of the math she had learned in high school—or, probably, how little she had learned in the first place. She had worked hard, however, and she thought she could get A's in the education classes as well as in a survey of American literature course, with maybe a B in chemistry if she continued to do as well as she had on the first two tests. Her bowling class might be another matter, at least if her grade depended on her rolling fewer gutter balls. But it was the only physical education class she could find in the morning, and she had to take morning classes so she could work afternoons.

She was walking to the library to get some reading done before she had to show up for her job in the Union Building at one o'clock. She was weary of her never-ending need to study, and she knew that she left Jenny on her own too often, just watching TV, but she hoped to graduate by the end of the school year. She wanted to be teaching by this time next year. Even though she knew the first year or two of teaching were going to be hard, she thought maybe the pressure would let up in time, and things might be easier once Jenny was in school.

Diane loved October days when the air was sharp and the sky was that brighter blue that came in the fall. She wished she had time to pick up Jenny from her grandma and take her to a park for a little while. Jenny loved to play in the fallen leaves, or even in dirt and puddles, but it was hard for Bobbi to take her very often, and Diane found time to help only on Saturdays, if at all. This day was more than full, so Diane didn't allow herself the time to stroll and breathe a little. She hurried down the sidewalk and was approaching the library doors when she heard a voice behind her. "Hey, Diane, you sure walk fast."

Diane stopped and turned around, then stepped out of the way of a girl who needed to get past her. The fellow who had spoken was standing straight, a briefcase in one hand and the other arm straight down at his side, like a sentry. Diane knew who he was; he was in her chemistry class. She had noticed him paying attention to her, rather obviously, but she was surprised he knew her name. Still, she did know *his* name. Professor Glade always called him "Mr. Lambert," and she had heard one of the students call him Ed. He was good-looking but newly home from his mission and probably twenty-one. Diane was only twenty-three herself, of course, but she *felt* vastly older. She smiled at him and, in a teasing voice, said, "I walk fast because I have places to be and things to do."

"Is this where you get your thrills and chills—in the library?" She noticed his stance relax slightly, his weight shifting to one leg, but he sounded short of breath. He had oak-colored hair, short but parted, and a smattering of freckles—probably why he looked so young. Or maybe it was his smile. The corners of his mouth turned up just slightly, hardly noticeable most of the time but childlike when he smiled—and he couldn't stop smiling right now.

"That's about as thrilling as it gets for me," Diane said. "Sad life, huh?"

Ed let her claim pass, with only a little laugh. But she could see he was trying hard to look serious. "Hey, do you understand the math Dr. Glade was showing us today? The more he talked, the more mixed up I got."

"I think I followed him okay. But my dad is good at math, so when I have trouble I drop over to see him, and he helps me."

"So you don't live at home?"

That was not the follow-up question Diane had expected, and the sudden turn toward her personal life took her off guard. She felt her cheeks warm and knew that her ears were probably turning red. She blushed way too easily. "No. But my parents are close by. I see them a lot."

"So you're from Ogden?"

"Yeah. I am." For some reason the answer, to Diane, implied that she had always lived in the area. She thought of telling him that she had been at BYU for a time, and then in Seattle, but she wasn't quite ready to reveal that she had been married and had a little girl. She had seen too many guys lose their composure when they found out, and she really didn't want to go through all that unless she had to.

"I'm from Clearfield," Ed said. "I'm living at home right now, but I think next year I might try to get an apartment with some other guys. Is that what you're doing?"

"No. I don't live with *other guys*."

Ed laughed, and Diane knew she had escaped again without having to say anything about her "living arrangements."

"I just got off my mission this summer. I was in the Central Atlantic States." He slipped one hand into the pocket of his cotton slacks, but he made the motion seem an effort—a failed attempt at casualness. He was wearing a brown sleeveless sweater that seemed tight on him, as though he might have gained some weight on his mission. Still, he had good shoulders and a strong chest; she had the feeling he had been an athlete in high school.

Diane nodded and waited, aware of the way his eyes were taking her in and conscious that his breathlessness was, at least in part, caused by what he was seeing. She still liked that, but she was reminded again how much more complicated her life was now than it had been the first time she had gone to college. Ed seemed to realize that he had started down a path of conversation that had no exact purpose, and now he was the one whose cheeks were reddening. "Anyway, do you think you could explain that math to me?"

"Well . . . sure. I don't have a lot of time, though. I work at the Union Building, and I've got to get some stuff done before I go to work."

"Hey, well, we could get together some other time." He took a step back, as though he was actually eager to escape the situation he had created for himself. Diane found that appealing. She had met enough slick guys in her life. She knew that things were going to get awkward if she didn't explain more about herself, but she didn't want to do it yet; this was a little too much fun.

The two walked on into the library and found a table. She sat next to Ed and explained the math rather quickly, essentially repeating what the professor had said. She had the distinct feeling that he wasn't actually listening, and yet he kept saying, "Oh, okay. I see what you're saying." And eventually he came up with, "I think I can do it now."

Diane couldn't resist. She did what she hadn't been able to do in years. She gave Ed a sly smile and said in a cute voice, "Ed, my friend, why is it I have the feeling you're a math major and you're putting me on?"

"No, I'm not." But he wouldn't look her in the eye now. "I don't know what my major is, but it isn't math."

"Is it chemistry?" She was still teasing him with her eyes, and he was doing what guys had always done for her: he was melting down.

"Okay. I admit, I probably understood the math okay. But I'm no brain in math, believe me."

"So what's up, Ed? Why would you want to deceive a poor little innocent girl?" Diane told herself she would play this out for a few minutes, tell him she was older and had a daughter, and then send him on his way.

"How do you know my name?" Ed asked.

Suddenly everything reversed. She was the one being discovered. She *had* noticed him. She had even smiled at him a couple of times, maybe to create this very moment—even though she knew that nothing could come of it. Her divorce had been final for quite some time now; that wasn't the problem. She simply knew how a young guy like Ed would react when he found out she had a child. Still, Diane was the one embarrassed, the one not looking directly back when she said, "I just heard someone call you Ed in class one day."

"I guess you noticed, I found out your name, too."

"I did notice that. What do you suppose all this means?"

"It could mean that I'd like to go out with you, but it scares me to death to walk up to someone like you and just ask."

So now it was time to tell him. But he really was cute, and there was something endearing about his admission. So she said nothing, just to see what he would do, and maybe to see what *she* would do.

"I've been scared because I figure that someone as beautiful as you either has about ten guys after her, or she's waiting for a missionary, or she's engaged—or something."

For a year now, and more, Diane had been telling herself that being pretty wasn't important. She wanted guys to find her interesting, show her respect, consider her attractive as a whole person. But this was sweet. "Actually, I don't have ten guys after me, and I'm not waiting for a missionary, and I'm not engaged." She was about to say, "It's the 'or something' that's the problem," but the words didn't come. She saw how pleased he looked, and it felt cruel to have strung him along all this time only to cut the string, all at once.

"Would you go out with me sometime, then?" he asked.

"Well . . . maybe."

"What about this weekend?"

"Oh. No. I can't."

"What about next weekend?"

She couldn't do this, but she did. "I guess so. Saturday might work."

Greg was taking Jenny that weekend. Diane would be on her own. It was just a date. It didn't have to mean anything.

"So, are you pretty booked up most of the time?"

"I didn't say that." But she let him believe it.

"A week from Saturday, then. That's great. I'm in Delta Phi. It's a returned missionary group. I think they might have something going on that night."

"Or we could just go to a movie."

"Yeah. Anything. Should I get your phone number?" He reached for a pencil in the leather briefcase he had set next to his chair, and Diane saw that his hand was actually shaking. She was amazed at how good that made her feel.

"So, what's your number?" He had his pencil ready.

He was looking at her with the ardor of a lovesick teenager, so she gave him the number. Ed thanked her, said he was excited and would see her in class, and then walked away, moving fast, as though he was afraid she would change her mind if he dawdled.

Diane knew she was in a mess. Ed would faint when he found out about Jenny. But for now, she liked the feeling that a guy was nuts over her.

❧

Kathy was sitting in her bishop's office. It was after Sunday School and he had stopped her in the hallway and asked if he could talk to her for a minute. Bishop Aldridge was a nice man—outgoing, friendly, aware of everyone. He never seemed to work at being bishop; it was as though he had been born to the job. He was older than most bishops Kathy knew, close to sixty, she thought, and he had bushy gray hair that seemed to have a will of its own. He didn't fuss much over what he wore, choosing ties that were much too narrow, considering what had happened with styles lately, and he apparently left home early on Sunday before his wife could make sure the color of his tie coordinated with his suit. But none of that mattered. He was actually handsome in his way, mainly because he smiled so easily and constantly.

"Kathy, how do you like your calling in the Primary?" Bishop Aldridge was asking now. But there was something in his look that said, "I'm up to something."

"I enjoy the kids. It's been hard to get over here on Wednesday afternoons some weeks, but my dad hasn't complained about my taking off early that day. I just go back later and finish what I have to do at the office."

"Would a Sunday job be better?"

"In some ways. But that's all right. I can always work things out."

"What if we made you choir director? President Thomas told me that's a job you loved when you were overseas."

"I would like that, Bishop. But you have to know, I'm no expert. I was working with people who had almost no singing experience over there, so they didn't know how bad I was."

Bishop Aldridge grinned. "I don't believe that for one minute. Sister Baker has some things coming up that are going to take her away for a while, so we need to find a replacement for her. She said you know your music about as well as anyone in the ward."

"Well . . . I doubt that's true, but I *would* like to try. I do love choirs."

Bishop Aldridge leaned back in his chair. He was smiling for no obvious reason, but he was looking away, as though something had come to mind and he needed to think it through. Kathy knew that behind her, on the wall, was a picture of Christ, and he was looking toward it. "What's happened to you, Kathy?" he finally asked. "I remember talking to you just before you left for the Philippines, and I have to say you were a different person back then. Your parents were worried to death about you."

Kathy suspected that Bishop Aldridge had never once in his life doubted the truthfulness of the Church, nor had he seen any good reason to be angry—about anything. He had taught her in Sunday School for a year when she was a teenager, and she had found him painfully satisfied, as though every piece of information he learned only confirmed his faith a little more. She had raised all sorts of questions in that class, but he had seemed to find that exciting. He had told her once how impressed he was that she thought so much about things. At the time, she had concluded that he wasn't very smart, that he didn't see the implications in her questions, but over the years she had noticed that there was a reason questions didn't frighten him: he had so much faith he trusted that every question had an answer—whether he knew what it was or not. He was willing to wait on the ones he hadn't figured out. Kathy had always liked him for his jovial good-heartedness, but she had struggled to respect him. She was surprised lately that she found him much more astute, even subtle, than she had suspected he could be, and also that his goodness was infinitely more important than she had recognized back in her growing-up years.

"I *was* upset a lot back then, Bishop. I still have some of that in me. I see things that are wrong, and it just seems like I ought to be able to do something to make them right."

"You can, can't you?"

"I don't know. Sometimes. But I was always mad about *ideas*. In the Philippines, I started to feel that people were a lot more important than ideas were. That's so obvious to you, you probably wonder why I couldn't see it all along."

He laughed as though he detected something deprecating in her assessment of him and didn't mind. "I'm a simple man, Kathy. I read the newspaper and I hear about all the things that are fouled up in the world, but I tell myself, 'I'll worry about the things I can do something about, and I'll let someone else worry about the rest.'"

"I know. That's more or less what happened to me while I was in the Peace Corps. For a while, I just gave up. I decided I couldn't fix what was wrong, so I quit trying, but when I stopped thinking about *things* that were wrong, I started paying attention to people, and I could hardly believe how happy that made me."

"That's the secret. Always has been."

"But there are still problems I want to work on. I want to be involved in the community, no matter where I live—the way I was in the little barrio where I lived in the Philippines."

"That's good. You sound like my wife. But what brought you back to the Church?"

"I never left—not completely."

"Still, you know what I mean."

Kathy thought about the question. What had brought her back? "I think it started one day when a woman asked me to pray for her little son who was sick. It wasn't something we normally did, but I told her I would. When I started to pray, I felt something come over me. I'd never felt anything like that—like I was inhaling so much air that I was swelling up and about to float away. After, I thought, 'So that's what everyone's been talking about all my life.'"

"You're telling me that you never felt the Spirit during the years you were growing up in this ward?"

"I don't know, Bishop. If I did, I didn't let it stay inside me. I would question the life out of my good experiences. But I needed a lift that day, and it seemed like God had given it to me, so I held onto it. I had another experience right about that same time. I took a bus trip into the Bataan Peninsula where my dad walked during the death march. It was as though I understood my father for the first time. It felt like he was whispering to me the whole way, 'I survived this so I could bring you to this earth.' I kept thinking that I was made of the same stuff he was, and I needed to start showing it."

Tears had come into the bishop's eyes. He nodded and then sat for a time. "That's wonderful," he finally said. "So tell me what you're going to do now?"

"Oh, Bishop, that's the problem. I don't know. I don't really like the work I do for my dad, but I don't know what else to do. I'm sort of lost. I've always had some immediate goal ahead of me, and suddenly, now, I don't."

"How old are you, Kathy?"

"I'll be twenty-five in December."

"I can think of one possible goal." He laughed, making a barely audible little noise, like rustling leaves.

"Don't say it. I hear it enough from my parents."

"But you do want to get married, don't you?"

"I really do, Bishop, but I've been home for four months and haven't even gone out on a date. I'm taller than about two-thirds of the men in this world—which seems to scare them off—and I think I'm too old for the rest."

"Don't forget to mention that you're smart. That scares some away too."

"Thanks. That's just the kind of encouragement I need."

He grinned and leaned back in his chair, his elbows pointed outward, like wings. "I'm just teasing, but it's kind of true. Remember though, it only takes one. You'll find him. I'd marry you in a minute if I was taller and younger and smarter—and wasn't already married."

"Hey, you're not supposed to give me a hard time. You're the bishop."

"I know. I'm sorry." He was making that breathy, scratchy little noise again. "Seriously, though, Kathy, you're perfect for someone. You've always been smart and attractive, but now you've found your way through those questions that troubled you so much, and you've made your commitment to the gospel. I think you're going to find someone, raise a wonderful family, and be a leader in any ward you live in."

The assessment was a little too simple. Kathy would never be finished with her questions. And frankly, it bothered her a little that people made her feel she would have worth only if she got married. But she didn't say that. She only told him, "It doesn't always happen, Bishop. You know that. I have a beautiful, smart aunt who's never married."

"I know. I'm just telling you what I'm feeling right now. Something's telling me—I hope it's the Spirit—that you're going to figure out what you want to do and you're going to find a mate to share eternity with—just the right guy for you."

Kathy sat for a time. She liked to think he was right, but she hadn't lost her ability to work up some doubt in response to the bishop's certitude. He had said it himself: he *hoped* the Spirit was speaking to him. It could also be wishful thinking. She knew lots of women who were amazing and who never found anyone. She wasn't going to let herself conclude that she could be happy only if a man validated her worth.

"Don't you know anyone at all you could interview for the job?"

"No applicants so far. There was a guy I dated a few times before I went east to college, and it turns out he's not married yet, but he knows I've been home all summer and he hasn't called."

"Can't you figure out a way to let him know you're interested?"

Kathy laughed. She had never known how to flirt or to "make the first move," but she had been thinking about that very thing lately, so she was pleased the bishop thought it wasn't a bad idea. "He goes to my grandparents' ward," she said. "I've thought about going to their sacrament meeting sometime just to see if we'd bump into each other. But that might be a little too obvious."

"Obvious is good, Kathy. Some fish have to have that bait dangling right in front of their noses before they think to take a bite. Go over there this Sunday. That's an assignment."

"I'm not sure I like the image of myself as *bait*. It sounds too wormy."

But Bishop Aldridge looked serious. He leaned forward, making his chair squeak. "Kathy, I shouldn't joke so much. I'm not talking about throwing yourself at anyone. I just think that if you have feelings for this young man—and you do want to get married—you should let him know. If he's not feeling the same way, you'll soon find out."

"But we only went out a few times, a long time ago, and since then . . . nothing."

"Hey, it's up to you. I can't tell you what to do. But maybe I'm getting inspiration. Maybe the Lord is giving you a hint here, through an old bishop who has no more sense than to get his nose in your business. It's possible, you know."

"I don't mind going over there sometime."

"All right. Next Sunday. Then come back and give me a report."

Kathy smiled. "All right," she said. "I'll go. But if it doesn't get me anywhere, I'm going to have serious doubts about your inspiration."

The bishop laughed hard, and then he said, "My wife has some doubts herself. So you won't be the only one."

◦∽◦

Hans Stoltz was standing in front of the door to the Dürdens' apartment. He had never been so excited in his life—and yet, he wanted to do this exactly right so it would be a day Elli would always want to remember. He took a breath and rang the doorbell, and for a few seconds he had the crushing impression that no one was home. But he heard movement, and in another couple of seconds the door opened. It was Sister Dürden, looking inquisitive before her face brightened with realization. "Hans! My goodness, I wasn't expecting you. Does Elli know you're—"

"No, she doesn't. Is she here?" he whispered.

"Yes. Come in."

"Could you ask her to come to the door?"

Sister Dürden's wonderful dimples appeared. "You have something in mind, Hans. I can see that." Her look seemed to say, "And I can guess what it is," but she quickly turned and walked off, calling, "Elli, there's someone here to see you."

Hans could smell red cabbage, he thought, or something sweet and strong. He wondered if the family had already eaten. He had hoped to arrive before they did.

More time passed than Hans had expected, and he wondered what Elli was doing, but he heard a door shut, and then he heard steps on the hardwood floor, coming from a hallway to the left. He cleared his throat, gripped his hands behind his back, then let go and dropped his arms to his sides. He was still trying to find a more natural stance when Elli turned the corner and looked toward the door. He saw the same curiosity he had seen in her mother's face, and then the same surprise—with more delight. "Hans!" She jumped toward him and put her arms around his neck. "What are you doing here?"

Hans held her for a time before he said, "I was wondering, would you like to go out with me tonight? We've never done that, you know."

"Go where? What are you doing, Hans? Did you get off work today?"

"Yes, I did. We could go out for dinner, if you haven't eaten."

"I have eaten, but I'll go with you." She looked into his eyes, as though to discover what she would find there. She began to smile, the way her mother had. "Tell me why you're here. Has something changed?"

Hans decided not to answer that question. "We'll go to the *Konditorei* down the street. They have some nice cakes in the window."

"Hans, tell me."

"I have *much* to tell you, Elli. Can we go now?"

"No, I need to change my clothes." Her clothes seemed fine to Hans, but he never had paid much attention to such things. His own clothes had been worn and barely presentable for a long time, but there had never been anything he could do about that. He wondered whether he could buy a new suit now.

He stepped inside the door and hoped Elli's parents would ignore him, not ask him questions he didn't want to answer, but Sister Dürden invited him into the living room, where Brother Dürden was sitting. Hans had the feeling that the Dürdens had already been speculating what Hans's presence might mean. But Brother Dürden only commented on the weather and asked about the branch in Leipzig. He didn't tease or even ask how Hans had managed to get away from his job on a Friday. Still, Sister Dürden was smiling for no reason, even glancing at her husband with apparent pleasure in his ability to be so serious at the moment.

Elli returned quickly with a blue dress on and her coat over her arm. She hadn't fussed, though, hadn't put on lipstick. She was so beautiful to Hans, and she seemed to know she didn't need makeup. He couldn't wait to tell her what he had learned that morning.

But he did wait. He walked with her down the street to the pastry shop, ordered *Küchen* with whipped cream, and let her ask several times what was going on. But he wanted to wait until they were almost finished with their cake, and then he wanted to tell her what had happened before they walked to "their place" by the river. It was dark, and it was cool outside, but it would be a better place than here, where other people were around.

He finished his own cake and watched Elli pick away at hers, talking way too much to make good progress, and then, finally, he couldn't stand to wait any longer. He said, "Let me tell you what happened this morning."

"Happened?"

"Yes. Something happened. I was working at my desk when my director walked in. He said, 'Hans, I have something to tell you.'"

Elli beamed. "I knew it would happen, Hans. I *knew* it would happen."

"Maybe he let me go. Don't be so quick to finish my story for me."

She grabbed his hands. "But he didn't. He gave you a better salary, didn't he?"

"Better than that." Hans loved watching Elli's delight, so he paused to let the excitement build. "He told me that a new project is beginning in Leipzig. Several tall apartment buildings will be constructed on the edge of the city."

"And *you* will design them!"

"Not by myself. But they want me to work on the project. My salary will almost double."

"And we can get married." She was still beaming, but tears were in her eyes. "I love you so much, Hans. And the Lord loves you. I *knew* this would happen."

"I didn't say anything about marriage." He was laughing.

"You don't have to. I did it for you."

"Let's take a walk."

"So you can ask me?"

"I asked you a long time ago."

"But I thought we would have to wait forever."

"I know. And I can still hardly believe that this could happen. I was told so many times that it never would."

"The Lord has blessed us, Hans. It's because we trusted him and we prayed so much. He wants us to be happy."

"And he wants us to do his work. Once we're married, we can do so much together in Leipzig. The branch needs someone like you, Elli."

"When, Hans? When can we get married?"

Hans laughed, let go of her hands, and stood up. "Let's take that walk."

"To our place by the river?"

"Yes."

So Hans paid the bill, and then they walked, and when they reached their spot by the little rock wall where they had watched the swans on the river so many times, he turned to her. There was enough light from a street lamp that he could see her face, shadowed and bright at the same time. He took her hands in his again. "Will you marry me, Elli. In the spring?" he asked.

"Oh, yes. Yes. But why not at Christmas, or—"

"We need to find an apartment, and—"

"I'll live with you in your tiny apartment. It will be all right for a little while."

"I thought of that, but I want to bring you home to something better. And we need to save some money. I'll be making more, but it still won't be a high salary. You'll have to find work there, and it would be nice if we could take a few days for a marriage trip."

"I don't need a marriage trip. I just want to be with you as soon as possible. I miss you so much the way we are now, so far apart all the time."

"I know. But we want everything to be nice. It's something we'll always remember."

He took her in his arms and held her. He could hear the river running, could imagine the swans. Long ago he had told himself that he could swim upstream the way swans did, gracefully, in spite of the current. Now he was making his own way against the current, much the same, and he was happier than he had ever imagined he would be.

CHAPTER 3

On a Saturday morning early in November, Greg Lyman was sitting on the living room floor of Diane's apartment. He had come to pick up Jenny, but he was playing with her first. Jenny had spent entire days with Greg a few times before, but she had never stayed with him overnight, as she was now about to do. Greg had wanted for some time to take her that long, as their divorce agreement allowed, but Diane had told him he needed to get better acquainted with her first, and to Diane's surprise, he had accepted her judgment and even done his best to get closer to his daughter. But after not seeing Greg for a couple of weeks again, Jenny, who had recently turned two, had acted shy around him when he first arrived. "I'll play with her awhile, here," Greg had told Diane, "until she warms up to me again." He had gotten down on the floor with her and asked the name of her doll. "She's *Dolly*," Jenny told him. "She need her bot-toe." She handed him the doll, along with a little plastic bottle. Greg glanced at Diane and smiled, and then he pretended to feed the baby. In a few minutes Jenny was jabbering about her crib and her other toys.

Diane stayed in the living room, but she sat at the end of the couch, as far from Jenny and Greg as possible. She wanted to let them have this time and not interfere. But Greg looked at Diane after a time and said, "Don't you think Jenny's unusually smart? I haven't been around a lot of two-year-olds, but it seems like she talks more than most kids her age."

"She really does. But girls usually develop speech skills faster than boys, and some kids just tend to be more verbal. It doesn't necessarily mean they're smart."

Greg grinned. "But I think she is. How could she miss—with genes from both of us?"

Diane couldn't believe he would say that. She hadn't forgotten Greg's accusations that she was empty-headed, back when they had been married. "Say what you really mean, Greg. She has *your* genes."

"Yours too. Look at all those A's you're knocking down these days."

Good grades were the sort of thing that impressed Greg. He had made a big deal out of her success every time she had seen him lately. Diane now wished that she hadn't said anything about that—that she hadn't felt the need to tell him. What bothered her even more was his obvious attempt to manipulate her. She could almost hear the wheels turning in his head, cranking out a theory: *She wants to hear about her brains these days, not her beauty, so that's what I'll play up.*

And yet, Diane did have to admit, Greg seemed to be changing. He was still arrogant, which came out in ways he hardly recognized in himself, but he had been surprisingly patient. Diane had expected Greg to come on strong by now and push for her to reconsider their relationship, but he hadn't done that, and he had been gentle and fun with Jenny. It was true that he could have looked out for Diane a little more. He had promised long ago to fix the cabinet doors with "kid latches"—to keep Jenny from pulling out all the pots and pans—but he had never gotten around to it, and now she was outgrowing that stage. Still, he'd had plenty of chances to show up in a bad mood, or to blame Diane for something he didn't like about the way she was raising Jenny, and he had never done that. The previous spring, when he had driven down from Seattle to talk to her, he had pleaded with her to keep open the possibility that they might get back together. He had promised that he could change and that he would prove that to her. She hadn't believed that then, and she was suspicious now that he was acting a role he thought she would buy into, but he had behaved better than she ever could have expected.

Diane didn't know what to make of all this. However annoying she found Greg, she was reminded of why she had fallen in love with him in the first place. He wasn't just good-looking; he had a certain power in him, an energy that tended to pull her along. That confidence was returning to him lately as he talked about his work, his future, and especially what he wanted for Jenny. Diane wondered whether he was dating someone and if that was why he wasn't pursuing her. Maybe that explained his elevated mood this fall. But he also dropped hints that he was actually willing himself forward and wasn't very happy. He had mentioned one day that he was thinking of buying a small house in the Salt Lake Avenues—just so he wouldn't be wasting money on rent. But then he had said, "I looked at some places, but they made me feel lonely just to walk around in them. A house needs a family." Diane had prepared herself for a pitch—but it hadn't come.

Diane could see after a time that the two were having fun, so she walked to Jenny's bedroom, prepared a diaper bag, and brought it to Greg. She had held off, maybe hoping just a little that Jenny would refuse to go. She explained about Jenny's eating habits and about putting her down at night, and then—suddenly, it seemed—Jenny walked out with him, holding his hand, still chattering. Diane stood in her little living room, alone. She had thought all week that she was looking forward to this time—a whole Saturday to clean house and get started on a paper she had to write, and a restful Sunday to herself—but she missed Jenny immediately. And maybe she missed Greg. The two of them were going to have fun today, and she wondered if maybe she would have enjoyed being with them.

Diane walked into the kitchen with the intent of making some toast, since she hadn't had breakfast, but she decided she didn't want to go to the trouble of getting out the bread and butter, even of making the hot chocolate she had promised herself. She sat down at the table. Her life was so busy that she rarely had time to think about it, but as the silence worked its way into her, she felt strongly what she usually sensed only in the back of her mind somewhere: This wasn't what she wanted. It was depressing to think of spending her life in an apartment, just she and Jenny. She wanted that fullness she had always pictured when she imagined herself with a family. Greg had said he was taking Jenny to Hogle Zoo in Salt Lake, and Diane remembered how much she had loved that as a kid, going with her parents and her sister. It was a pretty fall day, a day to be outside and doing things, to be with people. Diane had learned this past year to appreciate time of her own, time to study, but the weekend now looked long and empty. And yet, what bothered her just as much was that she had agreed to that strange date with Ed Lambert—the *boy*. Seeing Greg had only reminded her of how hesitant and awkward Ed had been.

Every day Diane had gone to chemistry class intending to talk to Ed—to break the date, or at least to tell him about her circumstances. And each time she had put off the inevitable, probably because she loved the way he looked at her, even his nervousness. The truth was, she wanted someone to fall in love with her again, and Ed was the only one who had shown any interest. It was his attention she was clinging to, and she knew that was pathetic. She leaned forward and rested her head on her arms. She thought again of Jenny, with Greg, riding next to him in the car, jabbering the whole way. Suddenly Diane was crying, and she hardly knew why.

But not for long. She did need to scrub her kitchen and bathroom floors, and she had to get started on that paper, so she walked to the bathroom, washed her face, and then went to work. She put in a full day, kept busy, and tried hard not to think. Ed was coming to pick her up at 6:30 so they would have time to get to the seven o'clock movie at the new Cinedome on Riverdale Road. *Lawrence of Arabia* had returned for a second run, and Diane hadn't seen it the first time around, but all day she was bothered by a vague feeling that she was doing something wrong. She actually worried that someone in the apartment complex would spot her leaving with a guy and . . . she didn't know what . . . maybe think she was starting to "run around." And there was still the other matter. She decided that she would come clean with Ed when he came to pick her up. She would tell him about Jenny and then see whether he still wanted to go out with her. What she allowed herself to hope was that he had done his research, already knew, and didn't care.

Diane didn't spend hours getting ready, but she spent more time than she had since she had been on her own, and she wondered about herself, that she still had that impulse. She tried on three outfits, then went back to the first, and was reminded that she really didn't have much to wear these days. She chose some fairly dressy pants to wear, with a blue and white patterned sweater, one she had loved back in her skiing days. She wondered whether she looked too "wintery," with the weather still nice, but it would be cool in the evening, and she didn't have a coat she liked very much. Besides, the blue in the sweater would bring out the blue in her eyes. It was hard not to remember how often guys had mentioned her light blue eyes and her blonde hair. She spent some time on her hair, too, even though it was so short now that it was hard to turn into anything special. But she teased it enough to give it some shape.

At the last minute she almost started over. What if he showed up in a coat and tie? Maybe she should have put on a dress. She wished she had asked him what he was going to wear. But when he arrived, he was wearing a sweater too, and dressy slacks, not cottons, so they had come up with about the same thing. And he did look good. He stood at the door, smiling, and suddenly she changed her mind about bringing him in to have that little chat she had planned. She stepped out before he had a chance to consider whether she had roommates. "Wow!" he said. "You look great." Diane was surprised how much she enjoyed that, even though he sounded a little too much like a high school boy picking up his date for the prom.

He walked her to the car without touching her, opened her door, and then walked around to his side. He was sitting behind the wheel before he seemed to remember that he needed his keys. He felt the outside of his front pockets, then twisted so he could reach into his right one, but the keys got away from him and slipped into the gap next to his seat. He laughed at himself, groped around for them, eventually with success, then said, as he finally got the key into the ignition, "So, how did you spend this beautiful day?" She had the feeling he had thought up a question ahead of time, just to get a conversation started.

She could have told him she had scrubbed her floors, but instead she said, "I worked on a paper all afternoon. Can you believe that?"

"No, I can't. You really take school serious, don't you?"

"Yeah, I do. I never did in high school, but I've started to in college."

"That's good. That's what I've got to do too. I'm doing okay, but I don't put in as much time on the books as I really should. I have better study habits than I did before my mission, though. I sort of blew away my freshman year."

Diane couldn't help wondering what Greg would think of a statement like that. It was hard to believe that Ed was going to amount to a whole lot. During her years with Greg, she had heard nothing but talk of high grades and big achievements. Greg had probably emphasized all that too much, but it was what she had come to expect. Ed had at least three years of college left and no clear major. It was hard to think of him as any sort of prospect for marriage.

On the other hand, she realized something about him she hadn't admitted to herself before. His simplicity and good nature made her think of Kent Wade. She had heard recently that Kent had finished his degree and taken a job as a high school teacher—a career Greg would have looked down his nose at—but she knew what a wonderful teacher he would be. She still thought of him sometimes, about the way he would have treated her and the nice family they might have had together. Maybe Ed was young, and certainly not the right one for her, but he was nice, and clearly, he thought he was getting a taste of heaven, just to be with her.

Diane worried as they drove downtown what kind of questions Ed might ask, so she pushed the conversation toward college, their chemistry class, and what was going on around campus. She also worried about running into someone at the movie who might drop a comment that would reveal what Ed didn't know—and she did spot an old Ogden High friend she managed to avoid—but they made it into the theater without saying much of importance. He took hold of her hand for a few minutes when they were standing in line, and she noticed that his hand was harder, thicker than Greg's, and at the same time less forceful, less sure. The little "move" was funny to Diane—a game she hadn't played for a long time. She was relieved when he didn't try to take her hand during the movie, and of course, also a little disappointed. But afterward, he gave her his arm as they walked through the parking lot to the car, which was clearly borrowed from his father since it was an almost-new Plymouth—a four-door Satellite, not a GTX.

"Would you like to get something to eat?" he asked when they were sitting in the car again.

"Maybe a little something. I'm not very hungry. I ate too much of your popcorn—after I told you I didn't want any."

He laughed. "Girls always do that." Diane wasn't surprised that he had called her a "girl," but she did wonder about his comparisons. High school girls, probably. "What if we went to Bratton's Grotto, up on Harrison?" Ed suggested. "We could get a bowl of clam chowder or something like that."

"That sounds really good. Bratton's is nice." Diane's thought was that he had a little more class than she had expected. She wouldn't have been at all surprised if he had suggested Rigo's, for pizza.

"To tell you the truth, I've never been there. It was my mother's idea. She's always trying to teach me how to do things."

Diane liked that almost better. Greg would have known exactly where to go. He would have taken her to the nicest place in town and then ordered for her. Diane liked that Ed wasn't so pretentious and controlling. And yet, it wouldn't hurt if he sounded a little less as though he were stretching just to pull off a little movie-and-a-dinner date.

Bratton's was crowded. Diane and Ed had to wait a few minutes and then were led to a small table by a wall. Greg would have maneuvered somehow to get a view, even if it was only of the street outside. Diane ordered a bowl of chowder and sourdough bread, and Ed followed her lead. He talked about his mom liking to bake bread, as though he was trying to think of *anything* to say.

"Your parents sound nice. Do you have a big family?" Diane asked.

"Not real big. I've got two sisters and a little brother."

"So you're the oldest?"

"Yeah. My two sisters are not much younger—twenty and seventeen—but Cory is only seven. He was a latecomer."

"That's how we are too. I've got a sister who's eighteen, and a little brother who's only eight."

Ed rubbed his freckled nose and took a look around the room, every move somehow seeming childlike, as though he didn't know what to do with his hands and didn't know what to say next. Finally he asked, "What does your dad do?"

There were so many dangerous questions, Diane was realizing. If she said he taught at Weber State, Ed would want to know what he taught, and if they pushed the matter a little, he might find out that Diane didn't have the same last name. So she merely said, "Both of my parents are teachers" and hoped he wouldn't follow up.

"My dad taught for a while, but he started selling real estate in the summers, and he ended up switching over and doing that full-time. He'd rather teach, but the money was better in real estate." Diane nodded, didn't comment, and she could tell that Ed thought he had made a mistake. "But it's not like my dad's made a killing or anything. We still have the same house we've had since I was a little boy. It's not fancy at all."

"Fancy doesn't matter much, does it?"

"No. But I'll tell you the truth, I thought you would say your dad was a big wheel in some company or something like that. You *look* like you've got a lot of money—or that you were raised with it."

"Not really," Diane said, and then she couldn't resist. "But I'm curious why you say that."

"I don't know. You're just so . . . amazing looking . . . and you seem really classy. Right from the first day of class, I started checking you out, and I kept telling myself, 'I really want to get to know her, but if I try, she'll laugh at me.'"

"So why did you try?"

"I don't know. Nothing ventured, nothing gained. When I told my mother about you, she said, 'A lot of beautiful girls are really nice. Don't make up your mind about her until you find out.'"

Diane gave him that sly smile she kept in waiting for such moments. "Do you always do what your mother tells you?"

There was nothing sly in his response. He blushed, the way he had that day in the library, and then he said, "No. Not always. But I figured she knew more about this kind of stuff than I do."

"What kind of stuff?" Diane knew she was being cruel, especially since she was teasing with her eyes, but it was an old pleasure she hadn't enjoyed in years.

"You know. Dating. I went out to dances and stuff before my mission, but since I got back, it's like starting all over—and it's sort of different now."

"What's different?" Diane was spreading a bit of butter on a slice of bread. Ed had eaten most of the little loaf. She was pretty sure he would have preferred a big hamburger over a bowl of soup.

"I don't know. In high school, I usually double-dated or went with a whole bunch of people. I never had a steady girlfriend. Back then, though, I was going out—you know, just to go."

"So what are you doing now?"

The answer, of course, was that he was looking for a wife, but he obviously saw where his own logic was leading, and he hedged. "I don't know. It just seems a little more serious now." And then he looked at her straight on and said the last thing she expected from him. "I'm nervous, Diane. I really want to impress you. I figure this might be my only chance. But I don't know how to do it."

"You just did. Not many guys would admit to something like that."

"Maybe that's all I have going for me." He was looking at the bread basket, as though he wanted to take the last slice but wondered whether he should. Diane pushed it over to him, and he looked up, surprised. Diane thought she knew what he was thinking: *This girl sees right through me.* But what he said was, "You're not like any girl I've ever known."

"What do you mean?"

"I'm not sure. You seem more grown-up. You seem—I don't know how to describe it—like you've really got yourself together."

"Well, that's nice of you to say. I guess I feel a little more confident than I used to. But I've had a lot to learn about myself."

Ed glanced around as though wondering why the waitress hadn't returned with the chowder. She had the feeling he had eaten too much in fast-food places. "Like what?" he asked.

Diane wondered. Should she tell him her story now? But she knew what would happen to their date. So she told a truth—just not the one she needed to tell. "You keep saying that I'm pretty. A lot of people have told me that, and I've listened to them more than I should. There was a time when I thought looks were *really* important. But they aren't. When I figured that out, I took a hard look inside myself and decided I didn't like what I had become. I had never developed the qualities I needed. Lately, though, I've been working on some of that, and I feel better about myself."

"What do you mean? What kinds of things?"

"I was a terrible student in high school, and—"

"I'm glad to know that."

Diane laughed. "Well, I'm trying to do better. I also thought I was religious because I always went to church. Now, I'm trying to find out what it means to be spiritual. I'm not sure I've come very far, but I'm trying to do more than just go through the motions."

"That's what my mission did to me. Before I went, the biggest things to me were sports and camping with my buddies—all that kind of stuff. I said I had a testimony, and I guess I sort of did, but I got out there on the East Coast where people believe different things, and some of the stuff I heard really blew me away for a while. People asked me all kinds of questions I couldn't answer, and I realized that my faith was about as deep as a mud puddle. In my homecoming talk, I told everyone that when I got to the mission field I stopped praying. Then I said, 'And I started *pleading*.'" He laughed at himself, looking wonderfully boyish again—and cute. His hair was cut short, but it still kept slipping onto his forehead, and he was constantly brushing it back with his fingers.

"Did the pleading work?"

"I thought it wasn't going to for a while. But yeah, it did. I learned *a lot* on my mission. At first, I was scared to death to talk to people about the Church, or to give lessons. I didn't think I'd ever be ready to be a senior. But I did okay. I got so I could—you know—teach pretty well. I'm not saying that's a big talent of mine, but I did all right."

Diane knew how Greg rated missionaries: by whether or not they had held positions of leadership. She was glad Ed hadn't told her that he had been a zone leader or an assistant to the president. Maybe that was only because he hadn't been called to anything like that, but she had the feeling that he wouldn't bring it up anyway.

"So what do you want to do with your life?" Diane asked.

"I'm not sure. I've got more confidence than I had before, so I'm thinking about things I never used to. It would take me forever, but I might want to go to medical school. That's why I've got to do well in chemistry."

"And that's why you need *my* help with your math. Right?"

He grinned with a little more self-assurance, didn't even blush much, and said, "Actually, I'm thinking I could use almost constant help with my math—all you're willing to give me."

Diane was surprised. This was Ed's first attempt at a more flirtatious tone. "You RM's are all alike," she said. "You know all the tricks."

"Hey, when I stopped you at the library, that was the first time in my life I'd ever done anything like that. I was so scared my vision was getting blurry."

Diane knew once again it was time to tell him the truth. He was clearly hoping this date was the first of many, and even though he might have a decade of school ahead of him—if he actually made it into med school—she knew he was imagining her as the wife who would share the hard years with him. Diane wasn't ready for that, of course, but there was something youthful and romantic in the little fantasy; she couldn't resist sharing some of the pleasure of it.

So she didn't pop his bubble, and he took her home, and at the door he said, "Diane, I feel like I've already known you for a long time. I've never had that feeling after one date with a girl. I hope . . . you know . . . that everything was okay."

"It was nice, Ed. But you don't *really* know me yet."

"Yeah. I guess that's right. And you don't know me. But I hope we can get to know each other a lot better. Will you go out with me again?"

"Sure." But she tried to make it sound like a routine thing for her, not something she was terribly excited about. She knew she had to do at least that much to keep him from building up his hopes. One of these first days, when his eyes weren't so full of awe, she was going to call him aside and tell him the truth.

When Diane walked into her apartment, she felt the dark and the emptiness again. She almost wished that Greg had been sitting outside in his car, waiting with Jenny, frustrated because Jenny had cried to come home. She wondered what Greg—and even Jenny—would think of her going out with someone else.

She didn't turn the light on for a time. She sat on her couch and looked at the floor, where a street lamp was casting its light in a big rectangle on her carpet. The unhappiness she had been fighting since that morning was filling her again. She had enjoyed being with Ed, but she couldn't go back and grow up with him. The irony was, Greg could give her all the things she wanted—instantly—and above all, he could step back into Jenny's life, a good fit. But she doubted he had really changed. It was always possible that when she walked out on Greg she had opened his eyes, and his effort to change was real. Still, she knew she could never love him the way she had in the beginning. She had feelings for him, if for no other reason than that they had been through a good deal together—and they shared a daughter. But she also had memories that would always haunt her.

The phone rang. Her immediate fear was that it was Greg calling with a problem or an emergency. Maybe he had been trying to reach her all evening. She hurried into the kitchen, flipped on the light, and took the receiver from the wall phone. But it was her mother's voice she heard. "Honey, I'm sorry to call so late, but I've been calling every fifteen minutes for a while. I knew that wouldn't give you time to come in and get to sleep."

"I just got here about five minutes ago," Diane said.

"So how was he?"

"Is that why you called?"

"Well . . . yes." Bobbi laughed at herself.

"He's very nice. And he's very young." Diane didn't want to go into any details.

"He's not *that* much younger than you are, Diane."

"If you talked with him for a little while, you wouldn't say that." Diane leaned against the wall, next to the phone. She didn't want this conversation to last very long.

"But think about it this way. Women usually live longer than men. It makes sense to marry a young guy who won't be as likely to leave you a widow."

"Mom, you don't even know him."

"I'm not saying you *should* marry him."

"Then what are you saying?" Diane could tell this wasn't going to be quick. She sat down at the kitchen table.

"Just that you shouldn't rule out all the men who are a year or two younger than you are. Most of the guys in college *are* more his age."

"Mom, he's thinking about medical school. If he gets in, he'll be in college forever. I don't want to start over like that."

"I understand what you're saying. But I think those things depend on how much you love someone. If something worked out between the two of you, all that wouldn't be as significant as you think."

Diane laughed. She put her elbow on the table and used her hand to brace up her chin. "He's a very nice boy, Mom," she said, her chin pressing into her hand. "He's honest and he's sweet. But I doubt he'll even make it into medical school. He's not exactly Albert Einstein."

Bobbi was quiet for a time. She finally said, "I'm sorry, Di. I shouldn't do this to you. I'm sounding like my own mom now. She worried herself to death when I got so *dreadfully* old and still wasn't married."

"I think this is a little different."

"It is different. I know. But I want so badly for you to be happy."

"I'm okay."

"I know." But neither said the other things that could have been said.

"He was really cute, Mom. He took me to Bratton's and we ordered chowder, even though I know he wanted a full meal. He's probably off buying himself a hamburger right now."

"And you've broken the ice. You've gone out once. That's a step forward."

"Yeah, I guess."

"But you haven't told me what he said when you told him you'd been married before."

Diane leaned back in her chair. Bobbi had a talent for questions like that—the ones Diane didn't like to answer. "I didn't tell him, Mom. I will before we go out again, but it would have made everything really awkward tonight."

"I understand." Then she said the obvious. "But you really do have to tell him soon."

"I know. I was going to, but he was just so—I don't know—*awestruck*. He made me feel pretty, and I haven't felt that way lately. He hardly asked me anything about my life. It was like he had an idea of me in his head and that was good enough for him. If he had asked the right questions, I would have answered honestly."

"But now you're in a bit of a predicament."

"I know." But there were things Mom didn't seem to understand. For one night Diane had felt like a college girl—the girl she had been the first time around, when everything was still ahead of her. It had been so nice just to let herself believe for a few hours that she didn't have a "past"— didn't have an image she hadn't chosen for herself. She had felt something like pain all evening—wishing that somehow she could do her life over and get it right this time.

Diane told her mother she was tired and wanted to get to bed, and her mother did seem to recognize there was nothing more to say. Diane said good-bye, got up, and hung up the phone, but then she sat down at the kitchen table again, where the light was bright. The rest of the apartment was so dark, and with no one there, not even Jenny, she felt not just alone but a little frightened. She had never liked to be alone, had never been good at it, but the dark beyond the kitchen seemed to represent her life now. It was what she had to look forward to. For the second time that day she bent over the table and rested her head on her arms. And also for the second time, she cried—much longer this time.

Kathy was on her way to Grandma and Grandpa Thomas's house. She had called that week and said, "Grandma, if you don't mind, I'd like to go to sacrament meeting with you this Sunday."

"Why is that?" Grandma had asked. "Do we teach better doctrine in our ward?"

But Kathy hadn't had to explain. Grandma Bea had been telling Kathy since she had come home from the Peace Corps that she ought to go to church with her and maybe have a chance to talk to Marshall. Grandma had some of the same doubts about Marshall that Kathy did, and most of those had come from things his own mother had said about him: that he kept changing his mind about his major—and his girlfriends—and still wasn't sure what he wanted out of life. Still, Grandma would always say, "He is a nice-looking boy, though, and smart as a whip. I think he's going to settle down to something one of these days. And the thing is, he asks me about you almost every time I talk to him. If you ask me, he's still interested."

By the time Kathy parked in front of Grandma's house she was nervous. She had driven a car that her dad had been letting her use lately, a '65 Ford Mustang that Wally had taken as a trade-in at the dealership. It was bright red and well equipped. Kathy sort of liked the idea of Marshall seeing it and getting a little different picture of her. She had even thought of offering him a ride. But if she did that, her excuse for being in the wrong ward was gone. She wanted to be able to say—if he should bother to ask—that she had dropped by to visit with her grandparents and they had invited her to come along to church with them. So why would they come in two cars?

Kathy rode with Grandma and Grandpa Thomas, and Grandpa insisted on driving, even though he was scary behind the wheel these days. He didn't seem frail; he looked as strong as ever. But he didn't pay attention at times, as though it was too much to think and drive at the same time. He seemed to go back and forth from doing one or the other. The fact was, his health wasn't good. He had been dealing with congestive heart failure for quite some time, and he got tired just walking up a few steps or doing anything else that exerted him. But in the car, Grandma Bea told Kathy, "Do you know what I caught your grandpa doing this week? He was out raking leaves. He didn't even tell me he was going out."

"Why should I have to tell you? You follow me every place I go. I have to hide in the bathroom just to get a little peace once in a while."

This was said with a gruffness that might have worried Kathy if she hadn't known the playfulness that underlay her grandparents' disputes. "Well," Grandma said, "you stay in there so long, I get worried. I might have to start following you there, too."

"Just try."

Grandma twisted in her seat as best she could to look back at Kathy. "Raking leaves. Can you believe that? Sometimes I think he wants to get to the spirit world as soon as he can." Kathy could see a hint of Grandma's dimple and knew she was on the edge of smiling. "I think he wants to find out whether the next life is all it's cracked up to be."

"That's about right," Grandpa said. "If I can't get up and do a little work once in a while, that's where I'd rather be. The Lord won't tell me that I have to rest. He'll give me a job."

"Now, Grandpa," Kathy told him, "don't be making travel plans. We need you here. You're the one who keeps us all on the strait and narrow."

Grandpa chuckled. Kathy could see his eyes in the rear-view mirror, wrinkled and squinting, but still very clear. "I never could keep *you* there. You've wandered all the way to hell and back a few times in your life."

"Not quite. I peeked in and had a look, but I didn't jump in."

"But you thought about it, way too long."

"I know. But I found out they didn't have choirs down there. I couldn't live without choirs." Kathy had held her first choir practice earlier that afternoon. Her singers were better than the ones she had led in the Philippines, but their enthusiasm wasn't nearly so strong. She was going to work on that.

Grandpa had begun fiddling with the mirror, moving it back and forth rather wildly. "What are you doing, Al?" Grandma asked him.

"I wanted to see who that is in my back seat. She sounds almost like Kathy, our granddaughter—the one who never would listen to a thing I told her. But it couldn't be her, not saying things like that."

"Oh, Al! What you won't do for a joke. Now you can't see a thing behind you."

"It doesn't matter. I don't look at that thing anyway."

Kathy and Grandma laughed, partly because they knew it was true. But Kathy kissed her fingers and then tapped Grandpa on the back of the head. "I love you, old fellow," she said. "And you're wrong. I heard every word you ever told me." She rested her hand on his shoulder. "And I paid about as much attention to your advice as you do to your rear-view mirror."

"That's what I thought," Grandpa said, and he chuckled again.

Kathy liked what she felt from Grandpa these days. The whole family was overjoyed that she was working in the Church, involved again, not sounding so strident as she had over the years. What Kathy wished was that it was as easy as it probably seemed to them. She did feel more committed to the Church than she had in a long time—since her early teens when she had accepted everything rather unquestioningly—but there was no returning to that kind of simplicity. She still heard people say things at church that grated on her so badly it was all she could do not to react.

After all these years of struggle for civil rights in the country, people still made comments about blacks that were condescending at best, downright racist at worst. She had called her friend Lester not long ago—the black friend she had known while she was attending college in the East. "I don't understand, Kathy," he had said. "How can you accept a church that says blacks are not equal to whites?"

"We don't say that, Lester. I know it seems that way, but—"

"But whites can be preachers in your church and blacks can't. It sure sounds like racism to me."

And then they had talked, but Kathy hadn't really known what to tell him. There were plenty of members who claimed to understand the policy of the Church. They said it had something to do with blacks being fence-sitters in the premortal life. But no one could trace that doctrine to its origins, and Kathy didn't believe it. She understood that a change could come only from the prophet, and that was something Lester saw as an excuse, but she did feel the way a lot of members felt: that the Lord would speak to his prophet and a day of change would come. Still, she knew members of her ward who claimed that hoping such a thing was wrong—and contrary to doctrine. The same people claimed not to have anything against blacks, but she was as skeptical as Lester about that.

Kathy spoke much less during Sunday School lessons than she once had, but she occasionally took positions that she had come to believe during her activist years—and not always to the other members' liking. But she kept her tone soft, and she reminded herself over and over that the gospel ran much deeper than any current "issue" did. She told Lester, "I had some experiences in the Philippines that changed me. I doubted God for such a long time, but I felt something real when I got back in touch with him. I just have to trust that. It's more important than anything to me now."

And it was what she felt again as the congregation at Grandma and Grandpa's ward sang "Lord, Accept Our True Devotion" before the sacrament was passed. Sometimes Kathy wished that church meetings could consist only of hymn singing. When people spoke, all too often they got off onto their own hobbyhorses—the same as she tended to do—but when the members sang together she felt a unison in their devotion. She had spent some years feeling lonely in the Church, and sometimes that feeling returned, but she now felt that had been her fault, and for a long time she had blamed it on everyone else.

Kathy tried hard to think about her own joy in the gospel as she took the bread and then the water, but another set of thoughts had intruded. She had sat with her grandparents in the pew where they always sat these days, about two-thirds of the way back on the right side. She had taken a good look around before the meeting started, and she hadn't seen Marshall. She was disappointed, but she told herself to forget about him. Then, just after the opening prayer, she had glanced back to see him come in through the door on the opposite side of the chapel. He found a seat close to the back. After that, it was a little hard to think entirely about "devotion" when she was also wondering how she could possibly meet up with him when the meeting was over. She could try to work her way toward him somehow, or maybe get to the parking lot in time to cross paths with him, but that wouldn't be easy the way Grandpa walked.

Kathy remained preoccupied all through the meeting, even though she tried to pay attention. That wasn't easy when a woman, Sister Dahlquist, used most of her talk to introduce her husband and herself and their five kids to the ward—offering details about her *special* children and her *special* husband and all the *special* experiences they had shared. Kathy still struggled not to gag on that much syrup. Brother Dahlquist's sermon was mostly an extended metaphor that compared running a race to living the gospel. He managed to throw in a few sports stories about Wade Bell, the Mormon distance runner, and stretch the comparison to the breaking point. But Kathy knew she was being too critical, as usual, and she tried to listen with more charity. Sometimes she wondered whether she would ever develop a better attitude—more patience with less effort.

And then, at the end, Kathy was reminded what the reward could be for staying in the right spirit. Brother Dahlquist told about the struggle he and his wife had gone through when they lost a daughter to leukemia. He described her gradual waning and her death. He was a big guy who would clearly rather watch a ball game than stand before a congregation, but he cried, and he thanked the Lord for helping him and his wife survive their loss. When he bore his testimony, Kathy felt it, and she liked him. She even liked his wife more than she had before.

Through all that, Kathy was still thinking about Marshall. Had he noticed her? She only allowed herself to glance over her shoulder three or four times, and she had never caught him looking her way. What if he planned to get away quickly right after the meeting? She couldn't keep coming back every week until she finally ran into him.

So when the final hymn was sung, and the closing prayer spoken, Kathy did the only thing she could think to do—short of pushing her grandparents out of their seats in a rush to get outside. She stood up rather quickly, one of the first to rise, and for once in her life she was glad she was so tall. What she didn't do was look Marshall's way at the same time. She had to keep a certain level of self-respect. But that meant, once she was up, she could only stand there waiting for her grandparents, since they were both closer to the aisle. Grandma had started talking to some people sitting in front of her. "Yes, I did hear about Floyd," she was saying. "He was healthy as could be, and then he just fell over, dead on the spot."

"That's the only way to go," Grandpa said.

As the discussion continued, with the two couples talking about the uncertainties of life, Kathy was no longer sure she was glad to be tall. She felt like a scarecrow. And so she did the only thing that didn't feel awkward. She sat back down and let go of her hopes. But just then she heard his voice. "Hey, Kathy, it's good to see you."

She turned and looked over her shoulder. Marshall had slipped into the now-empty pew, just behind her. "Oh, hi, Marshall. I didn't realize you were here."

Kathy's voice had come out tight and the final note, at the end of the sentence, had risen—the telltale sound of a really bad actor.

"I came in late, as usual. I was glad to see you were here."

"I came over to see my grandparents this afternoon, and they talked me into coming with them instead of going back to my own ward." Her tone was better this time, but she had been practicing the line.

"So Kathy Thomas is going to her church meetings. What's going on?"

Kathy turned a little more in her seat. But now her grandparents were getting up, and Grandma turned to say hello to Marshall. Then, with surprising skill, Grandma told a little white lie of her own. "Kathy, I need to see the bishop. You talk to Marshall. I won't be long."

Grandpa obviously didn't recognize that Grandma was inventing a fiction, and he began to sit back down, as though he figured he would wait with Kathy. But Grandma grabbed his arm. "Walk out with me, Al. We might have to wait in the foyer a few minutes until I can catch him." And then she tried a little too hard. "It's Relief Society business," she said, and the ring of the words was off-key. Kathy heard it clearly, but Marshall showed no sign. He simply said good-bye and then looked at Kathy again.

Kathy slid back along the bench so she didn't have to twist quite so much, but she was quick to get back to Marshall's question. There were things she wanted him to know. "I thought you knew, Marshall. I got active in the Church in the Philippines, and I've stayed that way since I've been home."

Marshall laughed. "Actually, I did hear that. Your grandma told me. I'm just teasing you." Kathy was thinking how good he looked—older and a little fuller in the face, but still with those dusky eyes, always so calm, and white teeth that looked so great against his tan skin. He was wearing a blue shirt with the top button undone and the tie not quite tight. He had always preferred to do things just a little his own way.

"What are you doing now, Kathy?"

"I'm working for my dad, just doing secretarial work. My degree is almost useless. I need to get a master's degree in social work, probably, if I want to find a job in something close to my field. The only trouble is, I'm not sure that's what I want to do. So I haven't applied to grad school yet."

"I'm in worse shape than you are. At least you have a degree. I can finish up next spring if I stay the course, but I've gotten back into history, and I don't think I want to be a high school history teacher. So that means I either have to go all the way for a Ph.D. and teach at a college, or I have to switch to something else again. My dad wants me to finish in history, then get an MBA, but to tell you the truth, the thought of it makes my skin crawl." He made a little shivering motion.

"I know what you mean. It seems like making a deal with the devil, doesn't it?"

He nodded, then leaned back and stretched one arm across the back of the bench. "I don't know, Kathy. In some ways, we're two of a kind. We like to learn. We just don't know what to do with what we know."

Kathy thought maybe that was more true of him than her, but she liked that he saw them as similar. And above all, she liked people who did love learning. Marshall would surely figure out a way to make a living sooner or later, but he would never lose his curiosity. She remembered how much she had loved talking to him during those weeks they had dated. She had never found anyone else quite like him.

"To tell the truth," Marshall said. "I feel a little lost right now. I joke about it, but it's actually kind of frightening."

"I know. I used the same words about myself when I was talking to my bishop last week. I managed to avoid thinking much about the future while I was in the Peace Corps, but since I've been home, reality has been staring me in the face, and I'm nervous about it. I'm an 'older woman' back here. I feel out of place." She hadn't meant to say that. She didn't want to imply that she was getting desperate.

"But is that what you want now?"

"You mean to get married?"

He nodded.

"Well, sure. I know how I used to talk, but I think I've finally out-grown my 'angry young woman' age. I struggle with a few things around here, but I know what I want, ultimately. It's what my parents have."

He nodded slowly, looked at her with so much understanding that she thought she had said the right thing. Maybe he was remembering his old feelings about her. He stretched his other arm out so that he was posi-tioned like Jesus on the crucifixes Kathy had seen so often in the Philippines, and in a rather sad voice, he said, "I'm the one who needs to grow up. I was engaged for a while. I guess you know that. But my girl-friend got so disgusted with me—when I kept changing majors and everything—that she gave up on me. The girl I'm going with now is a little younger, and maybe a little more patient, but I think she's starting to feel the same way."

Kathy felt her muscles relax, her hope suddenly gone. She had heard he was going out with someone, but mentioning this new girl he was dat-ing seemed his way of reminding Kathy that she was merely an old friend. Maybe she had been a little too obvious in the way she had been looking at him.

"In fact, I've got to get going. I was supposed to pick up Lisa as soon as church was over. For some reason, she accuses me of being late all the time."

Kathy tried to laugh, and she stood. She thought about shaking his hand, but she didn't. "You'll figure things out," she said. "I guess I will too."

And then he left, walking fast, hurrying back to *Lisa*. Kathy watched him go, made some silent resolutions, then walked out to find her grandparents in the foyer. Grandpa was confused when Bea was willing to leave without seeing the bishop, but Grandma only said, "I'll talk to him later," and then winked at Kathy.

On the way home Kathy had to answer all Grandma's questions. No, he wasn't engaged, but yes, he was serious about someone. And no, he hadn't said anything about seeing her again.

He actually had said, as he walked away, "I'll see you sometime, I'm sure," and when Kathy got home, she tried to make something out of that, but there had been nothing in his tone that implied it was anything more than a casual way to say good-bye.

So that was that. Kathy had tried not to build up her hopes about this little attempt of hers to see Marshall, but she had prayed about it all week, and when Marshall's voice had suddenly been there, behind her, and when he had talked about their similarities, she really had thought for a few minutes that he would want to see her again, soon.

Lorraine wanted to hear about everything too, and Kathy was really not in the mood. But she described the general tenor of what had happened and tried to say, in a level voice, that no sparks had flown. But she couldn't keep the emotion out of her voice, and Mom clearly heard it. "Well, honey, you've always said you two probably weren't right for each other."

"I know. And I'm sure that's true. But if you think about it, he's the closest I've ever come to having a boyfriend, and it lasted about a month and a half. I have this strange power over guys—to send them running away."

Kathy and her mom were sitting in the family room, Kathy on the floor with her legs stretched out and looking, to her, as though they were a mile and a half long. She was reminded once again that she was an ungainly freak of nature, taller than most of the males of the species, and not really brilliant but way too smart for her own good.

Mom was on the couch, sitting forward, looking worried. She was almost fifty now and still very pretty. She was so delicate compared to Kathy, and always graceful, always composed. Kathy had hated that quality at one time. She hadn't understood why nothing upset her mother, why she didn't have any fight in her, but Kathy had also envied her tranquillity, and now she wished she could be more like her.

Kathy hadn't planned to admit to her mom how disappointed she was, but she found herself saying, "I worked this up too much in my mind, I think. I kept remembering your story—how Dad went away to the war for so many years, and how you two ended up together anyway. Didn't he propose to you when you were engaged to another guy?"

"No. Not exactly." Mom smiled, and Kathy could see how much she loved the memory. "I didn't know for a long time whether your dad was still alive, and besides, we had broken up before he left for the army. I told myself to forget him—but I just couldn't. I ended up working in Seattle, and I met this really fine man—a navy officer and a member of the Church—and we got engaged. But I never felt quite as much for him as I wanted to. I delayed our wedding once, and then I found out your dad was coming home after all. I told myself not to think about Wally, and to keep my commitment, but when your dad and I talked the first time, all those old feelings came back. And he had really grown up. He looked awful, because of what he had been through, but he was so spiritual compared to what he had been."

"So how did he propose?"

"You know the story, don't you?"

"Kind of. But tell me again."

"We were at a church dance, and a friend of his made sure I danced with your dad. I had broken up with the man I'd been engaged to, but Wally didn't know. I kept trying to get him to see my finger—that there was no ring on it—but he didn't notice it for a long time. Finally, he realized why I was waving my hand under his nose." Lorraine laughed and looked so nostalgic that Kathy wanted to cry. It was what she had allowed herself to imagine this whole week, partly because the bishop had told her to find a way to see Marshall. "So Wally asked me to leave with him, but then he walked back into the recreation hall and asked the band to play this song that was a favorite of ours. Your dad was a great dancer, I guess you know."

"I've heard you say that, but I don't see the evidence."

"Well, we don't dance a lot now, but he's still a good dancer if we can get someone to play the old-fashioned songs."

"What was the song? You've told me before."

"'I Get Along Without You Very Well.'"

"Oh, yeah. That's such a great song. I wish we still had music like that."

"Your dad still likes to sing it to me sometimes."

"Dad? He sings?"

"Your dad is more romantic than you would ever imagine."

Kathy laughed, but the truth was, she had always had an inkling of that. "So how did he actually ask you?" Kathy knew. She just wanted to hear it again.

"He used the music to express what he wanted to say. You know, the song really means, 'I *can't* get along without you.' He told me that all during those horrible days as a POW, it was thinking about me that kept him alive. Then he knelt on one knee in the parking lot and asked me to marry him. We hadn't even had a real date yet, and we were engaged. We surprised our parents half to death."

"But they were happy for you, I'll bet."

"Oh, yes. And I'll be happy for you one of these days. I'm sure I will."

"Mom, I went away and Marshall forgot me. You would think I could have set off a little more of a spark than that. I've thought about him all these years, and what does he say to me? 'I've got to go pick up *Lisa*. I'm late.'"

"So let me see if I understand what you're saying. You two are not right for each other and you don't want him, *but* you want him to want you?"

"No." Kathy looked down at her legs again. "I don't know. Maybe. I let myself imagine this week that we might be right for each other after all. I guess I just want someone to love me. I know how obnoxious I've been all my life, but I'm getting better. I think I could be a good mother and a good wife. It's what I try to believe about myself, anyway."

"Kathy, I think you're spectacular. You're pretty enough and tall enough to be a model, if that's what you wanted. And you're brainy enough to do anything you choose. But above all—and it's what I've always known about you—you're good. I worried so much about some of the things you got involved with, but it was always because you cared about our world. The problem is, it's going to take a guy just as spectacular as you not to be scared off. Don't fret, though. He's out there somewhere."

"It's nice to get an objective opinion from my mother."

"I may not be objective, but I think I'm right."

Kathy didn't think so. She knew Aunt LaRue's story. LaRue was someone *truly* spectacular, and she had never married. "You're an optimist, Mom. Or maybe you have more faith than I do. But I'm well aware that things don't always work out the way we want them to." She pulled in her legs and stood up, feeling the effort. She was tired.

"I know," was all that Lorraine said.

Kathy waited a second, sort of hoped Mom would promise—based on her own faith—that things really would work out. But surely Mom knew better than to do that. She had tried too many times to argue with Kathy.

Kathy headed down the hall to her bedroom, and along the way did something she knew was stupid. She stopped at her old bedroom, Glenda's now. Nothing about it looked the same, but she thought again about the day Marshall had watched her pack to leave for college, and then—when she had finally hinted enough—taken her in his arms and kissed her. It was the warmest memory of her life, but she had to let it go. The fact was, most of the girls she had known in high school had children now. She had chosen to go away to college and chosen to go into the Peace Corps, and choices had consequences. She needed to stop feeling sorry for herself, make up her mind what she wanted to do, and then pursue the life she wanted. She couldn't base all her future choices on whether a man ever came into her life.

CHAPTER 5

By early December Diane had been out with Ed three times. He had actually wanted to see her much more often than that. She had hinted to him that her past life was not what Ed might expect, but he hadn't taken the bait and had never really probed. Diane kept telling herself that she had no responsibility to tell Ed everything. After all, she was only going out with him "socially"; he hadn't even tried to kiss her. In her BYU dating days she had learned to give signals to her pursuers, to accept dates for fun but to keep most guys at a distance so they knew they were wasting their time if they tried to get serious. She felt herself doing that now with Ed, holding herself remote, always keeping things light. She could also see that her demeanor was frustrating him, that their dating really couldn't go on any longer this way. The next time he called, she had decided for sure, she would tell him about Jenny and see how he reacted.

But he didn't call. He showed up at her door. It was a Friday, and she had come home from school early in the afternoon. Jenny had fallen asleep in the car, so Diane had carried her in and put her down, then tried to get a chapter read for one of her education classes. But the doorbell had rung, and there was Ed standing in her doorway, his neck hunched into a wool-collared coat and his eyes full of confusion. "Hi, Ed," she said, but she didn't have to ask him what was wrong.

"Why didn't you tell me?"

She stepped back and said, "Come in for a minute."

He came inside but stayed close to the door after he shut it behind him. There were flakes of snow on his hair and on the shoulders of his plaid coat. "What is it I didn't tell you?" Diane asked.

"That you'd been married before."

"Does it matter that much to you?"

But that seemed to stop him. He pulled his hands out of his coat pockets, seemed not to know what to do with them, then pushed them back in. "It's not that you were married that bothers me. I just don't understand why you didn't tell me."

"Why? Are we serious about each other? Were you thinking of offering me a ring for Christmas?" Ed's head actually jerked backward. She had won this little fight with one punch. That was another part of the old Diane, who had once possessed a knack for shedding the guys she didn't find interesting.

But she hated the effect of her words on him. He looked destroyed as he seemed to shrivel into the corner. "Look, I . . ." He shook his head. "I really like you, Diane. A lot. I *was* starting to think that something might happen between us—not by Christmas, but sooner or later."

He sounded like a little boy. But she couldn't resist saying, "That all came from you, Ed. I haven't led you on at all."

He nodded slowly and then looked at the floor.

"But I'm sorry. I really should have told you. Sit down for a minute." He hesitated but then walked over and sat in her living-room chair. He stayed on the front edge and didn't take his coat off. Diane sat on the couch across from him. "I've meant to tell you, but you were the first guy to ask me out since my divorce was final, and—"

"You told me you had another date that first weekend I asked you out."

"No, I didn't. I said I couldn't go that weekend. You were the one who decided I was going out with someone else."

"I said that, and you didn't say otherwise."

Diane thought that was probably true, but what was he trying to say now? That a person had to tell *everything*, right from the beginning? "Ed, I really am sorry. But I've seen how guys react when I say I've been married. They run for cover. You were nice, and I didn't know you, but it seemed like it would be fun to go out. That's all it was to me."

"But it was more than that to me, and you knew it."

"I guess I did. But think about it. You've only been home from your mission a few months. You're twenty-one. What's the big hurry to find the 'right one' immediately? You ought to plan on dating for a while and just meeting a lot of girls."

"Diane, the very first time I looked at you, I thought you *were* the right one."

Diane laughed. Now she was annoyed. "So that's how it works? You can check a girl out, decide you like her looks, and fall in love? Apparently, you didn't care what I had inside my head as long as I was cute."

"I could tell in class that you were—"

"That's not what you just told me. You said 'the very first time I looked at you.'"

She had taken the ground out from under him again, and she saw the color come into his face. "All I'm saying is that I was attracted to you, right off. But then, when we went out, I liked *everything* about you."

"But what if I'd told you in the library that I'd been married before?"

"I don't think that would have mattered. I don't care about that. I'm just upset that you lied to me—in so many words."

"Well, okay. That was my mistake. I apologize. Now . . . are you going to ask me out again—since everything about me is so wonderful?"

Diane saw his eyes drift away from hers and heard the loss of assurance in his voice when he said, "Yes. But I do want to know more about the whole situation. I think we ought to be open and honest with each other."

"Okay, fine." She leaned forward so she could engage his eyes. "I met him at BYU. He was a returned missionary. Right after we got married, we moved to Seattle so he could go to law school. He took control of my life—made me feel worthless. Then he got rough with me. He hit me. I stuck with him for a while after that, but when he beat me up again, I left him. What else would you like to know?"

"He really did that?"

Diane saw how much the thought of all that hurt Ed. He really was a nice boy. "Yes. I already told you I'm older than you, and I mentioned Seattle a couple of times. I sort of expected you to ask a few more questions, just so I would have to tell you. But the truth is, it was fun to go out, and I assumed the end would come as soon as I said anything about my past—so I was selfish." Diane knew how terse and accusing her voice was, and she knew she wasn't being fair. He *had* asked some of the right questions, and she hadn't responded the way she might have. But she wasn't going to lose her power in this little confrontation; she had seen the doubt in his eyes when she asked whether he wanted to ask her out again—no matter how he had answered. So she asked again. "So, do you want to keep going out?"

"Not if you don't have any feelings for me."

"I like you, Ed. But it seems unlikely that anything would come of this." Diane heard a faint little cry from the bedroom, but then nothing more. Jenny would be getting up soon. She wondered whether Ed knew about her.

"But why not keep going out and see whether something isn't possible?" Ed asked.

"We could do that, I guess, but only if you'll date some other people, and we just go out as friends."

"That would kill me. I don't want to be around you if you won't give me more of a chance than that."

"Ed, you have years and years of school left. How could you get married and still get through all that?"

"Lots of people have done it. My parents did." He gestured with both hands, letting his palms rise, and finally he sounded a little more convinced.

"And you're sure you can accept the idea that I've been married before?"

"He beat you up, Diane? I don't blame you for leaving him. If you'd just told me that, I would have been fine with it."

Diane wondered. But now she heard another little cry, and Ed heard it this time. She saw that baffled look again, the one she had seen on his face when she had first opened the door. "Just a minute," she said. Diane got up and walked to Jenny's bedroom. She picked her up and held her for a few seconds. "Did you have a nice nap?" she whispered. Jenny dropped her head on Diane's shoulder, not entirely awake yet, but Diane carried her out to the living room and stood in front of Ed. "This is Jenny, my little girl. She's two."

Clearly, Ed hadn't known this. He wasn't blushing now; the color was leaving his face. "Hi," he said, the sound hardly making its way from his throat. Jenny looked around at him, then ducked her head again.

"I suppose you want to leave now."

He didn't answer, and he didn't look at Diane. "She's really cute," he said.

"She's really *smart*. That's what I like about her."

Ed nodded, and Diane could almost see the thoughts flashing through his brain.

"You're in a little deep now, aren't you? What if I had told you about Jenny?"

"That doesn't matter. It doesn't make any difference at all."

"Try that once more, *with* conviction this time. I think you've lost your breath."

"I was just surprised. I didn't know."

"Okay. What you need is time to think about this. Give me a call if you want to go out, but you can see why I'm careful about getting involved with anyone again. I thought I knew my first husband, and I didn't. If I ever marry again, I need more than a good husband; I need a good daddy for my little girl. A lot of guys don't like the idea of raising another man's child. If you're so sure you want something to happen between us, you need to decide how you feel about that."

She expected him to make an argument, at least a lame one, or to defend himself, but instead he stood up and walked to the door. "I'll call you," he said.

But she knew he wouldn't.

❧

Aunt LaRue was in town for the holidays. Kathy wanted to spend some time with her, and she knew Diane would too, so she called Diane and then also invited Emily. A few days before Christmas, Diane drove down from Ogden, and the four had lunch together at the Hot Shoppes in downtown Salt Lake. Kathy loved LaRue and regretted that during her years at Smith College she had sometimes made things awkward between them. She had spent far too little time with LaRue, not only missing a chance to deepen their relationship but also to learn from her. LaRue was not only fun and interesting; she was wise.

The four sat in a high-backed booth with red upholstery, Kathy next to LaRue, and Diane and Emily on the other side. They talked a little about this and that, laughed a lot, and ordered their food before LaRue said, "Okay, let's get down to business here. Kathy, what happened when you went to church with Grandma? I never did hear. Was Marshall there?"

LaRue and Kathy had been corresponding by mail—just not very regularly. Right after Kathy's discussion with her bishop, when he had suggested that Kathy go looking for Marshall, Kathy had written. She hadn't made a big deal out of the "plan," but she had obviously said enough to inspire some interest. "Yes, he was there," Kathy said. "He came over and said hello. Then he told me he was late picking up *Lisa*. He needed to run."

"Ouch!"

"It's good you don't like him anymore," Emily said, and she let her eyes roll.

"Right." Kathy laughed at herself. "He did look really cute, but he didn't so much as say, 'I'll call you sometime.' At least I don't have to give any more thought to that subject."

"Have you dated anyone since you got back from the Peace Corps?" Diane asked.

"Don't ask cruel questions," LaRue said, and everyone laughed.

"Can you believe it?" Kathy said. "Wayne, the little brother I used to kick around, is married now, and I can't even get a date."

Wayne's marriage earlier that month had bothered Kathy more than she liked to admit. It was true that she didn't have many opportunities to meet anyone, but it was painfully disappointing that she was back in her hometown—back in Mormon country—and there wasn't one guy who had enough interest to ask her out. So Kathy forced the conversation in a new direction. "Now that we've dealt with my past, present, and likely future—with one easily answered question—let's turn to Aunt LaRue. She has something to announce."

"I do not." The super-composed LaRue looked surprisingly undone. "All I said was—"

"She's chasing a *man*," Kathy said. "She's come to Utah to hunt him down."

LaRue tossed her head and shook her dark hair, which was down on her shoulders these days, longer than Kathy had ever seen it. Her deep skin color usually didn't record her embarrassment, but Kathy saw some pink showing in her cheeks now. At the same time, LaRue clearly enjoyed the attention—she always had. She was dressed in a brilliant red blouse, with dangling reindeer earrings and lots of bracelets. For quite a few years she had restrained her impulses, but she apparently wanted to get back some of her old flashiness. She was a woman who loved the "life of the mind," but she had always been playful at the same time, and she was looking the part now, with bright red lipstick and her lively eyes that, however dark, were glowing like fireflies. "I am not *chasing* a man."

"What shall we call it then?" Kathy said. "I guess we could say, 'Giving a certain person of the male gender the opportunity to get to know you better.'"

"I'm home for Christmas, that's all." But now LaRue was unleashing her full smile, with a radiance that said, *Of course, I may be up to something.*

Kathy looked across the table at Diane and Emily. "She met this BYU professor at a conference in Philadelphia or somewhere—"

"Baltimore, actually."

"Okay, Baltimore. But he was this really sexy widower, with—"

"Wait a minute." LaRue held up both hands as if to say, *Whoa!* "Just let me say this. I didn't say he was *sexy*."

"You said he was good-looking. I added the sexy part."

"He's almost fifty. You girls would think he was an old codger."

"No way. You said he reminded you of Cary Grant."

Diane and Emily both brightened. Their response brought to Kathy's mind how much she liked the two of them. She wondered why she didn't call them more, or drive up to Ogden and spend time with Diane. Diane and Emily looked so different—Diane blonde, stunning without the slightest effort; Emily dark, simple, pretty more than gorgeous. They had always seemed very different, but Kathy saw something similar in them now, as though hard experiences had taken away their girlishness, making them seem older than Kathy, even though they were both younger.

"Yes, well," LaRue was saying, "'reminded' is not exactly the same thing as 'looks like.' It's really the gentlemanly way he talks, and the way he moves, more than his actual looks."

"But he does look good, right?" Emily asked.

"Sure. For his age."

"Be careful, Aunt LaRue. You're getting 'up in age' yourself," Kathy said, but now she really was teasing. LaRue was forty-two, but she was prettier than ever.

"Have you gone out on a date with him?" Diane asked. Kathy was feeling something from Diane. She was going along with all the fun, but she wasn't as animated as usual, and Kathy had caught her looking away at times, as though she had other things on her mind.

"Not exactly," LaRue said. "We just ended up spending quite a bit of time together at the conference. I found out he was from BYU, so I told him I was LDS, but at that point, I had no idea he was single. We came across each other in the coffee shop the next morning and had breakfast together—and then we met for breakfast on purpose the next two days, and lunch besides. He's smart and nice and he loved his wife very much. She only died about eight months ago. So it was sort of the same story as Kathy's. He liked me all right, I think, and liked having someone to talk to, but he didn't ask for my phone number."

"Yeah, but that's not the whole story," Kathy said. "She told him she was coming out for Christmas, and John—John Burbridge is his name—asked her to call him when she got to Salt Lake."

"Not exactly the big rush," LaRue said. "I had to call him." She leaned into the corner of the booth as if to say, "I'm not excited about this," but she was still smiling.

"You did call him, though?" Diane asked.

"Yes. And he's really busy. He's got two married daughters coming home for Christmas, with little kids, and a son coming home from college. He also has a daughter who's a high school senior, and I doubt she would be excited about the idea of her dad finding a new mom right away—if that has even crossed his mind."

"So aren't you going to see him?" Emily asked. She had picked up her napkin from the table, but she hadn't put it in her lap yet. She held it, waited, as though the question were really important. Kathy understood. The whole family had always dreamed that LaRue would find someone to marry someday.

"Actually, we do have a date. It's for New Year's Eve." And now her smile returned with some grandness.

"And get this," Kathy said. "She's thinking about moving back to Utah after the end of the school year. She's been talking to the colleges out here, trying to see whether anyone would hire her."

"Don't read so much into that, Kathy," LaRue said. "I've been gone a long time. I'd just like to be closer—especially with Dad not doing very well."

"And the sexy widower on her mind."

LaRue waved her hand as if to pass that off, but she seemed happier than Kathy ever remembered. "One thing's obvious," LaRue said. "If anything developed, it would happen slowly. I think John's scared of me. His wife sounds like she was a lot more . . . *traditional* . . . than I am. He's probably worried that he would have to move out of Provo just to protect his reputation." She burst into laughter, but then, more seriously, she added, "I don't think he even knows whether he wants to marry again."

"That's why she has to hunt him down, crack his neck, and drag him back to her lair," Kathy said.

Everyone liked that. Emily and Diane laughed, and LaRue mumbled that "enough was enough," with an unconvincing tone of annoyance.

"Really, though, do you feel like he's the right kind of guy for you?" Emily asked.

LaRue thought about that for a time. "Twenty years ago, I would have said 'absolutely not,' and ten years ago, 'not exactly,' but I've changed some, and I think I've started to realize that no one's the *perfect* guy. Two people have to make up their minds they want to have someone in their lives, and then they both have to work to make each other as happy as possible. Look at the pioneers. Brigham Young would tell a young man he needed to marry before he went off to settle a new town, so he'd go pick himself out a girl that afternoon, and they would get married a day or two later. Then they made the best of things."

Kathy was thinking how true that was. But Diane said, seriously, softly, "It's not always that simple."

The room suddenly seemed silent even with the sound of Christmas music from a distant speaker and the clink and ring of utensils. Kathy looked at Diane and nodded. "I know," LaRue said. "I'm sorry." And then after a moment, "Both partners have to have their hearts in the right place—and a lot of times that doesn't happen. But the other side of it is, I'm tired of being alone. John is a good member of the Church, a really nice man, and—"

"Looks like Cary Grant," Diane said, clearly wanting to reverse the seriousness she had created.

"'*Moves* like Cary Grant,' let's say."

"But that's *very* good. I love the way Cary Grant moves."

"Yeah. Me too." This time the pink in LaRue's cheeks was a little more obvious.

Diane said, "I know I'm only about half your age, Aunt LaRue, but—"

"Hey, don't say that. That sounds disgusting."

"Okay. I'm a *little* younger—and I don't like to sound like some 'voice of warning,' but I'd just say, get to know him really well. Being alone, however much I don't like it, is still better than being in a bad marriage."

"I know," LaRue said. "A lot of my friends got married happily-ever-after when they were twenty-one or so, and now way too many of them are divorced. I think that *is* tougher than what I've been through."

Kathy gave the table a little slap. "Wait just a minute here," she said to Diane. "My mom told me that *you* were dating someone."

"*Was* dating. A guy asked me out a few times, but I hadn't told him I had a daughter. He hasn't called since he found out. He's been in one of my classes, but he wouldn't even look at me after he found out about Jenny. I think he hurried through his final exam just so he would be sure he walked out before I did."

"I'm sorry, Di," Kathy said.

"He was too young—too . . . lots of things. I just liked going out."

Everyone was quiet, and then Emily said, softly, tentatively, "Diane's right about bad marriages. But there's no way of knowing what might happen." She glanced around at everyone. "I don't want to drop a bomb or anything, but I don't know if Gene and I are going to make it."

Kathy's breath caught. "What?"

"It's really hard, Kathy. I know how much you love Gene, and I do too, but he's not the same person I married." She hesitated and then said in an even softer voice, "He's angry. I don't think he would ever hit me, but he's really hostile sometimes. He can hardly deal with Danny. For a long time I refused to fight with him. I'd just tell myself it was his medication that was making him that way. But lately I've started fighting back, and we've had some really big arguments."

The four sat quietly for quite some time, and then LaRue said what Kathy was thinking. "Everything is turned upside down. I always thought you and Diane had ideal marriages. I didn't see any of this coming."

"I'm not saying it's coming," Emily said. "But lately I've started to think that I can't last this out forever, the way things are."

Kathy wanted to tell Emily to hang on, to be patient; she knew Gene's heart, and it was so good. But she didn't have the right to say that. She wasn't the one trying to survive Emily's life.

"The four of us are pitiful," Diane said, and she tried to laugh. "Kathy and I can't find anyone to go out with. Emily's hanging on for dear life, and LaRue has to cross the plains to find prey. I think we're a pretty classy group of women, and we're batting fairly close to zero."

Everyone smiled—a little. No one smiled a lot.

❧

Kathy knew when she left the restaurant what she had to do. Emily had mentioned that she had one more final the next day, and that meant Gene would be home with Danny. Kathy wanted to talk to him. So she took her lunch break early the next day and showed up on Gene's front porch. What she hadn't realized was that Alex and Anna had arrived home from Washington that morning. So she had to chat with everyone, and lost some time, but finally she was able to take Gene aside, into the family room, merely by saying, "I need to talk to Gene alone for a minute or two, if that's okay."

Gene looked surprised, but Alex and Anna said they were heading out to do some Christmas shopping anyway. So Kathy walked into the family room and sat next to Gene on the couch. She took hold of his hand. "Favorite cousin, we keep saying that we're going to talk, but we never do. I need to know, are you going to be all right?"

"Sure. I'm almost back to normal. I'm off painkillers—except sometimes to sleep at night." He pulled his hand away. "What did Emily say to you?"

Kathy had been afraid he might ask. "Gene, Emily loves you, but she's worried about you. Everyone is. We think it's time we start seeing Gene again, and we don't."

"That's what Emily said, didn't she?"

"It's what *I'm* saying. It's what the whole family feels. We miss the Gene we remember."

"Well, let's see . . ." He got up and turned toward her. "Supposing someone puts a couple of bullets through your gut—do you think that might have a little effect on the way you feel about life?"

"You're mad, Gene. I know you've had a lot to fight back from, but it's the anger that's changed you, not the bullets."

Gene stood for a time, looking down at Kathy. He shoved his hands into his pockets with a feigned confidence. "Let's see, Kathy, I thought you were the family expert on anger. I used to tell you to lighten up about the war. But it turns out, you were screaming then about the very things I'm questioning now." He walked over and sat down in his dad's big chair.

"I know," Kathy said. "And I still think I was right about a lot of the things I was fighting for, but the anger was pointless. It was hurting me and the people around me, and it wasn't changing anything."

"So what now? Do you plan to slip back into the Utah way of life and not bother people with questions ever again?"

Kathy actually did fear that that could happen to her, but it wasn't the point now. Gene needed to know, somehow, that he was about to destroy his life. "Gene, there's no question you got a raw deal. Every soldier who went to Vietnam did. Our government put you in an impossible situation. I was telling you that long before you realized it yourself."

Gene leaned back as though he wanted to keep all the distance he could from Kathy. "It goes deeper than that," he said. "It's one thing for a government to be wrong; it's another thing for leaders to lie to their own people. Have you read what Robert McNamara is admitting now? He was the Secretary of Defense, for crying out loud. Now he admits that he realized a long time ago that the war couldn't be won—clear back when Johnson was still president—and yet he went right on telling everyone that we were 'turning the corner' or 'seeing the light at the end of the tunnel.'"

"I know all that, Gene. But right now we're talking about you. The war is over for you."

"Oh, it is?" Kathy knew better than to reply. She could see the anger flaring in his eyes. But he shut those eyes and then in a voice like a hiss, said, "You don't know what my life is like, Kathy. I don't see the war in the daytime, but I see it over and over when I go to bed at night."

"You told me you didn't have dreams like that."

"I know what I tell people. And I didn't have the dreams at first, but they're coming every night now. I wake up, and I'm covered with sweat."

"Do you tell Emily that you—"

"No! And I'm not going to. I shouldn't have told you. I can deal with it. But I'm tired, and yes, I'm mad. I watched close friends die over there. And I saw a lot of them mutilated, worse than me. Now we're pulling out without accomplishing a single thing. How am I *supposed* to feel about that?"

"I don't know, Gene, but are you just going to fight it out alone?"

"Not *just*." He let his eyes go shut again, and he took in some air as though the conversation itself was setting off pain inside him. "I've gotten through the worst now—the physical stuff," he said more calmly. "My intestines work now, to some degree. Things are going to keep getting better. But I had to give up all those pain pills and that's been hard. I'm just hanging on sometimes. Emily thinks I'm not trying, but I've never tried so hard in my life. She says I'm cranky, and I try not to be, but you just can't believe what I feel sometimes." Tears squeezed from the corners of his eyes and trickled down the sides of his face, but he wiped them away quickly. "Kathy, the absolute worst thing I can do is talk about this stuff. It makes things harder every time. I've just said more to you than I've said to anyone—and I don't want you telling my parents I'm having bad dreams. You don't know how far I've come. All I need is to get back to work or go to school and start being a regular person again. It drives me crazy to be around the house all day."

Kathy sat for a long time. She had known what she wanted to tell him. It had been such a nice little speech. But now she couldn't give it. "Our lives weren't supposed to be like this," she finally said. "You were going to be the president of the United States, and I was going to save the world."

Gene looked at her as though the memory were too far back to find in a mind that had gone through so much torture. "I'll be okay," he said.

"Will you, Gene? I'm so worried about you."

"I just need to figure out what I'm going to do now that Plan A isn't working out. If I'm not going to be the president, I have to find some other line of work."

Gene smiled a little, and then so did Kathy. "Maybe vice president."

Gene nodded, his smile fading. "It sounds to me like you need to change your plan a little yourself."

"Yeah. I guess I do." She had come to help him—to tell him what he needed to do—but he was right. She didn't have her own life together.

CHAPTER 6

Hans stayed after sacrament meeting to sweep up the branch house. On one of the benches he found a hymnbook and checked inside the cover to see that it was the Gabler family who had left the book behind. He decided he would go out of his way, walking home, to take it by to them, since he knew they would worry. Recently the government had allowed hymnbooks to be printed in West Germany and then shipped into the GDR. Many families had managed to buy one, but they kept their books at home and carried them to church each week. There were never really enough, but people shared, and it was a wonderful thing to have books again after almost all the old ones had fallen apart.

Hans knew that President Schräder was still meeting with a branch member and would lock up the building when he left, so there was no need for Hans to wait. He decided he would not only walk to the Gabler's but take an even longer way home and enjoy the weather. It was a pretty March day, the best day of the year so far, and he hated to spend the entire evening alone in his apartment. His wedding was coming in May, just nine weeks off now, which was wonderful to think about, but his apartment seemed gloomier than ever now that he knew he didn't have to put up with it much longer. He had applied for a larger apartment, and he thought he might have a chance of being granted one before the wedding. If not, he and Elli would have to stay in the little room for a time. Elli kept telling him that was all right, but Hans prayed every day that wouldn't happen. He wanted things to start out right; he didn't want Elli to feel that she was giving up too much to marry him.

As Hans walked from the chapel, he saw his young friend Rudolf Greiner standing in the hallway, probably waiting for President Schräder. "So, Rudolf, how are things going?" he asked. The sun was angling low now. The hallway was growing dark. The old branch building had been a factory at one time and was awkward as a church, with few convenient windows. Hans thought of turning on a light, but it didn't seem quite necessary yet, and Hans never wasted electricity.

"Not bad," Rudolf answered, but he sounded subdued. He was a tall young man, mostly made of bones. His body was draped in a suit coat that was much too big for him. He was looking Hans in the eye, but that wasn't something he did with most people.

In the past couple of years Hans and Rudolf had talked many times. Rudolf had attended Hans's Sunday School class before Hans had been called into the branch presidency, and the two had found they were alike in some ways. Rudolf was seventeen now and a *Gymnasium* student. He was extremely bright but skeptical, and he had certainly been influenced by the rational, anti-religious approach to learning in the school system. He wanted to believe in God but struggled, so he had found solace in talking to Hans, who understood such doubts. The two had talked about issues Hans had dealt with in school and also about the renewed faith Hans had found during his days in prison.

"You sound a little troubled," Hans said. Hans gestured toward two wooden chairs that sat outside President Schräder's office. Rudolf folded himself onto one of the low chairs, his knees ending up almost as high as his chin. Hans sat down next to him.

"I always feel troubled—at least a little. You know me." He glanced toward Hans and smiled. He didn't seem quite so distressed as Hans had first thought.

"Yes, I do know you. And I remember myself at your age." Hans was aware that Rudolf hoped to become a scientist, and he was capable of being a great one, but membership in the Church could certainly limit his possibilities. He had admitted to Hans that it was something he worried about. Hans, of course, was living proof that those kind of fears were not imaginary.

"Hans," Rudolf said, "you told me about being in prison—and how that changed you. But before that, did you resolve some of the questions that were bothering you?"

Hans laughed quietly. "Yes. But I always had questions." He patted Rudolf on his bony knee that was sticking up so high. "I did develop a measure of faith at about your age. What prison did was knock the pride out of me. I turned to the Lord because I was desperate for help. The scriptures seemed to open up after that. I would read a passage from the Bible—the same words I had read before—and a deeper meaning would come to me."

"I guess that's good, but I think I might prefer to stay out of prison." Rudolf smiled again but didn't look at Hans, and then he said, "I hope I can find a deeper faith without going through something like that."

"You will."

"I'm not so sure, Hans. One day I feel as though I have a testimony, and the next day it all seems gone again."

"I know. I was like that for a long time. But I will say that after all the struggles, the Lord seemed to reward me for holding onto my faith. Just when it seemed I would never have the things I wanted out of life, he opened up a way. Now I have my wedding coming up, and I'm working at a job I like. Things couldn't be better."

"But you weren't allowed to finish your university training. You could have been an architect by now. I think the Lord has taken more away from you than he's given."

"Some of what happened I brought upon myself, Rudolf. We can't blame that on the Lord. And the fact is, I learned more in prison than I could have in *many* years at a university. In the next life, I'll be more thankful for the faith I found than for a career." Hans waited until Rudolf looked at him. "And I'll tell you this—eternity with Elli is a higher prize than anything else I can think of. I'm the most blessed man I know, if you ask me."

"She's pretty," Rudolf said. "I saw her when she was here."

Hans knew she was much more than that, but he didn't say anything; he didn't want to gloat. He really did feel sorry for all the other men in the world who had to settle for someone other than Elli. Besides, part of Rudolf's doubt about his life was the insecurity he felt about meeting anyone who would accept him for who he was. He had told Hans that.

"Rudolf, I'll make a promise to you. If you'll keep the faith, the Lord will bless you. I don't know how things will work out for you, or what you'll end up doing. I won't even promise that your career won't be limited in some ways, the way mine has been, but the Lord *will* bless you. You'll be thankful that you stayed true to the Church."

"Thanks, Hans." Rudolf lowered his head and said quietly, "My parents tell me things like that—but I don't think they understand what I've been going through. They can't imagine anyone doubting God. But you understand, so I trust your promise."

"Trust your parents, too. I think they understand better than you know." Rudolf nodded and then Hans got up. "You can talk to me anytime, Rudolf. I don't have every answer, but I suspect that any doubt you've had is something I've probably thought about. I had lots of time for thinking while I was in prison."

"All right. I would like to talk again—sometime soon."

"You're going to talk to President Schräder now?"

"Not about that."

"All right. Why don't we stay after sacrament meeting next week—for as long as you like. Sunday evenings are much too long for me right now."

"It's good. I would like to do that."

Hans left, and he enjoyed his long walk home. He strolled down

Gerberstrasse, then walked several blocks east to the Gablers' home. As he returned toward the center of the city, even though the sun was setting, he didn't take his usual way home, past the main train station; instead, he walked into the historic part of town, past the *Nikolaikirche*, where Johann Sebastian Bach himself had served as choirmaster. Hans often felt the absence of music in his life, not being able to afford the many concerts in Leipzig, but he sometimes sat in the old churches and listened to the choirs. Not today, however. He wanted to breathe and to feel the beauty of this city—which he had considered a kind of prison until recently. Now he would be happy living here and serving with Elli in the branch. The two of them wouldn't have a lot, but they would walk and look, and they would love the old parts of the city that hadn't been destroyed by bombing raids during the war. He turned east toward his favorite area: the opera house, the park around it, and the lake. He crossed *Goethestrasse*. Not only Bach but also Goethe had lived in Leipzig, and Richard Wagner. They had all walked these very streets.

Hans felt lightened by the softer touch of the air after the long winter. The change seemed symbolic of what he had been through and where he had arrived. Rudolf would experience the same growth, in time; he felt sure of it. Hans couldn't imagine himself any happier. He even trusted that bigger opportunities would open for him now that the former barriers had apparently been lifted. The sun was almost gone by the time Hans reached his apartment. He walked up the creaking stairs; built a little fire in his stove, since the night would still be cold; and then wrote a short letter to Elli—as he did every day. After, he read in the New Testament until it was time to go to bed.

When Hans got up the next morning, he fixed himself a little breakfast and then left early to walk to work. He had a great deal to do this week, and he wanted to get an early start. He knew he would be staying after hours as well, but he didn't mind. Right now he preferred his office to the tiny space in his apartment.

He was well into his project that morning when he heard a little tap at his office door. He looked up to see his supervisor, Herr Kraus, standing in the open doorway. "Hans, I must talk to you," he said. He stepped inside and shut the door behind him.

Hans didn't want to believe what he was seeing. Herr Kraus's face was pallid; he looked alarmed. He was a careful, nervous man who got upset easily, but this was something more. He didn't take a seat. He stood opposite Hans's desk, stiff, his hands gripped together. Hans got up from his chair and faced him, his stomach suddenly sick.

"They tell me that I have to give you up," Herr Kraus finally said. "You're to return to your former office, where you'll go back to your old work."

Hans tried not to panic. He had always known this could happen, and he had told himself many times that if it did, he would have to be strong. With Rainer in prison, under constant pressure from *Stasi* interrogators, Hans had known that something could go wrong. There was actually nothing new for Rainer to reveal, but there was plenty he could invent if the pressure was too much for him.

"Hans, I don't know how to tell you this, but the agent who called me—"

"Feist?"

"Yes. That was his name. He said you would go back to the lowest salary."

"And why won't I be going back to prison? Did he say anything about that?"

"No."

"If I had actually done something wrong, they would send me to prison. This is all just to show me who's in charge of my life."

"Hans, don't say anything more. They'll ask me what you said, and I'll have to tell them the truth."

"What difference does it make?" Hans felt a darkness in his brain, felt his strength seep away. The implications were too terrible to think about. He wasn't just losing his job. He was losing everything. He couldn't marry Elli now. The wedding would have to be postponed, at best, probably canceled. He could afford nothing now. It was a salary barely large enough to pay the rent for his apartment.

"I'm sorry, but you are to leave now. And I have no idea how I'll finish our project with you carrying so much of the load. They wouldn't answer me that. 'What am I supposed to do?' I kept asking Feist, but he said it was my problem, not his."

"I'm sorry."

"Hans, I don't know what to say."

"There's nothing to say." The weakness was ending for Hans, and anger was taking its place. But Hans knew it was pointless to take out his frustration on Kraus. So he picked up his valise from behind his desk, and he began putting in the few items that belonged to him.

"I'll do what I can—talk to anyone I can—but for now, you must return to your old supervisor. It's best if you go directly there and report to him. That was the instruction I received."

"I certainly will do that," Hans said, but he couldn't have said any more. The anger was already crashing toward despair. He would have to write Elli tonight. He would tell her that she should no longer think of him as a prospective husband. Perhaps, someday, he could work his way back up the system again, but it was doubtful, and certainly it would take years. How could he ask Elli to wait for that to happen? He wouldn't.

So he left. His only act of rebellion was to walk to his old office, not take a streetcar. It took him almost half an hour to make the walk, but it saved him a few pennies, and he needed all his pennies now. What he felt along the way was that he was walking into a cave, going deeper and darker into its emptiness with every step. He thought he had lost all hope the instant Herr Kraus had given him the news, but the gloom, the grief that came over him was worse than anything he had known in his life. At the worst moments in prison he hadn't felt this much sense of loss, and there was nothing to compensate, no trust that this was one more learning experience or that the Lord was trying to bring him to a better state. He had done his best for such a long time, tried to follow what he thought the Lord wanted of him—and now this.

He was almost to the old office when he realized what he now felt. "What God?" he asked himself out loud. How could a God be cruel enough to let him see what he wanted, almost reach it, and then jerk it back.

∽

Kathy was staring into her mirror, her hands on her hips, looking at herself. She had been wearing her hair short for quite some time now, but she had wanted to do something a little more with it tonight. She had curled it and tried to build some shape into it, but it was looking too much like a beaver dam. She decided to brush it out her usual way and forget about it.

Kathy had a date, and she was nervous, even though she doubted that she needed to be. A woman she worked with, an older woman named Florence, had lined Kathy up. According to Florence, the man—Florence's nephew—was "working on his master's in something or other" and was tall and handsome. So he had sounded good—even though Kathy had been guarded about believing all the claims—but as the time had grown closer, Florence had revealed that "Weston" was getting his MBA at BYU. Kathy was trying to overcome her lifelong prejudice against BYU—and was making progress—but she wasn't sure she could deal with a business major. People in business had always been foreigners to her back in her protest days, the very symbol of all that was wrong with American society. She had certainly relaxed her view—after all, her dad was a businessman—but she doubted that she would have much to say to this guy. "How about that stock market?" she whispered to herself.

Kathy wondered whether she should wear pants or a skirt. She didn't know where *Weston* would be taking her. He had called and mentioned going out to dinner, but she had no idea how fancy a place he might choose. She decided to go with something "in the middle" by choosing a cotton skirt and an oxford cloth shirt. As it turned out, however, he arrived in a dark suit, white shirt, and tie. "Hi, I'm Wes Washburn," he said. And then he reached out his hand as though they had just struck a deal.

Kathy shook his hand and said, "Do I need to dress up a little more? I wasn't sure where we were going."

"Oh, no. You're fine. We'll go someplace a little more casual."

A little more casual than what? Was he changing his dinner plans to fit her choice of clothes? "Really, I could—"

"I wouldn't think of it. Really. You look *spectacular*."

The word stopped Kathy. She gave him a little closer look. He really wasn't bad looking, although Florence had led her to expect just a little more. The only strange thing was that his hair was combed like a little boy's, with a nice wave in front that looked like it had been combed and then sprayed in place. But he was tall—six four or five, so Kathy didn't have to stoop—and the suit looked expensive, if a little more shiny than Kathy liked.

"I'm thinking we could take a drive down to Provo and eat in the Sky Room in the Wilkinson Center. You're looking very collegiate, and the food is excellent there."

"But I think you had other plans. It would be no problem at all for me to slip on a dress."

"No. Don't trouble yourself. I'm liking this approach better. I love the Sky Room, and the drive down and back will give us some time to get acquainted. I should have thought of that in the first place. I would only suggest that you take a sweater or a light jacket. It could be cool by the time we finish eating, and it's not easy to park close to the Wilkinson Center."

He seemed to think of everything, but there was nothing wrong with that. She walked back to her bedroom and grabbed a sweater. By the time she returned to the living room, Kathy's little brother Douglas had discovered Weston—a.k.a. Wes—and was asking him who he was. But Wes seemed comfortable about that. "I'm going out to dinner with your sister," he was saying, sounding a bit condescending but at least showing patience with Douglas's frankness.

Wes did seem to be nice, even accommodating. Kathy told herself not to be put off by his voice—with the volume set on "high"—and that firm handshake he had started out with. She noticed, too, that his nose seemed a bit excessive, but that could also be said of Joseph Smith, and he was considered a handsome man. Kathy reminded herself that she was too quick to judge people, even stereotype them; she needed to give Wes time to show what he was really like.

But in the car an interview began—or so it seemed to Kathy. Wes wanted, essentially, to know the history of Kathy's life. Kathy tried to stay with the *Cliff's Notes* version, but he kept probing for details. In some ways his questions were flattering because he took so much interest in her and seemed genuinely curious about her experience on the East Coast, but the persistent questioning kept her a little on edge. Finally, somewhere past the Point of the Mountain, she tried to turn the whole thing around. "Did you grow up in this area?" she asked.

"I was born in Salt Lake," he said, "but I grew up in Northern California. East Bay. Walnut Grove, if you know the area. After my mission—which I served in Australia—I wanted to be in Utah, so I came to BYU. I finished up my undergraduate work in accounting and then applied to the MBA program. I'm now more interested in marketing than finance, but ultimately, I'd like to own my own business—ideally, a small advertising agency." He finished with a little slap on the steering wheel, as if to say, "So that's that."

Kathy tried desperately to think of a follow-up question, but it had all sounded so complete. She could have said, "Why a small company?" but something in his tone had implied that he found it self-evident that small was better than big, and Kathy supposed she thought so too. "Well," she finally said, "you have it all figured out."

Kathy detected something a little nasty in her own voice and regretted it. He looked over at her quickly, but his squint showed he wasn't quite sure how to take the remark. "It's easy to plan. It's something else to make your plan happen. We'll see how things actually work out."

"I don't think planning is so easy. I'm not at all sure what I want to do."

"It's a little different for women, I think. You have your degree to fall back on, and you're getting some practical experience in the real world, which will—"

"But I'm not getting experience in my field. This is just a job I have for a while, simply to build up some savings in case I want to go back to grad school."

"I understand that. But when you study the social sciences, I think it's good to work for a business for a time—just to get your feet on solid ground. You know what I mean? Connect with reality a little."

"So advertising is your idea of reality?"

This time Kathy hadn't held back. She hadn't liked his little remark about "the social sciences," and she wanted him to know. But Wes paid no attention. "Sure it is. To me reality is meeting a payroll. In business you make a decision, and then you see the outcome. If you can't produce a profit, the doors have to close. It's not like these government agencies that get money from taxpayers and keep right on doing whatever it is they're doing, whether they accomplish anything or not."

Kathy resolved for at least ten seconds not to say anything, but finally, she couldn't stop herself. "So telling a guy he can't be truly happy or attract beautiful women unless he drives a certain model of car—that's *real*?" Wes began to laugh good-naturedly, as though he could accept the little paradox Kathy had pointed out. But she hadn't intended a mere clever rejoinder; she hated advertising. So she came back harder. "Apparently a lie becomes reality—if it produces a profit for the liar. Whereas, helping someone overcome a drug addiction—that's not real."

Wes slowly let his head turn toward her, even though he kept his eyes angled toward the road. He didn't have a bad smile now that a little humility was behind it. "Well," he said, "advertisers do 'sell the sizzle,' but it doesn't have to be a lie."

"Oh really? I watch the commercials on television and wonder how much damage they do to people. Every young girl thinks she has to look like a model to be of any worth. And every day we find out about some new odor we have to watch out for. If our bodies don't smell like plastic, there's supposed to be something wrong with us."

"Plastic?"

"We're not supposed to smell human. Our breath, our sweat—nothing can have its natural smell."

"Is that what you like—*natural*?"

Kathy was suddenly embarrassed. She had hauled out one of her old arguments—one she could fall into without even thinking. But the fact was, she did use deodorant. She backed off and said, "I'm just saying that clean might be enough—without convincing people they have to smell of all these scents we have now."

"I like a fresh, clean smell best of all," he said, but he sounded wary, as though he now recognized what he was dealing with: a "modern woman." He commented on the weather after a minute or two, then described the menu she could expect at the Sky Room, and for a few minutes Kathy was happy to let him squirm. After all, he had started it with his thing about people in government agencies accomplishing nothing. But she also knew she was hesitating about going to grad school because of suspicions of her own about that. She resolved again that she wasn't going to be a jerk tonight. By the time Wes parked the car east of the Wilkinson Center—

rather far east, as he had predicted—she had managed to move the conversation back to a more pleasant tone.

The dinner turned out to be very nice. Kathy ordered a salmon dish that Wes suggested, and it was moist and fresh, just as he said it would be. Kathy used the time to ask about life at BYU. Lately she had actually considered grad school at the Y. Her parents kept telling her there would be more available Mormon men, closer to her age. She had made so much fun of the school in the past, and she still had a notion that things were a little too beautifully "scented" on campus, but most of her former concerns were less important to her these days.

"I love it here," Wes told her. "I've spent my life surrounded by people who think what I believe is all wrong. It's nice to be around people who accept me."

"But would they accept *me*?"

She was being ironic, of course, but he said, "The sociology department would," as though he had her pegged and didn't feel the need to hide the fact. She spent another minute or two thinking that she really didn't like the guy, but then he said, "Actually, I wish I'd taken more classes in the social sciences when I was an undergrad. I keep thinking about what you said back there—about advertisers telling lies for a living. I don't think I ask myself enough questions about things like that."

Maybe he wasn't so bad.

Kathy looked out across the campus and thought how pretty the setting was. She had heard people at a nearby table talking about C. S. Lewis and about "Cartesian dualism." Maybe this place really wasn't a glorified Sunday School, as she had always liked to joke that it was.

After dinner, Wes walked Kathy outside and across the street to the parking lot. The wind was blowing, and the night had turned cold. Kathy was glad for the sweater she probably would have left behind. There was something nice about a man who thought ahead a little, who looked out for her. She had never been around anyone like that. Maybe he did seem a little too much like the salesmen at her father's dealership, but she needed to stop ruling everyone out on the basis of initial impressions. LaRue was right about that. Sooner or later, Kathy had to find someone acceptable and then work things out. Wes was a returned missionary, tall and neat and not bad looking—except that something about his mouth was strange, the way it wadded up in one corner and opened wider at the other. And of course, the nose. Still, he seemed the sort who would provide stability to a family. She even had the impression he was willing to listen to her and maybe change his mind about some things.

At the car, he opened the door for her—and it was a nice car, if a little practical: a Ford Fairlane, a few years old. She slipped in, and he shut the door firmly, then walked around to his side. As he turned the key and the starter motor chugged and then caught, he said, "I'm curious to know a little more about the Peace Corps. What kinds of help were you able to take to the people in the Philippines?"

But this sounded faked—as though he was trying to act open-minded even though he probably considered the Peace Corps one more example of government waste. "I think *I* got most of the help," Kathy said. She twisted in her seat and leaned into the corner, half against the door. She told herself that she wasn't going to get defensive again.

"Why do you say that?" Wes asked.

"I went over there with the idea that I needed to take *our* values to Filipinos, but I found out there are a lot of things they understand better than we do. They're very cooperative and congenial. They're not nearly as competitive as we are."

"I know what you mean. I saw that at times in Australia."

Kathy was surprised by Wes's response. She had actually been baiting him a little, and he had not only refused the bait, but he had also seemed to agree. "I really found my testimony in the Philippines," she said. "I wanted to change people without loving them, but it was only after I loved them that I saw change occur. So I was the one who ended up changing the most." She went on to tell him about working in the branch, but also about bringing some of the love from the branch back to the barrio.

"But isn't the idea to teach people skills and that sort of thing? I mean, what's the Peace Corps for, if we aren't teaching them anything?"

Kathy felt herself bristle a little, but she said, "We got some things done. I helped to get public toilets built in the little town where I was, so the place could be more sanitary, and I—"

"What did they do, go in the streets?"

"The children would. Even the men, at times."

"Wow. That's getting pretty basic. I didn't know things were that bad over there."

"It's not *primitive*. Americans just have different things we're used to."

"I'll say. But you must have had some bigger projects than outhouses, didn't you?"

He didn't sound critical so much as baffled, but Kathy resented his implication. Still, she controlled her voice as she said, "We worked mostly as teachers. We helped the kids with their English. In a lot of ways we were role models for the children in the barrios—so they'll place more value on education."

Wes was nodding his head, as if to say, "Okay, I guess that counts for something," but he was avoiding even a glance her way, as though he didn't want to show any direct censure. Kathy tried to think what else she could tell him, but she had wondered herself whether anything she had done had been all that significant. "I don't know," Wes finally said, almost apologetically. "I sometimes wonder. Americans have enough problems of their own. I think a lot of this foreign aid we send out just gets into the wrong hands anyway. Maybe we ought to stay home more and keep our money home—then cut back on our high taxes."

Kathy had been surrounded by liberals so long, this kind of talk was almost a foreign language to her. She tried to tell herself she didn't have all the answers, that maybe he had a point. But it wasn't working. She could feel her temperature rising, so she decided to give him just one little rebuttal and then let the evening—and Wes—go. "Wes, we represent about two or three percent of the world's population—something like that—and yet we consume almost half of the world's goods. We go into other countries, employ their cheap labor, then bring back the profits to America. If we throw around a little foreign aid, it's usually with strings attached. We don't do it out of the sheer goodness of our hearts."

"Uh, oh. You sound like a Democrat." He laughed, as if to make it clear that he was only kidding. "I guess that's what happens when you go east to college."

"Don't do that."

"Don't do what?"

"If you disagree with what I just said, tell me so—and why. But don't try to summarize me with a label."

"Fair enough." He laughed again. "And I guess you haven't ever assumed that you knew all about a guy just because he was a business major?"

"Actually, I have. The only trouble is, I've been right every time."

Kathy knew instantly she had said something stupid and unfair, and she thought of taking it back. She probably would have if she had liked Wes more. But this was not going to go anywhere. She had tried the whole evening to give him the benefit of the doubt, but she didn't like going to that much work just to avoid an explosion. So she let the tension ride all the way back to her home on Country Club Drive. She supposed that her address had been the beginning of the problem. He had expected something different from a businessman's daughter who lived in a "good neighborhood." He hadn't bargained for what he had gotten.

He walked her to the door and said nice things about the evening, even told her, "It was fun to spar with you a little. I hope I didn't make you mad." She denied being mad, thanked him, and went inside, and that was that: her first date since getting back to the States, and it was probably a good example of what was to come. She started toward her bedroom but made the mistake of stopping in the kitchen, where she found her mother sitting at the table drinking a cup of hot chocolate and reading the newspaper. "So how did it go?" Mom asked.

"Mom, I'm a freak. I really am. I tell myself that I've changed, but I don't know how to be this straitlaced little Mormon girl all the guys around here are looking for. I have opinions and I express them, and that doesn't work in this culture. I'm supposed to look pretty and keep my mouth shut."

Lorraine looked up and smiled. "You do look *very* pretty. That's tragic, I suppose, but I'm not sure what you can do about that. You are what you are."

Kathy let out a little sigh of disgust. "My mouth is the problem. I should have told him how much I love to cook and sew."

"What did you say that was so bad?"

"The guy implied that the Peace Corps was worthless, and then he started in on how we shouldn't be giving out foreign aid. What am I supposed to say? I have an opinion about that."

"I thought you came home somewhat dubious about the Peace Corps."

"Well, yeah . . . but he was making it sound like it was . . . I don't know . . . a complete failure." Kathy felt her indignation lose a little momentum.

"Or did you overreact?"

Kathy rolled her eyes, and then she smiled. "Me? Overreact? Mom, have you ever known me to pop off without thinking first?"

"Maybe once or twice when you were *much* younger."

Kathy sat down. "The guy wants to make a living in *advertising*. How can he claim that what I do has no value?"

Lorraine smiled gently, and she sipped her chocolate. "Want some of this?" she asked.

"Sure." So Mom got up, poured some milk in a pan, and then turned on the burner.

"I don't know what to do, Mom. I tell myself that I've changed, but I always do the same stupid things."

"You have changed. You're hardly the same person. And there's nothing wrong with having opinions. But why couldn't you have a *discussion* with him about foreign aid?"

"I could tell he was one of these right-wingers who—"

"Kathy."

"I know. I know."

"Just tell him what you know about foreign aid, and why you think it does have value—and for once admit that maybe it does get wasted sometimes, or that everything isn't one-sided and simple. If you'll do that, he will. That's been my experience. People who think they're polar opposites usually aren't, once they talk for a while."

"I know. I knew that tonight—even when I was saying some of that stuff. But it's too late now. I'm sure he'll tell Florence what a maniac I am."

"Did you like him at all?"

"I don't know. I kept trying. But there's no way he would ever be interested in me. Maybe it's just as well that he found that out immediately."

"And you would never be interested in him?"

"No." She looked at her mom, who was peering at her with her head angled to one side as if to say, "Don't answer without thinking." So Kathy tried again: "He isn't a bad guy or anything like that, but we would never be kindred spirits."

"Maybe. But if you're going to find a husband—and you tell me that's what you want to do—you have to back off a little and listen to what he thinks, then say what you think without so many absolutes and accusations."

Mom hadn't even been there, and yet she knew exactly what Kathy had done—and she was right. So Kathy drank some cocoa with her mother, and then she went to bed that night disgusted with herself—as she had been many times in her life.

CHAPTER 7

Gene and Emily had struggled through a difficult spring. Gene had continued to take care of Danny until Emily had finished her degree in April. Since then he had been working almost full-time for his Uncle Wally. He had felt good about himself at times as he tried to gain more self-control and build a better relationship with Danny. But every time he thought he was getting on top of things, his nerves would seem to shatter, and he would rage against Danny or Emily, or both. When that happened, a crazed voice would break from him, and his vision would blur with red again, as though his eyes were full of blood, but at the same time another self would watch and wonder, fully aware that he was destroying himself and his family. And when the rage was gone, he would plead again, and Emily would grant that he had been doing better before it had happened. But Gene knew this couldn't keep happening. He knew lots of things, but he also recognized that the anger, when it came, didn't care about reason.

It was June now, 1972, and Alex and Anna were home. They thought they would stay "two or three weeks," they said, but Mom had also spoken of staying longer—to avoid the sticky heat in Washington. Gene was increasingly aware that he and Emily needed to get their own place. Emily found it especially difficult to have family come and go, often with little warning. The frequent intrusions only added to the tension she and Gene were dealing with. For Gene, the worst was feeling that his parents were always watching him. Mom would talk to him about being more pleasant, not so curt with Emily, and Dad always wanted to "talk things out." Gene tried not to get mad about any of that, but he refused to let his parents work their way into his head. He didn't refuse to talk, but he found ways to avoid conversations that he knew would only bring back memories and make things worse for him.

After Gene's parents had been home a week or so, Uncle Richard and Uncle Wally showed up at the same time one evening, without explanation. Gene sensed immediately that something was up, especially when Dad brought the uncles into the family room where Gene had been sitting after dinner. Alex turned off the TV, and Emily and Anna suddenly took Danny and left the connecting kitchen, where they had been doing the dishes. Wally sat down on the couch with Gene, and Alex pushed an upholstered chair closer for Richard, then sat in his own favorite chair. The four were arranged in a cozy rectangle. Clearly, all this had been planned, but for the moment Richard and Wally only talked—self-consciously—about "news and weather."

Gene wanted out. He thought about telling them he wasn't going to let this happen, whatever it was going to be, but he waited, feeling a weight in his stomach, the onset of the nausea he often lived with. He decided he would let them come out in the open and say what they were up to, and then he would cut the whole thing off before they got him upset.

"Gene, how's your strength now?" Richard eventually asked. "Do you feel like your body is getting back to normal?"

"I think so," he said, trying to sound as congenial as Richard. "It's hard to remember 'normal' now, but I've been going for some long walks, and I can do that all right." He looked over at Wally. "I manage to put in some pretty long days at the office, don't I?"

"You do."

"I'm just processing paperwork, not doing anything physical, but last year I couldn't last more than a couple of hours doing stuff like that."

"That's great," Richard said. "Do you ever try to shoot hoops or—"

"No. I haven't. But I could." Gene heard the irritation in his own voice. He hadn't intended that, but he didn't really mind if Richard had heard it. He and Dad and Wally all needed to know that he didn't need their advice. They all seemed to think they knew all about him just because they had also been soldiers, but they were wrong. They had fought in the "good war" and then come home as heroes.

Dad had certainly picked up on the tone of Gene's reaction. He was suddenly more direct. "Gene, Wally and Richard came over tonight so we can all talk with you. It's about time we—"

"No, Dad. I'm not doing this. I've fought my way off painkillers by myself, and I'm going back to college this fall. I'm coming back all right. I'm moving ahead. I don't need to be preached to."

"We're not going to preach to you, but we do want to say a few things—and maybe give you a chance to get some feelings off your own chest. You've been promising me for a whole year that you would talk to us sometime, but you always find an excuse when I try to set something up."

Gene was sitting at the end of the couch closest to the kitchen. He had been reading the evening newspaper under the light of a floor lamp. The evening light, outside, was dimming now, leaving the other men shadowed, but the yellowish lamplight that was falling over Gene seemed to place him in the center of things, where he didn't want to be. "Listen," Gene said as calmly as he could, "I appreciate what you want to do. But I don't want to talk about the war. That's behind me now—just like it is for all of you. I'm looking ahead, not back, and I feel like I'm doing pretty well at that."

"You're in danger of losing your wife and son," Alex said. "You've got to know that."

"No. I don't know that. I know I was having trouble with my temper there for a while—I think those painkillers messed me up for a long time—but I'm doing okay now."

Alex ran his hands down his old khaki slacks, then gripped his knees and leaned forward. Gene could see the stiffness in the motion, but Alex spoke with his usual composure. "Gene, I've watched you this last week since we got home. You say things to Emily that Anna would never put up with. You sound downright hostile with her sometimes, and you're so impatient with Danny that he's afraid of you. That's not the Gene any of us remember. You wouldn't be acting that way if something pretty bad wasn't going on inside you."

Gene sat for a time, straining for the same composure, and then said in the calmest voice he could, "You don't need to come home and do *surveillance* on me, Dad. And you don't have to report to the whole family that I'm messed up. It's time Emily and I got our own place. I'm going to start looking tomorrow."

Uncle Wally was sitting with his head down, obviously embarrassed by the way this had begun. Uncle Richard was sitting back in his chair, but he was avoiding Gene's eyes, clearly just as uncomfortable. All this was Dad's fault. He should have known better than to drag people over to the house only to start making accusations in front of them. Gene knew as well as anyone that he didn't treat Emily and Danny the way he should at times, but he also knew how hard he was trying to do better—and he knew he was making progress. He had gotten himself through all the surgeries and most of the pain; now he just needed to gain more control of his emotions.

Richard cleared his throat with a little coughing sound, sat up straighter, and then in an equally careful tone, said, "Gene, when you and I talked over at the park that day—last year, on the 24th of July—I gave you some idea of what the three of us went through after we got home from our war. We each had our own demons to deal with, but we helped each other by discussing things we didn't feel we could tell anyone else. We've been thinking that it might be good to do something like that with you. Maybe if you find out some of the things we had to work our way through, that would help—"

"No. I've heard enough about all that. And I don't want to talk about the things that happened to me. I talked a little with Kathy one day, and it only made things worse for me. I know what I need to do, and that's to move forward. You all ought to be willing to respect that. I think I know what I need better than you do."

"The trouble is—" Wally turned a little more toward Gene "—when you try to force those memories down, you think they disappear, but they don't. We know all about that. Memories come out in dreams or in flashes, and the harder you try to contain everything, the more you find yourself feeling like you want to drive your fist through a wall. A lot of guys came home from World War II and ended up drunks or wife-beaters, or they just shut off all their emotions so they couldn't feel anything. Your dad and Richard and I have done pretty well, but it took some time. What we know is, we started to do better once we opened up to each other."

Gene stood. He wasn't going to yell at these men. He knew they meant well, but their war hadn't been like his. They would never understand that. "I've got to do this my own way," he said. "I'd like to think you would all be proud of me that I've come as far as I have, but the only thing I've heard from any of you, or from Emily, is that my best isn't good enough. If Emily is telling you she can't put up with me, then I guess that's just one more thing I'll have to deal with."

Alex stood. "Sit down!" he said. Gene was surprised by the anger he heard. "That all sounds a little too much like self-pity, Gene, and I'm tired of it. If there are any three men in this world who know what you're going through, it's the three sitting right here. But we did what we had to do to make sure we had good lives—good families. I would think you'd be happy to have a chance to speak to men who might be able to help you."

Gene stared at his dad. He was enraged by the accusation of self-pity, but he knew he couldn't say anything—not without exploding—and that would only convince everyone that Dad was right about him. So Gene sat down. He would let them have their say, but he wasn't going to "open up." He had enough knowledge of himself to know what worked and what didn't, and the real self-pity was going back over the things he remembered, harboring them instead of letting them go. He focused his attention on his father, but he let his eyes say what he was feeling: that he was not going to let him, or his uncles, into his head.

"Gene, I'm sorry," Alex said. He sat in his chair again. "It's hard to know what to say to you right now, but you have to let us have a try. We're worried about you."

Gene didn't change his look, didn't speak. The dark outside this little rectangle was gathering close, as though nothing existed beyond the glow of the lamp. Gene fantasized sometimes that he would walk away from this house, from Salt Lake, and just keep going. He would travel all his life, never settling anywhere, never dealing with people and problems, just looking about himself and moving on. He was tired of everything—of people, of family, of expectations, tired of shaping himself according to everyone else's idea of him. People kept telling him the same thing, that he wasn't himself any longer, but the truth was, he had no idea who he was or who he had ever been.

Gene liked the awkwardness he had created. He told himself he would let his dad and uncles talk to him if they wanted, but he didn't have to act as though this was some sort of testimony meeting and he was willing to take his turn. Gene had always liked these three, respected them. They had been giants to him as a boy: his famous father, the hero and congressman; Uncle Wally, the death-march survivor, Church leader, business leader; Uncle Richard, the thinker, professor, the gentle soul. Gene had compared himself as a teenager, wanted some of all of them, strove especially to *be* his dad. He hadn't resented them back then; he had even liked that they expected him to live up to their own achievements. But he resented them now. They were like Grandpa. They wanted another generation like themselves, upright people, *Thomases*. He knew what they feared: that he might somehow shame the family.

It was Wally who was clearing his throat now. "Gene, I talked to Kathy. She told me that you had some close friends get killed in Vietnam. I just wanted to tell you one thing that happened to me in the Philippines." Gene saw him blink, saw that his eyelashes were already getting damp. It was what Gene had expected. Wally was an outgoing man. He laughed a lot, liked everyone, and cried easily: in church, at family gatherings. He always seemed overjoyed with life, completely satisfied, and easily moved. It was as though he had done his time as a POW and found anything that came later something to be thankful for. Gene had always admired that, but lately he had also wondered whether the man wasn't just a little too good to be true. It was hard to imagine that there wasn't some anger hiding behind all that goodwill.

"I got sick during the death march and couldn't have kept going on my own. Two friends of mine got me through, sometimes carrying me along when they hardly had strength to walk. When we arrived at our first camp, the three of us relied on each other completely. We scrounged extra food and shared it, and we kept each other going emotionally—literally kept each other alive. Eventually, I ended up in a prison in Manila and finally got a little medical care. But before I was shipped to Japan, I met up with some guys from my first camp. They told me that my two partners had died. There's no way a man could be closer to anyone than I was to those guys, and they died needlessly, from starvation."

Wally had started out looking at Gene, but his head was down now, and Gene could see that his shoulders were quivering. But when he looked up, there were no tears on his face. What Gene saw was an immense sadness. "I've spent my whole life wondering why they died and I was allowed to live. For a long time it was hard not to hate myself for that, and I never have understood why I felt that way, but there's still some of that in me. Every time I think of those men, I feel guilt. I've had people tell me that feelings like that are irrational. They say it's all chance and could have happened the other way just as easily. But I'll tell you what bothers me sometimes, still. During that time, I would sometimes pray that I would make it home, and now it seems that I shouldn't have done that. It seems as though I should have prayed for us all, and then left it at that. It feels like God only had so many tickets home, and I was selfish enough to ask for one of them."

Gene saw his dad nod his head. Richard was doing the same thing. And Gene understood entirely. He had fought this very feeling, told himself there was nothing he could have done to stop the bullet that had taken Dearden, but it didn't feel that way inside.

"I've thought a lot about those kinds of feelings," Alex said. "I'm pretty sure every soldier, after a battle, sees a friend on the ground and feels horrible, but there's also this self-preservation mechanism that kicks in. You try not to let your brain say it, but you think, 'At least it's him and not me.' As soon as that thought comes to you, you start blaming yourself, and it feels like you killed the guy yourself."

"I'm glad you said that," Richard said. "We've talked a lot, but I don't remember any of us admitting to that. I've thought about that a lot of times, though." Richard looked at Gene, his silver-blue eyes clear but sorrowful. "I told you before, Gene, that when my ship was sunk I was put on a life raft because I had been burned. Men in the water were trying to climb onto the life raft, so the guys in the raft started to beat them with oars to knock them away. That's a terrible thing to remember, but I could always tell myself I wasn't the one who did it. The trouble is, my hands were burned, so I couldn't, so I've never known whether I would have. It's hard to remember exactly what I felt at the time. But I'm pretty sure I was relieved that someone else would do the dirty work for me and I didn't have to. What I know for sure is that I hated myself when I got home. I dreamed over and over about those guys in the water."

"So how did you stop thinking about that all the time?" Alex asked.

"I didn't." Richard looked at the floor. "Almost every day, in one way or another, the thought comes back to me that we left those men in the water, and half of them died. Their mothers got telegrams, and ours didn't. I got to come home and marry Bobbi and raise a family, and they didn't get that chance. I tell myself I have to live a good life, to justify my existence, but I've never been able to put all those thoughts aside."

Gene hadn't expected to say anything, but he couldn't resist. "So how is that supposed to help me?"

"Maybe it won't," Richard said. "But it was good for me, talking to Wally and your dad, just to know that I wasn't the only guy with feelings like that."

"I refuse to feel that way," Gene said. "That kind of stuff has crossed my mind, but I tell myself that when the bullets start to fly, anyone can get hit. It's not a man's fault that the guy next to him gets hit and he doesn't—not if they're both doing what they're supposed to be doing."

"Of course that's right," Alex said. "But what I've found out from living with my own feelings, and from talking to other guys, is that the way you feel about what happens doesn't have a whole lot to do with logic. Wally didn't do anything wrong, and neither did Richard, but emotions don't always listen to reason."

"That's my point," Gene said. "You can't just give in to all that. You have to fight it."

"It's like fighting a phantom, Gene," Alex said. "And your feelings can run the other way, too. I think you're furious that you had to take those bullets in the gut and go through all these operations when other guys sat at a desk or went into battle and never got hit."

"No. I don't care about that. The ones I can't stand are the guys who were back here burning the flag and cursing us soldiers for doing what our nation asked us to do. And it's the idiots who sent us over there in the first place. Those are the guys who burn me up."

"But that kind of resentment, you understand it," Wally said. "In time, you let it go. But you're alive. Don't you think about the guys who didn't make it—who didn't have a chance to marry, have children, do all the things they wanted to do in life?"

"I told you, that's just the way it is. Why should I think about that?"

"You don't have to *think* about those things. They're just there—all these conflicting emotions bubbling around—and you can't control them by denying that they exist."

"That's right," Alex said. "And that's what you're trying to do."

Gene felt the force of what they were saying, but he didn't want to accept any of his feelings: the hatred or the guilt. This was all too touchy-feely, as far as Gene was concerned. The thing to do was get over it.

"Gene," Alex said, "I've told you that I dropped behind enemy lines when our men were crossing the Rhine. What I don't ever tell anyone is that during that mission I killed a man with my bare hands. I know that when a soldier kills an enemy in war, that's not considered murder, but every time I read the words, 'Thou shalt not kill,' a little shudder goes through me. There's a dream I've been having for twenty-five years. I'm doing something normal in this dream, working in the garden or sitting at a desk, and I look down at my hands. They're soaked in blood, and the blood is dripping all over—on me, on my desk, on the flowers, or whatever. I try to shake it off my hands or wipe it on something, and the mess just gets bigger and bigger. When I wake up, I tell myself I didn't murder anyone, and I try to control myself when I start to wonder who the man was and whether he left a family behind, but I can't stop the dreams. It's as though my spirit is still repulsed by what my hands had to do."

"But you did have to do it, didn't you?" Gene asked.

"I think so."

"See, that's what you guys don't understand." He looked at each man briefly and then stared into his father's eyes. "We didn't have to do *any* of what we did in Vietnam. The whole war was a mistake—a *blunder*, everyone is starting to call it. No one needed to die on either side. How would you three like to live with that? I don't have to dream that up. It's what comes into my head every day of my life. I got shot for no reason, and my friends didn't have to die. I killed a sniper—blew his chest apart. And that poor guy didn't have to be there, didn't have to die. He probably didn't know whether he was a Communist or not."

No one responded. Gene felt a momentary sense of triumph, but as the silence stretched, he wished someone would say something, *could* say something, that would help. He looked around the room again, at each of them. When his and Richard's eyes met, Gene saw painfully little confidence, but Richard said, "Every soldier, every sailor, is at the mercy of his government. The guys out on the line don't think up the wars. Imagine how you would have felt if you'd had to fight for Hitler, just because you were a German citizen. Historians try to decide whether wars are justified. Soldiers just do what they have to do."

"Sure," Gene said. "But is that supposed to make me feel any better? It still means I lost friends who didn't have to die. And it still means I took two bullets in the gut when those bullets never should have been fired."

"How did it happen?" Alex asked.

"What?"

"What were you doing when you got hit? You've told me in general terms, but never in detail."

"I haven't told you because I don't want to talk about it. You know that."

"The letter I got from your CO said you went back into fire to protect one of your men who was down."

Gene let himself drop back against the couch. He crossed his arms. "That's stupid, and every one of you knows it. We were on a patrol. I was the team leader, and one of my men got hit. What was I supposed to do? Leave him there and run?"

"You could have," Alex said.

"No. You know I couldn't."

"But that's the point, Gene." Alex waited, but Gene refused for a long time to look at him. When he finally did glance up, Alex said, "People back here think war is about nations and flags and beliefs. At the front, it's all about a bunch of guys trying to keep each other alive. Maybe it never crossed your mind to leave your man out there, but that's only because you knew someone would come for you, if you ever got hit. That may not be heroism exactly, but it's the one good thing you can remember after a war—that you cared about the men you fought with, and they cared about you."

"But this situation was a little different. Estrada was hit, but not real bad. I just went back to cover for him, and another guy was right there with me." But Gene wasn't going to do this. He stopped himself. "And there was a lot more to it—not worth telling."

"What? Tell us."

"No. I don't want to get into all the—"

"What are you afraid of? Just tell us." Alex was leaning forward, as though he wanted to come to Gene, sit by him.

"All right. I'll tell you the whole story." Gene wasn't going to "open up," but he was sick of all the sweet talk. There were things these guys didn't understand about what he had faced. "Before I got hit that day, a lot of other stuff had gone down. Months before that, I got caught on a ridge with a six-man team—surrounded. But it was stupid. It didn't have to happen. Our CO messed the whole thing up. He was late calling in gunships to protect us, and while we tried to hold off the gooks . . ." He stopped and thought better of the word. "You know, the North Vietnamese . . . we got pounded with mortars and AK-47 fire." But Gene couldn't go on, not with this story. His anger had passed quickly, and now he could feel the panic he had experienced that day on the ridge.

"Go ahead. Tell us," Alex said.

"No. It doesn't matter."

"Yeah, it matters. Just tell us," Wally said.

Gene didn't want to dredge up a lot of stuff, but he did want his dad to understand. "Two of my friends got killed. One, a really close friend. And two more got shot up, really bad." Gene gripped his hands together, tightened his forearms until they shook.

"Officers mess up, the same as the rest of us," Wally said.

"I know. I've talked to myself about that a thousand times. But that's not what I'm saying. The point is, the whole mission was pointless from the beginning. We were out there running around in the jungle all the time, picking off a few of the enemy, playing games, really. There was no chance of winning the war that way. Even if the war had meant something, I don't know what good we were doing. We kept hearing that body count mattered—that if we killed enough of the enemy, the war would end. But that was a huge lie. We killed and got killed, and people gambled with our lives. It all turns out it was politics. People were saving face, talking about honor, and young guys were getting killed every single day we delayed the inevitable—which was to pull out. Guys are *still* dying over there, and there's no reason for it."

Gene could feel his breath coming hard. He hadn't said what he had set out to say, but he couldn't. He couldn't get it out, and it wouldn't do any good if he did. There was nothing anyone could say that would help.

"What do you see when you shut your eyes?" Alex asked.

"What?"

"You know what I'm talking about."

"I told you. We got shot up. All of us took hits."

"But what do you see?"

Gene wasn't going to talk about that. He knew what his dad was trying to do. Of all the things Gene tried to erase from his mind, it was Dearden on the ground. The harder he tried not to see him, the more the image came into his brain, the more he dreamed. He shook his head, but he didn't want to say any words. He needed out of this whole thing—now.

Dad came to Gene, knelt down in front of him. "Gene, tell me. What is it you remember—visually. You need to tell us."

"No, I don't." Gene stood up again. He was going to leave the room this time.

But Alex was up just as quickly, face to face, and he grabbed Gene by the shoulders. "You need to say it, Gene."

"Dad, let go. I'm not talking about that."

"Say it, Gene. Just say it."

"Dad, I'm not going to—"

But his dad was leaning into him, his face close. He shouted, "*Say* it, Gene!"

Gene screamed back at him, "They blew his head apart, okay? His forehead was gone. Blood and brains were all over the ground!" Gene's voice cracked, but he fought the tears. He wasn't going to cry about any of this. "What good does it do to talk about it? His head was blown apart and no one can do anything about that."

Wally and Richard stood up. Richard was next to Alex and Wally next to Gene. "It's better to talk about it," Wally said, and he put his arm around Gene's shoulders. "I didn't think so at first either, but it is better. There's no reason to go around telling everyone, but it helps to tell the people who understand."

"There's a group, Gene," Alex said. "They're Vietnam vets. They meet down at the vet hospital. They get together and talk things out. Your war *was* different from ours, but these guys will understand all that. I feel sure it will help you."

"I don't believe that."

"But will you try it—at least once? Just go down and talk to these guys and see whether that doesn't start to relieve some of what you're feeling."

"I don't need it. I'm moving ahead now."

"No. You know you're not. Will you go—just once?"

Gene wanted this over. There was no way he was going to spill his guts to a bunch of wacked-out vets. But Dad was going to stay after him, and his uncles weren't going to leave until he gave in. So Gene said, "Yeah, okay, I'll go once."

"Give it a real try," Richard said. "If that doesn't work, try it with us again. But you need to work through this stuff."

Gene knew that he had never said what he had started out to tell them. He had gone back for Estrada *because* of Dearden. Gene had lived and Dearden had died—and the helicopter had taken off without Dearden. The team had left his body out there on the ground. In Gene's mind, Dearden was still out there and always would be. But he was glad he hadn't told them that. These were the things he had to *stop* feeling, not indulge.

"Gene, you're on the verge of ruining your life," Alex said. "You're driving your wife and son—and the whole family—away. You've got to do something now or it will be too late."

That wasn't true. Gene was making his way through this mess. He was slogging forward, no matter what it took. But he said what he figured he had to say. "Okay. I'll go. I'll give it a try."

CHAPTER 8

Jenny was standing a few feet away from a little boy about her same age. The boy had been throwing little rocks into a creek nearby, and so far Jenny had only watched, but finally she bent down, found a couple of pebbles, and tossed them both, one with each hand. Only one actually reached the stream. Diane was worried that Jenny might move closer to the water—although the stream was little more than a trickle. She started to get up, but Greg said, "She's okay. I'm glad to see her trying something. She doesn't really know how to play with other kids."

It was true, and it was something that sometimes concerned Diane. She liked that Greg was paying attention, thinking what was best for Jenny. Greg had continued to take Jenny one weekend a month, and he had driven up from Salt Lake now and then to spend a little more time with her. Diane had feared that he might start pressuring her to rebuild a relationship, but now that it was June and he had never brought up the subject, she wondered whether he had lost all interest. When Diane watched Greg gaze at Jenny, smiling a little at her awkward tosses, she found herself liking him, and she remembered how interesting and exciting he had been back when she was dating him at BYU.

Jenny took a step closer to the little boy and said something to him. Diane and Greg were sitting at a picnic table not far away. The patter of water splashing over rocks made it difficult for Diane to hear, but Jenny, at two-and-a-half, was difficult to understand anyway. The little boy paid no attention to her. He was not as prim as Jenny; his orange hair was scattered and wild, and his bare knees were caked with mud. But he seemed much more confident. Jenny spoke to him again, and Diane heard the word "rock," but the boy only took a brief look at her, as if to say, *What do you know about rocks?*

Greg had been twisting around to watch, but now he turned toward Diane. "It's so fun to watch her figure life out," he said. "She likes to be around kids, but she's not sure what to do."

"I want to put her in a play school this fall—you know, just for a few hours a week. I think that will help her."

"Have you checked out any of those places, though? Some of them, from what I hear, aren't very well run. If you find the right kind, she could get a jump on learning her letters and numbers and all that sort of thing."

"I guess. But mostly, they're just for learning to socialize. I don't think we should try to push her too hard."

Diane watched Greg and waited. She had learned over the years to expect an argument when she expressed an opinion. But he let the comment go for a few moments, and then he said, "I need to be careful. I have this idea in my head that she's really intelligent and we've got to give her a chance to excel. You know how I am about stuff like that. But she might be better off if she's just a happy kid. If she is smart, she'll do fine without me pushing her."

"I'll bet you wouldn't say that if she were a boy." This was more direct, and Diane knew what she was up to. She wanted to know whether he could handle her disagreeing with him.

Greg smiled and said, "You're probably right. But she catches on to anything we try to teach her. I've got a feeling the sky is going to be the limit for her."

"That's why we need to pass the Equal Rights Amendment."

"Are you serious? Do you believe in that?"

She watched him, trying to see any sign of disdain or anger. The truth was, she wasn't entirely confident that the ERA was a good idea, but it felt good to take a stand about something, just to see how Greg would handle it. "Why shouldn't I?" she asked. "All it asks for is fairness. It passed the Senate almost unanimously. Both parties supported it."

Greg laughed. "You must have been hanging out with Kathy too much lately."

She heard a hint of his old condescension, but none of the force she had expected. "I haven't seen Kathy for a while. We've never even talked about this."

He continued to smile, to watch her, as though he was curious about what she was up to. He was wearing a navy-blue knit shirt, and she could see that in the last year he had slimmed a little, tightened. He had told her that he worked out in the evenings sometimes, and he had started to jog. He looked very good, and his eyes kept passing over her with obvious pleasure. She found herself liking his doing that more than she wanted to, and maybe that's why she felt such a need to challenge him.

"So if you're not talking to Kathy, where are you getting your information?" he asked, trying to sound playful.

Diane caught the little insult, and it fired her temper. It was his old view of her, that she didn't know anything. "I read, Greg. And we've talked about this issue in some of my classes."

"You read *Time* magazine, which is slanted to the left—just like your professors—so you get a warped view of everything."

"Greg, women get paid about half as much as men for doing the same work. That's just a fact. There's no way to *slant* that kind of information."

Greg was still smiling, and Diane was reminded again of his patronizing manner, but he didn't respond. He turned to look at Jenny. She and the boy were finally talking about something, and their rock-throwing had evolved into an interest in the rocks themselves. The boy was stuffing them into his pockets. Jenny, without pockets, was holding all she could and still trying to pick up more. Diane and Greg both laughed. When Greg turned back, however, he said, "Actually, I agree with you. It isn't fair that women get paid less. But a woman's income is usually a second income, and—"

"I *hate* that argument. A lot of women have to raise children alone these days, and they end up on welfare because they can't earn enough to provide for their families. A job ought to have a certain value, and if someone can do it, the pay ought to be the same, no matter who it is. If I can drive a truck, then give me truck-driver's pay. And you watch—women are starting to do things like that."

"I can't quite see you behind the wheel of an eighteen-wheeler." He grinned, and that irritated Diane again.

"Why not? It doesn't take big muscles to drive. And don't start in with any of your 'women driver' remarks."

Greg leaned his head back and laughed hard. "Wow," he said. "You *are* getting feisty these days."

"Why is it feisty to want what's fair?"

"It's not. But women want more than that. They want men to run around opening doors for them, and they still think men should pay for their meals. Then they go to work and suddenly expect 'equality.' They can't have it both ways."

"Fine. We'll open our own doors, and we'll go half on lunch. Just pay us what we deserve. Teachers don't make anything because it's considered 'women's work.' I think your dad ought to hire the best new lawyers coming out of law school—even if some of the best are women—and then he should pay them the same as he would a man."

"Fair enough." He crossed his arms and nodded his head ponderously, making some sort of parody of his willingness to reason with her. "I'll admit, I've seen some pretty good women lawyers. But I've seen them bring too much emotion into their work, too. It's hard to find a woman who can be as hard-nosed as an attorney has to be."

Diane liked how much she disliked Greg again. "Greg, that's just your *stereotype*. When women have the chance to compete on level ground, you'll find out how tough they can be. And I know plenty of soft-hearted men. I wish I knew more. If lawyers weren't so hard-nosed, as you call it, maybe more problems could get worked out."

Greg was laughing again. "Well, maybe so. I guess we're going to find out. But the ERA isn't the answer. If you do away with every law that takes gender into account, you're just going to create chaos. The simple fact is, women have babies and men don't, and that will always create an inherent difference. The law has to take that into account. Besides, the amendment will have to go to the states, and it'll never pass in enough of them to become law."

Diane had read enough to know that Greg might be right, and she did see some logic in what he had said about the difference between men and women. She realized she needed to read more, that she needed to understand the amendment a little better before she pretended to have all the answers. But when she didn't respond, Greg seemed to sense that he had come on a little too strong. "Still, though, you make a good point. If a woman can run a company, she ought to have the chance, and she ought to make the money she's worth. I think most men believe in that. They just don't want a woman to get the job *because* she's a woman."

"That almost never happens, and you know it. But lots of men get the job over women just because some boss can't imagine a woman filling roles he hasn't seen them in."

"Yeah. That's probably true."

Diane could hardly believe that Greg had admitted that much. It was amazing to think they had had a little debate and he had respected her opinion—or at least pretended to. But where was his anger? She thought she had had him where she wanted, ready to ignite, but it hadn't happened.

"I think you've been around your parents too much," Greg said, and he winked at her. "You're turning into a Democrat."

"You must have been around *your* dad too much. You're as annoying as ever."

He laughed, but she thought maybe she had stung him that time. He didn't flinch, but he looked away, and his laughter didn't last long. Diane was not sure what to think of him. She could feel how hard he was trying to change and at the same time how easily his old self emerged.

Jenny had actually knelt down on the wet earth, next to the boy, and Diane thought of stopping her before she ruined her pants, but she told herself that Jenny needed to get dirty sometimes, needed to throw rocks with the boys. She wished she had learned a little more of that herself, a lot sooner. "I don't know what party I support," she told Greg. "But I don't think much of Nixon."

"But history will. He's getting us out of Vietnam—where Kennedy and Johnson led us—and he—"

"Wait a minute. You've been telling me for years that you *support* the war. Now you're praising Nixon for doing what all the protestors you hate so much were saying we ought to do a long time ago."

"Yeah, well, if the war had been run right, it might have served a purpose, but now it's a matter of getting out, and Nixon is doing that the only way he can. And look what he's doing to improve relations with China and Russia. No one expected anything like that from Nixon, but he's done more to create peace in the world than the so-called 'doves' have ever done."

"The problem with Nixon is that he's such a liar. I never believe anything he says."

She saw the glare come into Greg's eyes, and for a second or two she was ready for an attack, but the tightness in his jaw gradually relaxed. "I don't love the guy, Diane," he finally said. "I'm not sure anyone does. But I think he's been a lot better president than Johnson."

Diane thought of saying something about all the legislation Johnson had passed, and what he had done for civil rights, but the fact was, her knowledge really was pretty shallow about all that, and even more important, Greg was offering an olive branch of his own, and she had lost her desire to bait him. So she said, "Well, I'm not sure George McGovern is the right answer. And it looks like he's going to be nominated."

The fact was, Diane had only started thinking about politics in the past year or so, and a lot of that came from talking with her parents, who really were devoted Democrats. Even though she had some opinions about certain issues, she often found herself confused by current events. A lot of people in the country, even in the north, had supported George Wallace, who was looking for a backlash vote of whites who harbored a resentment against the whole civil rights movement and especially the idea of bussing kids for racial balance in the schools. But Wallace had been shot down by a would-be assassin that spring. He was alive but out of the campaign. To Diane, McGovern seemed too much of an extreme the other way, almost naïve in his idealism. Her parents preferred Edmund Muskie, and Diane had liked him too. That spring he had defended his wife against Republican attacks. He had gotten emotional and had even shed a few tears. It was constantly in the paper after that—that he had cried—and his campaign had lost all its momentum. Diane found that incomprehensible. Couldn't a presidential candidate cry?

"Diane, this is fun. I like you this way."

Now he was trying a little too hard. "You think you just won the debate. That's what you like."

"Of course. But you think *you* won, and I like your confidence."

Diane liked his smile—and wished she didn't. She wasn't sure she had held her own in the argument, but she liked trying, and it seemed that maybe he really did like it. Either that, or this was another one of his manipulations. How could she ever be sure?

Some older kids had wandered over to where Jenny and the boy were playing. Diane wondered whether she should go get her and bring her back, but Greg seemed to sense what she was thinking, and he said, "She'll be okay. We'll keep a good watch on her."

Diane did like the gentleness in Greg's voice, the way he looked at Jenny, and then the way he looked at her. She remembered the devotion he had shown her before they got married. That had won her over more than anything—just the realization that he had wanted her so very much.

"There's something I want to talk to you about," Greg said. He reached across the table and put his hand on hers. This was something new, and Diane was taken by surprise. "I don't know whether you remember, but last year I told you I wanted to give you time to see whether I could change, and to prove that I could be a good dad."

Diane pulled her hand away from his. "Of course, I remember."

"Well, I gave myself a year. I made up my mind that I wouldn't ask for anything more out of our relationship until then. I know it hasn't been quite a year, but I'm wondering whether enough time hasn't passed. What I'm hoping is that you'll agree to start seeing me a little more now. You know—go out to dinner, just the two of us, or go dancing. I guess I want to court you again, if that doesn't scare you too much."

Diane was suddenly nervous. She had told herself thousands of times not to be taken in by him again. "I don't know, Greg."

"Everything can be at your own pace. I won't put the rush on you the way I did back in college. I've grown up a little since then. And if you want to pray about this, I'll grant you your own answers. I understand now what a tough position I put you in by telling you what my answers were."

Diane looked down at his hand on the table, still reaching toward her. "For now," she said, "I'd still prefer that all three of us do things together."

"Sure. We'll keep doing that. But how about maybe next weekend, we just go to dinner together, so we have a full evening to talk and get to know one another better again. I can't believe how much fun it is to talk the way we've done today. You might change my mind about all kinds of things. I'm about half in favor of the ERA now that I've listened to you."

But Diane wasn't buying that. She knew Greg. She knew how he behaved when he was in a sales mode. Still, the thought of a nice dinner and a night out sounded good. And it was satisfying, whether she liked to admit it or not, to see him working so hard to please her. He certainly had done everything he could to prove himself. "I'll check with Mom. If she can watch Jenny one night next weekend, then that would be okay, I guess. I want to be friends with you, Greg. We have a daughter to raise. But I'm not sure I could ever feel the things for you that I once did."

"I understand that. But forgive me if *I* feel *everything* I ever did—and more. I'll try very hard not to say so." The smile again. The charm. He was so obvious.

But she did react. It was like watching a sappy movie and willing herself not to cry—and then crying anyway. She felt a stirring of emotions she didn't think she was capable of—memories, as much as anything, of how much she had once felt for him. But she wasn't going to look shy and impressed, wasn't going to flirt. "Don't do that, okay?" she said, and she saw the air go out of him.

He sat for a time, looking past her, and then, when some older boys walked toward the creek, he turned to check on Jenny. When the bigger boys started throwing rocks into the creek, he got up and went to her. He didn't move her away, but he made sure the boys kept their distance. He even crouched next to Jenny and said something that made her laugh. Maybe he knew it—and maybe he didn't—but it was that little action that reached Diane more than anything he had done that day, and it was the memory that lasted all week until the night of their "date."

On Saturday night he came for her after Diane had already dropped off Jenny. Diane thought that would be easier, since she felt awkward bringing Greg and her parents together. She knew that her mom was still very skeptical about Greg. As Diane had left the house, Bobbi had said, "Be careful, all right?" Diane, of course, knew what she meant.

Greg usually drove a Pontiac Firebird, but tonight he was driving a black Cadillac. "It's Dad's," he told Diane. "I just thought you might like the smooth ride. I know this is kind of a roundabout way of doing things, but I thought we'd drive back to Salt Lake and eat at the Country Club. I'm not a member, but my parents are. Dad got me a reservation."

"That's fine," Diane said, and now she was glad she had dressed up. She was wearing an ice-blue satin sheath, with pearl earrings and a pearl necklace—her mom's. She told herself she wasn't trying to impress Greg, but she knew he liked nice places, and she didn't want to show up looking like the poor single mom she was.

As they walked to the car, Greg said, "Diane, I know I'm not supposed to say things like this, but just allow me one. When you opened the door just now, my knees got weak. You were gorgeous in college, but you were a kid. I don't think I've ever seen a more beautiful woman than you are now."

Diane said nothing, but she thought of the times when they had been married and he had told her that she had lost her looks, that she was fat, that he had gotten a bad deal in choosing her. If she took all his current overtures too seriously and bought into what he was obviously working toward, how long until she heard those same kinds of accusations again? And yet, the words "weak in the knees" stayed in her mind.

On the way to Salt Lake, Greg kept things light. He talked about Jenny, as always, but he also played the radio. When Gilbert O'Sullivan sang "Alone Again (Naturally)," he sang along, and she knew what he was saying to her without pressing the matter.

The Country Club was beautiful on a June night, with the light lingering and the tables glimmering with candles and shiny silverware. What she had forgotten was that Greg knew everyone in the better social circles of Salt Lake. He greeted some from a distance, waving and mouthing, "Hello, nice to see you," and he stopped at some tables to introduce her, always calling her merely Diane and avoiding any explanations.

Diane knew the surnames she heard. They were "old Salt Lakers," and prominent.

"How do you keep track of so many names?" Diane asked when they sat down.

"I grew up with their kids. That's the way I know most of them—and from coming here with my parents all my life. We also represent some of their companies. Mr. Walker, the one with the bad toupee—we're defending him right now in a civil suit."

"You like all that, don't you?"

"What?"

"Knowing all the well-off people in town. Circulating. Shaking hands. Glittering when you walk."

Greg rolled his eyes. "I like people. You know that. It feels comfortable to come to a place like this, where I know so many. But remember, Richard Cory went home and 'put a bullet through his head.'"

He had gotten her allusion to "glittered when he walked," and that surprised her a little, pleased her more. "I'm not saying you're going to do that. I'm just saying that you really do glitter."

"But you also know what the poem is about: people we envy, who seem to have everything, even though they're actually miserable. I admit, I like being in a place like this, but I don't make the mistake of thinking that any of this is real. It's smoke and mirrors." He gestured with his hand, made a broad swing. "You know what my life is like. I live in a perfectly nice apartment—with beautiful appointments and a lovely view of the valley. But I stand there sometimes at night and wish that life could mean something to me again. The only time I enjoy the place is when Jenny is there with me." He hesitated, and his lips actually quivered. "But I'm not supposed to say things like that. We're supposed to keep the conversation on the surface."

"I didn't ever say that, Greg."

A waiter was approaching. The man made a spare smile and said,

"Good evening, Mr. Lyman." Then he presented a menu to each of them, named the soup of the day, and recited a short list of entrées not on the menu.

When the waiter walked away, Greg said lightly, "I'm tempted to order for you, but in the spirit of the ERA, I'll only suggest that you give some serious thought to the rack of lamb or the shrimp scampi. And the house salad is the best I've eaten anywhere."

"Greg, I didn't say we had to stay on the surface. I just want to talk, honestly, and not play games. And I don't want to be pushed."

"I know. I understand."

"But do you? Greg, we went through some terrible times together, and I can't just put that aside because you tell me you've changed."

She saw the focus come into his eyes, that hard stare she remembered. She could tell he didn't like being reminded of such things. She waited for his reaction—almost wanted it, just so she would know. His jaw tightened, as though he were biting down on the words he wanted to say, but finally he said, "I did put you through some terrible times, Diane. I just hope there were some good ones, too."

"Of course there were."

"I don't know whether anyone can change completely. I can't promise that. But I've spent a lot of time trying. I think I understand myself better now, and that's something I never had much insight into when we were married. Still, knowing isn't doing. That's something I have to prove. The only thing is, if you always expect the worst from me, maybe—sooner or later—that's what will come out. And I don't think that's fair."

"Greg, be careful. You seem to be saying that if you do the wrong thing, it will be my fault. A lot of men have arguments with their wives, but they don't hit them."

Greg stared at her, holding back, his jaw clenched again, but someone was walking toward the table, a middle-aged man with graying hair and a three-button suit, perfectly pressed. "Greg, I just noticed you over here," he said.

Greg stood and shook the man's hand. "Great to see you, Frank," Greg said, and now he was glittering again. "Let me introduce you to Diane."

"Oh. You mean . . . ?"

"Yes. That Diane." Greg looked at her. "This is Frank Bowman. He's also an attorney. We spent most of last year working on a case together."

"I'm *very* glad to meet you," Frank said. "It's great to see you two together. But my goodness, when he said you were beautiful, I thought he was exaggerating. You light up this whole room, Diane."

She shook his hand and thanked him. And she liked all this. She had seen the way people had noticed her as she had walked in with Greg. And Frank hadn't been the first to tell her how beautiful she was. She hadn't shined this bright in a long time, and she had forgotten how much she had once thrived on those moments.

Frank chatted with Greg for a couple of minutes and then walked back to his table. Diane saw him talking to his wife and another couple, and she saw them all look at her. She could almost hear him saying that he was excited that Greg and she might be getting back together, even telling them to see how pretty she was. It was a fairy tale she knew about, had been caught up in at one time, and yet it had all faded during these years of diapers and Kraft macaroni dinners. Greg thought that *he* had been through a hard time alone, but he had kept the glitter in his life.

Greg let a little time pass, and Diane watched his solemn look return. Clearly, he hadn't forgotten what Diane had said to him. "I know I hit you, Diane," he finally said. "It's the worst thing I've ever done in my life—the worst thing I ever will do, I feel sure. And I don't blame you that you can't let it go yet. All I ask is that you don't rule me out, that you continue to let me prove I'm not the man who did that."

Diane nodded. She *was* trying to give him that chance. But did he have any idea how much more he had done to her than just hit her? And what did he mean that he didn't *blame* her that she hadn't let those memories go? Was that another way of saying that she was the one who was wrong? She looked around the room. Life would be so much easier if she could come here on Saturday nights, and if she could live in the kind of home Greg could buy for her. All this was so tempting. She knew she had to watch herself. Once before, she had chosen Greg because he promised to carry her off to a pretty future, and he hadn't kept his promises. Now he was hinting at new commitments, and part of her wanted to believe he really could change. But she had seen the anger in his eyes a couple of times that evening. Could he really get through life by clamping down on his instincts? She thought of what her mother had told her: "Be careful." That was clearly what she had to do.

CHAPTER 9

When Hans came home from work on a Saturday afternoon in August, he saw a man waiting outside his apartment building. He felt the usual jolt of fear, and then he told himself that it didn't matter, that there was nothing else anyone could do to him. But he had walked only a little farther when he recognized the stance of the man, the build. It was his father. He picked up his pace and waved, but he was worried now. Why would his father come so far to see him? Was there more bad news?

"Papa," he said from some distance, "what brings you here?" He saw concern in his father's face. Peter looked old to Hans, older than the man he kept in his mind. He was not yet forty-seven, but he was wearing out, it seemed to Hans, looking like a man of sixty.

Peter waited until Hans came close. "I just wanted to talk with you," he said, and then he took Hans into his arms.

"Is everything all right?"

"All is fine with us. It's you I'm worried about."

Hans understood that, of course. He hadn't written much since March. He had tried not to show self-pity in the letters he had written, but that left him with little to say.

The two walked upstairs, and Hans unlocked the door to his little room. As Peter stepped inside he said, "Is it always so hot in here?"

"Summers are bad," Hans said. "With only one window, there's no way to get any ventilation. But it all averages out. During winter I freeze." He tried to smile but didn't do very well. He walked to the window and used both hands to hoist the bottom sash, which often got stuck this time of year. It was a still, humid day. The open window would make little difference. Nights had been terrible lately, and Hans hadn't slept well. That left him tired all day, every day.

Peter sat down on Hans's bed. "My boss gave me the day off," he said. "I left early. I have to travel back on a late train tonight so I can be back for my church meetings tomorrow."

"Can't you miss them for a day and spend Sunday with me?"

"I would, but our branch president is on holiday now. I promised I would return."

"You didn't need to come, Papa. There's nothing for you to worry about."

"I think there is. We received a letter from Elli. She says you want to cancel your wedding, not just postpone it."

"I haven't said that. Not exactly. But I've told her it's what we should consider. And it is, Papa. She should marry someone who won't keep her in misery all her life."

"Hans, I blessed you that things would work out all right. I'm certain that they will."

Hans walked from the window to the lone chair at his little table. He sat down and used one elbow to lean on the table. He didn't want to have this conversation. "Prayers aren't always answered, Papa. You know that."

"It wasn't a prayer. It was a blessing. And it's what God wanted me to promise you."

Papa's faith was simple, and that was supposed to be good, but Hans was weary of relying on faith. For so many years, every time he had raised his head a little, he had gotten it beaten back down. "We'll have to see," he said.

"Don't you believe in the blessing?"

Hans didn't want to answer. He knew that his father wouldn't like what Hans had allowed himself to think lately. He had gone through hard times in prison, and he had doubted God as a young man, but he had never known such hopelessness as he had felt these past few months. "Papa, I'm not sure what I believe. I'm trying my best, but it's difficult to be optimistic about anything right now." Hans could see sweat beading on his father's forehead, trickling down one temple. Like an old man, he was wearing a suit, the only one he owned—heavy enough for winter in Schwerin. "Take your coat off, Papa. You'll melt in this room."

Peter nodded, stood, and pulled his coat off, as though he hadn't thought of it until now. He laid the coat out on the bed and then sat down again, pulling a handkerchief from his pants pocket and wiping his forehead, his cheeks, the sides of his nose. "Hans, you're the one who has held to your faith even in the darkest hours. You've been a strength to all of us. Can't you do that now?"

All summer Hans had fought with himself and prayed for faith, but his chest felt hollow, as though his heart had stopped pumping. He got up each morning knowing that all his days would be the same now, that he would never have what he had thought was his. "Papa, I don't understand God. Does he like to joke with us? Does he turn us over to be battered by Satan, the way he did with Job?"

"No, Hans. I don't believe—"

"Papa, in prison I realized I would have to survive a meager mortality and wait for something better in the next life. I accepted that. But then God gave me everything: Elli, a good job, hope. He let me fall in love with all that, and then he withdrew it. I suppose he wants to see whether I will curse him for it. Sometimes I want to. I try to do my church work, but my heart isn't in it now."

"Hans, don't blame everything on God. It's *Stasi* agents who have done this to you."

"But God could have stopped them. You blessed me that I would have Elli, that we would marry in the temple someday. How can God merely step aside and let the *Stasi* have its way?"

Peter got up and walked to the window. His steps seemed heavy. Hans hated the burden he was bringing to the man. Nothing in Papa's life had been fair either, and yet he kept trudging ahead. Hans hated to look at his father's eyes, lined with wrinkles, the color all gone. Papa never changed, was never buoyant and never disheartened, but steady. Hans had never heard him complain in any serious way. He simply moved forward, always doing what he had to do. He was looking out the window now as though he expected a little air to move. "I don't know how you live in this little jail cell of a room," he said. "It's not good for you to be alone, Hans. That's why you're discouraged. You and Elli need to set a new date, get married, and make the best of things. You'll be happy if you're with her."

"Papa, she earns very little, and yet it's almost twice what I get paid now. Between the two of us, we couldn't afford an apartment—not unless we stayed here."

"Then live here. She wouldn't complain. She loves you, Hans; she only wants you. She'll be true to you forever, no matter what the two of you have to go through together."

"But that's selfish. How can I offer her this room? You said yourself it's a jail cell. I can hurt her a little now and make her much happier over time. She'll find someone else."

"You're meant to be together, Hans."

Hans stood up, angry, but he caught himself. He waited a few seconds and then said, "Papa, you want it to be that way, but you don't *know* that it is. We talk about the Spirit all the time—and the answers we get to prayers. But maybe we only believe what we want to believe. I'm not sure there's a God making things happen. I should probably accept what my teachers taught me in school—that God is superstition. Then there's no one to hate but the *Stasi.*"

"You'll take your teachers' opinion over what our prophet tells us?"

"I don't know. That's all I'm saying. I simply don't know what I believe now."

"Do you know we have a new prophet? President Harold B. Lee?"

"Yes. I heard it last Sunday."

"When I heard his name, I felt something burn inside. The Spirit told me, immediately, he was called of God." Peter walked to Hans and took him into his arms again, held him against the heat of his chest. "I know what it is to doubt God, Hans. During the war, I—"

But Hans pulled away. "Papa, I've heard those stories all my life. I know what you went through, and I know you think you were guided to Mama. But look at all the people who died in the war. Is that also what God wanted?"

Peter put his hand on Hans's shoulder. "These are questions you asked me when you were studying at the *Gymnasium*, Hans. But that was before the Lord touched your heart. You know better than this. God has spoken to you. He's guided you through the greatest of tests. He'll help you through this one, too. I understand why you want to give up, but I also know that you can't do it."

"I wish I had gone to Salt Lake City when I had the chance. It must be easy for people who live there to believe. I could have lived better if I'd gone, and Elli might have found a man who could give her what she deserves."

"But God told you to stay, didn't he?"

"I don't know, Papa. I thought so."

"You *do* know. You knew then, and you'll know again if you stop denying what you experienced. Things are going to get better. I promise you that."

"Nothing is so sure as that, Papa. I thought I heard words in my mind, telling me to stay here. But what does that mean? People believe all sorts of crazy things."

"Hans, that's enough. You know. Just remember what you know."

Hans could say nothing more. He was too angry. His father seemed such a fool to him at the moment.

"Son, you aren't the first to have a hard life. Many people do. We should be thankful for our tests. It's the way we learn. After we—"

"Papa, don't. I don't want to hear it. I know all this. I've told it to myself for years. And I'll get by. I'll stay with the Church if I can. But don't ask me to like it. If there is a God, he doesn't treat us all the same. He chooses some to bless and some to curse."

"It only seems that way. But it's the meek who will inherit the earth. We have to look at the whole picture, the way he does."

Hans wanted to accept that idea, the way he once had, but he was tired of acceptance, tired of meekness. He wanted to rant at God. He wanted to confront him and demand an explanation. But he didn't say that to his father. He shut his eyes and let his breath flow out. He knew he did have to get back to the spiritual state he had once reached when he had been thankful to live in a dreary world rather than a prison.

Peter let his hand drop from Hans's shoulder, and he walked back to the bed, where he sat down again. "Hans, I understand your doubts. When I was about your age, I was in Utah and had the chance to stay. In some ways my life would have been much better if I had done that. I chose to come back to Katrina, and I've never regretted that, but my life, for the most part, has been long and colorless. My work has never satisfied me. My salary has always kept us from having the things many people have. But I have your mother; I have you and Inga; and I have my church work. Those are the things that give my life meaning. You can do the same. Just trust a little and—"

"That's what I've lost, Papa. I can't invent trust when I don't feel it."

"But you can. Faith is an act, not just an attitude. Exercise some faith and a way will be opened."

Papa's logic was all so clear, and yet it wasn't really logic at all. If faith was an act, where was the muscle that could start it moving? Hans had tried all summer to change the way he felt, but nothing worked.

"Hans, I came here to give you another blessing."

"No, Papa. You've blessed me enough. It wouldn't do any good now anyway. I'm too angry to feel the Spirit, even if such a thing exists."

"Then I'm going to pray for you," Peter said. He slipped to his knees, facing Hans. He gripped his hands together, bowed his head, and stayed that way a long time. As he prayed, some of Hans's anger passed away. He tried to pray himself. He told the Lord, as he had many times that summer, that he wanted to believe. He didn't ask the Lord to make the first step, didn't ask for blessings or changes; he only asked that he could feel the Spirit again. And he talked to himself. He had to *exercise* faith, do something positive. But underneath his thoughts was the skepticism he had fought not only lately but for much of his life. Faith had to be something more than merely willing himself to accept things he didn't know, couldn't know; it had to be an actual force, the one he had believed in without effort these past couple of years.

Peter got up from his knees. "Let's go away from this room for a time, Hans. Let's find some air and have a nice meal before I have to catch my train again."

So Peter took Hans to dinner and bought him a nice *Schnitzel* at a nearby *Gasthaus*. The two ate outside in a garden area under a great sycamore tree. The air wasn't moving, but it seemed more breathable, and Hans, when he let his struggles alone for the moment, did feel some joy in being with his father. The two talked quietly about Schwerin and Hans's good friends there, about Mama and Inga. After their meal—the best Hans had eaten in many months—they walked to the main *Bahnhof*. Along the way, Papa again told Hans to trust, to move ahead, to set a date for his marriage. Hans promised to think about doing that.

After Hans said good-bye to his father, he felt sorry that he hadn't allowed him the satisfaction of giving the blessing. Papa had come all this way for that, and Hans should have let him do it. Hans started to walk home but couldn't stand the thought and decided to stay out until the temperature cooled a little. He walked to the park by the opera house again. The sun was going down, and the hazy air was glowing a soft honey color. He stood by the big pond, and, as he had often done in his life, he watched the swans on the water, the sinking sun eventually turning the water—even the feathers of the swans—a richer, rosier tone. He tried to allow the beauty to penetrate him, and he tried not to think. He remembered those swans long ago that had made their way against the current. He didn't know now whether he could find much strength, but he had to move ahead as best he could, just as his father had told him. It was the other advice that he simply couldn't follow. He was going to write to Elli and end her hope that they would ever be together. It was simply the right thing to do, and once he did it, however painful it would be, they could both give up the illusion that was making them miserable. Once he had released her of her promise, his life would be simple again, and without hope there was numbness, not pain. He had been there before, had known hopelessness, and it was something he could survive. Always in his life, it had been hope—longing—that had made him unhappy. So he began to compose the letter in his head. He told Elli, "I know it's hard to believe right now, but you still have a chance for happiness. I can't take that away from you."

✧

Kathy and Diane were lying in the sun on a hard concrete slab by the swimming pool at Lagoon, an amusement park between Salt Lake City and Ogden. They had taken Jenny on some of the kiddie rides, and then they had taken turns watching her while they each rode alone on the grand old wood-construction roller coaster. Kathy was glad for a day like this. She and Diane always had plenty to talk about, and she liked doing something that relaxed her without making her feel on edge—the way dating did. Wes had actually asked her out a second time, but Kathy hadn't seen the point, and she had turned him down. Unfortunately, others had taken pity on Kathy—women at work, even her mom—and she had been lined up three more times that summer. She had gone on three dates with three different men, all as awkward for her as the date with Wes. In fact, Wes had been quite charming compared to the others.

Kathy was lying face down, allowing her back to get some sun. The sun was much too hot and the pavement uncomfortably hard under her towel, but she and Diane had both decided they were way too white. The only trouble was, Kathy could tolerate a good deal of sun without burning, and Diane couldn't. Diane was sitting up now with her shoulders covered by a towel, but she was allowing the fronts of her legs to get just a little more exposure. She was also watching Jenny, who was splashing in the shallow children's pool. "So what about this guy you went out with last week?" she asked Kathy. "Did you like him any better?"

Kathy laughed. "Better than what?"

"Those other guys you got fixed up with."

"Well, let's see. I guess I'd say I liked him better than 'Mr. Hands.'"

"Which one was he?"

"The one who talked about nothing but his mission the first half of the evening and showed me all his best moves the rest of the time."

"Oh, yeah. You told me about that. But what about this new guy? What was his name?"

"His name is Ray. And dear Ray is—how shall I say?—*eager* to get married. You might even say *fixated* on the subject. He's a twenty-nine-year-old single guy who drives a station wagon. When I asked him about that, he said, 'I thought I might as well get the kind of car I'll need when I start having kids.'"

"Does he plan on doing that alone?" Diane asked.

"Oh, no. He wants a *wife*, and he wants her now. If I had applied for the job, I would have had it, on the spot."

"No forms to fill out?"

"No. But he did give me an interview."

"What did he ask?" Clearly, Diane was loving this.

"First off, we'd hardly gotten into his station wagon when he asked me how many kids I wanted to have. I said, 'Oh, I don't know. Seventeen sounds like a nice round number.' He didn't even crack a smile. He said, 'I only want eight.' It sounded like he was saying, 'Sorry, ma'am, but you're not getting seventeen from me.'"

Diane was laughing hard by now. "You should have told him you were holding out for someone who could give you at least a dozen."

"He would have started bargaining toward ten," Kathy said, but all this wasn't as funny to her as she wished it were. Ray had actually asked her to quote her favorite scripture and had seemed suspicious when she had joked that she liked the New Testament and would recite all of it if he had the time. But he had put her in her place by quoting Doctrine and Covenants 84, about the oath and covenant of the priesthood.

"What else did he ask you?"

"How many guys I'd kissed."

"Are you serious?"

"Yes. I didn't dare tell him that I'd only kissed a couple of guys. I was afraid if I did, he would propose, right then and there."

"It sounds like the guy's frustrated. He's got his standards, but he also has his *needs.*"

"Definitely." Kathy rolled over. She couldn't stand lying there any longer. Besides, her back had probably taken enough sun after getting very little all summer. She was wearing a two-piece swimsuit, but a conservative one. Still, each time she had stood up, she felt naked, maybe just because she was so tall. Diane, of course, looked stunning in her bright pink suit and her blonde hair, but she didn't parade around in it the way she would have done when she was a teenager. She claimed she had stretch marks, but Kathy didn't see any.

"But you *would* like to meet someone, wouldn't you, Kathy?"

"Sure I would. I don't like being alone any more than you do. And I have *needs* of my own."

"Do you think much about that?"

"Oh, yes. But it's kind of sickening to think how little I know about that sort of thing. The only really serious kiss I've experienced in my life was with Marshall, and that was the year I left for college. I guess you could say I have a lot of pent-up willingness to learn, if I ever met the right guy and got married."

"It may not be as easy as you think. I married the guy I thought was right, and I couldn't make him happy. That's part of what scares me about getting married again."

Diane had hinted at such things before, but she had never said anything quite so direct. Kathy decided to sit up. She shaded her eyes and looked at Diane. "Things couldn't have been too bad, the way Greg keeps pursuing you."

"I wonder about that sometimes. I'm not sure he doesn't try to get me back just because it hurts his ego to know I'm the one who divorced him. If I told him I was interested in marrying him again, he might back away."

"I doubt that. I mean, I'm not saying you ought to marry him again, but he's been persistent for a long time, and I'm sure, with his money and looks, he wouldn't have trouble finding someone else."

"Greg's a complicated guy."

"Well . . . at least someone wants you."

"Hey, we weren't going to do this today," Diane said. "We promised not to talk about men. Life really is a lot simpler without them."

"I think I've had enough simplicity to last me forever. I want something really *complicated* to happen—if only for the entertainment." Kathy pulled her knees up and rested her arms across them, and then she put her forehead against her arms. The sun was too bright, and the quick summary of her life was depressing.

"I'm not going to comment—although I could," Diane said. "That would be more talk about men, and I'm not going to do it."

"Okay. But just answer me this: Is that part of marriage pretty nice? Because I sure want to believe it is."

"Kathy, I don't know." Diane was looking away, watching Jenny, who was trying to splash water in her direction. She laughed at Jenny, but her voice sounded almost mournful when she added, "I could never find much pleasure because I was too worried that I was disappointing him. I want to believe it could be really wonderful, but I'll just say again, Greg is complicated. Maybe all men are."

"Okay. That much of a warning puts the fear back into me. Now let's talk about makeup and hairstyles and the cute shoes I saw at Auerbach's yesterday—you know, 'girl talk.'"

"I think instead of that, I'll go take a dip in the pool, just to cool off. Can you watch Jenny for a minute?"

"Sure."

So Diane walked off to the deep end of the pool, and Kathy watched everyone around the pool—male and female—follow Diane with their eyes. Kathy edged closer to the kids' pool and put her feet in. She splashed a little water in Jenny's direction, and Jenny laughed.

Diane dove into the pool and then stroked through the water. She swam to the shallow end, then walked up the stairs and started back toward Kathy. But Kathy saw a man moving toward her. He was a big guy who had spent a lot of time in the sun, his skin a sort of dirty brown. He was pulling in his stomach, but he looked a little paunchy. His hair was long and black, slicked back now but still drooping over his ears. He looked like some sort of gangster on holiday. All that was bad enough, but his skimpy black swimsuit was embarrassing.

He said something to Diane—something Kathy couldn't hear—and Diane made a quick reply but continued to walk on by him. He was following, however, and as they got closer, Kathy heard him say, "I think I saw you here last week, didn't I? Do you live around here?"

"No," Diane said. She smiled toward Kathy and kept walking.

"Are you just here on vacation or something? I'm not really from here myself."

Diane had not quite reached Kathy, but she stopped and turned toward the water. Kathy could see she was going to dive back in, to make an escape.

"Hey, don't run off," the guy was saying. "We're just getting acquainted." He reached out and took hold of her arm.

Diane spun toward him, pulling her arm away at the same time. "*Don't touch me,*" Diane said with force. "Leave me alone."

"Hey." He held his hands up, palms forward. "I'm not doing anything. I'm a nice guy. I just like to meet people. And I gotta tell you, I haven't seen anyone in this whole state I wanted to meet quite so much as you." He smiled, shrugged, and angled his head to the side, clearly trying to be charming. "My name is Harv. What's yours?"

"I'm going back in the pool."

"Okay, fine. I like the water. It's hot out here. I'll go in too, and maybe we can chat just a little. I'm not too acquainted around here, you know. I need a few friends."

Kathy saw the dilemma. Diane glanced at Kathy. If she dove back in, he would only follow. She needed to get rid of the guy.

And then Kathy knew. She lifted Jenny out of the pool. "Go give your mommy a hug," she whispered. And then she looked up at Diane. "Jenny wants her mommy," she said.

By then, Jenny was running to Diane. She threw her arms around Diane's legs and said, "Mommy, I swimmed."

Harv was suddenly looking confused. "Is this your little girl?" he asked.

"Yes."

"Pretty," he said. "Very pretty. It was nice to meet you." And then he was gone.

Kathy laughed first, and then Diane started. Diane sat down by Kathy, held Jenny on her lap, and leaned against Kathy. Both laughed for a long time, and Jenny joined in without asking what was so funny.

But the three decided they had had enough sun for one day. They showered and dressed, bought cotton candy, let Jenny go on some more rides, and then ate hot dogs. Kathy put mustard and onions on hers, which didn't mix well with the cotton candy. Still, she and Diane found lots more to laugh about, and they joked about Harv the rest of the day—breaking their rule just a little about talking about "men." Kathy enjoyed herself, but she knew she was making an effort to do just that, and in truth, the pleasure didn't run very deep.

CHAPTER 10

In September, 1972, Kathy finally did what she had needed to do for some time. She moved from her parents' home into an apartment of her own, near the University of Utah. She wanted to return to college fairly soon. The trouble was, she still wasn't sure what she wanted to study, and if she cut back on her work hours, she wasn't sure she would be able to afford the apartment. Still, she needed to be on her own. She got along with her parents better than she ever had in her life, but she had always been an independent person, and her mom and dad sometimes had trouble remembering that Kathy was an adult.

Wally had gradually given Kathy more responsibility at the dealership. She was now the executive secretary, running the main office, and she was surprisingly good at it. What she had learned about herself was that she had a gift for keeping track of details. She was also realizing that she wasn't nearly as creative and impulsive as she had always preferred to think she was, and she was better at being "the boss" than she expected. Maybe that was because most of the secretaries were younger and less experienced.

All that was interesting to learn about herself, but the fact was, Kathy found almost no satisfaction in her work. At nine o'clock in the morning she was already checking the clock, disappointed that only an hour had gone by, and at four in the afternoon she could hardly believe that she still had another hour to go. "The girls," as all the male employees called the secretaries, were a chatty bunch, who loved to talk about the cute salesmen who worked out front. The talk always quieted when Kathy came near, and that made Kathy feel like the "matron" of the staff, but she had little interest in the discussions. She did sometimes talk to Gene, who was working part-time and back in college that fall, but she had no one else she felt close to, no one to share lunch with and talk about the things that interested her.

Kathy sensed that the clock was ticking on her life. She would be twenty-six in December, and she was going nowhere. She had dated a guy a couple of times lately—a man in his early thirties named Leon Powers—and she had accepted a third date, but only because he had asked her to go to a Utah Symphony performance, and that had sounded too good to pass up. He was an insurance agent and he seemed to have a lot of money. He wasn't pushy, didn't seem desperate to marry, wasn't even bad looking. And he was tall. His only problem was that he never said a word that Kathy found vaguely interesting. It was as though he didn't let life get inside his skin, didn't feel anything. He could comment on current events, the weather, or anything else; he just didn't seem to care about things. Kathy had commented on their first date that she hoped Henry Kissinger's negotiations with North Vietnam would finally end the war. Leon had glanced at her and said, "They'll have to work something out before too much longer. If not this year, next year, I'm sure." When Kathy had wondered out loud how many more would die by then, he had taken a longer look at her. "I guess, coming out of Smith College," he had said, "you were into that whole anti-war thing." But she hadn't answered, and he hadn't probed any further.

Kathy was home late one Saturday afternoon when Aunt LaRue called. "Hey, I'm in Salt Lake," LaRue said. "Are you going to be home for a while?"

"Yes," Kathy told her. "I've got a date in a little while, but not for an hour or so. Come on over. How long are you going to be in town?"

"That's what I want to talk to you about. There have been a few changes in my life."

"What?"

"Never mind. Let me tell you in person."

Kathy liked the excitement in LaRue's voice. It seemed a good sign, given how frustrated she had been all this past year. She had gone out with John Burbridge, the BYU professor, while she was home for Christmas, and she had flown to Utah again at Easter time, but he had been entirely noncommittal, and LaRue had gradually backed away. She had returned to Salt Lake for a while in the summer, but once again John had done little to encourage her. Still, it seemed likely to Kathy that the excitement in LaRue's voice must have something to do with him.

Kathy tidied up her little living room while she waited. She had rented an unfurnished apartment and then dragged in cast-off furniture from her parents and other relatives, so the place was something less than elegant. Her couch and chair were quality pieces, but old, and the fabric, a tan plush, had been rubbed rather bare on the arms. She had also absconded with her bedroom furniture from home, including a comfortable old leather recliner, itself a hand-me-down, once used mostly by her father in her parents' family room. She had placed it in her living room with a table and reading lamp, and that was where she spent a great deal of her time. She didn't mind any of that. She didn't need anything fancy, and she liked having a place of her own—and yet, she often felt a twinge of depression when she arrived "home" after work. The little apartment seemed to symbolize her present life—and it didn't fit any picture she had ever imagined for herself.

Kathy heard a car door shut. She looked out her front window to see Aunt LaRue walking to Kathy's ground-floor apartment, taking long strides. She was smiling absently, as though something pleasant was on her mind. Kathy thought again how beautiful she was. She was wearing yellow jeans with a gauzy, loose top. She looked striking, but not exactly like a BYU professor's wife—and a little too chic for a Smith College professor. Kathy opened the door and waited. "You look like the cat who swallowed the mouse," Kathy said.

LaRue laughed. She hugged Kathy and then held her shoulders as she said, "You won't believe what I did." Then she walked inside and turned all the way around as she took a look at the apartment.

"What?" Kathy asked. "Did you get engaged?"

"No, no. Nothing like that. But I retired from Smith."

"You can't retire. You're only forty years old."

"Plus three. But I did it. I've never had much to spend my money on, so I've put plenty away. And my money from the family businesses has been building up over the years. Just between you and me, I'm kind of rich."

"Sit down," Kathy said. "Tell me what you're going to do."

"I like what you haven't done with your place," LaRue said, and she laughed. "Does it have to be so dark in here?"

The only window in the living room was on the north side, and the combination of a rather dim ceiling light and the little reading light didn't brighten things much. Kathy was reminded how dismal the place was, but she didn't want to talk about that, so she ignored the comment. "Sit down. Tell me what's going on."

LaRue dropped onto the couch, leaned back, and spread her arms, like a movie star about to be interviewed. Kathy had thought she would sit on the same couch, but LaRue was commanding the position, so Kathy sat in her chair across from the couch, even though she felt too far away. "I talked to the economics department at BYU. They said they could use me to teach a few classes. It won't be full-time, but I don't want full-time."

"Will they let you in at BYU?"

"Why wouldn't they?"

"I've heard what you've said about the place sometimes."

LaRue laughed again. "I know. But I've been unfair. John tells me that he has wonderful students at the Y. And frankly, spoiled little rich girls are starting to wear me out. I don't know what happened to the revolution. Instead of activists, we're getting *prima donnas* at Smith now."

"Are you actually going to *live* in Provo?"

"I'm not sure. I haven't made up my mind. I quit just before school was going to start, and everyone at Smith is really mad at me. I just did it all on impulse. I saw the list of my classes, and all of a sudden I said, "I don't want to teach the same courses again. I've done them too many times. And if I don't need to, why should I?"

"But this is all about John, isn't it?"

"No. Not exactly. But when I called him, he was the one who made arrangements so I could teach some classes, and he told me he was excited I was coming . . . well, actually, I think he said 'pleased' . . . but at least he didn't tell me to stay away."

"LaRue, I worry about this. It sounds like he's being awfully careful. He might think you're after him."

"I know. Trust me, I've thought about all of that. But I didn't come out here because of him. I came for me. I wanted to be home, closer to my family, closer to all the things that have turned out to matter to me a whole lot more than I ever thought they would twenty years ago. I don't know how long Dad will be around. I've fought with that man since the day I was born, but there's no one on earth I love more. Mom's easier to get along with, but Dad's like an anchor who keeps the family from drifting off with the tide, and I want to spend some time with him before he's gone." LaRue slipped toward one end of the couch and seemed to pull into herself a little more. "But it's strange what actually forced me to a decision."

Kathy came closer and sat at the other end of the couch. "What?"

"I've been really hopeful about the arms limitation agreement Nixon has been working out with the Soviets, but this thing at the Olympics scared me."

Kathy knew the feeling. A group of Arab terrorists had murdered eleven of the Israeli athletes at the Munich Olympics in August. Film of the attacks had been on television, and to Kathy, the raw hatred behind the killings seemed to say that the violence and hatred in the world would never get better, that the trouble in the Middle East would never end.

"The situation in our world keeps getting worse," LaRue said. "I was sitting in my apartment in Northampton watching all that, and suddenly I just wanted to run home. I really do feel safer here." LaRue turned and hiked one leg onto the cushions of the couch. Her arms were folded now.

"It's going to be wonderful to have you here," Kathy said. She turned toward LaRue the same way, pulling her own knee onto the couch. "We never did spend enough time together when I was back there with you."

"I won't comment on whose fault that was."

"Hey, I was eighteen when I got there."

"And one of the world's leading authorities on *everything*."

Kathy laughed. "Guilty as charged," she said. She was aware that Leon would be arriving in little more than half an hour, but she wished he weren't coming. She wanted to get comfortable and talk all evening with LaRue. "Can I get you something?" she asked.

"If you happened to have a Coke, I'd take it right now. I got in sort of late last night, and I don't think I slept for five minutes. I'm just too excited about all this."

"I do have some Coke." Kathy stood up. "But LaRue, you'll have to give the stuff up before you walk onto campus at the Y. They can smell it on your breath."

"I don't think so. John said some of the departments have refrigerators in their lounges and keep a stash with their lunch sacks. BYU doesn't pay people enough so they can afford to buy lunch."

"But they keep *Coke* around the place? That's a scandal. I'm going to report them to the *Trib*. It'll make headlines."

They both laughed more than was warranted, but LaRue was laughing about everything today, and Kathy couldn't help laughing with LaRue. Kathy got up and walked to the refrigerator, got out a couple of Cokes, then pulled an ice tray from her freezer compartment. As she was getting the ice out of the tray, LaRue called to her, "What's going on with you, Kathy? Who's this guy you're going out with tonight?"

"His name's Leon Powers."

"First date?"

"Third."

"Ah. Something new. Are you in love?"

"No." Kathy poured Coke into both of the glasses, then waited for the bubbles to die down. "He's not a bad guy. He takes me to nice places. But he has all the passion of a brick."

"You know what I told you. You need to stop writing men off so quickly."

"I know. I tell myself that all the time. And Leon is better than some of the weirdos I've been out with. But he's just so unexciting."

"Maybe he's intimidated. You're a strong woman, and strong women scare a lot of guys. I'm the expert on that subject. Give him credit for asking you out a third time."

But Kathy didn't sense that Leon was scared of her. She had expressed some rather strong opinions on their second date, and he had reacted very little. She had made a point of telling him she was voting for McGovern—"mostly as a protest against Nixon"—just to see how he would respond. But he had only said that he didn't like either candidate very much. And then he had added, "I vote mostly for Republicans. A guy is crazy not to if he's in business for himself."

"But what if you live below the poverty line?" Kathy had asked.

Leon had smiled rather slyly and said, "Fortunately, that's not my worry. What bothers *me* is how much I'm giving the IRS every year." He had followed that with a number of comments about how well he was doing financially, but he never did express any concern for the poor. Kathy hadn't expected him to shed tears, but he could have at least expressed an opinion on the subject. Even Wes, the guy she had gone out with in the spring, would have said something reactionary about poor people being too lazy. Kathy finished filling the glasses and brought them to the living room. She handed one to LaRue and then sat down on the couch again.

LaRue took a long drink, then shut her eyes and smiled without saying why. "Kathy, I'm going to sound like some visitor from outer space now—and I never thought I would say something like this, but here's what I've noticed. Most married couples aren't really 'soul mates.' They sort of live in their own worlds, and once kids come, they don't talk all that much about anything but keeping their bills paid and what the doctor said about little Suzy's fever. A lot of women make the best of their situation and create their own world with their children, and even with other women."

"Sure sounds wonderful."

"Okay. I know what you mean. But I talked to Mom last night, and she was bubbling about Joey and Janette having their baby. She measures life by the number of her posterity. I hear that and I think, 'I'll never have that. I really wish I could have had children. I'll never be the wise old grandma with an ever-growing family. I'll never have anyone to teach what I've learned out of life."

"You have me. You give me advice all the time. And frankly, a lot of it's not that good."

"Hey, it doesn't matter whether it's good or not. Who ever cared about that? But in my situation, I'm the eccentric aunt—the liberal from the East, the cautionary tale of what happens to a Mormon girl who doesn't live her life the way she's supposed to. And I have to say, one of my great worries is that I've led you right into the same predicament. I really want you to find someone—and soon."

Kathy sipped at her drink. She was glad for the coolness of the day. When she had moved in on September 1, she had had to turn on a window unit that was supposed to blow cold air, but the contraption had never seemed to understand that. Mostly, it had just made noise. It was late September now, and the season for air conditioning seemed over, but Kathy had signed a year's lease, and she wasn't sure she could handle the summer next year. "So what are you saying—I need to find someone before it's too late for me, the way it is for you?"

"Well . . . yes."

"Are you sure it's too late for you to have children?"

"Let's just say, probably. And my understanding is, it takes a woman *and* a man to make a baby." She smiled, but the fun had gone out of her voice. "A man who's almost fifty may not want to start again with a new family anyway. Maybe that's part of what scares John."

"You haven't talked about anything like that, have you?"

"Are you kidding? We haven't even discussed the possibility that our 'friendship' might go somewhere." She reached over and patted Kathy's arm, which was draped over the couch back. "But let's get back to you. Are you sure you want to run this Leon off? I turned some men down who have ended up sharing good lives with other women. I look at them now and think, 'Maybe they weren't so bad.'"

Kathy had thought the same thing. Maybe that's why she had agreed to go out with Leon more than once—just on the hope that something about him would start to appeal to her. But still, when she thought about him showing up soon, she couldn't imagine that he was capable of surprising her tonight—in any way. "LaRue, I've got to get ready for my date. But don't leave yet. Talk to me while I get ready. I want to ask you a little more about John."

LaRue had finished her Coke already. She stopped in the kitchen to refill it, but then she followed Kathy into her little bedroom—as dark and dingy as the living room—and she talked about John. "I'll admit," she said, "I like him more than I let on. But don't tell anyone I said that."

"I'll just tell Grandma."

"Don't you dare." LaRue sat on Kathy's bed.

Kathy was looking through her closet but couldn't think what she wanted to wear.

"John's not at all like me," LaRue said. "He's soft-spoken and sort of predictable, but he knows the scriptures better than anyone I've ever known, and he has interesting thoughts about theology. It's amazing to me how much I like to talk to him about those things. He thinks carefully about religion and doesn't just emote the way so many people do. He's the same way about other things. He believes strongly in civil rights, for instance, but he can talk at great length about the complexity of making real change. I'm tired of young people who can only discuss issues in bursts of emotion." She laughed in one of those little explosions of hers. "See, I told you I'm getting old."

Kathy wondered. Was Leon's evenness actually a good trait? She finally picked out a gray dress that she hadn't worn since the previous winter. She was so tired of wearing the same clothes. While she changed, she listened and LaRue continued to talk. Kathy wasn't just hearing praise for John; she was hearing something wistful in LaRue's voice. The woman was in love.

But then the doorbell rang. Kathy had moved to the bathroom and started on her hair, but she was far from ready. "Oh, dear," she said. "Answer the door, will you? Introduce yourself and tell him I'll be ready in five minutes."

So LaRue went out, and Kathy heard her say, "Hi. I'm Kathy's Aunt LaRue. I'm afraid I've talked to her too much and I've made her a little late."

Kathy couldn't hear what Leon said first, but as he stepped inside, he said, "Kathy has mentioned you, it seems to me."

"Oh, really? Did she reveal any of my dark secrets? I'm the family disgrace, you know—the one who went to the East and lost my way."

Kathy heard Leon's brief, controlled laugh. "That's not quite what she told me," he said. "She said you were a teacher, I think."

Kathy cringed. *She's a professor, Leon, at Smith College, for crying out loud.*

"Yes. You're right about that. That's what I am. Sit down, Leon. She won't be long."

There was a rather long silence, and finally it was LaRue who came up with something to say. "What is it you do, Leon?"

"I have my own insurance agency."

"Oh. Well, I guess you don't have to struggle along on a *teacher's* income."

Kathy cringed. Leon had clearly said the wrong thing, calling LaRue a "teacher."

"I've actually been very fortunate," Leon said. "I've been able to grow my little company much faster than anyone could have expected."

"So I guess you have a degree in business?" LaRue asked.

"Actually, no. I did major in business, but in my senior year I was doing so well selling insurance, I couldn't see the point of continuing with college. I knew a lot more than most of my professors by then—just from being out there slugging it out on the front line—and most of the classes they wanted me to take to graduate were ridiculous."

"You mean business classes, or—"

"No. The business classes were worthless too, but I took those. I just couldn't see the point of taking literature classes and all those group fillers—physical and social sciences, and all the rest."

"I think the idea is that a person who gets an education is expected to be—you know—*educated.*"

A long silence followed, and Kathy knew she'd better hurry. LaRue was only at the sarcastic stage. All-out battle might not be far away.

Finally, as though Leon had begun to make some guesses about LaRue's reaction, he asked, "And what is it you teach?"

"Economics."

"Oh, I see. I took a couple of economics classes."

"And I suppose they were *worthless*?"

Kathy heard Leon's brief laugh. "Well, let's just say that every econo-
mist seems to have a different theory, and *no one* knows what's really going
on. For the guy who's trying to make a living, all that theory doesn't really
help much."

"So if I understand what you're saying, the only information you
wanted from college was the kind that would earn you a buck."

"No. Not necessarily. But—"

"Do you ever like to learn something just for the joy of knowing?"

"Sure. But I can read. I don't like to pay for classes that . . . you
know . . ."

"Don't give you a return on your dollar?"

"That's one way to put it."

"Well, you've got a point. People who *know* the most are usually not
paid the most," LaRue said.

"It depends on how you look at it." Kathy hesitated, waited. She
knew something nasty was coming, and she feared an explosion. "A lot of
the people who *pretend* to know so much are really just full of hot air."

Kathy gave up on her hair, swiped on a little lipstick, and then hurried to the living room. But as she headed in that direction, she heard
LaRue say, "And I suppose *salesmen* are the guys we can trust to speak the
truth."

"Okay, should we go?" Kathy asked. Leon stood up. He laughed again
and glanced at Kathy, as if to say, *So what's wrong with your crazy aunt?*
And then he said to LaRue, "I did take a class in 'music appreciation,' and
now I like classical music." It was the kind of statement that might have
helped to make peace, except that his tone, as usual, was far too superior.

"I'm glad to hear it," LaRue said, and she waited until Leon was turning toward Kathy to add, "And the nice thing is, most of the people at the
concerts have money. It's a good place for a salesman to make contacts."

Leon smiled. "That thought has *certainly* occurred to me," he said. He reached into his suit-coat pocket and pulled out a white business card. "If you're ever looking for insurance, give me a ring."

Leon extended the card to LaRue, but she didn't take it. She looked toward Kathy. "Have a *lovely* evening," she said.

"It's been good to see you, LaRue," Kathy said. "We need to get together right away and talk some more."

LaRue had begun to smile. "You know what I was talking about earlier—about making the best of things in order to have babies and all that?"

"Yes."

"In this case, I wouldn't," LaRue said. She gave Kathy a hug, then without so much as glancing at Leon, walked out the door. Kathy was thinking that LaRue had come on a little stronger than she had needed to, but she was also thinking that LaRue was right. Kathy did need to be careful about where she got her babies.

❧

Gene was sitting in his dad's big chair, bent over, with his elbows on his knees and his head in his hands. He and Emily had just had another raging argument and he wondered what was going to happen to them now. He had enrolled in college that fall, intent on taking some classes he would need before applying for law school, but he had hated every minute of it and had not done well on his first set of tests. He couldn't seem to concentrate, and he hated the young guys in his classes who thought they knew everything. That morning, as students were chatting among themselves before class, one of them had made a negative comment about the soldiers in Vietnam. Gene had almost blown apart. He had denounced the guy with an intensity that shocked everyone into silence, and then he had stalked out of the classroom and skipped the class. The whole thing was wrong for Gene, going back to school when his brain still wasn't working right. That was finally clear to him, so he had walked to the administration building and withdrawn from the university.

When he had told Emily what he had done, she had been very upset, and that had only made him defensive. He had yelled at her more fiercely than he ever had before, had found himself on the edge of grabbing her, unsure what he wanted to do if he did, but crazy to do something destructive. Danny had run into the bedroom where Gene and Emily were shouting at each other. He was obviously alarmed but then he had looked up at his father as though he were a monster. Gene had screamed at him to get out, and the poor little guy had run away in terror.

Gene was pulling himself back together now, and he knew he had to go to Emily and apologize. He had to get his anger under control—the way he had promised so many times. He waited a few more minutes, let himself calm down some more, and then got up and walked back to the bedroom, where he had left Emily.

But when he looked inside, he saw that she was packing her clothes in a suitcase. "Oh, Emily, please. Don't do this," he pleaded.

"Gene, I'm sorry. I've tried for two years to deal with this. But you're not getting better; you're getting worse. I can't put Danny through this any longer."

Gene didn't know what to say. There was no way to justify his fury with her, or the way he had yelled at Danny. But Emily and Danny were all he had left. "Please stay. Let's talk this out."

Emily brushed some loose hair from her face. She looked tired; she looked older than she was. Gene knew what he was doing to her. "I'm not sure you didn't die in Vietnam," she said. "What's left of you has no resemblance to the man who went over there. But the worst thing is, I don't think you want to come back to life. The only thing you care about now is that you're a victim. I know what you've been through, but if you can't let it go, your life is already over."

Gene knew all that. He talked to himself about it every day, and he was *trying* to get over it. He really was. Couldn't she give him that much benefit of the doubt?

"I can live with you losing your temper, Gene. I can tell myself that I just need to be more patient. But I can't let you scream at Danny that way. These are crucial years for him; he's nervous all the time, and he gets upset by things that most kids shrug off. I can't let him go through any more of this."

Gene didn't like to think he was dead, but he felt now that he was dying. He could feel his body shutting down, the strength leaving his muscles. He stood looking at Emily, his arms hanging limp. "What are you going to do?" he asked.

"I'm going to Bountiful. I'm going to live with my parents for a while. I won't file for a divorce yet; I'll wait to see what you're going to do with your life. But dropping out of school was a signal to me that you aren't ready to move ahead. You've been promising me for a long time that you would be all right once you could get your life back to normal."

Gene stepped closer to Emily, but he didn't dare touch her. He had violated her just by the thought that he wanted to hurt her, not yet fifteen minutes ago. "I'm trying, Em. I go to those discussion groups even though I hate them, and—"

"And you come home angry every time."

"But those guys are so messed up. I'm not like them."

"You don't say anything, Gene. You've told me that. You're supposed to be getting some things out in the open so you can deal with them, but the only thing you do is sit there and hate all the guys who complain."

All that was true, but why couldn't she try a little harder to understand? He pushed his hands into his pockets and balled up his fists where she couldn't see them. He didn't want to get mad again. "It's not what I need, Emily. I go because you and Dad want me to go, but it isn't helping."

"Nothing is. So I'll give you some time to see what you can do with yourself, but I'm taking Danny to live with people who love him." Her voice had taken on a hint of anger again, but then Gene saw her eyes soften, and she said in a kindlier voice, "He needs that, Gene."

"I love him. No one loves him more than I do." Gene wanted to let himself drop to the floor. He wanted to curl up and cry, but he had the feeling that if he ever did, ever let go like that, he would slip into madness. It was the one thing he couldn't do. But didn't she know? Did she really think he didn't love his son?

Emily turned and looked into an open drawer, but she didn't reach for anything. It was as though she had forgotten what she was trying to do. After a time she looked back at Gene and said in a voice that was little more than a whisper, "Don't say that. You don't love anybody. I haven't felt any love from you since you came home. I think you want to love me. You remember that you once did love me. But something has gone out of you. You're self-contained, Gene. You're like a mannequin. I try to reach you, but you feel hard as plastic."

Gene knew it was true. But it wasn't what he wanted. He couldn't help it if he didn't feel the way he once had. "Please, Emily. I can't live here by myself. I'll go crazy." His legs let go, and he dropped to his knees, beginning to cry. He hadn't cried for a long time, and the release that came was more than he could handle. He felt himself slipping to the floor, curling up—the very thing he had feared.

He cried for at least a minute, there on the floor, more alive because he was feeling something other than anger, but not alive enough to do anything. Emily finally knelt next to him, touched his shoulder, then sat on the floor by his side. She stroked his hair, and the soft touch opened something deeper in Gene. He cried harder than before and reached his arms around her waist. "Please stay. I'll do better."

Emily waited a long time and let him cry. Gene could feel that she wasn't leaving, and he was relieved, but he was still scared.

"What's going to make the difference, Gene? What's it going to take for you to make some headway on this thing?"

Gene breathed, stopped crying. "I'll talk at the next meeting. I'll tell those guys what happened to me in Vietnam."

"I think that would be good, Gene. But what are you going to do with your life? You thought college was going to help you."

"I don't really want to be a lawyer, Emily. I kept thinking, 'Why am I doing this? It's not what I want.'"

"But you don't have any other ideas, Gene. We've got to figure this out."

"That's right. We can think about it together. I'll go back next semester and study something else."

"Gene, you always say that, but then you won't talk to me. If I ask you what you're going to do, you bite my head off."

"I know. I've done that a lot. But I'll try harder."

"Gene, you can't get over this just by *effort*. We've got to find some answers." Gene knew that, of course. But he was afraid of looking for those answers. It always seemed to involve looking inside himself, and he had been trying to do it the other way, by looking outside, looking ahead. "Let's talk right now. Let's see if we can't think of some steps we can start to take. I have to have that, Gene. I have to believe that something is going to change."

"Okay. Let's do it." He got up from the floor and walked with Emily out to the family room, where he found Danny sitting stiff, watching television, focused in as though he didn't want to see or feel anything else. Gene knelt by him and hugged him. "Daddy's sorry," he said. "He loves you."

Danny continued watching the screen, as though unaware that Gene was even there. Gene wondered whether that wasn't something he was learning from his dad. He kissed Danny's head, and then he joined Emily on the couch.

"Can you think of anything else you might want to study?" she asked.

He didn't want to say no, but he had tried hard to think what he wanted to do, and he really had no answers. "Uncle Richard thinks I would be a good professor. I've thought a lot about that. I might like that, but I don't know what field to go into."

"There's something I've been thinking about." Emily put her hand on his arm, and the affection almost caused him to cry again.

"What's that?" he asked.

"I think you ought to write something about Vietnam. It's on your mind all the time, and you hate the things you hear people saying. Why don't you write an article and explain how veterans feel about what happened to them over there? I think most people are gradually recognizing that they haven't treated Vietnam vets the way they treated men who came home from other wars, but they don't really understand what you guys went through."

"But the more I think about things like that, the angrier I get. I'm not sure it would be good to write about it."

"Maybe it would work the other way. Why don't you try to put something down on paper and see if you can figure out what it is you're feeling. Don't just let it eat you up all the time."

Gene didn't want to do this, but he didn't dare say that to Emily and get her upset with him again. "What would I do—try to publish it?"

"Sure. Send it to magazines. People need to understand, and you have something to say to them. I think you could publish it somewhere."

The idea scared Gene, but he didn't say so. He had to show her that he was willing to make an effort. "I could write something, I guess, and then you could tell me where I'm getting too extreme or too angry."

"Just write it. Then let your vet friends read it. They could help you get it right."

Gene agreed. But everything was wrong with what she was saying. Those guys in his group were not his "friends." And he had never thought of himself as someone who could write. He doubted that anything would come of this, but he said, "Okay," and he put his arms around Emily. "I love you," he said. "I honestly do." And the words brought his tears back. In his own mind, he had never stopped loving Emily, but it had been a long time since he had really *felt* that love—or anything else. But he felt something stirring in him now—gratitude at least, that she would stay, and the residual effects of all the emotion he had allowed himself this past hour. He felt human, and that was frightening, but it also felt familiar, even good.

CHAPTER 11

Diane was relieved when Lloyd Ewing, her home teacher, called from the kitchen, "Okay, your faucet is working fine now. No leak." But she had stayed out of the kitchen while he was working. Lloyd was a nice guy, but Diane could guess what her bishop—or the elders' quorum president—had been thinking in assigning Lloyd to her. He was thirty or so, and single. He had a steady job; he was active in the Church; and, as everyone in the ward knew, he certainly ought to be married by now. There was nothing wrong with him, either. His face was a little too narrow, and his front teeth were bunched a little oddly, but he had nice dark hair and eyes. The truth was, what bothered Diane most was the way he combed his hair, the way guys in her junior high school had once done—with a wave in front and combed back on the sides. It somehow established Lloyd as a small-town boy, and he was that. On his first home-teaching visit, a few months back, he had told her about growing up in Hyrum, Utah, in Cache County. "That's where I'd go back and live if I could, but I can't find any work up there," he had told her.

That was fine. She liked him. He seemed not only nice but also devoted to the Church and desirous of being a good home teacher. But he seemed a little too attentive, and that made Diane nervous. When she walked into the kitchen to see what he had done, he turned from the sink and leaned back against the cabinet as though he planned to hang around and chat for a while. "Thanks so much, Lloyd," Diane said. "The landlord told me he would fix that faucet when I moved in—and he's promised about ten times since—but I'm not sure he even knows how."

"Naw. It's not that. Anybody can put a new washer in one of these things." He held up a little rubber donut. "The guy is just lazy, that's all."

"I don't doubt that. But it's going to be nice not to have to listen to that tonight. So *really*, thank you very much." She tried, with her voice, to make this last "thank you" the final one. It was Saturday morning, and she needed to do her grocery shopping and get her apartment cleaned up. Greg was coming to take her out again that night, and before then, she needed to prepare a Sunday School lesson. She was teaching the ten-year-old kids in Junior Sunday School, and she loved doing that, but it added to the busyness of her Saturdays.

Diane turned to see Jenny walk into the kitchen and look up at Lloyd. She had liked him since he had paid so much attention to her when he had first come home teaching with one of the bishop's sons. Now he crouched in front of her and said, "Hello, Jenny. How's my friend?"

She didn't say anything, but she smiled at him. It was October now, 1972, and Jenny had turned three. She could be a chatterbox, but she was usually shy at first around visitors, especially men. Diane worried sometimes how much she loved Lloyd's attention, as though she longed for a full-time father. "Can you tell Brother Ewell what you've been doing?" Diane asked, aware that she was extending the time he stayed—but not wanting to be impolite either.

Jenny looked up at her mom as though she wasn't sure what Diane meant. "Were you playing with your dump truck?"

Jenny looked back at Lloyd and nodded. "Uh-huh," she said.

Lloyd laughed. "You like to play with a dump truck?" he asked.

"Uh-huh."

"Her grandmothers have given her a whole collection of dolls, and she hardly looks at them, but she picked out this dump truck when I let her choose her own toy, and that's what she plays with all the time. She's got a fire engine, too, and she likes that. I guess she's a liberated woman."

Lloyd was still grinning at Jenny, obviously delighted with the idea, but he glanced at Diane and said, "Better watch out. She'll be voting for the ERA."

"That may not be such a bad idea." Actually, Diane had pretty much decided against the Equal Rights Amendment. She and her mom had talked about it a lot, and maybe Mom was getting more conservative in her old age, but she had some worries about the way the amendment might be used. Still, Diane enjoyed baiting Lloyd.

"Are you kidding? Are you really in favor of it?" he asked.

The rural twang in Lloyd's voice was grating to Diane. He had a college degree, but he sounded like an old rancher. "I might be," she said.

"I don't see how you could be. The Church is against it."

Diane decided not to address that argument. Instead, she said, "You need to start listening and learning from me, Lloyd, and pay less attention to your hero—old Spiro Agnew."

Lloyd grinned. "I think you're one of those 'nattering nabobs of negativity' Spiro likes to talk about," he said.

"Well, you're not the 'silent majority.' You've got more than enough to say."

Lloyd shrugged, and then he said in a softer tone, "The truth is, I don't know much about politics, and I really don't care. I just think Agnew makes a good point once in a while."

But Lloyd was quick to turn his attention back to Jenny. He didn't get much more out of her, but it seemed to Diane to be his way of hanging around—and changing the subject. "Say," he finally said to Diane, with an obvious attempt at casualness, "next Saturday we're having a dance for all the single people in our stake. You ought to go to that."

Diane didn't think she wanted to go, but she said, "We'll see," and that opened the door.

Lloyd slid his fingers into his front pockets and looked down as he said, "Some of us are going over together. If you'd like to go with us, I could maybe introduce you to some people and help you break the ice a little."

"I don't know, Lloyd. I'll have to see how busy I am next weekend."

"You really ought to go, Diane. It's a good way to get to know people."

Diane's mom had been telling her that for a long time now. Most of the men she met at the college were too young for her. She needed to meet men who had started their careers. It had crossed Diane's mind that maybe she ought to go to one of these functions and at least see what they were like. If nothing else, she could tell her mom she had made an attempt. But she didn't want Lloyd to think he had a date with her. "Who's going?" she asked.

"I'm not exactly sure, but Elaine Norton always goes, and so does Gaye Shivers."

They were both at least ten years older than Diane. She wondered how old the crowd would be. "I don't know. I might. Is it at the stake center?"

"Yeah. But we'll come by for you. It starts at eight. We could pick you up about a quarter to, or something like that."

"Maybe you'd better call first. I'm not sure."

Lloyd didn't push the matter, and that actually eased her mind a little. She didn't want this to mean too much to him. She certainly didn't want another situation to develop like the one she had gotten into with Ed. "While I'm here, do you have anything else that needs fixing?" Lloyd asked.

"No. That was the only thing that's been worrying me."

"What about doors that squeak? Or windows that don't open right. I can even patch up holes in your walls."

"Well, actually there is one thing. In Jenny's closet, the rod I hang her clothes on is coming loose from the wall at one end. I don't dare hang much of anything on it."

"Let's have a look at it."

That turned out to be something else he could fix, and before he left, he lubricated the compression closer on the storm door so it finally closed all the way by itself. All that was very helpful to Diane, and she did like Lloyd's goodwill, even the pleasure he seemed to take in making things better for her. She expected him, at some point, to start flirting or suggesting they go out, but he was careful about that—or maybe he really was just trying to be a good home teacher. She wanted to think so.

∽

That night Greg took Diane to hear the Utah Symphony orchestra perform at the Tabernacle in Salt Lake. Most of the men wore suits, not tuxedos, but Diane knew very well that Greg loved black-tie events more than he loved the music itself. And he did look good in a tux; he knew that as well as she did. He actually drifted off during the performance, his head dropping to his chest more than once, but afterward he gushed about Maurice Abravanel and the quality of the orchestra. Then he walked Diane up the street to the Hibachi—a Japanese restaurant Greg liked, with separate little screened-off dining areas and seating on the floor. During dinner Greg asked Diane whether she thought the war in Vietnam would end in the next few weeks, as Nixon and Kissinger had promised. The ground troops were now withdrawn, but the bombs continued to fall. It was strange for Greg to ask Diane about something like that. Back when he and Diane had been married, Greg would have told her what to think about current events, and he would have made her feel stupid about her questions or opinions. Now he asked seriously, and Diane wasn't sure whether he cared what she thought or whether he merely knew she would like to have him ask. Either way, she did like the change, and she ended up with the feeling that she knew more about the issues of the war than he did. She told him she thought it was probably another empty promise, with the elections coming up, and probably didn't mean much. Greg told her he thought she was probably right.

What worried Diane was that Greg was touching her more, holding her hand, putting his arm around her shoulders. When he brought her home that night he was clearly hoping for their first kiss since they had started seeing each other this way. Diane made a joke of that. She pushed him back with her hand against his chest, and she said, "We haven't been dating long enough for that, young man." He tried to laugh, but she saw something else in his eyes—a little flash of anger that lasted only a second. Then he thanked her for a "great evening," and he walked quickly to his car. Diane wanted to think that he was learning to control his anger, but it was just as likely that he was holding back a flood that would break loose sometime.

Diane thought about the date all the next week. She did wish there was someone like Greg in her life—someone who liked what she liked, someone she could talk to, be with. But she was still scared of Greg. How could she take a chance on him again? She thought again about the singles' dance that weekend and decided she would go. She even prayed that if there was someone right for her, he would show up at the dance. For such a long time she had told herself to accept her life and concentrate on raising Jenny, but these times with Greg had only reminded her of what it meant to have a richer life and a partner.

When Lloyd came to Diane's door to pick her up on Saturday night, he walked her out to a big Ford station wagon. Ross Warner, a man certainly over forty, was driving. He had already picked up Elaine and Gaye, and then he stopped to pick up a woman named Florence Goddard, who was older yet, probably fifty. Diane was glad the number of males and females was not equal, but she wondered whether everyone at the dance would be older than she was. It wasn't until she walked into the cultural hall at the stake center, however, that her concern turned into alarm. She saw no one who looked under thirty, and some of the people had white hair. Diane tried to think of an excuse to turn around and leave, but she had no way to get home unless she wanted to start a long hike.

There were some sad attempts at decorations, with a little trellis laced with fall leaves—plastic ones—at the entrance, and a refreshment table with some mottled gourds as a centerpiece. Someone kept counting to three on a sound system but never got around to saying anything. As people kept coming in, however, and Diane looked at the men, she hoped the sound system was broken and the music would never start.

"Don't panic," Lloyd told Diane. "All the oldest people come on time, and the younger ones don't show up for a while."

"Which are we?" Diane asked.

Lloyd grinned. "I have this bad habit of going everywhere on time. It's the way my whole family is. I always know we should wait until eight-thirty or so, but if the announcement says eight, I'm usually there at eight. Or five minutes early, waiting for someone to open the door."

Most people were gathering in little groups, close to the entrance. Diane decided to walk to the opposite side of the hall and maybe drift away from Lloyd, but he stayed by her side. She wondered whether he was planning to dance with her all evening. "Is anyone *my* age going to come?" Diane asked. Her question was directed at Lloyd as much as anyone. He might have been five or six years older than she was, but for all she knew, he could be ten years older. He really did seem too old to Diane, and she wanted him to know that.

"A lot of people our age—especially ones who haven't been married—don't find much interest in our dances. It's usually people like you, who have a child, who feel like they fit in here a little better."

"But you haven't been married. You don't have children."

"No. But I'm just saying that people who are maybe just out of college don't usually come." He stood for a moment with his hands in his pockets. He was wearing a rather nice-looking plaid sport coat, but the tie he had chosen was too busy, and he had tied it so it hung too short. "Actually, I don't think *any* people like that come."

This was getting worse; Diane was trapped. She glanced around to see whether there was a way to slip out without being noticed. It wasn't *that* long of a walk back to her apartment. But it was cool outside, and she hadn't worn a coat.

A balding, middle-aged man began blowing into the microphone, and then he said, "Hello, everyone. Oh, just a minute."

The sound had been much too loud, and there had been a whistle of feedback on the speakers. It took another few seconds to back off the sound. What had all that counting one-two-three been about?

"Okay, is that better?" Actually, it was only a little better, but he went ahead: "Welcome, and thanks for coming out. I'm Brother Burdick. The committee made me get up here because I'm the one with the biggest mouth. We expected a little better turn-out, but I guess we'll get some more folks here on Mormon Standard Time." Most everyone laughed as though he had just said something original. Diane rolled her eyes.

"We're going to have an opening prayer by Herb Hymas of the 76th Ward. I've told him not to pray that he'll find a wife here tonight, but I'm still a little worried that he might try to work that in somewhere."

Diane's muscles were tensing, and Lloyd seemed to notice. "He's just kidding. It's what everyone thinks about us." Diane wondered. She thought of her own prayers that week, and she wondered why the Lord hadn't sent her a warning.

Brother Hymas said the prayer in a voice that was like a series of explosions, and then Brother Burdick took the microphone back. "Okay. We're going to start with a snowball so the fellows don't waste too much time looking everyone over. Me and Lonny Smart will dance first, and you know how it goes from there. I know we have more women than men, but you men can kind of spread yourselves around enough so everyone gets to dance."

Diane knew how these "snowballs" worked from her days in Mutual when the boys wouldn't ask girls to dance and someone had to force the issue. Diane stepped closer to the wall, and Lloyd followed. As the recorded music started with a big-band tune—the kind of music Diane's parents liked—Diane saw Brother Burdick looking over his partner's shoulder, scanning the crowd, and he zeroed in on her. The instant someone lifted the needle from the record, Brother Burdick looped around Lonny and headed straight for Diane. There was absolutely no way to hide, and she certainly couldn't turn him down, so when he held out his hand and said, "May we?" she followed him onto the floor.

At least the guy kept his distance, but he held her like her father might have, with his arm held high and wide—and he said, "As you just heard, I'm Ralph Burdick. I don't think I've met you before."

"No. You haven't." Brother Burdick was losing his hair, but he wasn't going down without a fight. He had combed as much as he could from low on one side all the way over to the other, and he had plastered it down with something that looked wet. In spite of the loss of hair on his head, he had an abundance in his nose, which was showing in two dark, protruding tufts. He had a similar excess in his wild eyebrows.

"I'm sorry. What was your name?"

"Diane." She was going to make him work for anything he learned. She wasn't going to offer up both names automatically.

But he got her last name and the number of her ward, and then he said, "Tell me—not that it's any of my business—but . . . have you ever been married?"

"Actually, several times," Diane said. "Once a year or so."

That was her way of saying, "You're right; it is none of your business," but Brother Burdick didn't seem to understand that. "I think you're pulling my leg, Diane. And I don't need one to be longer than the other. I'm a poor enough dancer as it is."

Diane laughed, but she didn't respond. That needle would be coming off the record soon, she hoped, and she didn't have too much longer to stall.

But Brother Burdick was suddenly looking serious. "Diane, I'm kind of a cut-up, I guess you can tell. And I say things I shouldn't. I shouldn't have asked you about being married. But I hope we'll get a chance to get acquainted. After this snowball—"

But the music stopped, and Diane escaped immediately. Her horror was that she was now expected to choose someone else. She did the safest thing she knew to do, although she wouldn't have thought so ten minutes before. She walked to Lloyd and held out her hand. He smiled shyly and walked onto the floor with her. "I'm the worst dancer in the world," he said, as he reached for her. She had the feeling he might want to pull her a little closer than Brother Burdick had, so she established the distance as far away as possible without losing touch entirely. Lloyd needed to understand her intentions—or lack of them.

Lloyd said almost nothing, and he danced as badly as promised. The expression on his face was distant, as he probably counted out the fox-trot steps in his mind. Diane had gotten used to all the fast dances that had come along when she was in high school—the twist and the pony and the mashed potato. Mostly, these days, college students did their own free-lance "stomp" dancing, with little or no design. She had lost track of all that during her years with Greg in Seattle, but she still would have been more comfortable out of reach and moving on her own. Lloyd danced with stiff legs, making clunky steps, the music hardly a factor in his timing, and Diane felt awkward trying to follow what he was doing.

But the music ended quickly this time as the snowball had to keep rolling. Diane thought of slipping off to the side this time, but there were still not enough on the floor for her to get away with that. She decided to ask Brother Warner to dance, and he turned out to be a smooth dancer and shy about talking, which was just what Diane needed. When the music stopped next time, Diane was in trouble. Most of the men were on the floor by then, and the choices were getting slim. She spotted the oldest-looking man she could, assuming that he might also be the safest. He was a short little man all dressed up in a dark suit, a white shirt, and a dapper, if old-fashioned, red tie. He had a deep wrinkle extending down from the corners of his mouth that made him look as though he were frowning. That all changed, however, when Diane approached him. Those lines turned upward, and he grabbed Diane with more force than she had expected. She was suddenly in his grasp, very close, almost touching in front, and he was saying, "I'm Bradford Miner. And who, my enchantress, are you?"

Enchantress?

"Diane Lyman," she said. "Eighty-first ward. I'm divorced. I have a little daughter named Jenny." She was only giving up what he would probably ask anyway, and she hoped the mention of Jenny would scare him off quickly.

"Oh, my. And is this little girl as gorgeous as her mother?"

The man danced very well. He knew how to lead and how to hold her as he twirled—and he did like to twirl. "She's very cute," Diane said.

"Tell me, did you kill her father and bury him in your backyard? Or did he simply realize that he was no match for a beauty like you?"

Diane tried to think of a witty answer, or a blunt one, or some way to deal with this man, but she was caught in a whirlwind of motion, and his cheek was almost touching hers. "I married a ravishing woman," he said. "But she was frail. She died a year ago, and I'm the loneliest man on this planet. But I have more life than most men. I have miles to go before I sleep, young lady. Miles to go."

"Twirling all the way," Diane said.

"Yes, yes." He started another spin. But the music had stopped and Diane had had enough; she was getting dizzy. As she walked away, Brother Miner was saying, "Save another dance for me, sweetheart."

Not every man was dancing, but quite a few women were left over, so Diane slipped over and stood next to Gaye Shivers.

"Brother Miner is quite the dancer, isn't he?" Gaye said.

"Yes, he is that," Diane said. "But I think he's a little off, mentally. He kept—"

"Oh, no. He's just dramatic. He's done a lot of acting, you know. I always like to dance with him, but he goes after the youngest girls. You'll be seeing him again."

That turned out to be a solid prediction. As soon as the snowball ended and another Guy Lombardo tune began, Diane saw both Brother Miner and Brother Burdick making their way toward her. She was actually thankful that it was Brother Miner who got to her first. Maybe he lived in his own world, but he seemed a little less likely to try to get her phone number.

Brother Miner whisked her off, and then he whispered, "Ah, my lovely, each second away from you was a burden to me."

At least he was laughing. Was this all in play? But the grip he had on her didn't feel playful, and they were twirling again. But not for long. Brother Burdick allowed about a minute, and then he cut in. "Ah, true love never did run smooth," Brother Miner said, and Diane decided maybe he was just having fun. She wanted him back. Brother Burdick was now staring into her eyes with great sincerity. "Diane, I feel terrible about the way I embarrassed you before. I have such a problem with this big mouth of mine. It's just not any of my business whether you've been married. Sister Norton was just telling me that you had a lout of a husband who mistreated you, and you're raising a little girl by yourself."

Apparently that *was* his business.

"There are some real crumbs in this world, Diane. I'm sorry you ended up with one. I chose wrong the first time too. I married a woman who didn't think I provided well enough. I could work six jobs and she could spend it all—and yet, it was never enough. But I shouldn't get into all that either. We should get acquainted first and talk about all those things later."

Diane was holding to her new theory: don't say anything. Just wait for someone else to cut in.

Before the tune had finished, a lanky man much closer to her own age—within, say, fifteen years—tapped Brother Burdick's shoulder. "Hello, I'm Ron," he said. "I looked around for the prettiest girl here, and it didn't take too much looking to know you were it."

Diane didn't even look at him.

"What was your name?"

"Diane," she said, mumbling on purpose.

"Like I said, I'm Ron. I moved here just a short while back." When she didn't respond, he added, "I'm in real estate."

Diane nodded, ever so slightly.

"I just got started, but so far it's going real good. My ex-wife got most everything I had, but that's the way it usually goes. When we broke up, I decided I was going to start a whole new life and do things my way this time. I wanted a career with good opportunities, you know, and more freedom than I had laying carpet. I said to myself, why think small, why not step into a whole new field of work? So that's what I've done. I've made some pretty good sales already, too. You know, I can't say it's enough to make a full-time living yet, but my ex takes most of what I get anyway. I figure, let her try to live on less, the same as me. So tell me about you."

Diane cleared her throat. She even tried a cough. She kept thinking that the next shoulder tap couldn't be far off. But it didn't come, so she said, "I'm going to college."

"That's good. There's nothing more important than an education. I wish with all my heart I'd finished high school and then kept right on going. But what does a guy know when he's seventeen and a man offers him good money to lay carpet? I mean, I made a decent living. It's not that I didn't, but—"

Thank goodness. Lloyd was tapping on Ron's shoulder, and Lloyd suddenly seemed surprisingly normal. "I should have known this was going to happen to you," he said. "No one quite like you has been here before. These guys are foaming at the mouth."

"Could you borrow Brother Warner's car and drive me home? You could hurry right back."

"Look, I'm sorry. After a few dances, maybe things will settle down."

"Another guy's coming. Please, let's go."

So Lloyd took her arm and walked quickly toward the door. "You go to the ladies' room, and I'll go back and get Ross's keys," he said. Diane glanced over to see the heavy-set man who had been working his way toward them. He stopped, and he looked disappointed, but she avoided direct eye contact. The trouble was, she had to walk right past Brother Burdick, who was looking shocked and hurt, probably assuming way too much about her leaving with Lloyd.

But she looked straight ahead and kept going, and then she hid away until Lloyd returned. It was only outside that she finally took a breath. "Thanks, Lloyd," she said. "I'm glad you understood."

"It was like a room full of hungry dogs—and you were a side of bacon."

Well . . . something like that.

Lloyd drove her home, and he didn't have much to say as he drove. When he pulled up in front of her house, he didn't get out to open her door, and Diane thought for a second that he was going to let her walk to the apartment alone—which she preferred—but as she reached for the door handle, he said, "Diane, I thought it might be good for you to do something other than stay home on a Saturday night. I should have thought about you being a lot younger than everyone there. I didn't remember it quite so much that way."

"It was okay, Lloyd. No harm done."

"Well, I'm not so sure about that. If I can help you in some way—I mean, other than fixing your faucets, I hope you won't be afraid to let me know."

Diane couldn't quite figure out what Lloyd actually had in mind. Was he telling himself that to be a good home teacher he had to make her life better? Or was he actually interested in her? Either way, she decided to put a few more of her cards on the table. "Lloyd, I do go out now and then. My ex-husband takes Jenny sometimes, but he also comes and takes me out. I'm not sure I'm ever going to trust him enough to marry him again, but it's a possibility."

"Probably a better one, after tonight."

"No. Not really." But Lloyd had a point. Suddenly a future without Greg did look more bleak than ever.

"Well, anyway, I hope you know I'm someone you can turn to if you need any help."

He sounded sweet—and disappointed. She had a feeling that he hadn't liked hearing about Greg. But that was all right. Chances were, she wouldn't end up going back to Greg, but chances were much greater that she would never be interested in Lloyd. He might as well know that.

Lloyd got out and walked around to her side of the car, opened the door, and walked with her. He waited until she found her key and opened her front door. "What about Jenny?" he asked. "Where's she tonight?"

"My mom has her. I'll drive over and get her now."

"Oh, shoot. I should have thought of that. We could have stopped by for her."

"It's okay. You need to hurry back to the dance."

"Not really. Do you want me to drive you over now, so you won't have to go alone?"

"No. I'm fine. I might stay over and talk to my parents for a while."

"Well, okay. I'll see you then." He gave her a little pat on her shoulder and then walked away. Diane thought again how considerate he was, not wanting her to be out at night alone, as though he felt a need to protect her. She doubted that impulse had anything to do with home teaching. It seemed more an instinct, and one that not all men had.

Still, when she arrived at her parents' house and sat down with her mom at the kitchen table, she knew the honest answer to Bobbi's immediate queries about Lloyd. "He's good as gold," Diane said. "But he's not my type at all. I've never heard him say a word about a book he's read or an idea he's been mulling over."

Bobbi laughed. "I'm sorry, Diane, but no matter how hard I try to get used to you saying things like that, I still think of all the years I spent trying to get *you* to read—and think."

"Maybe it finally worked."

Diane had gotten back much sooner than anyone had expected, and Jenny didn't want to leave yet. Bobbi said Richard was supposed to be watching her, but he was actually reading a book, and Ricky was playing with Jenny. For a ten-year-old, Ricky had amazing patience with Jenny, and Jenny loved him. Diane was sure it was Ricky who had taught her to like trucks and cars and Lincoln Logs more than dolls.

"It seems to me," Bobbi said, "you could have a little more patience with someone who isn't a big reader. You keep saying how nice Lloyd is to Jenny, and—"

"Come on, Mom, don't do this. You've never even met him. He's got this slow way of talking that makes you think of a boy right off the farm, and he combs his hair like one."

"That's the *bad* stuff?"

"No. Not really. But we have nothing in common. I don't have the slightest interest in him. So don't start thinking that I could. You got all excited about Ed, and you can see now what happened with him."

"What worries me is that Greg keeps showing up, and he stops you from considering anyone else."

"Not exactly. But let's face it, in most ways, Greg is what I've always wanted."

Bobbi shook her head slowly, looking disgusted. "That's right. He's great—except for that one little habit he had of slugging you and tossing you against walls."

"Yeah. There was that." Diane smiled. "Actually, though, that's not true. Greg made me unhappy long before he hit me."

"You aren't letting him talk you into anything now, are you?"

"No. But he's pushing me a little harder to consider the possibility that we could end up back together. So far, I just backpedal, but sooner or later I'll have to let him know one way or the other. I will say, he's been very patient."

"Maybe so. But he deserves whatever he's going through now. Don't let him sweet-talk you into anything this time."

"I'm older now, Mom. And I'm probably more skeptical about him than you are. I'd like to think he can change, but I can't say I believe that yet."

"I think you'll find out one of these days. He's not the type to be patient forever."

"You expect the worst, don't you?"

"Yes, I do."

"Well . . . I don't blame you. But remember, I've got to decide."

"That's what you said last time."

"I know. But it's still true. And I'm not the same little girl I was back then."

Bobbi put her hands on the table and leaned forward, forcing Diane to look directly into her eyes. "Can't you at least consider someone like Lloyd, who would—"

"Mom, don't do that to me. I've told myself all the reasons I *ought* to consider him. It doesn't help his cause one bit for you to push him at me."

"I wasn't *pushing*. I'm just saying—"

"I know exactly what you're saying. But I've got to decide about him, too."

"Okay. Okay. I'll keep my mouth shut."

But Diane doubted that she would.

CHAPTER 12

Kathy had decided that she wouldn't go out with Leon again. She knew that nothing was likely to come of their relationship, and since the day LaRue had locked horns with him, Kathy had been trying to get up the resolve to turn him down when he called next time. But it was always easier to put off doing that—mainly because he took her to such nice places. At first he had seemed satisfied merely to date and had shown no obvious interest in getting serious, and she had been content to have someone to go out with on weekends, just so her life wasn't quite so dull. On their last date, however, he had finally pressed the issue. He had kissed her good-night at her door, which she allowed, but he had tried to hold her longer than she wanted, and he seemed annoyed that she had pulled away so soon. It was that kiss that had forced a decision. She was going to break things off. The only problem was, she had more or less talked him into buying tickets for the Nutcracker ballet. It seemed shabby to back out before Christmas and leave him with tickets she knew he hadn't really wanted.

As it turned out, when she and Leon did see the Nutcracker at Kingsbury Hall, she spent the time wishing she had made the break sooner and maybe bought the tickets from him. She had seen Ballet West's performance once before, and it was a favorite memory, but seeing it with Leon was difficult. When he had picked her up that evening, Kathy was not in a good mood. Nixon had begun to bomb Hanoi that week, just when the war had seemed about to end. For Kathy, the thought of conducting bombing raids at Christmastime was disheartening. But when she told Leon what she was feeling, he had said, "It's not Christmas for them. What difference does it make? If you're going to bomb people, one day is as good as another."

"Why bomb them at all?" Kathy had asked.

"If it were up to me," Leon said, "I'd bomb those people off the face of the earth. That ought to make our peace negotiations a lot easier."

"What a lovely thought for Christmas. Peace on earth—achieved by killing civilians."

"You can't make peace with Communists. They'll only stop fighting when they know they *can't* defeat us."

Kathy hadn't replied. All this time she had been wanting Leon to express some stronger opinions, and now he had finally done it. She had the distinct feeling he was tired of her and wanted this to be the last date, the same as she did. But she really didn't want to argue, and she didn't want to watch the ballet when she was feeling full of anger. "Could we drive through downtown on the way to campus?" she had asked. "I want to see the Christmas lights." She had looked out the window of Leon's car and tried to concentrate on the lights, on anything but bombs falling. She liked to remember how she had felt about Christmas when she was a little girl and she would go shopping downtown with her mother. The world had seemed very different then. She remembered walking along the streets in the cold air, wearing snow pants and a stocking cap. She and Mom had made their way through the crowded aisles in ZCMI, had eaten lunch in the Tiffin Room, and finally ended up at Woolworth's, where Kathy could find presents for her brothers and sisters. The world had seemed so good then, and Christmas had felt right. How was it possible that she could be sharing this time with a man who felt no regret at all— even if he believed it was necessary—that America was dropping bombs on human beings just a few days before Christmas?

Kathy and Leon seemed to disagree about almost everything, but this was the first time they had openly argued. That was partly because Kathy was so tired of her own anger. There were times when her old fire welled up, but more often she simply felt regret that the world couldn't be kinder and more Christian. And worse, she was starting to lose hope that things would ever change. She did feel that headway had been made in civil rights, her old cause, but racial division had not ended, and no amount of fighting could change the hearts of those who still hated. And the national division caused by the war ran so deep, she wondered whether a healing could ever come. She felt sad and powerless, more than angry, and her temptation was to hide away from all the issues, sit in her apartment in the evening, and read books that took her away from all the problems she didn't know how to solve.

Kingsbury Hall was nice and, as usual, Leon had bought very good tickets. The Nutcracker was exactly as Kathy remembered: delightfully light, playful, magical. But Leon yawned through the whole thing, clearly bored. When the ballet ended, Leon applauded with everyone else, but as soon as the sound began to die down, he stood, as if to get out as quickly as possible. But their seats were in the middle of the main floor, so there was no getting out quickly. "Do you want to get something to eat?" he asked.

"I don't think so. All the places around here will be crowded."

"Not if we could get out of here quickly." He looked down the row left and then right, but neither direction looked promising. He shrugged, seeming to resign himself to the idea that their exit was going to be slow. When people on their row finally began inching forward, Kathy walked ahead of Leon, slowly making her way to the aisle. She was almost there when she heard someone say, "Kathy, hello."

Kathy looked to her left, unsure who had spoken, and then saw Marshall, who was stuck in the aisle, having come from farther down front. He was with a pretty, dark-haired girl who was standing in front of him. She was short enough that he could see over the top of her head. Kathy had always longed to be that petite, and this girl had pretty eyes, pretty skin, and a cute sort of "little girl" look. "Hi, Marshall. How are you?" Kathy asked, but she didn't want to talk to him. She couldn't think of anything worse than having to introduce him to Leon.

"All right." The line in the aisle moved forward a little, and Kathy decided to let Marshall go on by, then get in line well behind him.

But Marshall said, "Go ahead," and Leon was pressing her, so Kathy moved into the aisle and Leon worked his way in too. Kathy hoped that would be the end of the little encounter. She was feeling bad as it was; she didn't need to watch Marshall with his pretty little girlfriend.

But Marshall had moved to the left, in the aisle, and he managed to slip ahead as the forward progress improved. When he got close enough, he said, "Kathy, I haven't seen you for a long time. What's going on with you these days?"

Kathy had to twist a little to look back at Marshall. He was wearing a blue blazer with an oxford cloth shirt and a blue-and-red striped tie, and he was carrying a camel-hair topcoat over his arm. He looked *really* good compared to Leon, who seemed to think that polyester double-knit was the new standard in fashion. "Not much," Kathy said. "I'm working for my dad and . . . I don't know . . . still trying to figure out what I want to do with my life. What about you?"

"I finally finished my degree," he said, and he laughed. "I have enough hours for a Ph.D., but all I have is a B.A. to show for it."

Kathy was gradually getting farther ahead of Marshall—so that Marshall and Leon were walking shoulder to shoulder and Kathy was next to Marshall's girlfriend, but Kathy still didn't want to start any introductions. "Are you going on to grad school?" Kathy asked, glancing back again.

"I'm not sure. That's been my plan. But I've got this nutty idea in my head right now. Last summer I went to work for a carpenter. It was supposed to be a temporary job, but I loved it, so I've stayed with it for now. We do finish carpentry—mostly cabinets—and that's something I always liked in my high school shop classes. I just didn't think it was something I would ever do for a living."

Kathy had finally reached the lobby. She was curious about Marshall's possible career change, but she still wanted to walk away and escape the situation. Just as she was about to stride out more quickly, with renewed pressure on her back from Leon, Marshall said, "Kathy, how's Douglas? I think about him all the time."

Kathy stopped. It touched her that Marshall would think of Douglas. Leon probably didn't even recognize the name, even though she had talked about Douglas a few times. "Marshall," Kathy said, finally capitulating, "this is Leon Powers. Leon, this is Marshall Childs. We've been friends for many years."

"Yes, we have," Marshall said. He laughed as though he saw some irony in the description. "This is Lisa Griffith," he said. "And Kathy Thomas. I can't remember whether you two have ever met."

"I don't think so," Lisa said politely, but Kathy had the suspicion that the girl knew her name.

People were having to work their way around the four of them now that they had stopped in the middle of the stream of things. A man, trying to put his coat on, knocked Kathy in the shoulder, then looked at her as though she were the problem, but the worst was over now, and Kathy did want to talk to Marshall. "Douglas is the same. You know how he is. Always simple and lovely—always a child, and he'll never get any older."

"He's got such a perfect spirit. He'll be a great man in the next life when he has all his capacities."

Kathy was thinking about Marshall's smile. It had always done things to her—those great teeth set off by his dark complexion. But she was also responding to what he said about Douglas. It was something she had always thought, and she loved that Marshall would think of the same thing. "You two were good friends," Kathy said. "He always liked you."

"I've meant to go see him. But I haven't for a long time."

Kathy nodded. "Well, it's good to see you, Marshall." She felt Leon take a step, now pulling her by the elbow.

"So you're still working for your dad, huh?"

Kathy turned back and Leon waited again. "For now. I want to go to graduate school, but I still can't make up my mind what I want to study. It seems pointless to go back until I know what I want to do."

"You sound like me."

Kathy saw Lisa smile and raise her eyebrows. The girl was painfully cute, but Kathy saw her disdain for Marshall in the little gesture. How did he put up with that? "But it sounds like you've found something you want to do now."

"Maybe. You know me. I'll probably change my mind again, but I can't believe how much I like working with wood. When we finish a set of cabinets, I feel like an artisan. No ideas; no confusion; just the pure stuff. And I like to bring out the grain in the wood—you know, the sanding and staining and polishing. I feel like I'm uncovering the beauty God put there. It's like being a photographer. The beauty is there, in nature, but no one focuses on it until the photograph isolates it and forces you to see it." He stopped and laughed. "I'm not sure that makes much sense, but I've been thinking a lot about all this, as you can tell."

"It makes *perfect* sense," Kathy said, and she instantly felt her face heat up. She had spoken with too much fervor, had felt too much and hadn't hidden it. The truth was, it was funny for him to talk about something he called simple and use so many words to describe it. But that was Marshall, and of course, it was also Kathy.

The pressure from the crowd was easing a little. Marshall took the chance to slip on his topcoat, and that seemed to say he was about to move on. But he was saying, "I'm thinking that I want to learn from my boss for a year or two, even though I don't get paid much, and maybe learn enough to open up my own little cabinet shop."

"You might want to think that through a little more," Leon said, his voice like a sudden clash in Kathy's ear. "The building trade goes in cycles. You can invest a lot of money into equipment and then hit a downturn and lose your shirt."

Marshall hesitated and smiled at Leon as though he saw something comical in his words. Kathy knew he was thinking how odd it was for her to be with a guy like that. "Maybe," Marshall said. "But when building slows down, people start remodeling, and cabinet guys usually stay busy. Right now, my boss is turning away customers. He can't keep up with all the work."

"But there's no way for a small operation to turn out enough volume to produce a serious income. A guy has to settle for a lot of hard work with little hope of building much equity into his business. If you could develop a method of mass-producing quality cabinets that compete price-wise with all these cheap pre-fabs that are coming out, then you might have something. But that would take a lot of investment capital and a heavy monthly payroll. Besides, you'd have an even bigger problem if the economy went south and sales slowed."

Kathy wanted to elbow Leon in the stomach. She wanted to tell him to leave Marshall alone. And above all, she knew she would tell him *tonight* that there was no point in the two of them going out anymore.

But Marshall was smiling. "That's probably all true," he said. "But I'm not worried about a *serious* income. I want to keep my life simple. I'd like to live in a small town, get up every morning, eat breakfast with my family, then go out to my shop and spend my days doing something I like to do. And in the evening, instead of pushing myself to death, I'd like to have time with my kids—then maybe read a good book for a while before I go to bed with my wife. I see guys making a lot of money, but they're running themselves ragged and working twenty hours a day. And they're still over their heads in debt, trying to build a house the size of Buckingham Palace—just to show everyone how successful they are. I'm not interested in that kind of life."

"I agree, Marshall," Kathy said. "I never thought I'd like a small town, but I lived in a little barrio in the Philippines and loved the way people knew and cared about each other. Lately I've been thinking how much good a person could do in a small town. If you're on the library board or the town council, or something like that, you can really help make a town work at the grassroots level. I learned the hard way that I couldn't solve the world's problems, but I don't want to give up on doing some good with my life."

"That's what I keep telling Lisa. She's lived here in Salt Lake all her life, so she has these negative stereotypes about small towns. But I think—"

"You've never lived in a little town, Marshall," Lisa said. "You've got this whole fairy-tale idea about them. I've got cousins who live out in Duchesne, and there's nothing for the kids to do out there. The biggest thing in the world for them is to come down to Salt Lake."

She had a little voice, sort of nasally, like an elf. An angry elf. It was annoying. Kathy could tell that the two had had this conversation before.

"It depends on what you call 'something to do,'" Marshall said. As he spoke, he pulled his tie loose and unbuttoned the top button on his shirt. "You know me. I'd be hiking and taking the kids fishing. If we had the right attitude about it, and didn't worry whether we saw all the movies right after they came out, it would be great."

"That's how I feel," Kathy said.

Lisa had been about to say something, but she stopped herself. She was looking at Kathy with the same disdain she had directed at Marshall, and some very clear resentment. A little fantasy jumped into Kathy's head: Marshall and Lisa would quarrel tonight—and break up.

"The thing is," Leon said, "small-town life may have some advantages, but you would have to stay close enough to a major metropolitan area or you would never find enough work. My own experience has been that these little towns sound great until you get there. Everybody knows everyone else, but they also know everyone else's business. All this love Kathy talks about is no more prevalent in a small town than it is in a nice neighborhood in a bigger city. After all is said and done, it's the ward you live in that counts, and some of these small towns have pretty ineffective wards."

"That's exactly right," Lisa said. "That's what I've been telling Marshall."

Kathy had a solution. Leon could take Lisa and live in a *nice* neighborhood. Kathy would run off with Marshall and live in a small town. But the thought wasn't as funny as Kathy wanted it to be. She was in love with Marshall all over again, or really, had never stopped, and there was stunning little *Lisa* standing in front of her, confident that ultimately she was going to win this one. She would talk Marshall out of his plan, get him back into school to become manager of some company, and Marshall would end up trying to pay for a house big enough to satisfy the "better class of people" in Salt Lake.

And then Marshall said something beautiful. He let the whole conversation go, ignored Lisa and Leon's little speeches, and said, "Kathy, I've been just sick this week about Nixon starting the bombing again. What a nice way to say 'Merry Christmas,' huh?"

"What do Communists care about Christmas?" Leon repeated, now with more disgust, but Kathy was nodding to Marshall, and she was trying to tell him with her eyes that he was meant for *her*, not for Lisa with the elfy little face.

The lobby was emptying out. Kathy had noticed by then the smell of the Christmas tree nearby, and for the first time she felt as though it really was Christmastime. But Leon was starting to tug on her arm again. "Well, it was nice to see you," Kathy said.

And then Lisa took revenge. "Kathy, we need to get your address," she said. "We'll send you an invitation to our wedding."

Kathy couldn't speak. She merely nodded, didn't even make a passing attempt to state her address or even acknowledge the stab she had taken. And then Leon took her away. Kathy wondered whether the wedding date was actually set, whether they were officially engaged, or whether she was merely firing a shot over Kathy's bow, just in case she had ideas. Whatever the case, Kathy knew she had lost another battle in her decade-long struggle over Marshall. If only he hadn't seemed so appealing tonight, and if only the life he had described hadn't sounded so wonderful.

But Leon was walking faster than usual. "Maybe we can still get into a restaurant if we drive out south a little way—or downtown."

"I'm tired, Leon. I'd rather go home."

"You didn't seem very tired when you were talking to your old boyfriend back there."

Kathy didn't answer. She was relieved that Leon had gotten the picture and glad that he had struck the first blow.

The walk to the parking lot was rather far, and yet Kathy was glad for the time, especially since Leon wasn't saying anything. She was telling herself to enjoy the cold. She wanted to go downtown tomorrow and finish her Christmas shopping, and get back into the Christmas spirit. She couldn't let this evening ruin the season. She had lost Marshall long ago; she wasn't losing him again.

When they reached the car, Leon opened the door for her, still without a word, but when he got in on his side, he looked over at Kathy and said, as though he were continuing where he had left off somewhere, probably in his own thoughts, "The thing about a guy like that, he learns a little woodworking and likes it, and immediately he thinks he knows how to run a business. Most of these little subcontractors are the same way. They know plumbing, maybe, but they underbid jobs to get work, and then they can't figure out why they aren't making anything. Most of them would be better off to work for someone else and bring home enough of a salary to buy a little house and get by."

Kathy wasn't going to discuss this with Leon.

"And the thing about this Marshall fellow, he doesn't even have the skill. You don't pick up cabinetmaking in a few months. It's a highly developed craft. You watch what happens. He'll lose his excitement when he finds out what it takes to learn what his boss already knows—from years of work."

Kathy had heard enough. "And why would that make you so happy, Leon?"

"What are you talking about? It wouldn't make *me* happy."

"Then why are you still ranting about it? Lisa is the one who has to decide if she's okay with what he wants to do—not you."

"I feel sorry for her, that's all. That guy will never make a living. It sounds like he wasted his time in college and took forever to get finished. That's the way he'll live his whole life, no doubt."

"Leon, you know what Marshall likes to do? He likes to learn. He would rather know things than *not* know them. He's curious about his world. That's something incomprehensible to you, isn't it? Everything my Aunt LaRue said about you was true."

Now it was his turn not to answer. It was the first time she had ever said anything to him that was so clearly hostile. The silence was evidence that they both understood what had just happened.

Leon kept driving and was almost to her apartment before he said, "Kathy, you don't like me. Why have you bothered to go out with me?"

"It's not that I don't like you," she said. "We're just too different."

"And Marshall is your idea of what the ideal man should be, I suppose."

"Actually, yes. And I know you didn't like him. But I guess that says something about both of us."

"Well, I feel sorry for you, but it's probably good you didn't end up with him. He's going to marry Lisa, and she's going to make sure he doesn't go off the deep end. If you and Marshall had gotten married, I'd hate to think what might have happened."

"You're probably right."

"But your heart is going to break when you get their wedding invitation. I can tell that."

"Yes. I guess it will. Won't you feel wonderful, knowing you're right?"

"No, Kathy. I'm sure you can't imagine it, but I have a heart of my own. And it's not feeling very good right now. I like you much more than you seem to understand, but I don't like ballet, and I don't feel bad about dropping bombs where they need to be dropped, and I fear that I make a very good living, which would embarrass you to death. So I guess it's best that we go our separate ways."

She was glad he had said it so she didn't have to, but his assessment of her situation was much too accurate, and the skill with which he had brought her down was startling. "I drive you crazy, Leon. I have no idea why you've continued to ask me out."

She heard him take a breath, saw his chest expand, and then he said, "I never have found a girl who liked me very much. At least you kept going out with me. It seemed sort of hopeful." He took another breath, then added, "That's pretty pitiful, isn't it?"

Kathy could only think to say, "I'm sorry, Leon. I really am."

But afterward, back in her apartment alone, she realized that until now she had also found some strange hope in the fact that Leon had kept calling for two or three months. At least she had been able to say to people that she was "dating someone." Now what?

Kathy wished she had never seen Marshall, had never heard him talk about what he wanted to do. And at the same time, she wished she hadn't heard what Leon had had to say about him. Leon was probably right. This idea of making cabinets was probably just one more passing notion in a long line of Marshall's ideas. Marshall was lovely—so ardent and idealistic, so curious, so in tune with her idea of what was worthwhile in life—but he was something of a flake and probably always would be. It was deflating to think that Marshall was the one love of her life. She had scared away every other man who had ever found her interesting, and she had met no one else who appealed to her the same way. Lisa hadn't been wearing a ring, but she must have been expecting one for Christmas or she wouldn't have talked so confidently about the wedding. So that was that.

Kathy was a Smith College graduate working as a secretary for her father. She lived alone in an apartment with almost nothing to look forward to and little to hope for. At least Aunt LaRue had pursued a dream. Maybe the dream had taken her to a place she now regretted at times, but what was Kathy's dream? She didn't even know what she wanted to study or who she wanted to be. She had spent her life arguing with people, convinced that she knew more than they did. It was somehow a fitting punishment that she would now be alone, with no one to offend—no one even to talk to. Kathy's mother had called that morning to tell her that Dixie, Wayne's wife, had had a baby boy during the night. Kathy's little brother had a family. Sharon, Kathy's younger cousin, had never dated much in her life, but she had gotten married in the summer, and she and Joel would be having babies before long, no doubt. Kathy was already becoming LaRue—the old-maid aunt.

CHAPTER 13

Gene was working at the dealership. He had spent the day processing paperwork, completing loans, and taking care of other things he had no real interest in. But he liked that he could put in a full day now, and he really was beginning to feel some strength return. He had done a lot of walking during the fall, and as the days had gotten colder he had actually played a little basketball. He usually just shot a few hoops by himself and then jogged for fifteen minutes or so. Twice he had tried playing pickup games with some younger guys in his ward, but he hadn't lasted long. The running wore him out, but besides that, these guys were banging pretty hard, and he found he didn't have the muscle to stay with them. He hated that sense that he was frail, that he didn't dare go all out, but he tried to remind himself that a year before he had wondered whether he would ever be able to do anything physical again.

The truth was, Gene didn't like to play with guys like that for another reason. The second time he got in a game, one of the boys—a kid about eighteen—had hacked him hard across the arm when he had made a move to the basket and then had bellowed, "What are you talking about? I didn't foul you." Gene had grabbed him by the shirt and spun him around, and he still didn't know what had kept him from knocking the boy down. He knew right then, however, that he didn't want to test his anger control that far again.

Life, of course, wasn't back to normal, but then, Gene hardly remembered what normal was. One thing that helped was that his physical relationship with his wife had improved, and he realized how much the limitations on their intimacy had hurt their sense of closeness. Still, every part of life seemed a test of Gene's control. He struggled to be patient with Emily and especially Danny, but he also got upset with the cocky salesmen at work. And lots of things fired his temper—traffic, long waits in a line, stupid comments on the news, dozens of other things. He had talked to guys at the vet hospital, and some of them were having a worse time than he was, but it seemed a common problem. It was as though they had learned to react with intensity and violence to enemies in the jungle, and now, turning off those reactions was not as easy as they had expected.

Gene kept telling himself that he had been home a long time, and that he should stop responding like a soldier, but twice that fall a banging noise had sent him sprawling on his chest. That had happened once at the dealership. A salesman had dropped a driver's manual, and it had slapped on the floor in the showroom. Suddenly Gene was on the floor, his eyes wide and searching. A couple of guys had seen him, and they had hurried over, but he had retreated to his office as quickly as he could. He was sure they thought he was some sort of psycho.

He was still having dreams, too—replays of things he had seen, or whole new scenes, not even necessarily from war, but threatening and chaotic. One night Emily turned over in her sleep and flipped her arm against his face. He had grabbed her arm hard and rolled toward her, ready to strike. He had awakened in time to realize what he was doing but had still come close to throwing a blow at her. Emily had been terrified.

But in a way that was good. Emily had come away from the experience a little more aware that his reactions were trained and that some of the things he did were beyond his will. They had talked much of the rest of that night, and Gene had described some of his dreams and some actual experiences in the war that he had never told her about before. Then, early in the morning, they had fallen back to sleep, holding each other, and Gene thought they had gotten along better since then.

Today Gene was about to file away some forms on his desk before he left to go home, but then the phone rang. He picked up the receiver and heard Emily's voice. "Gene," she said, "I just got home, but as I was walking into the house the phone was ringing. It was a guy who wanted to talk to you. He said if you called now he would still be in his office, but he's leaving soon. He was calling from Boston."

"Boston? Who was it?"

"I don't know. His name is Jack Atwood. That's all he said."

Gene didn't know anyone named Jack Atwood. "Was he selling something?"

"I don't think so. He sounded sort of businesslike."

"Well, I don't know. He might be some—"

"No. Call him. I promised him you would. I thought you might be on your way home or I would have had him call you at your office."

"Okay. I'll call him, and then I'm getting out of here." Emily gave him the number and Gene hung up and made the call. The phone rang a couple of times, and then a man with a raspy voice said, "This is Jack."

"Mr. Atwood?"

"Yes."

"This is Gene Thomas. I had a message that I should call you."

"Oh, yes. Thanks for calling back. Just a second." There was a pause and Gene waited skeptically. But out of habit he set a note pad in front of him and got out a pen. After a few seconds, Atwood said, "Say, listen, I'm an editor with *Atlantic Monthly*. I just read your article this afternoon. I like it very much and plan to run it."

"Oh." Gene hadn't thought of that. He had submitted his Vietnam article, but he hadn't thought that an editor would call him. He had expected a letter; in fact, he had expected a rejection letter.

"I can only pay you three hundred dollars. Can you live with that?"

"Oh, sure. That's . . . well, I hate to admit that that's more than I expected, but it is. I've never written anything before." Gene had written "*Atlantic Monthly*" on his notepad. Now he added "$300." He liked the look of it.

"That's interesting. You've got a nice writing style. You don't try to be clever or flowery; you're direct and straightforward. Still, your article hits very hard. We need things written from the point of view of Vietnam vets, but most of the articles we get are either reactionary stuff—way too defensive—or they're pure anti-war material, full of too much rhetoric. You've done a good job of balancing what you want to say and doing it in a voice that sounds reasonable."

"That's what I tried to do. I'm glad you think it came out that way."

"Listen, the reason I called you was not so much about the article. I was wondering what other things you might have written, or what your plans are. But you say this is the first thing you've written."

"Yeah, it is." Gene was thinking about Emily now—wanting to tell her all this. He had written "likes my style," "balanced," and then "wants more."

"Would you have any interest in doing some more articles for us—not every month but maybe two or three times a year?" Gene stopped writing. "I'd like to see you do some articles on other aspects of Vietnam. You could do more things about coming home and adjusting, the way you did this time, or you could write about the experience you had in Vietnam and how it's going to affect our veterans. You could interview other vets, or you could describe some of your own experiences—whatever you'd like. There are some pretty hot topics that are not going to go away for a while: Agent Orange, veterans' benefits, this post-traumatic stress disorder we're hearing about now. I'd have to approve your ideas, but that wouldn't be a big problem."

Gene could hardly believe what he was hearing. "That does sound sort of interesting," he finally managed to get out. "But I'm not sure I'm the right guy. I had some things I wanted to say, but I don't really know anything about journalism."

"Are you using your G.I. Bill to go to school now, or what are you doing?"

"I actually finished college before I went over to 'Nam, but I might be going back to school again. I just can't decide what to major in."

"Why not journalism? I think you ought to write a book. Most of the memoirs coming out are like I said before—too far on one side or the other. We need a really accurate, fair portrayal of the experience men had over there."

"I don't know, Mr. Atwood. I don't even like to talk about those things."

"Exactly. It's the guys who *don't* like to talk about it who ought to write the books—not the braggarts or the protesters. It might be a good thing for you to sort out how you feel about your experience and get those ideas down on paper—the way you did in this article. You don't have to think long-term on this. If you have another idea or two of things you would like to do, write me back and tell me what they are. We could pay a little better on future articles."

Gene was flattered, but he was still too stunned to know what to think about any of this.

"Anyway, what do you think about doing some more articles for me?"

"Well . . . I'm interested. I guess I've got to decide whether I think I can actually do it."

"Here's something to think about. Why don't you go back to school, major in journalism, and write some stories for your assignments? If you tell your professors you've got an article coming out in *Atlantic Monthly* and a deal to do some more, they'll be impressed. Meantime, you can be learning more about writing techniques. Just don't let them ruin what you're already doing."

"Wow. That's a lot to think about. I need a day or two to consider all this. Would it be all right if I call you after that?"

"Okay. And I'll send you a contract for the first American rights to the article you submitted. But maybe I should pay you less, since you didn't expect that much." He laughed in that rough voice of his.

"No, that's all right. I don't mind taking the three hundred."

"You'll still have the rights to this material. You can use the contents in your book, when you get around to writing it."

When Gene put down the phone, he leaned back and stared for a time. He looked at the electric clock on the wall, with the second hand, black and heavy, swinging in a slow circle, but the time didn't register in his mind. He finally looked down at the pad of paper, just to check what he had written. He wished he had kept jotting notes. Had the guy really said all that? Gene had done all right in his English classes in high school and college, but no one had ever encouraged him to be a writer. This was amazing. He had been looking for a direction to go, praying about it, and suddenly someone was standing there with a flag, waving him onto a new fork in the road—as though the Lord had placed him there. It was hard not to feel that he'd better go where this Atwood guy was pointing.

So Gene left the scattered papers on his desk and drove home. He wanted to talk to Emily. As he drove he tried to remember what the man had said, but it kept coming back to him in a jumble—which is more or less how it came out as he tried to tell it to Emily. She was in the kitchen, trying to get something started for dinner, and Danny was vying for Gene's attention at the same time, but the more he talked the more excited he felt, and the effect on Emily was dazzling. He hadn't seen her look so happy since he had returned from Vietnam.

She finally placed a Pyrex dish in the oven and walked to Gene. She sat down sideways on the kitchen chair next to his, put her hand on his arm, and asked, "Would you want to do that? Write a book about Vietnam?"

"I don't know, Emily. Until half an hour ago I would have said absolutely not—and the truth is, I don't think I could do it—but he kept telling me I could, and it was pretty exciting to think so."

"Gene, I *know* you could do it."

"Oh, come on. Why would you say that?"

"Have you ever tried to do anything you didn't do well? That's who you are, Gene. That's who you've always been. You go after something, and it's not long until you can do it better than anyone else. Look at what just happened: You write your first article and it gets published."

"Em, I can't believe you're saying that. I've done a terrible job of adjusting to my wounds. I've been a rotten husband ever since I got home. You know that."

"It's the one time in your life that you were held back, when you had to be patient and accept that you couldn't barrel on at full speed. It doesn't surprise me that you weren't good at sitting at home. You were trying to convince yourself to go into business, or go to law school, but you don't have any real passion for that. As soon as you tried something you wanted to do, you did it well. I look at your face right now, and I think, 'That's my Gene. That's how I remember him.'"

He was sitting at the table, grinning at her. He felt stupid, being quite so kid-like, but he couldn't help it. "Do you need me to make a salad or something?" he asked, mainly to change the subject.

"No. I'm heating up some of the casserole we ate last night. I've still got some Jell-O salad left over too. What I want you to do right now is sit right where you are and keep smiling. It's the best thing I've seen in a long time."

"But we need to think about all this. I don't know anything about journalism. I don't know what a newspaper reporter makes, or a columnist. It's never seemed like anything I would want to do."

"We'll look at all that," Emily said. She kissed him on the cheek and then stood up. "But when an opportunity opens up like this, it seems like it's meant to be."

"I know. That's exactly what I've been thinking."

Danny seemed to sense the change in Gene. He leaned against him and said, "Throw the ball with me, Daddy."

"Okay. Just a minute." He looked back at Emily. "What would you think if I enrolled at the U. for winter quarter? I could try some journalism classes. If I liked that, I could maybe even finish out another degree so I'd have a credential. That way, if I wanted to look for a job at a newspaper, or something like that, I might have a chance."

"I think that's a great idea, Gene. I can keep working for a while, and you could go back to part-time at the dealership. Plus, you could do some more articles, and bring in some income that way. After a quarter you'd probably have a better idea whether it's what you want to do."

"I could be a sports writer maybe, if nothing else."

"No. That's not you anymore. You have things you need to say, Gene. Before you went into the service, you sort of took life as it came. You talked about politics, but you didn't really know the issues that well. I think the day is coming when you're going to be thankful for everything you've been through these last few years. You're a man with a lot more depth than you used to have. Once the anger passes away, you'll still have that."

Gene wondered. Would he ever really be thankful for all the bad days he had suffered? Emily had suggested that idea before, but he had found the thought ridiculous until now. He still wasn't sure he believed it, but it did seem a possibility.

Gene went out to the backyard and threw a ball with Danny, who was already showing signs that he was going to be a good athlete himself. Gene had noticed it before but saw it more clearly today. The kid could wind up and really toss a ball. It sometimes went in directions he hadn't intended, but he had an arm on him. And he didn't mind mixing it up either. He loved to have Gene play football with him and wrestle him to the ground. But Gene had some reservations about sports being as central in Danny's life as they had been in his own.

It was cold outside today, even though December had been quite warm so far, so Gene and Danny didn't stay out too long. They came back in and ate Emily's warmed-over dinner, which actually tasted better the second time around—or maybe it was life itself that was suddenly tasting a little better—and they talked more about journalism, about writing a book, about all the possibilities. Gene was picking up his plate to take it to the sink when Emily said, "Are we still going over to see your grandpa tonight?"

Gene had forgotten about that. Grandpa Thomas had been at LDS Hospital for a few days and was supposed to come home today. His heart had been acting up, going out of rhythm, and Grandma had had quite a scare when he had collapsed at home. Gene had wanted to visit Grandpa in the hospital, but he couldn't get himself to go. He just hated the smell of those places—and the memories. But he had promised his parents, who had called from Washington, that he would go see Grandpa tonight, now that he had recovered enough to go back home. Alex had thought about flying out immediately, but he and Anna were coming home in a couple more days for the Congressional Christmas break, and Grandma had reassured Alex that Grandpa was going to survive his little crisis.

Gene was actually not sure he wanted to see Grandpa. He was feeling happy tonight, and so often, since returning from Vietnam, his experiences with Grandpa Thomas had been difficult. He decided that he would talk with Grandpa about family matters, but he wouldn't bring up this whole journalism idea. It was just like Grandpa to have some reason he didn't think it was a good idea, and Gene didn't want that tonight.

So they cleaned up the dishes and then drove over to Grandma and Grandpa Thomas's house, but on the way, Gene told Emily, "Let's not stay very long. He probably needs his rest, and I'd like to have some time at home tonight—just to talk a little more."

"And maybe make out a little," she teased.

"Maybe a lot."

But some of the wind went out of Gene's sails when he saw Grandpa. He didn't look good. He was pale, and his face was puffy. Over the years, his hair had stayed dark, but lately Gene had been seeing more and more gray come into it. "How are you feeling, Grandpa?" Gene asked. He stepped close and patted him on the shoulder.

"I'm fine. And I wish everyone would stop fussing so much. I'm not dead yet, and I don't have any plans to be." Grandpa was sitting up in his chair downstairs, with a blanket wrapped around him. He was holding a newspaper on his lap, as usual.

Emily bent and kissed Grandpa on the cheek, and he let her do it, but he showed no response. Emily and Gene sat down on the couch, and Emily pulled Danny onto her lap. Danny was a little wary of old Grandpa Thomas with the booming voice and the gruff manner.

"He's too mean to die," Grandma said. "The Lord doesn't want him until he straightens out his attitude." She sat down in her chair, not far from Grandpa's. It was where she often sat in the evenings to do needle-work or read.

Grandpa smiled a little, but he said, "She says I'm an old grouch, and I think maybe she's right. But she hasn't been up there in that hospital, letting people stick needles into her all day long."

"I'd be nicer than you about it."

"I don't doubt that. But you're the nicest woman who ever lived, and *no one* ever accused me of anything like that. I don't have a reputation to keep up."

Gene and Emily laughed, but Gene thought Grandpa wasn't far wrong. Grandma Bea never seemed to change. She didn't have bad moods. She could be feisty—and even shockingly honest sometimes—but that always came off as another aspect of her love. What Gene did know was that Grandpa loved him too, even if he wasn't very charming about the way he expressed himself. Grandpa certainly deserved his reputation for being a grouch, especially in recent years, and yet he hovered over the family like an old guard dog, barking away all the bad guys who tried to intrude.

"Come here, Danny," Grandpa said. "I want to talk to you."

Danny hesitated, so Emily set him down, even pushed him a little. Danny stepped a little closer, but he kept some distance. "I'll race you to the kitchen and back. The winner gets a nickel."

Danny seemed confused. He didn't move.

"Okay?"

Danny nodded.

"Are you ready?"

He nodded again.

"Get on your mark, get set, go!"

But Danny still didn't move. "Run to the kitchen and back," Emily said.

Danny looked around at her.

"Run to that door and back."

So Danny ran at half speed, touched the door, and then walked back. "Okay, you beat me," Grandpa said. "But I'll beat you next time. Do you want your money?"

Danny looked back at his mom again, obviously unsure what he was supposed to say.

Grandpa was fishing in his pants pocket. "You can't buy anything with a nickel anymore," Grandma told him. "Give him a quarter."

"Not on your life. He didn't beat me far enough for that."

Gene laughed at that. This was all Grandpa, through and through, the stuff he had been doing with Gene his whole life. And for the first time in a long time, it felt good.

"Guess what, Grandpa?" Emily said.

He had found a dime in his pocket by then, and he held it out to Danny. "That's for this time and for the next time you beat me. But one of these days I'm going to beat you."

Danny took the dime and looked at it, and then he stepped back and handed it to his mother. By then Grandpa was looking at Emily.

"Gene wrote about his experience coming home from Vietnam, and he sent it to *Atlantic Monthly* magazine. He found out today that it's going to be published. He's getting paid three hundred dollars for it."

Gene hadn't thought to warn Emily not to say anything about that. He found himself catching his breath, afraid of what Grandpa might say.

"Is that right? Well, that's great. What did you have to say in the article, Gene?"

Gene leaned forward and grasped his knees. The house was way too hot, as always, and Gene was feeling it. "I just tried to explain to people what a lot of vets are going through. I didn't attack anyone for doing the wrong thing, but I tried to help people understand what it's like for a soldier to come home."

"Well, maybe you should have set them straight a little more than that. There are way too many people these days who aren't giving soldiers the respect they deserve. They go off to preserve our freedom and get spit on by a bunch of traitors who should have been over there themselves."

"Well . . . I don't know. It's been a different kind of war. We've talked a lot about that before, Grandpa. I just think most men coming home feel like they did their best in a strange situation, and they don't deserve to be called 'baby killers.'"

"Of course they don't." Grandpa had something more to say, but he had started to cough, and he couldn't stop himself for quite some time.

"Al, don't get yourself all excited. You know what the doctor said. You've got to take it easy for a while."

"What am I doing? I'm just sitting here. I can't take it any easier than that."

"Well, don't get all worked up."

"Worked up," Grandpa mumbled. "Who's worked up?" But he began to cough again.

"Gene's thinking about going back to the U. to take some classes in journalism," Emily said. "The editor who called him wants him to do some more articles, and he suggested that maybe Gene could write a book."

"Book about what?"

"Vietnam—you know, a personal account of what he experienced over there."

"We've got enough of these peaceniks writing that stuff. I hope it wouldn't be something like that."

Gene glanced at Emily and gave his head a little shake. He didn't want to get into all this with Grandpa.

"Gene, that sounds wonderful," Grandma said. "Do you think that's what you want to do—go into journalism?"

"I'm not sure. But it's something to think about. I've never considered anything like that until today, but the editor I talked to seemed to think I would do all right at it."

"Of course you would," Grandpa said. "You'll do very well at anything you take up. But it's no way to get rich, I can tell you that. You'd be better off to take over our parts plant, the way I've told you before. We need someone who can get that place going again—either that or we're going to have to sell it off."

"But it's not what he's interested in, Al," Grandma said. "I think he could be a wonderful writer. And some of these books that come out make a lot of money."

"It *can* be a way to make a name for yourself," Grandpa said. "Jack Kennedy claimed he wrote a book—although people in the know said he had a ghostwriter do it for him—but he used that to launch him into politics. You've got the same thing going for you, Gene. You're a decorated war hero, like Kennedy was, and if you wrote the right kind of book, who knows what that might do for you? I've always told you, you need to run for office."

Gene took a long, even breath. It was the same old tune, and Grandpa ought to know that it was. The last big argument the two had gotten into had started with almost the same words. But Gene said, "My dad's not as rich as Kennedy's was." He laughed—or tried to. "I'd have to start a little smaller."

"Well, you've got a point there. Old Joe Kennedy did buy that presidency for his boy. But there have been plenty who didn't start out that way."

Gene knew it was time to change the subject. "So Grandpa, what's the doctor telling you? Is your heart going to be all right now?"

"He says I'm going to die. But I didn't have to pay him to tell me that. We all die sooner or later. I'm just going to last a little longer than he thinks."

Gene laughed, and he looked over at Grandma. "What *did* the doctor say?"

"His heart isn't good, Gene. We all know that. But if he'll take his medicine and watch what he tries to do, he'll be all right for a while yet."

"Would you write for a newspaper or what?" Grandpa asked, ignoring everything that had just been said.

"I don't know, Grandpa. That's one of the things I'd probably consider doing."

"I hope you wouldn't be one of these muckrakers. Some of these guys who have it in for the president are trying to find anything they can to make him look bad. It's lucky the Democrats put a man as stupid as McGovern up against Richard Nixon. No one could have lost to that guy. But these liberal newspaper people are nipping at Nixon's heels like a pack of stray dogs. They don't seem to have anything better to do."

Gene wanted to let that one go by, but he couldn't get himself to do it. "I don't know, Grandpa. I've been reading more and more about this break-in at the Watergate building. Those burglars had their pockets full of hundred-dollar bills, and that money's been traced back to the Committee to Re-Elect the President."

"Where did you hear that?"

"The *Washington Post* has been running articles about it all—"

"That ought to tell you something right there, Gene. That's a liberal paper if there ever was one. Katharine Graham, who owns the paper, hates Nixon and will do anything to make him look bad. Her reporters smear the man, and the Republican Party, every time they get a chance."

"That might be true, Grandpa. I don't know. But I don't know why a bunch of guys would break into the Democratic Headquarters just for the fun of it. And when evidence comes out that these guys were getting money from the Republican Party, *someone* had better keep looking into the matter. If Nixon has nothing to hide, he ought to cooperate, but he's fighting the investigation every way he can."

"But the presidency itself has to be protected or our whole system will fall apart."

"No one wants to ruin the presidency, Grandpa. But there have to be limits to what the president can get away with."

"Oh, come on, Gene. Think about it. How stupid do you think Nixon is? He had that election won from the day McGovern was nominated. Why would he—or anyone in the party—need to break into the Democrats' offices? That doesn't even make sense."

Grandpa had started to cough again, and Grandma was telling him to calm down. But Gene had to say one thing. "Grandpa, if I do become a reporter, I'm going to look at things objectively. I'm not going to start with the assumption that every Democrat is a bad guy and every Republican is pure as snow." He stopped himself, but then he couldn't resist, and the rest spilled out. "You say those writers have their minds made up, but so do you. And I think this time you're going to have to eat some humble pie. Something is just not right about this whole thing. You wait and see what's going to come out in the next few months."

Grandpa was staring at Gene, his face whiter than before, and Emily was saying, "Gene, it's okay. We don't need to talk about this right now."

Gene was taking quick little breaths, trying to calm himself. He had said enough. But he had kept his voice calm, no matter how much anger he was feeling. The strange thing was, it suddenly occurred to him, he was going to be a journalist. He had just made up his mind about that.

"I love you, Grandpa," Gene said. "You've taught me to think about things."

Grandpa was still staring at him. "Maybe so," he said. "But not one of you kids agrees with me on much of anything."

Grandma chuckled. "Gene didn't say you taught him *what* to think. He said you taught him *to think*."

Slowly Grandpa Thomas smiled, but only a little. "I should have worked harder on that first part," he said.

"Grandpa, if I write some things, I'll try to be fair. I promise you that. And I'll come over and get your opinion."

Grandpa nodded. "I wish you would," he said. "And your dad's opinion, too. He's back there where he hears things others might not know."

"All right. But I'm going to do my own thinking."

"No doubt," Grandpa said. "No doubt." And his smile got a little bigger.

CHAPTER 14

Diane dressed up a little more than usual for her date with Greg. He had told her he was taking her to the Paprika, the restaurant where he had proposed to her five years before. It was February now, 1973, and during the holidays and since, Greg had been asking Diane out more often. Clearly, he was trying to rebuild their relationship at a faster pace. He was still not pushing too hard, but he liked to talk about the day when he and Diane and Jenny could be a family again. Diane was sometimes caught up in the prettiness of that image: the three of them together as she had once assumed they always would be. She was certainly realizing how unlikely she was to find someone else who could give her and Jenny all that Greg could. Maybe—though she didn't like to admit it to herself—that's why she was taking so much time with her makeup and hair tonight. But she also kept reminding herself that she had once let Greg overwhelm her with the force of his personality, and she didn't want to make another decision she would come to regret.

Diane felt at times that maybe she could—and even should—forgive Greg for the way he had treated her while they were married. After all, he was now fighting against his darker impulses. As she began to feel better about him, however, images and memories would flash back to her: the day he had finally slugged her with his fist, and the months before that, when he had made her feel so worthless. When he told her how nice she looked, how interesting she was to talk to, how much he liked being with her, she couldn't help remembering the insults he had thrown at her during that last dreary year in Seattle.

Diane had continued to see Lloyd. He came by her house with Marc, the bishop's son, once a month, but he stopped over more often by himself. He shoveled her walks some mornings even though the apartment manager was supposed to do that, and he had put some badly needed weather stripping around her front door. More often, though, he simply played with Jenny for a while and talked with Diane. He never really hinted that he expected anything more than friendship, but Diane saw the way he looked at her, and she knew that he was feeling more than he expressed. Lloyd knew, of course, that Diane was seeing Greg, and maybe Lloyd was trying to win her over with kindness rather than trying to compete directly, but he was, at best, a helpful friend and, at worst, an annoyance. He usually dropped by without calling first, without seeming to take into account how busy Diane's life was. She sometimes had to tell him that she needed to study and just couldn't spend time with him. That's when he would stay and play with Jenny, which was actually helpful, but irritating, too. If he thought that Diane would learn to love him because Jenny did, he was wrong, and it seemed a strangely manipulative approach.

When Greg arrived, he was dressed in a handsome suit, dark with pinstripes. He not only looked sharp and smelled good, but he seemed especially happy and confident. When she walked outside with him, she saw why. Greg had told her about a car he had bought, but this was the first time she had seen it. It was a pale yellow 1959 Jaguar MK 9. He had bought it a few months back and since then had been getting it overhauled, painted, and repaired. It really was an exquisite car. He walked Diane around it so she could get a good look, and then he opened the door for her. "Just look at the inside," he said. "It's even nicer than the outside."

It *was* impressive, with leather seats and polished walnut paneling on the dash. "It's nice. Really nice," Diane said as she got in. But she didn't want to sound overly pleased. It was hard not to guess what Greg was thinking: *Just think, Diane, this too could be yours.* But Diane's thought was that he had gone into a lot of debt. He wasn't making *that* much money yet. She had learned too much about economy in the past couple of years—forced by Greg's stinginess, especially at first—not to see the irony in his showing off this way. Life with Greg, no doubt, would always be about the *things* he could acquire.

Greg must have sensed from Diane's unwillingness to gush that she was thinking such things. Once he got into the car, he said nothing more about it. On the way to Salt Lake he talked about a new idea he said he'd been thinking about. "Here's what I have in mind," he said. He liked to sit well away from the steering wheel, with his seat leaning back more than seemed safe, as though he were resting in a lounge chair instead of driving a car. "I don't think I want to stay with my dad's firm all that much longer. I feel like the errand boy around there sometimes. And I don't like a lot of the cases I get involved in. I'm not sure it's good for a man to spend his whole life *arguing* and *contending* with people—and that's what most lawyers do."

"What would you rather do?" Diane asked.

He ignored the question and continued with his train of thought. "Even if I'm not the one to litigate the case, I'm always writing the arguments and figuring out some way to defend a guy who's gotten himself into some sort of mess. What drives me crazy is that no one wants to write a contract and then just hold to it. Someone's always coming to us and saying, 'Isn't there some way I can get out of this?' And we rarely say, 'No. Just do the right thing.' We usually try to find some loophole in his contract."

"But what would you do instead?" Diane asked again. She had never heard him express any concern about arguing. In fact, it had always seemed what he loved to do.

"If there's one thing I love to do it's manage money. I've done some investing this last year, and things have gone well. I have this friend—a guy I knew in high school named Roger Erskine. I think you might have met him." He glanced at her and Diane shrugged. She didn't know the name. "He's become a broker, and he's helped me with some investments, but half the time I've been the one to choose where I wanted to put my money. Roger is getting really busy, and he talked to me the other day about going partners with him. He says he needs someone with a legal background—for contracts and all that sort of thing, but especially for tax planning. That's getting to be a big field now. You not only help people invest, but you plan out their retirement for them, and you manage their whole estate."

"Can you do as well at that as you would practicing law?"

"I think *I* would. And I'd do it two ways. I'd not only help other people get rich by managing their money—which I, of course, would get a cut of—but I'd be right on top of managing my own wealth. Guys who get rich don't get that way by working. They make sure their money works *for* them instead of *against* them. Most people make money, spend it all, go into a lot of debt besides, and end up at the end of a career with nothing to show for forty years of labor. I like to spend money—you know that—but I'm smart enough to set something aside every month, and I'm already building up something of a portfolio that way."

Diane wondered. She had seen signs that he was spending *plenty*.

"This car is a good example," Greg said. "I like it, and I'm going to keep it for a while, but I bought it because it's an appreciating property—and most cars aren't. The money I've put into it will double the value. I'll have the fun of driving it for a while, and then I'll make a profit when I sell it."

It was all rather difficult for Diane to imagine. She survived each month on what she got from Greg and from her little job at the Union Building, but the end of every month was a worry, and she sometimes had to borrow a few dollars from her parents. She had loved expensive clothes at one time, but she never shopped at the nice Ogden stores now. It actually embarrassed her to be seen in J.C. Penney or Sears, but she had no choice. That's where she bought Jenny's things, but it was also where she now bought her own. And she got by without most of the things she really wanted. She had seen a dress in the window at Castleton's recently. She knew it would look great on her, but she didn't even walk in to ask what it cost. She knew better.

Diane also knew that if she had said something to Greg about the dress, he would have bought it for her. He had started bringing her nice things. In fact, the black dress she had on tonight was one he had bought her for Christmas—along with a beautiful string of pearls. He had bought expensive little outfits for Jenny, too, and they were things he had picked out himself. He loved to shop, especially for Jenny, and Diane certainly didn't resist his doing that for her, but he never offered to increase her monthly check.

A little flurry of snow was falling as Greg passed the mouth of Weber Canyon and ascended onto the mountain road toward Farmington. Diane thought Greg was driving faster than he should, but she decided not to say anything. That was something that always annoyed him when they had been married—her "nagging" him, as he always called it, about his driving. "So are you thinking you might leave your father's office quite soon?" Diane asked.

"I don't know. I'd like to. But my dad is going to hit the ceiling. He wants me to take over his office a little more all the time so he can cut back on working so many hours. Or at least that's what he says. The truth is, if he spent more time at home he'd go crazy, and so would Mom. They hardly bother with each other anymore."

"Really? Is it that bad?"

"Diane, it's exactly what I want to avoid. It's one of the reasons I want to change my own pattern of behavior. I'm too much like my dad, and I don't want to fall into the same trap. You know how I was in law school—always putting in the extra hours so I could ace the tests. I'd never lived in a home where the father was around the house. You kept wanting that, but it just wasn't something I'd ever learned from my dad."

"But couldn't it be the same in this new business?"

"I don't think so. Roger puts in pretty much an eight-hour day, and then he goes home to his family." He glanced at Diane and smiled. "You get your money working for you, and you let *it* put in the overtime."

"But there's always that temptation to do just a little more, take on a few more clients and all that."

"Sure. And during tax time in the spring, guys who do taxes can really get snowed under. But I know one guy who takes time off right after April fifteenth every year. Last year he took his wife on a trip to Europe, and the year before that to Bermuda."

What a thought. Diane had always dreamed of seeing beautiful places: Europe; Australia; the Holy Land. When she and Greg had been married, it was something they had talked about: the day when he was doing well enough for them to travel to places like that. Sometimes now she thought of being a teacher and single mom and how many of those kinds of opportunities would always be closed to her. Maybe later in life she could travel some; she knew retired teachers who did that. But "later in life" seemed a poor compensation for what she might have been able to do with Greg.

"Here's the thing," Greg said. "I'm trying to rethink what I want my life to be. And I know I have to get some of my excesses under control. I can be exactly like my dad and work sixty or seventy hours a week all my life, or I can take some steps now. I think I'd like to be in a different kind of business and make a fresh start that way."

Diane did like the sound of this. She knew she tended to be skeptical when Greg talked about changing, but she was impressed by the way he was thinking.

"Diane, I know you don't want me to give you a sales job, but just let me describe the future the way I imagine it." He glanced at her as if to get her permission, and she nodded. "My problem right now is that it doesn't matter whether I go home at the end of the day or not. I just go back to an empty apartment and a television set—so a lot of times I just stick around at work the way Dad and the other guys in our office do. What I need is a *home*." He turned and took another look at Diane. "I need my *family*. I need a reason to live. I play with money now, and it's fun for me, but I'm not saving for anything particular. Just think if I were saving so I could retire early and take my wife all over the world." He hesitated, this time looking straight ahead. "You don't have to say anything in response to what I'm about to say, but I want you to know how I feel. What I need more than anything in this world is some indication that I have a reason to hope for a better life than I have right now—just the hope that you and I and Jenny will all be together."

Diane trusted what he had said—that she needn't respond—but she did feel sorry for him. His life did sound empty, and there wasn't much doubt in her mind that he was trying hard to be a better man. So she touched his hand, only to say, "I'm sorry this is so hard," or something of that sort, but she sensed his reaction. He nodded to her, and his eyes filled with tears, as though he was interpreting her touch as a much stronger signal than she had intended.

Or at least that's what she told herself. But she might have been flirting. She might have been thinking of the travel, the house, the good years that would be hers if she wanted them. She had to admit that it was not easy to think of herself showing affection to Greg again, trying to satisfy him in the way she never had been able to, but she did feel a warmth for him that had never entirely disappeared. She remembered what it had meant to her to move with Greg to Seattle, excited to start a new life, and she thought of the day they had brought their baby home together, both of them aware that they had found a new level of meaning in their lives. The idea of retrieving the future they had once planned really was appealing—as though the past couple of years had been the aberration and "normal life" could return after all. But it was hard to trust dreams, the way she once had. It was the thought of picking up a day-to-day life with Greg that made her nervous. She told herself to be careful; she had to keep her head tonight.

But Greg had a great knack for doing things right. He had somehow arranged to have the same table at the restaurant where they had sat on the night he had proposed. When they sat down in the muted, golden ambiance of the Paprika, Greg said, "Would you like to have the lobster with me this time, or the trout almandine?"

Diane understood the question—and she was amazed that he remembered such details. Diane had asserted just a little independence that night, not letting him order for her. But either answer she might give had implications, and so she tried to be certain he wasn't reading too much into that hand touch earlier. She didn't want the meal to end with a little cake being delivered to her table; that's how he had proposed last time. "I think I'd like to look at the menu," she said.

Greg smiled as if to say, "That's okay. I can still be patient." Diane liked that. But then Greg said, "Just a sec. I hate to do this, but there's someone here I *have to* say hello to—a client."

He got up and walked to another table. Diane saw a beautifully dressed couple, much older than Greg. She couldn't hear what was said, but she watched Greg laugh and talk with them. There was something so adept about the way he fit in everywhere in Salt Lake, and yet something so stylized and calculated in his manner. She thought of the night at the singles dance, how awkward all those men had been. This was probably better. At the same time, she wondered when Greg was ever genuine, whether he even knew what it was to be himself. She had been bothered a good deal lately by Lloyd's attempt to reach her through his kindness. But he *was* kind. She never doubted that.

Greg came back after a few minutes and said, "They wanted to know who the beautiful woman was. I told them you were a Hungarian princess."

Diane recognized the reference to My *Fair Lady*, and she smiled. "We girls from Ogden, once we get cleaned up and learn proper English, can almost manage in Salt Lake society."

"You can pass for a princess anywhere, little flower girl."

But Diane didn't like that. Greg had told her too often how ugly she was—back in those darkest days of their marriage—and such praise only reminded her of that. She sipped at her water glass and looked around at the paintings that covered the walls.

Maybe Greg knew what she was thinking. After he and Diane had ordered, he said, "You know, Diane, there's something else I've been thinking about. I've always put my religious life in one part of my mind and my career goals in another. But if a person can't bring the two together, life really is pointless. I've always had this drive for achievement and, at the same time, religious ideals that actually contrast in a lot of ways. It's strange how it's never been clear to me until now that the two actually work at cross purposes."

"So what do you plan to do about that?"

Again, he didn't answer. He merely stayed with his own thoughts. "What's the point of making money if it only makes you prideful and materialistic? In the long run, you pay for what you get. You sell your soul."

"But you were telling me in the car that you like to make money."

"I like to invest. I like to *manage* money. But I'm seeing the purpose more clearly now. I want to provide for my family, first, and then do some good in this world. If I could retire early, my wife and I could not only travel for pleasure, we could serve a mission. I'd love to be a mission president, and you would make such a wonderful . . . or . . . I'm sorry."

"What?"

"I didn't mean to put you in the picture. It's just the way I tend to think."

"But do you think you would like to be a mission president?"

"Sure. And who serves in that role? People who can afford to go. But there are a lot of other good things you can do if you have the money and the time. If a guy could get himself set up early enough, he could spend the rest of his life doing good."

Diane never knew what to think of Greg when he talked this way. He was clearly trying to rebuild all those idealistic dreams they had once had, even adding elements he knew would appeal to her now. He was painfully transparent no matter how sincere he could sound. And yet, it was flattering that he would work so hard to get her back into his life. Diane touched her hand to her neck, felt the smoothness of the pearls Greg had given her. "I think most people who make a lot of money tell themselves that's what they'll do—you know, do a lot of good with it—but they get so wrapped up in making the money, they don't want to quit, and they spend more than they have, no matter how much they make."

"I know. My dad's the classic example of that. But that's why I'm thinking I want to go another way. I just want you to know how I'm thinking about life these days."

The waiter had arrived with salads. Greg thanked the man and joked with him, and then, as though he sensed it was time to back off again, he asked Diane about Jenny. He told a story about his secretary asking him where the best places were to shop for kids. He ended by saying, "She told me, 'I figured you're the one who would know.'"

Maybe this was calculated to remind Diane of what a good daddy he was, but at least he had stopped making his case. She appreciated that.

As they ate, Greg asked Diane about school and about her family, and Diane asked him what he thought of the recent Roe v. Wade decision that had legalized abortion. Greg got a little worked up about that, but he remembered to ask Diane what she thought, and then—as though he wanted Diane to see how fair-minded he was—he offered a little criticism of President Nixon for not being more forthcoming about Watergate.

When they were waiting for their desserts—a dish of chocolate mousse that Diane promised to eat a little of—Greg said, "Diane, I know, being here, we've both been remembering the night I proposed to you. And you know very well that's exactly why I brought you here. But you'll notice, I didn't order a cake and place a ring box in it. I'm still trying to be patient about that. But I hope you can see that everything I do now, everything I think about, is part of my way of preparing for a day when the three of us can be a family again. I think I've proved a lot over the past year and a half. I hope you think so too."

"I do appreciate your patience, Greg. I hope you understand how difficult this whole situation is for me."

"Diane, I hurt you. I hurt you emotionally, and I hurt you physically. Wounds like that take time to heal. I'm not out to win you over with a nice dinner. I'm on a long campaign to prove to you that I want you forever, and I'm going to do everything I can to make myself worthy of having you." He hesitated and looked into her eyes. "But you never say anything. You never give me any idea what you're thinking. I'd just like to know where I stand at this point."

"Greg, I feel a lot better about you now than I did when I filed for divorce. You've worked hard to be a good father to Jenny, and you've treated me extremely well. I hated you at one time, and I don't hate you now. I enjoy these times together."

"But?"

Diane hardly knew what to say. She didn't want to hurt him, didn't want to ruin the evening, but she felt she had to be honest with him. "When we were in college, and you wanted to marry me, you made it a campaign then, too. And I trusted you. I accepted what you told me. I wrote that letter to Kent when I still liked him a lot. There are times when I can't get it out of my mind that I'm heading right back in the same direction, letting you win me over—and then I wonder if the same things might start happening again."

"Don't you think I've changed?"

"It seems so. But it scares me to say that. I made up my mind at one time that I'd made a terrible mistake to marry you and I had to get Jenny away from you. It's very hard for me to face the idea that I could put all of us through the same mess again."

He nodded. "I know. I understand that. And that's why I've given you such a long time to see how different I am now." His voice sounded soft, controlled, but she thought she heard a bit of effort to hold onto that control. "But how long do I have to prove myself? When can we at least start considering the possibility of marrying again?"

"I am considering it, Greg. I think about it every day of my life."

"That's good to hear." But she saw something more stoical, maybe sad, in his face. He had worked hard to create an atmosphere tonight, and Diane had probably popped his bubble with the things she had just said.

"Are you praying about it?"

"I am, Greg, but I'm not feeling what I'd call an assurance. I just get more confused, the more I think about it."

Greg sat for a time. He took a drink from his water glass. But he didn't touch the dessert. He pushed it toward Diane. She took a couple of little dips into it with her spoon in an attempt to ease the tension, but Greg was staring at her without seeing her, obviously lost in his own thoughts.

"Do you wish you'd married Kent?" he finally asked. "Is that what you were saying before?"

"No. I don't think about Kent anymore. He's happily married."

"But you must have wished a lot of times that you had married him instead of me. You must have thought plenty about that, up in Seattle."

It was true, of course, but she also felt what he was doing—finding a way to accuse, maybe even taking the first step toward starting an argument. So she didn't answer, and she saw his stare become focused, his thoughts seeming directed toward her now—not on himself. "I can't do this forever," he finally said. "It's making me crazy. I love you and Jenny, but I can't stand living by myself, wondering whether I have any hope at all to have you back."

"I know. I need to give you an answer. But I'm not ready to say yes, and you keep telling me not to tell you no."

Greg waited for a time again, but now Diane could see a clear change. He was losing interest in "managing" the situation. She could see his jaw setting, his eyes taking on a sternness she remembered, even some color rising in his cheeks. "What would it take, finally, to convince you? What do I have to do?"

"It's not that, Greg. I'm not trying to make you jump through hoops. But I need to be in love with you again." She watched him take a hard breath. She was afraid what might happen next. "Greg, please, think about it from my point of view. You tell me that you love me, but every time I think about us being together, I remember how dissatisfied you were with me before. I don't know if I can show you the kind of intimacy you want from me. Maybe there's something wrong with me that I wasn't . . . the way you wanted me to be . . . but I don't know whether I can do any better—especially if I still have all those memories in my head."

Greg looked across the room, sat quietly again for a long time, and then he spotted the waiter and said, "Could we get our check?" When he looked back at Diane, he said, "I see no end to this. I crossed the line. I hit you—more than once. You gave up on me, and you aren't going to forgive me. So I might as well quit thinking that you ever can."

The words were bad enough—the accusation and the self-pity—but the tone was frightening. He was letting go a little more all the time, not trying to hide his anger. Diane knew she would be better off not to say anything, but she tried again. "I don't know if that's true, Greg. I think I have forgiven you. But that's not quite the same as saying I love you. I don't want to get married again just because Jenny and I would be better off financially. I want to feel the kind of love I had for you when we got married."

"Okay, fine. I'll keep groveling for a few more years and wait to see whether you can *love me* enough. Never mind that I'm trying to hold onto a temple marriage, and you don't seem to care about that." Diane could live with the sarcasm, but she knew Greg's pattern: the outrage would come next, and then the violence. Diane felt a fear of him she hadn't known for a long time.

Diane saw the muscles in Greg's arms swell, and she knew he was gripping his hands together. She knew he was fighting himself. He paid the bill, although his style had changed toward the waiter, and he got up, took Diane's arm, and guided her from the restaurant. The next couple of minutes would be crucial, and Diane didn't want to set off an explosion. She hated this feeling, and her first thought was that she just wanted to get home and get away from him forever, but that thought set off another fear. If he broke now, he might or might not hurt her, but he would do and say things that would end the dream forever, and all evening Diane had been feeling twinges of hope. She *had* married him in the temple, and she did like to think there was some possibility, however remote it seemed right now, that they could go back to the beginning and start again. At the very least, she didn't want things to be ugly between them. She wanted Jenny to have a good dad who cared about her.

She tried to understand all her complex feelings as Greg drove down 21st South and onto the freeway. He wasn't saying a word, and she could see a door closing that she hadn't wanted to close, so she turned and touched Greg's shoulder. "Greg, I'm sorry. I didn't mean to ruin the evening. Everything you did was so nice. I'm not saying that I *can't* love you again; I was just saying that it's been difficult for me. But I've felt so positive toward you tonight, and that seemed the beginning of feelings I really do want to have for you."

"You're really enjoying this, aren't you?" he said, without so much as glancing toward her. "I'm the bad guy, and I'm the one who has to prove myself. You can dangle that little carrot in front of my nose—that you just might love me again someday—and lead me around forever. That way you can get what you want from me and avoid what you *don't want*. And we both know what that is."

"Greg, come on. That's not what I'm trying to do."

"Do you think I don't date anyone else?"

"I don't know. I have no idea."

"Well, I do. And there's a very pretty lady in Salt Lake who is just waiting for me to pop the question. The Lord keeps telling me I ought to salvage my temple marriage, and that's what I've been trying to do, but let's see, that's one of the things I'm not allowed to mention: that I pray and then try to follow God's promptings. If I tell you that, I'm trying to manipulate you."

"That's twisting what I've said, Greg. You know it is."

"Well, I'll tell you this much. God *has* forgiven me; you're the one who won't. So I think it's time I move on with my life. I want a family, and I want more children. I'm tired of this life you're making me lead."

"Greg, would you really want to marry me before I'm ready to be close to you again?"

"*Close?* You don't know anything about closeness, my old friend. You're made of ice. I'm dating a woman right now who can hardly keep her hands off me. It's all she can do to wait until we're married. I keep telling myself it would be better for Jenny to be with the two of us—and not alone with a mother who has no feelings—but I guess not. You've tested my patience, all right, but you played it wrong, little girl. You just lost your free ride."

Diane leaned back in her seat and laughed. "Whew!" she said. "What a wonderful feeling this is. This is the Greg I remember. You had me halfway there tonight. I'm just glad I didn't let you sell me a bill of goods."

"You think you just won, Diane, but you haven't seen anything yet. I know people who know you, and they say you've had your little home teacher friend around the house a lot lately. I'll make a case that you're sleeping around and leaving your daughter, and I'll get her away from you. She loves me more than she does you already. She'd be glad to come with me."

Diane shook her head back and forth, amazed. But she wasn't scared now, and she liked that feeling. "That's a nice plan, Greg. If I were you though, I wouldn't look too deeply into my lifestyle—because you won't find what you're looking for—and I wouldn't let Jenny see what you're really like. If you plan to beat up on your new wife once in a while, be sure to do it when Jenny isn't watching. It might bring back a few memories for her."

Suddenly Greg hit his brakes, and Diane flew forward. She caught herself with her hands as best she could, but her forehead struck the windshield. For a moment she was dazed, and she wasn't sure how badly she was hurt, but Greg had only hit the brakes hard for a moment and then had swerved to the side of the freeway. "Get out and walk home," he said.

She was holding her head, trying to think, but she thought getting out might be the smart thing to do. She could hitchhike and be in less danger. She reached for the door handle, but suddenly he popped the clutch, and the Jaguar screeched forward. He blasted ahead, shifted, then hit the gas hard again. "That's a better idea, Greg," Diane said. "Take me home and then get out of the car and knock me around for a while. That's exactly how I want to remember you."

"Shut up!" he shouted. "I've done so well for so long, but you know how to get to me better than anyone in this world."

"Yup. It always was my fault—in your mind—and always will be. I'm the one who *makes* you hit me."

He kept driving and didn't say another word all the way back to Ogden. She could feel the rigidity leave him gradually, watched him slump more and more, and she knew the rest of the pattern was completing itself. Now would come the regret. When he finally pulled up in front of her house, he said, in a voice hardly loud enough to hear, "It's my fault, not yours. You know that. But maybe my only hope is to start over with someone else."

"Okay." Diane opened the door, but then she looked over and said, "Good luck, Greg. I hope things do work better with someone else."

"I'll try to be a good father."

"I know you will, Greg," Diane said, and then she added, "I'm sorry for how all of this turned out."

"I do love you, Diane. That's the part that makes me so furious with myself."

"I don't know, Greg. I'm not sure what the word means to you. You can't say those things you said to me back on the freeway and then just take them back. It doesn't work that way."

"I know."

"I *did* love you, Greg. And I love the daughter you gave me. I hope we can always be civil to each other."

"Sure." And then as she got out of the car, he added, "Diane, I *am* sorry. I hope things turn out okay for you."

"Thanks. I hope the same for you," Diane said, but by then she was crying. She walked to her apartment, found her key, and opened the door—and then walked into the darkness. She sat down on her couch and cried as long as she could. She wanted this one cry, and then she knew she had to move ahead. But it was hard to cry enough. Her life seemed a tragedy all over again. But she eventually walked to her bathroom, washed her face, and took a look at her forehead. She decided there wasn't much of a bruise, so maybe her mother wouldn't notice, so she waited for her eyes to dry a little better and then drove to her mom's house to get Jenny.

It wasn't until Jenny was in bed sleeping, her breath coming in lovely little puffs, that Diane had a better talk with herself. She realized that she felt free, and that brought some relief. She didn't see a lustrous future ahead, but she had been tempted toward something that would have been bad for her and worse for Jenny. At least she had had the good sense to resist the danger this time—even if she had been sorely tempted. And in the end Greg had done such a lovely job of showing himself for who he still was that she didn't have to question her decision. She felt sorry for the man; she really did. But she wanted to be Diane, whoever that was, and tonight she felt that she had taken another step toward finding out.

CHAPTER 15

K athy was lying in bed on a Saturday morning. It was after eight o'clock and she had been telling herself for half an hour that she needed to get up and start cleaning her apartment. When the telephone rang, she rolled over and picked up the receiver from the phone on her nightstand.

"Kathy, are you up?"

Kathy recognized Aunt LaRue's voice. "More or less," she said, in a voice that sounded, even to herself, not quite "up."

"No you're not. Get hopping, girl; the day is wasting."

"When did you turn into Grandma Bea?"

"My dear niece, you've hit very close to the truth—closer than you could ever imagine. I need to talk to you about some . . . things. Can we have lunch together."

"What's going on, Auntie? You sound *awfully* perky for this time of the morning."

"Whatever do you mean? You know I'm *always* perky on Saturday mornings." But she didn't give Kathy time to respond. "I'm going to call your mother, too. I'll take you both to lunch at the Hotel Utah. Meet me in the lobby at . . . what? Eleven-thirty?"

"Do you have an announcement or—"

"No questions now. Just meet me down there. I'll call your mom right now."

So Kathy got up and made herself some toast. Her mom called after a few minutes and said she would drive, but neither speculated about LaRue's reason for wanting to see them. The fact was, Kathy was fairly sure she knew what LaRue was going to say—even though she hadn't expected it quite this soon—and it was hard not to be a little jealous. But that was the wrong attitude and Kathy knew it, so she got busy cleaning the kitchen and told herself how happy she was for LaRue.

Kathy and Lorraine arrived at the hotel first and sat down in the stately old lobby. After a couple of minutes Kathy spotted LaRue walking toward them, looking excited. It was a mild March day, but breezy, and LaRue's hair looked a little windblown. She was wearing a breezy yellow and white skirt—chiffon, or something of that sort—with a white vest. She looked terrific—like someone in a TV commercial striding across a grassy field, overjoyed by her new toothpaste. "Let's just go down to the Coffee Shop," LaRue said from a distance. She turned and motioned for Kathy and Lorraine to follow. LaRue had always possessed a vitality that could change Kathy's mood immediately, but today there was something new. She seemed younger, and she was flowing more than walking.

In the coffee shop a hostess seated the three at the back, near the big semicircular fish tank that Kathy had always liked to look at. She loved the simple elegance of the room, the white linen tablecloths, and she liked the look of the people, most of whom seemed to be out-of-towners, people going somewhere. Kathy had been itching lately to do something new, maybe go on a trip—anything to break up the dull routine of her life. That desire wasn't eased at all when she looked at LaRue and felt those little jabs of jealousy again.

Kathy was tempted to burst LaRue's bubble and simply tell her that she knew very well what this was all about, but she knew LaRue wanted to do this her own way. So Kathy allowed the small talk until after the waitress had taken their orders. But as soon as the young woman walked away, LaRue said, "There's something I want to tell you. I talked to Mom and Dad this morning, and I called my sisters, but I needed something that felt like a little party, so I thought of you two." She was trying not to smile but was losing the fight. Kathy also realized LaRue had been keeping her left hand out of sight.

"Gee, LaRue," Kathy said, "I just can't guess what it is you have to tell us."

"Maybe *you're* not surprised, but *I* am." LaRue finally let herself smile openly. The entire room must have taken on light; Kathy wondered whether people weren't turning to look. "John asked me to marry him last night." She brought her hand up from under the table and revealed a solitaire diamond—and not a tiny one—in a pretty gold setting.

"So you accepted without asking for time to think about it?" Kathy asked.

"Actually, I did take some time to think. About half a second."

Lorraine had reached across the table by then and taken hold of LaRue's hand. She looked at the ring for a moment, and then she said, in a soft voice, "Oh, LaRue, I'm so happy for you." She stood, walked around the table, and hugged LaRue.

Kathy realized it's what she should have done, and so she got up too, and also embraced LaRue. Kathy noticed that most of the people in the coffee shop *were* looking at them now.

By the time the three sat down again, the tears had begun—and the search for tissues. Lorraine found hers first, and shared, and that made everyone laugh. It really was wonderful that after all these years, something had finally worked out for LaRue. Suddenly Kathy *was* happy, maybe even hopeful. But she didn't want to cry. "Here's what I need to know," she said. "How many cows did John offer to Grandpa?"

LaRue laughed. "He didn't mention any cows, but he told me he would buy a new house for us—so we can start a new life together."

"In Provo?"

"Somewhere in Utah County. I'd like it if we found something kind of north, so it's not quite so far to Salt Lake."

Kathy laughed at the thought of feisty LaRue moving from

Massachusetts to Orem or Lehi. A few years back Kathy couldn't have imagined that happening. "You're really in love, aren't you?" she said. "Anyone who looks at you right now knows you got engaged last night."

"Oh, please. Don't be silly." LaRue let her eyes go shut for a moment, and she took a deep breath. "But yes. I'm in love. At first I liked him and thought we were a good match—you know, in spite of a million differences. But I don't know what's happened lately. I stopped considering all the ramifications and just allowed myself to *feel,* and I think John finally let go of his past. For quite a while he seemed afraid that he was doing something wrong to love anyone but Pat—his wife who died—but he's looking ahead now, and it's partly, I think, because his kids all like me and keep telling him it's okay."

"How old are his kids?" Lorraine asked.

"He has a daughter who's twenty. She's the youngest and the only one not married. He's got another daughter and two sons, and those three have a total of seven children. So it's kind of strange to me to be 'Mom' to kids that old, and especially to be an instant grandma, but I love the kids, and I'm getting used to the idea of becoming a new bride and an old grandmother all at the same time."

"But I talked to you a few weeks ago," Lorraine said, "and nothing much was happening."

"I know. So I took matters into my own hands." She laughed as she made a grabbing motion, with her fingers bent like claws.

"What did you do?" Kathy asked.

"Well . . . you know. I just—how should I say?—moved things along."

"No, I don't know," Kathy said. "Explain it to me, because I seem to be missing a gene that controls a woman's instinct for catching men."

"Hey, you're talking to forty-plus-and-still-single LaRue. What do I know?"

"You knew something. So tell me what it is."

The waitress brought a glass of water for Lorraine and soft drinks for

Kathy and LaRue. LaRue picked up her Coke, took a sip, and then set it down. She seemed to be waiting for the waitress to walk away. Finally she said, "I'm not sure I should give you this advice in front of your mother, but what I did was kiss him, and after that, everything seemed to change between us."

"*You* kissed *him*?"

"Well, sort of. We were about four feet apart, and I cut the distance down to about an inch. He finally bridged the final gap, so he probably thinks that *he* kissed *me*."

"Now let me get this straight," Kathy said. "John is this intelligent, rational man with a Ph.D., and he's struggling with his emotions about his dear departed wife, so you trick him into kissing you and suddenly all his doubts are gone? Explain that one to me."

LaRue was looking delighted with herself. She seemed too beautiful for any man to resist. "Kathy, you must have learned somewhere along the line that love isn't rational. He had all sorts of concerns when he analyzed the situation. I got him to start thinking with his heart—the way I was trying to do."

"I don't want to sound skeptical, dear old Aunty, but I think I can come up with some biological explanations that might be equally plausible."

"Well, sure. Love's emotional, but it's biological too. I like John's looks, and I like his kisses very much. And I really think I'm going to like being with him all the time. You know how it is. I want to stay up late and talk economic theory with him." She winked.

Kathy was shaking her head, still laughing, but Lorraine said to Kathy, "Honey, you *think* too much about everything you do. There does come a time when you have to let your heart do the leading."

"Hey, my heart led me into breaking up with Leon when you were telling me I should consider what a solid guy he was—with a *good future*."

"That's because she didn't meet him," LaRue said, and everyone laughed.

"My heart works just fine, ladies," Kathy said. "But it keeps leading me right back to thoughts about Marshall, and Marshall is taken."

"What's happening with that?" LaRue asked.

The waitress had arrived with chef's salads for everyone, but she realized that she hadn't brought utensils and had to go back for them. Kathy looked at the tropical fish in the tank, all seeming to understand, by instinct, what their lives were about. She wondered how female fish attracted the right male. They probably knew about some little wiggle, or maybe they hid in the coral and played hard-to-get.

"So what's the situation with Marshall?" LaRue asked. "You told me at Christmas that he was getting married."

"I know. He is. Grandma talked to his mom, and I guess he's not officially engaged, but he and cute little *Lisa* are definitely planning to get married. His mom thinks the wedding will be this summer, 'if Marshall doesn't change his mind again.'"

"Hey, he's still legal game, if you ask me."

"Not really."

"But you had that wonderful conversation with him at the ballet that night."

"It was wonderful to me. We were really on the same wavelength—and *Lisa* was all put out with him and sarcastic. I think she's really kind of . . . well, never mind. The fact is, he left with her and never has called me. So she won."

"Why don't you call him?"

"Oh, sure."

"Look, Kathy, I'm getting married, but it should have happened a long time ago. And why didn't it? Because I waited for some guy to decide he wanted to marry me. This time I quit my job and moved across the nation, and then I took some chances."

"And kissed him first."

"Yes. And kissed him first." She smiled as she chewed for a time, and then she said, "Surely, you can make a phone call."

"What, and ask him out when he's more or less engaged?"

"It's the seventies, little girl. Don't you know that? Women are liberated. You don't have to wait for him to make the first move."

Kathy looked at her mother. "I can't do that, can I?"

"You don't have to ask him out," Lorraine said. "Call him for some other reason."

Kathy laughed. "Mom! What are you talking about? You're the one who taught me all these rules about girls not calling guys."

Lorraine did seem a little embarrassed. "I know. But sometimes a woman has to let a guy know what he can't figure out for himself. If you're a better match for him than his girlfriend is, you need to make sure he doesn't make a *tragic* mistake."

"There's your justification," LaRue said. "You're only thinking of him. And besides, all's fair in love and war—and finding a husband is both."

"I'm not going to call him. I can't."

"Kathy, you're in love with this guy, and he must be having his doubts about the girl he's going with or he wouldn't keep delaying. You said yourself that you had this great 'meeting of the minds' when you saw him. So figure out a way to talk to him, and let him have another taste of that. How can you live with yourself if you don't help him find out he's about to marry the wrong girl?"

Kathy was laughing, but she had been saying pretty much the same thing to herself all winter. Lisa was so wrong for Marshall, and Kathy and Marshall really did think alike. She loved his smile, and she loved his easy manner, but that was not the point. She liked the way a lot of guys looked; she just hadn't known any who were so deeply curious about their world, and this new idea of moving to a small town and getting involved in the community—it was exactly what Kathy had been thinking she wanted to do. "But what could I say to him?" she asked, looking at LaRue and then her mother. "How could I explain why I was calling?"

"He'll *know* why you're calling," LaRue said.

"I know. That's what embarrasses me."

"It'll flatter him. He'll like it. So any excuse will do."

"No. I can't."

But on Sunday evening, she did. She waited until later in the evening and hoped he wasn't still with Lisa, as he probably had been much of the day. And she did catch him at home. But as soon as his mother said, "Yes. Just a moment," Kathy's frail confidence disappeared entirely.

"Hi," he said when he answered, sounding relaxed.

Kathy was afraid he thought she was Lisa. "Hello, Marshall, this is Kathy Thomas." She had wanted to sound sort of business-like, but her voice echoed back to her, brittle and high-pitched.

"Oh, Kathy, hello. How are you?"

"Fine. I was wondering if I could talk to you sometime. When I saw you at Christmas, you were rethinking what you were going to do with your life, and I liked what you had to say. I'm trying to sort things out for myself, and I just thought it would help me to have a chat with you about . . . the things you said that night." She had memorized this little speech, practiced it at least a dozen times, but it had tumbled out breathlessly, and she had gotten lost toward the end and hadn't said it right.

He laughed a little, and she wondered whether he was laughing at her, but he said, "Hey, I'd love that. I'm actually in the middle of that whole process again. Lisa thinks I'm nuts to pursue this cabinetmaking thing, and she doesn't want to live in a small town—so I don't know. I may have to go another way."

"Are you still working as a carpenter?" At least she had sounded a little more natural this time.

"Yeah, I am. But I'm not quite so idealistic about it as I was when I saw you last winter. If I had to work for someone else all my life, I'm not sure I would like that. It's having my own shop that appeals to me."

"It appeals to me, too."

"What?"

"I just mean it sounds like a good thing for you."

"Well, maybe. I don't know. Have you started back to school?"

"No. I'm still working as a secretary, and it's not very satisfying to me. I'm trying to decide what to do." Kathy was still standing stiff, but at least she had managed a breath between sentences.

"Well, I'm not sure how much help I can be, but I'd love to spend some time with you—and just share our thoughts."

"Good." Kathy knew she shouldn't ask, but she had to know. "When are you and Lisa getting married?"

"Oh, Kathy, who knows? My mom says I have problems making commitments. But half the time I'm not even sure that Lisa and I are right for each other. I think we're getting married in August, but Lisa gets really disgusted with me. We've come pretty close to breaking up a couple of times lately."

"Oh, that's too bad."

Marshall laughed rather hard. Was it because she had sounded as unconvincing to him as she had to herself? She was humiliated again just when she had started to gain a little composure. "Well, anyway . . ." she said, without a sentence to follow.

"This week is really busy for me, Kathy. But what about the weekend? Maybe Saturday, during the day."

"That would be fine."

"Okay. I'll call you on Friday. Do I have your number?"

"No," Kathy said, but she had forgotten the number herself. She stuttered for a moment and then remembered it was written across the dial on her phone.

"Hey, you know what we ought to do? We ought to drive up to Alta."

"They're still skiing up there, aren't they?"

"Sure, but we could drive up and sit in the lodge or something. It's just a thought."

Just a perfect thought, that was all. It was romantic, and he knew it. It was nostalgic, and he knew it. It made her stomach feel full of butterflies, and he probably knew that, too. When she put the receiver down, her excitement was almost greater than her humiliation. Marshall and Lisa had almost broken up a couple of times lately. Why would he tell her that? And he had thought of Alta, where she and Marshall had lain on the grass and looked at the stars on their first date. Why would he want to go back there? She knew he had probably chosen a time during the day because he spent every weekend night with Lisa. But hey, as LaRue said, all was fair in love and war. At least she was going to have a chance. That thought, however, made her think of trying to kiss him, and that sent the butterflies into another flurry. She told herself there was no way she could be that obvious. She had to engage his mind and his heart this first time and then find out whether he wanted to come back for the kiss.

❦

The week was long, and Kathy lost a little more confidence each day. She tried on all her clothes on Monday night, and then on Tuesday, after work, went shopping. What could she wear for a drive to a ski resort—if they weren't going to ski? She could wear ski pants, but since she hadn't skied in years, she didn't have any, and if she bought new ones, he might recognize they were new, and that might look like she was trying too hard. She thought of those after-ski boots she had seen, and maybe a ski sweater with regular pants, but he had only said they *might* drive to Alta. What if they went to lunch somewhere else around town? She could get herself all fixed up like a ski bunny and end up down in the valley on a day that was seventy degrees.

She bought nothing on Tuesday and shopped again on Wednesday, and this time only got more confused. By the time she got home, she knew she had to talk to Diane, who knew everything about dating. She called her up and told her she wanted to come up after work on Thursday to get some advice. "Advice? From me?" Diane said.

"Yes. It's about guys and about clothes for a date—plus my hair, and a few other things."

"Kathy, I haven't dated in years."

"But you understand this stuff, Diane—better than anyone I know. And I'm in desperate need of help."

"Well . . . come up. We can talk. But who's the guy?"

"Marshall."

"*Marshall?* Do you have a date with him? I thought he was getting married."

Kathy was sitting on her bed. She dropped onto her back. Diane's question reminded her how stupid all this was. Marshall probably had nothing in mind more than a chat with an old friend, and Kathy was acting as if he had asked her to a sweetheart ball. "He probably is getting married. And this is not really a date. The truth is, I'm trying to be the 'other woman' and see if I can't steal him away from his girlfriend."

"Excuse me? Who is this calling?"

"I know. This whole thing is just not me. That's why I'm calling you." She thought of that fish who knew when to wiggle. "I need some fast training."

Diane was laughing. "Well, come up tomorrow night, then. I think I know a few things."

She certainly did. And Kathy held out that hope all day on Thursday. But on the way to Ogden, she wondered what in the world she was doing. She couldn't change herself in an hour or two. But if Diane could at least help her figure out what to wear, that would be a step forward.

When Kathy reached Diane's place, she sat down in her little living room and explained her dilemma—all about the weather and the possible drive to Alta. Diane listened, asked a few questions, and then said, "Kathy, I see your problem, but you're asking all the wrong questions. You're doing what women always do—worrying about the things men don't even think of."

"Like what?"

"A guy doesn't care whether you pick the perfect clothes for the occasion. He doesn't care whether you wear ski pants or shorts. He just wants you to look good."

"I can only do so much in that department."

"Oh, Kathy. You don't know." Diane slipped off the couch and sat on the floor next to Jenny, who was trying to wrap a baby doll in a little blanket. As she helped Jenny, she said to Kathy, "Most women *want* to look like you. Tall and thin is so 'in' these days. And what man doesn't like those long, long legs of yours? Your problem is, you don't like being tall. You don't wear things that show your shape."

"I could wear some of those ribbons they wrap around a maypole."

Diane laughed. "Don't give me that. If you put on a slinky dress, you'll knock his eyes out."

"But it's a daytime thing—like a lunch date."

Diane placed the doll into a little crib and smoothed the blanket out, but Jenny pulled the blanket off and grabbed the doll by one arm and carried both to Kathy. "Wap it up, okay?" she said.

Diane told Kathy, "She likes to 'wap' her baby up, but then she can't think what to do next, so she starts over."

"Well, it *isn't* very interesting to wait for a doll to sleep."

"I'm just glad she's taken some interest in dolls lately. I thought she was going to play with heavy equipment all her life."

"Well, women have wider interests these days. That's good."

"You know, it really is," Diane said, "and I hate what I'm telling you about *attracting* men. I always did it by trying to look pretty, and you know the kind of guy I ended up with."

Kathy had wrapped up the baby, and now she handed it to Jenny, who took it back to her crib. "Have you heard anything from Greg since that night he got so mad?" she asked.

"Yes. He came to get Jenny last Saturday. But he only wanted her for the day, and not the weekend. He told me he'll probably be getting married before the summer is over—to the woman who can't 'keep her hands off him,' I'm sure."

Kathy had heard the whole story. "That's good in a way, Diane. That'll close the whole thing."

"I know. I just hope things will be okay for Jenny. But listen . . ." Diane's voice suddenly took on some enthusiasm. "If a guy loves your brain—and only your brain—he'll become your buddy. And having a few buddies is nice. But he won't want to marry you unless he *does* find you attractive. I mean, let's face it, women are the same way. You've probably heard about the birds and the bees, haven't you?"

"Someone mentioned something about that. But right now, I just want you to tell me what to wear."

"Okay. It's still winter up at Alta, but it's spring down here. So dress for the valley, and then just take a coat if he wants to drive up the canyon. And when I say 'for here,' I'd say a pretty spring dress that's slim and light. Then, if you end up in the snow, you can tiptoe, or whatever you have to do, and he'll think you look cute—and probably sexy, the way men think."

"Diane, I'm not sexy. That just isn't me."

"You *are* sexy. You just do everything you can to hide it. Like your hair."

"I like it short."

"I know, and that's okay. But you need to make it look more feminine."

"I have no idea how to do that."

"We'll experiment in a few minutes. But we need to talk a little more about a basic philosophy."

Kathy laughed. "What kind of philosophy?"

Jenny had apparently lost interest in the doll. She brought a puzzle to Kathy and said, "Help me, okay?"

It was a simple little wooden puzzle—a little scene of Snow White and the Seven Dwarfs. Kathy slipped onto the floor as Jenny scrambled the pieces. But Jenny obviously knew the puzzle well. She started putting it together without Kathy's help.

"I'm sure Marshall loves to talk to you," Diane said. "You're always up on current events, and you have interesting opinions. So that's good. But I remember those days when you would come home from college, go out with him, and then get in arguments with him about politics. Marshall obviously likes you, but you've made him into your debate partner, not your boyfriend."

"I know. That's exactly right. I pretty much called him stupid a couple of times back then. That's when he first lost interest in me. I know I've got to be different this time, but I don't know how to reverse what I've already done."

"You don't have to change all that much. He obviously likes that you're smart. Just de-emphasize some things. Listen to the guy. Let him tell you his opinion, and if you disagree, don't jump all over him about it. Just once in your life, say, 'That's interesting. I've never thought of it that way.'"

"I don't want to marry some guy and then have to act stupid all my life—just so he won't think I'm as smart as he is."

Diane leaned back against the couch and stretched her legs out across the carpet. She was wearing some threadbare jeans and a faded sweatshirt, and she still looked great. *Attractive*. "I know all about that," Diane said. "Greg wanted me to bow at his feet and tell him how brilliant he was. I didn't dare disagree with him. But it doesn't have to be like that. It's all right to say what you think. Just don't put him down. And it doesn't hurt to make him feel manly and wise once in a while."

Kathy tried to think about that. It sounded a little dishonest, and yet, she had been learning since she had come home from the Peace Corps to control her zeal and listen to people. Besides, whatever she had been doing wasn't working. So she asked the one question she had been worrying most about. "I told him I wanted his advice. But once we're together, how do I let him know that I'm interested in *him* and I'm not just there to have a chat about my future?"

"He probably suspects that already, but he needs some signals so he'll know where he stands."

"What signals?"

"You know. Touch him, or—"

"What?"

"When you say something to him, touch his arm. Let your hands bump against each other when you're walking. Sit close to him. Whisper something to him. If your lips touch his ear, that won't hurt a thing."

"Diane, come on. That's so obvious."

"And how has 'subtle' been working for you so far?"

Kathy rolled her eyes.

"It's like a mating call to guys. They're like any other animal. First you let the male of the species know that he's big and strong and desirable. Then you strut your stuff a little. From that point, his instincts take over."

"I shouldn't go for a kiss, should I?"

"Uhhhh . . . no. Not in the daytime, under these circumstances, but leave him wishing he could kiss you."

"And the touching will do that, and the whispering in his ear and all that?"

"Oh, yes."

"All right. I'll look for a dress tonight. LaRue was wearing a pretty spring outfit last Saturday. I'll find out where she bought it. Now let's see what we can do with my hair."

"Okay. But Kathy, remember, don't make *too much* of all this. You're an amazing woman. You're not *desperate*, so don't act like you are."

Kathy smiled and nodded. She could remember when she had thought of Diane as her cute but kind of dumb little cousin. "Diane, you're the amazing woman," she said. "I'm so impressed with what you've become." Jenny had finished her puzzle—twice—but was still sitting next to Kathy. Kathy pulled her close and hugged her. "And if a guy ever wins your heart, he'll also get this beautiful little bonus."

Diane smiled at Kathy. "We're going to be all right," she said. "Let's not either one of us feel sorry for ourselves."

"Okay."

❧

Kathy did find a pretty but simple dress that night—one that emphasized her long lines, didn't hide them. She liked the way she looked in it, and that gave her some confidence. She just couldn't picture herself touching Marshall's arm or, especially, whispering in his ear. So she told herself she couldn't do it by the numbers; she would have to see what felt natural to her.

On Friday evening, she didn't leave her apartment, not for a minute. As the hours stretched and Marshall didn't call, she tried not to despair. But by ten o'clock, she was giving up and trying to be philosophical about it. And then the phone rang and it *was* Marshall. "Say, Kathy," he said, "I'm sorry to call so late."

"It's not late. That's fine."

"Listen, I'm afraid tomorrow's not going to work for me. Do you think we could get together another day?"

"Oh, sure," Kathy said. "There's no big rush or anything. I was just . . .

you know . . ." Why was she letting him off the hook so easily? But she didn't know what else to say.

"Okay. I'll call you. I'm not sure when, but soon. Okay? I've got way too much going on right now."

"Sure. I understand."

And Kathy did understand. Marshall was not going to call. He had thought things over and realized that he was only getting himself into a mess, going out with Kathy behind Lisa's back. What Kathy knew was that she had let another of her fantasies get out of control. She could hardly believe how stupid she had been all week. Marshall would never change; she should have known he would cancel out. She wasn't going to let herself think about him anymore. She was going to move ahead with her life—go back to college. She would also keep the dress and wear it when she met someone else. Or if that didn't happen, she wasn't going to feel sorry for herself. Most important at the moment, she wasn't going to cry. So she wiped away the tears that were already on her face.

CHAPTER 16

Spring quarter at Weber State had begun, the term for Diane to do her student teaching. She was assigned to Lewis Elementary, in Ogden, which was close enough to be convenient, but it was in a part of Ogden she had never known much about. The kids were mostly from working families in the old part of town, and there were more minority children than she had ever been around. She soon gained the sense that most of these kids had parents who struggled to get their bills paid each month. Growing up, she had never known anything like that, but it's who she was herself now, and she felt the connection. Diane's child-support money kept her going, but if her parents hadn't helped at times—and if Greg's parents hadn't bought so many things for Jenny—Diane knew she couldn't get by. Since her confrontation with Greg, he had decided to switch jobs, as he had told her he might. But he was talking poverty now, buying nothing for Jenny, and hinting that he might have to go back to a judge and get an adjustment in the amount he sent Diane each month.

Diane knew what was going on: Greg was getting married in June. Diane had heard about the wedding from Greg's mother, but a Salt Lake friend had told Diane that Greg had bought a beautiful house in Holladay. It was clearly extravagant for a man who was talking about hard times.

Diane knew that Greg had vowed to be a good father, but she also knew that he would always look out for himself first. If his own money got tight, no matter how nicely he was living, he would try to find ways to keep his child-support payment as small as possible. She didn't know whether he would, as he had threatened, put up a fight for Jenny at some point, or whether he would forget Jenny once he had children with his new wife. Either seemed possible, but Diane was already seeing hints that the latter might be more likely. She had tried for a time to believe that Greg had changed, and she thought he did have a conscience, but expediency usually triumphed when he wanted something. He could twist anything to his own point of view, justify almost any behavior. Diane was sure that he had told his fiancée all sorts of terrible things about her, minimizing his own "mistakes."

What Diane wanted was to make herself as independent from Greg as she could, and she didn't want to depend on her family—or his. That meant that she, as a schoolteacher, was not likely to have very much to live on. It also meant that Jenny was going to grow up more or less like the kids in her school—a child who couldn't afford the nice things Diane had come to expect as normal in her own childhood. Jenny wouldn't have a fancy place to live, and she might not have much opportunity for travel, for lessons and instruments, for ski passes and all the other things Diane had known. Maybe Jenny and Diane would end up living in a neighborhood like this one. Diane told herself that was okay, and she certainly felt thankful every day that she hadn't let herself get drawn closer to Greg, but she did worry that Jenny might miss out on some things that Diane would love to be able to give her. Of course, Diane never stopped wondering whether she would find someone who could give her and Jenny an easier life. She certainly longed to have someone close to her again. But it wasn't helpful to think in terms of someone stepping in to save her.

On Diane's first day of class with her fourth-grade students, Mrs. Jones, Diane's cooperating teacher, had introduced Diane to the kids. That day Diane had only observed, but during math time, Mrs. Jones had asked her to work with one little boy who was struggling with his arithmetic. Diane had taken a chair and sat next to him, and she had used flashcards to help him memorize his times tables. The boy's name was Donald, and he was not just shy but almost silent. He would give the answer when he knew it, but if he didn't, he would say nothing at all. And he wouldn't look at Diane.

Diane had felt a sense of failure with him that day, but during the next couple of weeks, as she and Mrs. Jones continued to share the actual teaching, Diane had continued to work with Donald in the hours when Mrs. Jones was in front of the class. He had gradually become a little more able to talk to her, though he was still quiet, but he had taken to staying close to her whenever he could. During recess, he had little interest in playing with the other kids. Diane would turn around to find him standing nearby. She would try to make him laugh then, and he would sometimes respond to that. Once he had even tried to play catch with Diane, when she had gotten out a softball and asked him if he would play. He had been awkward and embarrassed about it, and Diane had the feeling it was something he had never done before.

One morning Donald came to class in the morning looking a little brighter than usual. "How are you this morning, Donald?" Diane asked.

Donald looked away from her, as always, and said, "Okay." He only seemed to have two sets of clothes, but they were always washed. Diane could see that someone combed his hair each morning, but she could also see that his mother had cut his hair with scissors and it was nicked up pretty badly most of the time.

"Did you walk to school?"

"Yes."

"It's warm this morning, isn't it?"

He nodded. They were standing by the classroom door, and she was surprised he hadn't slipped away by now—off to his desk in the first row.

"Who did you walk to school with?"

Donald looked up at her. His eyes usually seemed colorless, but she saw the hazel tones when he let himself look at her directly. "My sister," he said.

"Is she a big sister or a little sister?"

"Little."

"What grade is she in?"

"Second."

Diane felt she had made a step forward, just to have that much conversation with him, so she tried another approach. "Tell me about her," she said.

But Diane saw the surprise, the fear. He looked away.

"What's her name?"

"Teresa."

"Do you two like to play together?"

He seemed unsure about that, but he finally said, "Yes." He pushed his hands into the front pockets of his jeans. They were not the Levi's most of the boys wore but were cheaper-looking, probably purchased just down the street at the Grand Central store.

"What do you and your sister play?"

Again, he seemed to be making an effort, as though he wanted to answer but was terrified to come out of himself that far. "She plays dolls," he said. It was a whole sentence.

"Do you play with her sometimes?"

Diane knew that fourth-grade boys weren't likely to admit such a thing, but he said, "Yes," and she didn't know whether it was true, or whether it was just a simple answer so he wouldn't have to explain any further. So Diane put her hand on his shoulder and waited for him to look up again. When he did, she said, "I like you, Donald. You're a nice boy. And I'm glad you're nice to your sister. I have a little brother, but I didn't have a big brother to walk with me to school. I would have liked that."

And then, to Diane's surprise, he said, "I help her cross the street."

"That's great. You *are* a good brother."

He let his eyes linger on hers, and she saw the love. Later that day, when she was sitting next to him, she saw him rest his arm next to hers on the desk, and finally felt the warm skin of his forearm touch against hers, and she understood how much the little guy needed someone to love him. She was glad she was a teacher at that moment, but she also knew she would soon be up front full-time, and she wouldn't be able to give Donald as much individual attention. That afternoon, after school, she told Mrs. Jones what she was worried about.

Mrs. Jones was sitting at her desk. She was over fifty, Diane thought, but she had told Diane that she hadn't taught when her own kids were young. She was a strong-looking woman, with big hands and substantial hips, but she was gentle with the kids. What impressed Diane, however, was that she was always in control and the kids knew it, even though she didn't raise her voice to get them to pay attention.

"I don't know the whole story on Donald," she said. "But I know he's smarter than he seems sometimes. His mother is raising him and his little sister by herself, and I think she's trying hard, but I noticed when I talked to her that she seems almost emotionless, as though she's making her way through life but isn't quite connected to anything. My guess is that her absentee husband was beating her and her kids before she got away from him. I've seen way too many of these abused little kids—and battered wives. They react in different ways, but none of them comes away unscathed."

"Donald wants someone to love him," Diane said. "You can feel it in everything he does."

"I know. And he's fallen in love with you. But a teacher can only do so much. You'll have to be careful with him. He needs to get love at home, and I'm not sure that's ever going to happen."

"What will happen to him, then?"

"I don't know, Diane. There are so many of these kids now. They're so sweet in fourth grade, but they have to find someone to connect to, and by junior high all the little castaways seem to find each other. That's when the drugs and the acting out start—or anger finally starts showing up. Chances are, he'll stay along the edges, the way he does now, and never be accepted by the popular kids. Then who knows? Most of the time, it's not good."

"But there must be something we could do."

"I heard what you told him this morning—that he was a good brother. He needs to hear things like that. And he's got one thing going for him. He's actually quite a good reader. If we can keep him going on his math, and give him some confidence there, that can make a big difference. If kids do well in school—in spite of problems in their homes—they gain some self-confidence, and it's something they can build on. I've seen a few kids like Donald really blossom. Just not many."

Diane was left feeling empty. She thought about Donald as she drove home. She worried about him—worried about all the little kids in this world who were starting life with brutal fathers or loveless mothers, and the emotional damage they were receiving. She couldn't help thinking of Jenny. She hoped that the things Jenny had seen as a baby wouldn't stay inside her, wouldn't affect the way she thought about herself and about life. She hoped too that growing up without a dad in her home wouldn't impair Jenny in some way, and she hoped that going back and forth, spending weekends at times in a big house in Holladay, wouldn't warp her values. Greg was likely to use his wealth to buy her love and influence her attitude toward Diane, if nothing else to make her look bad for divorcing him. What would those things do to Jenny? It was all very frightening because Diane could only control so much of the situation. But at least she hadn't gone back to Greg, and at least she wasn't so battered and discouraged, or so emotionally destroyed, that she was unable to give Jenny love. And she had the family backing that could make a difference. Her own dad would be a wonderful father image for Jenny.

Diane thought of Lloyd. He did love Jenny, and if given the chance, would provide for Diane. She had never seriously considered Lloyd as a possible husband—no matter how often her mom told her that she ought to—but she gave the idea some thought now. She told herself she needed to think of Jenny, not just herself, and she needed to be more open-minded. So what if Lloyd quoted Spiro Agnew or didn't read the newspaper? She had been condescending toward him—because of the boyish way he combed his hair, as much as anything, and his funny accent when he spoke. But how important was that? She had to get it into her head that she wasn't twenty, and she wasn't asking herself whether she wanted to marry a future lawyer or stick around college long enough to be the homecoming queen. Life was what it was now, and she was seeing a whole new reality at her school. Maybe it was time she humbled herself and took a new look at Lloyd.

❧

The following week, the singles in Diane's ward were going to a play at Weber State—"The King and I"—and Diane had told Lloyd that she didn't think she would be able to go, but she decided that maybe she would after all. When he checked back with her, she told him to count her in. In the back of her mind was the ordeal at the stake singles' dance, but she thought the ward group was less awkward for her, even though she was, by far, the youngest. Everyone seemed to think of Lloyd as her friend—if not her boyfriend—and the older men hadn't made any overtures, at least so far.

On the night of the play, Diane dropped Jenny off with Bobbi and Richard. She found her dad in the family room, downstairs. Mom, he said, had gone to the grocery store. As Diane was about to leave, her dad asked, "Are you going out with that fellow in your ward?"

"No. Not really. It's all the single people in our ward. We're going to a play."

Dad had been sitting on the couch watching the evening news on television. He had taken off his tie, but he was still wearing the dress pants and button-down-collar shirt he had worn to the college that day. It was funny how often Diane heard comments on campus about how handsome he was, and he was in his fifties now, halfway to sixty. He was a farm boy from Springville, Utah, but he always had the look of an aristocrat. Most professors were dressing down these days, but Dad still wore tweed jackets, nice slacks, and Florsheim shoes. "Your mom tells me," he said, "that he likes to look out for you."

"Yeah. He's nice about that. He's my home teacher."

"But Bobbi says you're not giving him a chance to be more than that."

Diane smiled. "The thing is, I don't want to do what Mom did—marry any old guy, just because he's good at fixing faucets."

"Yes. That is my specialty." Jenny walked over to her grandpa, and he pulled her onto his lap. She nestled in against him, her head against his chest.

"I'm trying, Dad. Lloyd really is good with Jenny."

"What do you mean, you're *trying?*"

Diane sat down on the couch next to her dad. "Lloyd is nice, but he hasn't exactly set my heart on fire. Maybe I need to change my attitude about him."

Dad took his time to respond, as always, but Diane had learned to wait. He usually said things to her that made a difference. "Watch out for your mom, Di. And for that matter, don't listen to me too much. You know what you feel toward this man. I wouldn't marry him just because he's been kind to you. You're still awfully young, and marriage lasts a long time—long after your kids are grown up, and long after this life. I think it's a mistake to marry someone merely because it's *practical*. You *do* have to feel some fire in your heart, honey. Remember all those doubts you felt about Greg? I think now you wish you had listened to them."

"Oh, Dad, you shouldn't do this to me. I've been telling myself all week I've got to give Lloyd a chance—you know, because of Jenny."

Dad wrapped his arms tight around Jenny. "She's only going to be happy if you are."

"But it's not like last time. I can't go to my college classes and check out all the guys while they check me out. Every time these young guys at Weber get a little interested, they find out I have a child."

"I know. It's a lot more complicated this time, but as far as I'm concerned, you and your sister Maggie are the prize 'catches' on this entire earth, and I don't want you to settle for someone simply because he's there and he's willing. I ask the Lord every night to tell you what to do with your life. If your spirit isn't responding to this man, I'd say that's a stupor of thought, at best, and take that as an answer."

"I know you're probably right. But I'm really confused. Mom and Aunt LaRue have been telling me that the pioneers picked themselves a mate and made the best of things."

"Yes. And ask your mom and LaRue if that's what they did. LaRue is all twitterpated about John now, and the last I remember, your mom fell *in love* with me. I don't remember her deciding that I wasn't a bad sort—and better than nothing."

Diane laughed. "I know. And that's a danger in my situation. I do start thinking about 'better than nothing.'"

When Diane heard her mother come in, she kissed Jenny and then walked upstairs. She had asked Lloyd to pick her up at her parents' house, so he could drop her off there later and she wouldn't have to drive back over to get Jenny. She chatted with her mom, but she purposely didn't tell her what Dad had said, if only to avoid the discussion that might follow. But she found herself feeling confused when she walked out to the car with Lloyd. She had made up her mind really to try tonight, but now she had Dad's warning in her head.

Lloyd was his usual polite-but-quiet self, and Diane was, as always, too self-conscious to sit in a car with someone and say nothing, so she did a monologue about teaching, about her students, and about Mrs. Jones, whom she liked so much. Lloyd would converse sometimes, but he seemed to find nothing to say tonight. He listened and didn't ask any questions to keep Diane going, so she had to come up with her own little connections to start another comment. Diane told herself that that was all right, that her own father, whom she loved more than any other man in the world, was fairly quiet himself.

Diane had mentioned Donald before, but she told Lloyd now what Mrs. Jones had said about him. Lloyd listened, but when Diane decided she wasn't going to do all the work to carry on the conversation, he waited for a time and then said, "Well, he might turn out just fine. You never know."

The one thing she always said about Lloyd was that he was nice, and that he cared about Jenny, but what kind of response was that? If he was so nice, couldn't he feel a little more concern about a kid Diane had come close to crying about as she had described him? Maybe Lloyd didn't say much because he didn't think much, or worse, because he didn't feel much. Could that be it?

But that wasn't fair, and Diane knew it. Donald was an abstraction to Lloyd. The guy was genuinely caring toward Jenny and attentive to everyone in their singles' group—even some people who weren't that easy for Diane to like.

Diane watched Lloyd all evening. Even though he was shy, he spoke to everyone, and afterward, when the group met at Sister Lawrence's house for pie and ice cream, he was the one carrying folding chairs, dipping ice cream, making sure everyone had napkins. So what if he didn't talk a lot? He was looking to see what needed to be done, and he was doing it. Most of the men were sitting on their haunches, letting the sisters—and Lloyd—serve them. Lloyd was like Martha, more than Mary, and the world needed lots more Marthas—people who did the work that needed to be done.

After everyone was served, Lloyd sat down next to Diane. "You didn't tell me—how did you like the play?" he asked, and Diane had the feeling he was chiding himself for not having had more to say all evening. Diane liked that. He had initiated a subject, and something in his tone made her feel that he was concerned for her enjoyment, not just interested in an opinion about the play. But that made her wonder what he had thought about it, so she said, "You tell me first. I'm curious to know whether you liked it."

"Oh. Well, I don't know. Musicals never quite make sense to me. It doesn't seem like people would sing so much—you know, in normal life."

"Of course they wouldn't. But that's what you have to expect when you go to a musical. It's not realism; it's a kind of fantasy."

"Yeah. I can see that."

"But did you like it?"

"Yeah. There were some good songs, and it was kind of funny."

"What about the woman who played Anna? Did you like her singing?"

"Sure."

"Did you? I thought she was rather weak. Her voice would almost pinch off when she tried to hit the high notes. You can forgive someone who isn't a great actor in a musical—because the singing is so important—but I didn't think her voice was strong enough to play Anna."

"Yeah. I guess that's probably right. I just . . . I don't know . . . I just don't worry much about that kind of stuff. Like you said, it's not real anyway."

Diane let it go. And she tried not to grind her teeth. She certainly couldn't reject a guy because he didn't like musicals. But could she live with a man for time and all eternity who would always be saying things like that? "It's not real anyway"? What did that mean? But she had to remind herself that she had never been a huge fan of musicals herself, and once in college she had gone to see *The Merchant of Venice* with a guy who wanted to talk about the racism in the play—and all the symbolism—while eating ice cream at the CougarEat. She had vowed never to date another English major as long as she lived. So what was she now? The big authority on theater?

But it wasn't so much that Lloyd didn't care about musicals; she worried that he wasn't interested in much of anything. If he had a passion for something, some interest that occupied his mind a good deal, even some hobby he liked to talk about, she could accept that. But he was the polar opposite of Greg, who had an opinion about everything. Lloyd waited for Diane to say what she thought before he committed himself, and then he usually just agreed with her. She had asked him once how he felt about Nixon, and he had said, "He's not my favorite, but he's better than 'McGovnern' would have been." McGov-*nern*?

Diane had spent her whole life thinking that everyone knew more than she did, that she wasn't smart, that she ought to be careful about expressing an opinion—because someone in the room might put her down. Now, here she was skeptical about Lloyd because he didn't seem well-informed and didn't care as much as Diane wanted him to. Was that fair? Diane didn't know, but she did know that she found Lloyd's attitude more than just a little bothersome, and that was a serious problem for her, whether it *ought* to be or not. She thought again of what her dad had told her.

Later, as they were driving back to her parents' house, Lloyd said to her, "I'll bet you're under the gun right now, trying to prepare every night for your classes after you get home from a long day at school."

It was the best thing Lloyd could have said because it reminded her how empathetic he was. He really did seem to put himself in her place and care how she was doing. That was a trait Greg had never shown any sign of possessing, and it could mean so much in a marriage. "It is difficult," she said. "I don't think most people have any idea how hard a teacher works. It just takes everything out of you to be in charge all day. Then you get home and have to prepare every night for the next day. I know it gets easier after you've been doing it for a while, but I can see why a lot of teachers burn out."

"What if one night a week—or even two—I just came over and took

Jenny for a while? We could go to the park or something, and you would have a little time to get prepared without having her to distract you."

He had hit on the exact problem she had been having. Jenny wanted all her attention when she got home, and by the time Jenny was in bed, Diane was so tired it was all she could do to force herself to stay up late enough to prepare. One night a week, maybe in the middle of the week, would be a huge help. And Jenny did like Lloyd. But that would still be one more babysitter for Jenny, and Diane wasn't sure that was a good idea. "That's really nice, Lloyd," Diane said. "And it would help me. But Jenny's shifting back and forth all the time. I think, at the end of the day, she wants to know I'm there with her."

"Well, then, what about this? I could come over and play with her in another room. She would know you were right there, but she wouldn't be bothering you."

Diane almost said yes. She even thought she should say yes, but there was something about all this that didn't sit quite right. She had felt it before. Lloyd was trying, in his own way, to win Diane. He wanted her, but he knew better than to woo her the way most men would. What he was doing was moving into her life, making himself necessary and helpful. It was lovely, in its own way, but maybe it was just one more style of manipulation. Maybe Greg's techniques were worse, far more egocentric, but still, Diane sensed that another man was trying to make a sale. Diane wanted to love someone. She wanted to have someone to share her life with. But she didn't want to feel indebted to that man—and certainly not so indebted that she agreed to marry him out of mere appreciation. Dad was right. Maybe some marriages started with convenience and worked their way into love, but Diane was just as sure it could go the other way.

"I don't think so, Lloyd," she said. "I want to give Jenny my full attention for a while each day. And that's a break for me, too. I'll just have to plow my way through this quarter, staying up late and getting by. But I've done that for three years now. I can hold out a little longer."

Lloyd didn't press the issue. But then, Lloyd never pressed issues. He seemed to sense that longevity was on his side, and if he never made Diane angry with him, he could stay in her life. Diane had no idea what to do about that, but she was pretty sure she had to do something.

CHAPTER 17

ene was eating a bowl of cereal when Emily walked into the kitchen. She looked concerned as she held the morning paper out to him. "I'm afraid you've done it now," she said. "Look what the *Trib* wrote."

Gene took the paper from her and saw his picture—one of him in his army uniform—on the *front* page. The headline on the article next to the picture read "Republican Congressman's Son Speaks Out Against Nixon." And a subtitle added, "Decorated Vet Claims Government Lied About Vietnam." Gene was surprised that the story was on the front page, but he had known that something of this sort was coming. During winter quarter at the University of Utah, he had started writing a column for the student newspaper, and then, for his first commentary in spring quarter, he had written his opinion about the growing Watergate scandal. It was May now, and Gene had granted the *Tribune* permission to reprint his column, but the big story seemed to be that Gene, considering who his father was, would take such a strong stand.

Gene's first thought was that he hadn't said anything all that shocking—nothing that hadn't been in papers all across the country—so he scanned the column itself, printed on an inside page, just to see how strong it sounded. He knew, of course, that a lot of Utahns were defensive about accusations against President Nixon, and he recognized the section of his column that would bother some people:

> Many Utahns blame the current accusations against
> President Nixon on the news media or on ill-spirited

Democrats. Increasingly, however, the evidence is turning against the president. Facts are piling up that he and
his White House advisors avoided justice by hiding critical information from police and FBI investigators. John
Erlichman and H. R. Haldeman have resigned from the
White House staff, and John Dean has been fired. Nixon
would have us believe that the "bad apples" have all been
purged, but I am not convinced that Nixon kept himself
clean from the Watergate mess.

According to the *Washington Post,* James McCord has
revealed to Senate investigators that John Mitchell himself approved the break-in. John Mitchell, let us remember, was head of CREEP at the time, but before that he
served as Attorney General of the United States. As
such, he was the chief law enforcement officer of our
country. It's shocking to think such a man would approve
and financially support a criminal act. I hear Utahns
screaming that McCord is lying. But why would he do
that? He has been convicted of a crime and will gain
nothing by his admissions.

Maybe it's time to admit that the evidence is stack-
ing up against Nixon and goes far beyond accusations we
can blame on the press. In the next few months, as the
Senate Select Committee begins its open hearings, I
doubt that many of us are going to remain convinced
that Nixon has been forthcoming with all he knows.

Gene had then gone on to describe further evidence of other buggings
and political sabotage by the Nixon administration, and then he talked
about the danger of trusting government officials unquestioningly. He
argued that Republicans, of all people, should want their party purged of

members who didn't uphold the values most members claimed to espouse. Gene didn't mention his father, but he did write that many decisions in Congress over the past decade had been made out of trust, and part of the reason that Vietnam had been mishandled was that false information had often been disseminated to Congress from the executive branch of the government, both by Democrats and Republicans.

Gene turned back and read the rest of the front-page story. He found nothing in it that wasn't true. A reporter had called him and asked for a quote, but Gene had simply said, "I think my column speaks for itself," and that quotation was in the article. The only thing that bothered Gene was all the talk of political ramifications. Would Alex Thomas be hurt by his son's perceived disloyalty? One state party official was quoted as saying, "He's young. He's a college student. He has a right to his opinion. I don't think this hurts Mr. Thomas at all." But the head of the Utah Democratic party was quoted as saying, "It's definitely an embarrassment for Congressman Thomas. But it won't be long until the real embarrassment will be that he's not as forthcoming as his son. I think the rats are going to be jumping the ship before long, and no one will want to tie his political future to Nixon."

It was the end of the article that bothered Gene. The reporter had written a little summary of Gene's life. He said that Gene had been a sports hero and student body president at East High who had become a decorated war hero in Vietnam. He said that Gene had been badly wounded and, "according to one friend," was bitter and angry about his experience in the war. Gene hated the idea that a "friend" would make such a simplistic assessment of him. The question was whether Gene was right, not whether he had been wounded, and not even whether he was angry.

Emily sat across from Gene and waited for him to read the article. When he looked up, she said, "I only glanced through it. How bad is it?"

"I don't know. I guess it depends on how you look at it. I said what I thought in my column, and I knew that someone might want to make something out of it—you know, because of Dad. But I'll tell you what: I'm going to start looking a lot smarter as the months go by. People who get upset about this right now are soon going to be telling me I was right all along."

"Are you really sure of that, Gene?"

Emily's worried look irritated Gene. He also needed to get going. He didn't have a class until ten, but he had a test, and he wasn't ready for it. Lately he had been too preoccupied with his work on the newspaper to study for his classes as much as he should have. "Em, I've been reading every word that comes in about Watergate. Woodward and Bernstein, those two *Washington Post* reporters, have been writing stories almost every day since last summer. Now, everyone is picking up the story, and more facts are coming out. All of it just keeps adding up."

"But I keep hearing there's no proof that Nixon knew what was going on." Emily hadn't dressed yet. She was wearing a red silk dressing gown he had bought her for Christmas, but her face seemed pale and her eyes dark. Was she really that worried? "Maybe the whole thing stops with John Mitchell."

"No way. The connection into the White House has already been established. McCord said he got directions not just from Mitchell but from John Dean, the White House lawyer. Now Dean is singing like a bird to this new Senate committee. People in the know say he's going to implicate Nixon."

"But wouldn't it be better for you to stay neutral for now and not cause all this fuss?"

"No! I'm going to say what I think. If you don't like that, you shouldn't have told me to start writing articles." But this had come out much too strong. Gene knew he had to be careful.

"Gene, I'm proud of you for what you've been doing. But it's hard, too, the way some of the people in our ward look at us. It's going to get a lot worse now after this thing in the paper today."

"Telling the truth ought to be the easiest thing we ever do. If people in our ward can't handle that, it's their problem."

"But I think it would help if you went to all your church meetings. When you don't go to sacrament meeting, or skip Sunday School, people get the idea that you're falling away from the Church. Then they—"

"Emily, I can't have this conversation right now. I'm not falling away. You know that."

Gene watched Emily make the decision not to push the issue. Instead, she said, "I do like the look in your eye, Gene. You seem alive again."

"Emily, I feel like I'm a whole new person. I'm finally moving forward again."

"That's good. But I wish you would be here to answer the phone. I know what's going to happen today. We'll get calls from all over the country."

"No way. You're making way too much out of this. If you do get some calls, just say what I told the reporter for the *Tribune:* 'His column speaks for itself.'"

"Okay. But aren't you going to dress up a little bit more today? You might have guys showing up to take your picture."

"Emily, lay off, okay? Is that all you worry about—what *other* people think of me?" When Gene had taken business classes, he had gone to school fairly well dressed. This time around, studying journalism, he usually wore old jeans and sports shirts—or even ratty sweatshirts. He knew she didn't like that. But Gene liked the comfort, and the truth was, he liked the image that went along with the casual look. He was tired of everyone summarizing him as the congressman's kid. And he was sick of Emily buying into all that. Still, when Emily ducked her head, seeming frightened, Gene knew that his voice had gotten too intense. He had to be careful. "I'll put on a better shirt, okay?" he said, and then he got up and set his cereal bowl in the sink and headed to the bathroom to brush his teeth. He was in the middle of doing that when he heard the phone ring. He knew he had to make his dash now. But Emily called out, "Gene, it's your dad."

Gene knew he had to face this sooner or later anyway, so he walked to the kitchen and took the phone from Emily. "Hi, Dad," he said. "News travels fast, doesn't it?" He laughed, but he was nervous. He didn't know what to expect. He stood facing the wall phone, gripping the receiver tight.

But Alex laughed too. "Yes, it does. I've had some people call my office this morning—a couple of reporters, but mostly constituents. The most common opinion is that you're a mouthy young pup and I ought to put a muzzle on you. On the other hand, I've had a few say that you're writing the truth and I ought to come out in your support."

"Those must be Democrats."

"No. Not at all. Some Republicans are running pretty scared right now. They feel like Nixon is self-destructing and he's going to take the party down with him."

"What do you think?"

"I'm speaking to a reporter; I'd better watch what I say." Alex laughed, but then he said, "I haven't read your article, but one of our staff guys out in Utah read part of it to me over the phone. I didn't find anything I disagreed with. I think the evidence against the administration is looking pretty bad."

"I didn't know everyone would make such a big deal out of this."

"I know." There was quiet for a few seconds, and then Alex said, "Gene, here's why I called. I just wanted to tell you to write what you believe. Use your own judgment and your own good sense, but don't ever ask yourself how your writing might affect me."

"What drives me crazy is that people don't want to hear the facts. They'd rather be loyal to their party than know what's really going on."

"That's partly the fault of us politicians, Gene. We throw around a bunch of slogans and vapid clichés, and people get used to that. It's all sort of terrifying to me. We believe the people should decide, but then we assume those same people are too stupid to understand what the real issues are."

Gene turned and leaned his shoulder against the wall. He glanced at Emily, nodded. He needed to talk to her before he left and apologize for the way he had responded to her about the shirt. "Dad, I appreciate your confidence in me. I'm going to think a little more from now on about what might happen to the stories I write."

"No. Really, don't do that. Write what seems important to you. I'm just glad to see you up off your bed and fighting. I've been grinning all morning about this story because it tells me my son is going to be all right."

"Thanks, Dad. That means a lot to me."

"Okay. Keep up the good work. This nation needs people who are willing to knock us out of our simplistic notions. That's what you can do. I think you've got a great future ahead of you as a writer."

"I hope so. Thanks." His dad's words meant much more to Gene than he admitted. He had actually expected his father to be upset with him. He said good-bye and hung up the phone, but as he did, it began to ring immediately. "Can you take this, Em?" he asked. "Just tell them I'm gone." He picked up the phone and handed it to her. Then he headed for the bedroom to change his shirt. Before he could get very far, however, Emily was calling to him, "It's your grandpa."

"Hey, tell him . . . no. Never mind. I'll get this over with." He walked back and took the phone. "Okay, Grandpa, have at me," he said.

"Well, no. I'm not calling to chew you out or anything like that," Grandpa said. His voice sounded weak over the phone. Gene hated to hear him like that. "In my opinion, a lot of what you said was right."

"But?"

"Well, you know very well. You're not just any young man. Your father is a congressman who may run for the Senate or the governorship one of these days. He doesn't need extra baggage to carry around with him."

"Grandpa, Dad just called and said not to worry about that. He wants me to write what I believe and not ask myself how it will affect him."

"Well, sure. That's Alex. He's an honest man, and he doesn't like to play politics. But sometimes the rest of us need to watch out for him a little."

Gene wasn't sure what that meant, so he didn't respond. He pulled a chair away from the kitchen table and sat down. Emily sat across from him. Gene could see in her eyes that she was worried again—obviously afraid of what Gene might say to Grandpa. He understood that, but it would be nice if she would trust him once in a while.

"The thing is, Gene, most of what you said was all right. We don't want to protect people who've done something wrong. But let's wait and see what this Senate committee comes up with. I don't see why you want to start calling Nixon a liar until we get the whole story."

Again Gene waited. He thought of some things he could say, but he decided to keep his mouth shut.

"Why don't you write another column and follow up with a little explanation. You could just say that you don't want to protect those who've done wrong, but you don't want to convict anyone until he's proven guilty either. And maybe say that others around Nixon made mistakes, but there's no proof against the president, himself."

"Even Dad has his doubts about Nixon, Grandpa. He's admitted that to me."

"Well . . ." Grandpa was breathing hard. Gene could hear the little gusts break up his sentences and then the long pulls for air when he hesitated. "As I said, Alex has never liked party politics. He's said things about Vietnam that he would have been better off avoiding."

"But Grandpa, we know now that Nixon lied about Vietnam—the same as Johnson. He was bombing Cambodia and Laos right while he was saying that he wouldn't do that."

"Gene . . ." Grandpa took a longer breath. "In time of war, a president has to be allowed some latitude. He has to consider matters of national security."

"It's one thing to hold back information to protect the troops, Grandpa, and it's a completely different thing to say one thing and do another."

For a time, Gene thought Grandpa wasn't going to respond, but his breath was still heavy, and Gene waited. "Gene, you can't keep thinking about politics like a naïve kid," Grandpa finally said. "There are all kinds of reasons politicians say what they say—and truth is not the only priority in certain situations. Read a little history. Roosevelt surely didn't tell people everything during World War II."

"Grandpa, if we say that, we're just—"

"Now wait just a minute." Gene did wait. "All I'm asking you to do is write another article. Say you've had a big reaction. You didn't think so many people would read what you wrote. You've thought things over. You'll wait till the facts are in. You know—just try to smooth over this fuss."

"I've already written my column for next week, Grandpa, and I've got some things in mind after that. Dad said to write my honest opinions, and that's what I'm going to do."

"All right, Gene. You do what you want. You used to think I knew a thing or two. But not anymore. Since you came back from the war, you've made up your mind that you have *all* the answers. But you might consider your family. This is embarrassing for the rest of us."

Gene was gripping the phone hard now, and he was staring at Emily, who was shaking her head, obviously afraid of what he might say next. Gene was as mad at her as he was at his grandpa when he said, "Well, thanks for your nice call, Grandpa. I appreciate your opinion." He stood up.

"I don't need your sarcasm, Gene. I think I deserve a little more—"

"Grandpa, I'm late. I'm sorry, but I've really got to go. I'll talk to you again later." He hung up the phone.

Emily was cringing, but Gene figured he could have done a lot worse. He had come within a breath of shouting into the telephone, of telling Grandpa he was sick of the control he tried to put on the family. But he hadn't done it. He had stopped himself. He felt his stomach churning, his hands shaking, but he hadn't let the lid blow off. He stepped to Emily as she stood up from the kitchen table and in the most controlled voice he could manage, said, "Good-bye, honey." He gave her a kiss, then added, "Go ahead and take the phone off the hook."

"I might do that," she said.

She was trying to sound relaxed, but he could sense that she was still upset with him. There were things he wanted to say to her, but he wasn't going to let himself blow up. He was going to get through this. He walked toward the front closet. He was going to grab his jacket and go, not say another word.

"I thought you were going to change your shirt."

Gene stopped, swung around. He wanted to shout, but he didn't. "Emily, this shirt is fine. I'll keep my mouth shut. I won't embarrass you or Grandpa—or my honored Thomas name. I'll be a good soldier. But you can't keep talking to me like I'm an idiot. I can figure a few things out for myself."

"I don't think you're an idiot. You said you were going to change your shirt. I thought you'd forgotten."

Her face was white. She was gripping her hands together. And Gene knew why. She always expected the worst from him. She had made up her mind he was a keg of dynamite, just waiting to explode, but all that did to him was light the fuse. "Emily, just think what I *could* have said to Grandpa. Give me a little credit."

"I didn't say anything about that."

"Oh, but I know what you were thinking."

"Gene, don't do this. I have a right to my opinions too."

Gene couldn't believe this. "Is that what you call an *opinion?* That I should wear a nice shirt—in case someone wants to take my picture?"

"Oh, Gene, never mind. Just go. I'm sorry I said anything at all."

"Emily, you can't keep treating me this way!" But Gene had shouted, and he knew he couldn't do that. He shut his eyes, let some air into his lungs. In a quieter voice, he said, "You tell me you believe in me, but you don't. You're just sure I'm going to mess up and *embarrass* you. First it's 'what will people in the ward think'? Then it's 'don't offend Grandpa' or 'what if someone takes my picture in an old shirt'? I'm sorry, Em, but that's just stupid. I'm trying to keep my promises to you, but you've got to give me a little more room to be myself."

Danny had shown up somewhere in the middle of all that. He was barefoot, still in his red plaid pajamas, his hair a mess. He had heard Gene shout, no doubt, and now he was clinging to his mother's legs, looking scared. Gene hated that look—the same as Emily's. Both of them expected the worst of him.

"Gene, it's okay. I'm sorry I—"

"Don't be so *careful*, Emily!" Gene yelled. "You don't have to talk like that to me." But now Danny had started to cry. And something went off in Gene. "Shut up, Danny!" he screamed. "I'm not going to hurt you. You don't have to be such a little boob all the time." But that was crazy and Gene knew it. He stopped himself, took another gulp of air, and said, "I'm sorry. Daddy's very sorry. I've got to go now. But tonight we'll play together, okay?"

But Gene wasn't surprised when Emily said, "We won't be here, Gene."

Gene's first impulse was to plead with her, but he couldn't do that anymore. "Fine," he said. "I'm tired of the threats. I'm doing the best I can, but that obviously isn't enough for the two of you. So do what you've got to do."

Gene walked out, got into his car, and drove toward the university, but his anger didn't last nearly long enough, and he wasn't halfway to campus before he knew he had ruined his life. He turned off 13th East onto a side street, stopped the car, dropped his arms onto the steering wheel, and then his head onto his arms. He broke down and began to sob. But he couldn't think of one thing he could do to reverse what had just happened.

CHAPTER 18

Kathy was getting ready to go to bed. It was only 9:30, but she was tired, and her evening had seemed long. The summer solstice was only a few days away, and twilight seemed to last forever. She had sat in her living-room chair and read Chaim Potok's *My Name is Asher Lev* all evening. She loved the book, found so many things that had been similar in her own life, but her eyes were tired, and something in Asher Lev's sense of isolation had begun to depress her. In the middle of a paragraph, her head suddenly dropped, and she knew it was time to go to bed. She was growing increasingly tired of her daily routine at work, and she had vowed many times to start graduate school that fall, but she hadn't applied. She knew that one of these days she had to find her direction in life and move ahead. But not tonight. She was going to get a good long night's sleep so she wouldn't hate getting up in the morning so much as she did most days.

She was brushing her teeth when the phone rang. She was sure it would be her mother, who called almost every night and, all too often, offered advice. Kathy thought of not answering, but then her mother would only worry and call back again later. So Kathy rinsed her mouth quickly and walked out to the kitchen. She picked up the phone and said, "Hi."

"Kathy?" It was a male voice.

"Oh, I'm sorry. I thought you were my mother."

"I guess I do sound a little like her."

Kathy's system took a jolt. "Is this Marshall?"

"I'm afraid so. I'm really embarrassed to call you. The first thing I need to do is apologize. I meant it when I told you I would call you back—whenever that was—two months ago, or something like that. It's been . . . I don't know . . . kind of a strange time in my life."

"That's okay. I'm sure you're busy. I just wanted to chat about a few things, but if you don't have time, it doesn't matter."

"No. It's not that. I do want to talk to you. In fact, I was wondering whether you happened to have any time tomorrow evening."

"Tomorrow? Well, let's see. Let me consult my appointment book. I actually do have an opening tomorrow night, since I was planning to do . . . nothing whatsoever. So I guess I can fit you in." Tomorrow was a Friday, and Kathy knew she had just admitted more than she probably should. Maybe she should have told him he would have to wait a week. But that was stupid. He probably wanted to have a good brother-sister chat before he got married, so what was the point of playing games? Kathy had heard from Grandma that Marshall was officially engaged now.

"Okay. I'll pick you up at what? Seven?"

"Sure."

"Maybe we can grab a little something to eat—and just talk for a while. I really have been wanting to see you."

Kathy wondered what was going on. Was *Lisa* away for the weekend, shopping for her honeymoon wardrobe? "Sounds good. Do you still have my address?"

"I'm not sure I have the number, but I know where you are."

What did that mean? Kathy found herself inventing a little fantasy that he drove by every day, looking longingly at her apartment but not being able to work up enough courage to knock on her door. Somehow, though, that didn't seem likely. So she gave him the number, and he said, "I know you expect me to be late, but I've turned over a new leaf. I'm not like that anymore." He laughed at himself.

Kathy doubted he had changed all that much, but she told him she would see him at seven. She hung up the phone and tried to think what could be going on. She tried to convince herself that it was nothing, but suddenly she was wide awake. She went to her closet and tried to think what she would wear. She still had the spring dress she had bought for the Saturday "date" he had broken. She wondered whether she should wear it now. At least he wasn't talking about Alta, and the weather was warm. But the dress seemed just a little too swishy—especially for "*grabbing* something to eat."

Kathy fussed with her decision for more than twenty hours, including most of the hours when she should have been asleep. And she consulted once again, by telephone, with Diane. A simple skirt and blouse—or pants—made the most sense, but Diane thought the spring dress would "knock his eyes out." Kathy told herself that this was an engaged man, a friend, and they were getting together to talk about their careers. But in the end, she couldn't resist wearing the dress. She wanted him to see her in it, partly because she had imagined herself wearing it on the date that had never happened, but also because she couldn't forget Diane telling her how men thought. If this was her only chance to see him, she might as well look her best. Of course, she saw the danger in thoughts of that kind, and she kept telling herself to relax before she acted like an idiot the whole evening. This was the guy she had written off several times in her life and recently had concluded to put out of her mind *forever*. Still, she worked for a long time on her hair, which she had been growing out a little more this spring. She found it easier now to tease some shape into it, and she decided to let her bangs swoop toward one eye, the way Diane had showed her.

Kathy had a full-length mirror on her closet door. She had spent most of her life avoiding those things, but she looked tonight, even turned around and let her skirt flow—and she did think she looked good. But then the doorbell rang—on time—and she walked to the door, suddenly feeling stiff, not swishy. And when she opened the door, Marshall was standing there in jeans, a rather faded knit shirt that wasn't even tucked in—and tennis shoes.

"Hi," he said, and she could see the surprise in his eyes.

"Oh," she said. "Maybe I should change . . . or—"

"No. You're great. Wow, you look good."

Kathy liked that, but she felt strange as she walked with him to his car. He was tall enough to allow her to stand straight, and the weather was right for the dress, but anyone looking at them would have to wonder how they ended up together. When Marshall got into the car, he said, "I got thinking that we still ought to drive up to Alta. But it gets pretty cold up there in the evening, even this time of year."

"I could go back in and—"

"No. We don't need to go up there. What I did, though, is pick up some Kentucky Fried Chicken over at Harman's—you know, to take with us. Why don't we just take it over to Liberty Park instead?"

Kathy decided not to apologize any more—and only add to her embarrassment—but she wished she had thrown on a pair of old slacks and hadn't acted so much like she was going out on a date. Clearly, he hadn't been thinking of it that way.

They drove to the park, and along the way Kathy tried to think of things to say. Marshall never minded silence, and that was probably good, but it made Kathy feel that she needed to fill the void. She had little to talk about, however, except life at the dealership, and she caught herself telling him how boring her life had been lately. She knew that would probably only convince him that she was as boring as her work, but she couldn't seem to stop herself from babbling.

At the park they found a picnic table and sat across from each other. Marshall had actually gone to more trouble than he had let on. He had a checkered tablecloth and a basket full of food to go with the chicken—a nice salad he admitted he had "tossed together," and A&W root beer in a gallon container, which he poured into two mugs. There was a small pie, too, which he said he had stopped by his "favorite bakery" to pick up. Kathy liked the idea that Marshall had a favorite bakery, and she was impressed that he would think of the mugs—always better for root beer. More than anything, she was pleased he would go to this much trouble for her. "Were you going to take all this up to Alta?" she asked him.

"I was thinking about it. But there's probably still snow up there. It was probably a bad idea."

"No, it wasn't. That was a wonderful night, that time we drove up there. It's one of my favorite memories."

"That *was* a great night," Marshall said. "But man, it was a long time ago. We were such kids."

That was true, and yet Kathy didn't know how to read what he was saying. After all, he *had* wanted to go back. Was he merely nostalgic about his "childhood"? But Kathy couldn't resist telling him how she had felt. "I thought you were the coolest guy ever born. No one I knew in high school would have done anything like that."

"I was pretty cool, wasn't I?" He laughed. "At least until Christmas. Remember when you came back from Smith and told me what a loser I was?"

"I did not."

"Actually, *loser* would have been a kinder assessment. You thought I was *mindless*. But then, maybe that's because I was."

"No, you weren't. I thought everyone was mindless in those days. Anyone who wasn't threatening to burn the world down, I considered *irrelevant*—and there was nothing worse than being irrelevant."

"And now you've returned to the fold."

Actually, Kathy didn't like that summary of her. Yes, she had come back around to her faith. But a fold was a place for sheep, and Kathy liked to think there was still some sheepdog in her—just enough to nip at a few heels when Church members became too secure in their assumptions. Besides, he sounded as though he were making fun of a long process that had not been a mere teenaged rebellion followed by a simple capitulation. Still, she thought of what Diane had told her. This was no time to start telling him that he didn't know what he was talking about.

Kathy found herself brushing her bangs away from her eye, feeling self-conscious about the way she looked—with much more makeup than usual—but Diane's advice was also spinning through her thoughts. "Marshall, I think you're the one who's kept his head through all these years. I was really impressed with the things you told me that night at the ballet. I hope you stick with your plan to be a cabinetmaker."

Kathy really meant that, but she could feel herself blushing, and maybe it was because she had made a conscious attempt to build his ego.

Marshall had set out the plates, and now he held the bucket of chicken out to her. "I'll let you choose what you want," he said.

"Is it okay if I eat it with my hands?"

"I don't know—this is a pretty nice place. The other diners might be offended. Still, I think I'm going to use my fingers—and then *lick them.*"

Kathy laughed, and then she took a thigh piece, which she decided she could handle without too much mess. At least Marshall had thought to bring plenty of napkins.

There was a family not far away—the only other "diners"—and they had already eaten. The parents were sitting on a blanket on the grass while two boys and a little girl were tossing a rubber ball around. "You throw like a *girl*, Connie," one of the boys yelled to his little sister. Kathy felt a little flash of disgust. If a girl threw awkwardly it was only because she didn't play ball as often; there was nothing inherently different about the way boys and girls threw things. She thought of saying something about that to Marshall but decided it was better to let it go—and not get off onto one of her women's rights speeches.

Marshall took a bite out of a breast piece, set it down, and then did lick his fingers, making a bit of a show of it. "Finger-lickin' good," he said. But he sounded serious when he said, "It's interesting you would say I've kept my head, Kathy. I'm glad you think that. Most people think I'm a confused mess. My parents are about to disown me, and Lisa is having second thoughts—or probably more like *twentieth* thoughts—about whether she wants to marry me."

"Really? Why?"

"You know how I've been over the years. I've changed my mind about my major a dozen times, and then when I finally did get a degree, I started talking about being a carpenter. Almost everyone I know thinks I have a screw loose."

Kathy didn't know whether she was hearing more than Marshall meant, but he seemed to be implying doubts about his marriage, and she could tell he was pleased with what she had said about him. This really did seem her chance, and somehow she wanted him to know that she still had ideas about the two of them ending up together. She thought of what Diane had told her, made a decision to touch his arm, then hesitated. "Marshall," she said, and she reached across the table and rested her hand on his forearm for a moment, but she had paused just long enough that the little move seemed mistimed. "If you ask me, too many people think there's something wrong with working with their hands. Everyone wants to do something 'professional' in order to feel good about themselves. But if you developed your own little company and trained yourself to be a fine craftsman, to me, that's beautiful. It would be a career and a service and *art*, all at the same time." This was a phrase she had thought about during the night when she was imagining this conversation, and it was a nice expression of what she believed, but her voice sounded a little too intense, as though she were romanticizing more than was natural to her.

"That's kind of how I think of it too," Marshall said. "But I think that whole idea is probably down the drain. Lisa wants me to go to law school. What she'd really like is to see me go to med school, but I didn't do well enough in organic chemistry to think seriously about that—although, that was one of my temporary career choices, way back in the beginning." He laughed at himself and looked relaxed and wonderful. He was talking about Lisa, and yet Kathy felt something in the way he kept looking at her. It was hard to believe this was only career talk.

Kathy chewed on her chicken, then wiped her fingers and lips on her napkin. She tried to think what might be the best thing to say. "Marshall, if I were you, I wouldn't listen to everyone else. I think you ought to follow your own heart. You have good instincts; you ought to trust them. Maybe the reason you've changed your mind a lot is because you've been trying to satisfy everyone else."

Kathy meant this, too. So why did it sound so sticky sweet when she said it? She hardly knew whether she was doing what Diane had told her to do or whether she was speaking for herself. She did know that she was trying to look into his eyes, on purpose, and she was also very aware that he was looking back. She had shaded her eyelids with a blue tint, the way Diane had taught her, and she hoped he liked that, hoped she hadn't overdone it.

"I don't know," Marshall said. "I like working with wood, but I'm not sure I'm improving my skills as much as I expected. Maybe I don't have the knack for it. My dad's always been a smart businessman, so maybe I have the right makeup for that—even though I've never thought so. If I got an MBA or a law degree I could maybe go into some kind of business with him."

"Is that what your dad wants you to do?"

Marshall thought about that. "Not exactly. He's a little more like me. He's always tried something, done it for a while, and then moved on. He could have been rich a few times, but he sold out too soon and someone else made the money off his idea. But he has no regrets. He likes developing a business more than running it."

"Couldn't you do that with a cabinet shop? Why not try it, if it's your dream, and see whether it works out or not?" She wanted him to know that she wasn't like Lisa—always second-guessing him. Kathy liked that he was willing to experiment, stay open to possibilities, and he needed to know that. She leaned forward and tried to express her confidence in him with her eyes as much as with her voice.

"I don't know if cabinetmaking is my *dream*—you know, like a kid who starts out in life wanting to be a major-league baseball player or something like that. The idea just appeals to me. But it's not just the work; it's the whole concept of living in a small town where I could get involved in the community. I'd be out there meeting the people I built cabinets for, and I'd see my work in people's houses. I don't know, maybe I'm overly idealizing all that; that's what I tend to do."

This time the arm touch felt almost natural, but Kathy saw him glance at her in surprise, as though he wondered what she was up to, and that made her decide she wouldn't try it again. But she did say what she thought. "In the Philippines, I started out feeling really superior to the people. I was supposed to be there to teach them a better way of living. But once I found out they had as much to teach me as I had to teach them, everything changed. We all started working together to make the little barrio a better place. I think that could happen with you." She had come so close to saying "us" that it scared her. She had to calm down. "Once you knew people, and felt close to them, you could serve on the city council or something like that, and you could be a tremendous service to everyone in town."

Marshall was nodding, thinking. "Maybe," he said. "Or they might think I'm just some outsider. In a lot of little towns, they don't consider you a 'local' until you've been there for about three generations. That's what people tell me, anyway."

"But what is it you want exactly? Isn't it the community lifestyle? It doesn't matter whether you're on the city council or not. You can work through the Church, too. In my ward in the Philippines all I did was lead the choir, but it's what they needed at the time. I became a big part of everyone's lives."

"Yeah, I guess. Or maybe I wouldn't fit in. Who knows? I think Lisa would have a really hard time if I didn't make all that much money and she found the people too—you know—'down to earth,' or whatever you want to call it."

Kathy didn't like what she was hearing about Lisa, and her memory of her wasn't good either, but the fact that Marshall was still talking about her suddenly brought Kathy back to reality. She did like to imagine the life Marshall was talking about, but it was pointless to try to talk him into it if he was doubting the idea himself. Kathy also knew she had started to sound too forceful and opinionated. "Well," she said, "you know yourself. You know what you need out of life. I feel sure you'll make the right decision."

Marshall laughed. "I don't know why you would say that. I wander through life like Hamlet, never able to kill the king and get it over with."

That was actually true, from what Kathy knew, but she loved Marshall's quandaries, the very fact that he considered lifestyle factors in his decision and didn't just pick a major and march forward. She loved the fact that he found so many things interesting, that he found it hard to settle on one thing. And she loved the way he looked, with that knit shirt showing the strength he had developed in his arms and chest this past year, and those soft eyes that seemed to be watching her so carefully.

But then he said, "The thing is, Lisa would have to like the idea as much as I do. I can't just force her to go live in some little place if she really hates the idea."

Kathy felt herself give up. This really was all about Lisa. Kathy had only been seeing things in Marshall's eyes that she wanted to see.

One of the little boys nearby threw the ball too high, over his sister's head. The older brother ran close to Marshall and picked it up. "Connie, I'm not going to let you play anymore," he yelled. "You can't catch."

The boy was apparently tired of running after the ball, but his attitude bothered Kathy. "The little brat," she said. "He's such a little sexist."

"What?"

"Didn't you hear him before? He was telling her that she threw the ball like a girl."

"Actually, she does."

Kathy couldn't believe Marshall would say that. Suddenly she wasn't so enthusiastic about him after all. Maybe Lisa was welcome to him. "There's no *girl* way of throwing a ball," Kathy said. "She just doesn't know how. He ought to teach her."

Marshall was grinning, and Kathy wasn't sure why. "He *was* trying to a little while ago. But she won't pull her arm back right. She tries to push it—like a shot put."

"And that's a girl's way?"

"Yeah. It sure seems like it." He was still smiling. "I think boys get the knack of that kind of stuff a lot easier."

"Of course. Their fathers are always out there working with them. They . . ." But she wasn't going to do this. She wasn't going to remember that the last time she was with Marshall she had gotten into another argument with him. "Well . . . I don't know. Maybe there is something built into the sexes. Not many boys want to play with dolls."

But now Marshall was looking surprised. He shook his head and laughed, and then he said, "You're really going to let me get away with that?"

"With what?"

"Oh, nothing."

"Come on, tell me. I think you're laughing at me, and I want to know why."

"You've got to admit, you've been a little strange tonight."

"Strange? What are you talking about?"

"I've never seen you back away like that—especially when you know darn well I'm wrong."

Kathy wasn't sure what he was saying. Hadn't he meant what he had said? But she didn't want to admit what she had been doing. "I just get too defensive about gender issues sometimes," she said. "I think that comes from my years at Smith. But boys and girls are different in some ways, right from the beginning. I think you're right about that."

"So I'm right and you're wrong. Is that what you're telling me?"

She laughed. "Marshall, I'm not the Kathy you remember. I can admit when I'm wrong, and I don't get mad about everything the way I used to. I always liked the way you would listen and not be so absolute in your opinions. I admire you for that. You're smart, but you don't always think you have the last word on a subject. I want to be more like that."

He was staring at her now, looking dubious. "Or maybe you're trying to change yourself and struggling a little to do it."

"I think you're right about that, too."

"Hey, you forgot to touch my arm when you said that."

Kathy felt as though Marshall had just stuck a giant needle in her chest. The air was all leaking out of her, and she hoped she ended up in a heap under the table. At least she wouldn't have to look at him. He seemed amused more than put out, but that only made things worse. He really was laughing at her—and Kathy didn't blame him.

"I think I read somewhere that boys *will* play with dolls if they're given the option," Marshall said. "At least until they get old enough that other boys start to tease them about it."

Kathy nodded. "I know. I've read that, too." She couldn't look at him now. She just wanted him to take her home.

"Then why did you tell me that boys don't like to play with dolls?"

"I don't know. I'm just trying not to argue as much as I used to."

"We're not arguing. Just tell me what you think."

She had no idea what Marshall was trying to do. But he still seemed to be making fun of her. So she looked him straight on and said, with a little heat in her voice, "All right. I will. I think there's way too much testosterone pumping through men's bodies. It makes them aggressive and causes little boys to talk to their sisters like that boy was just doing. And little girls take too much of that kind of stuff without fighting back— because they always feel they have to be peacemakers. Men, for the most part, run this world, and they're making a mess of it. I think it's time to elect more women as leaders and see whether *Mother Earth* won't be a better place."

"But women are way too emotional. No woman would make a good president." He crossed his arms over his chest and tried to look resolute, but the smile was in his eyes.

"You know that's baloney. Men hide under a mask of rationality when they're actually motivated by ego and greed more often than not. Women have proven that they care about communication and cooperation more than most men ever do. I think you could make a case that the sexes aren't equal at all. Women have more stamina. They live longer, can deal better with hardships, and nurture more selflessly than men. If there's anything this world needs it's more nurturing and less *grappling*."

"Then why is it that in literally every field of endeavor, men are known for being the best? And it's not just in physical activities. Look at science, art, literature, even cooking—the great ones are almost always men."

That little smile had never left his face. She was pretty sure he was putting her on. But she hated his argument; she had heard it put forward seriously. "That's such a crock. Little girls get pushed out of virtually any field before they get a chance to show what they can do. It's only been in recent years that women have even been allowed to compete with men, and they're doing very well. Give us another generation or two and then get ready to eat our dust."

Now Marshall was laughing out loud. "I've got a feeling you might be right," he said.

"Oh, sure."

"I mean it. But if you're going to make me eat your dust, how come you're working at a job you hate and wondering what you're going to do with your life? You've got to get moving."

"I know that." But she had no idea where this conversation was going or even where it had been. Marshall was playing games with her, she knew, but she couldn't see what his point was. This whole thing had been so humiliating. She had dressed wrong, made herself up too much, and he had seen right through her little arm touches. She already knew she was going to remember this night the rest of her life—and cringe every time she did.

"Kathy, let me tell you a couple of things," Marshall said.

"Okay. Go right ahead."

"Do you want some more chicken, or—"

"No." She was looking at the checkered tablecloth, not at Marshall.

"I think you're a great-looking woman. In fact, I think you're beautiful."

Kathy wished that she didn't like hearing this. It was insulting to bring up something like that right now. Was this his reply to their gender dispute? She looked up at him and tried to show her disdain for whatever it was he was trying to do now.

"I think you should dress however you feel comfortable. And I've always liked that you keep your hair really simple and don't wear a lot of makeup."

"Thanks for the advice," Kathy said. "I'll be sure to remember. And I certainly won't touch your arm again."

"I don't care if you touch my arm. Just don't think about it when you do."

Kathy nodded. "All right. I'll remember that, too. Would you mind taking me home now?"

"You know what I've always liked best about you?"

Kathy didn't answer. She didn't even look at him.

"You've always taken me on when I said something stupid, and because of that I've ended up rethinking things I thought I was sure about. You're the only woman I know who's like that. Lisa gets what she wants from me, but she does it by using her 'feminine wiles,' or whatever that's called. But you say what you think, and you don't try to manipulate me. I'm glad you're softening your opinions, because you used to make me feel so stupid, but I want to spend my life with a woman who *thinks*—and challenges me to think."

Now she looked at him, and he looked back at her for a long time. He wasn't smiling. He seemed to be taking in her face, as though he were the one touching her now. Clearly, he knew what he had just said, and she did too, but she was having trouble switching gears.

"I'm having a lot of doubts about my relationship with Lisa, as you can tell. So I've got to decide, soon, what I'm going to do."

Kathy nodded.

"Do you want some more chicken?"

"Uhhh . . . yeah. I think I do."

"And some pie?"

"Yes."

But he didn't pass the chicken. "Kathy, I shouldn't have done this. I should have made up my mind about Lisa, once and for all—you know, before I called you."

"Well . . . maybe. But I was the one who called you first, and I knew you were planning to get married."

"But I feel like I'm going to hurt someone, either way, and I don't want to do that."

"I took a chance, Marshall. I called you even though I knew I shouldn't. So I guess I opened myself up for some hurt."

She wanted him to offer just a little hope, but he sat quietly for a time, and then he reached across the table and touched her arm. She loved that, even if it was just a joke.

"Kathy, I'll call you," he said. "I feel like I've got to straighten out a few things in my life, and then we need to talk again."

"I'd like that," Kathy said, but she was still wondering what he had meant—that he was going to hurt someone. She didn't want to be hurt again.

CHAPTER 19

Hans knew what he had to do. It was June now, and he had let too many months slip by while he had held out hope that somehow his situation would change. It was difficult to resist hope when Elli was writing so positively. But nothing was getting better, and there was no reason to believe that it ever would. He had told himself for a long time that Elli was young, but the fact was, she would be twenty-two in the fall. She had reached an age when she needed to have a chance to develop a relationship with another young man in the Church. Most young members in the GDR knew her, but for a long time she had been "spoken for," and Hans realized that she needed to be known as a prospect again.

Hans had continued to serve in the branch presidency, and gradually he had let go of the bitterness he had felt for a time. He was not a child any longer, and it was pointless to throw a tantrum because he wasn't getting from God what he wanted. He told the Lord every day now that he would accept whatever came into his life, and he would prove his own commitment and strength. The Lord had once whispered to Hans that he should stay in the GDR, and so he had stayed. But it was Hans who reached the conclusion that he had been meant to marry Elli, and now it appeared that he had been wrong about that. The strongest people Hans knew had given up something significant in their lives, and that test had often proven their making. He couldn't predict what life would bring him, but poverty was most likely, and he knew he could accept that. The important thing now was that he couldn't ruin Elli's life while he was clinging to his own notion of what he wanted from God.

So Hans made the trip to Magdeburg on a pretty Saturday evening, and he sat with Elli in a little garden area in the *Hof* behind her apartment building. "I know why you've come," she said. "It's why you always come to see me."

"That's not true. Once I came to ask you to marry me."

"And then you didn't do it."

Elli could be frustrating at times. She had never had to pay rent or buy groceries. She had always lived at home. When he tried to talk practicalities with her, she simply refused to listen. "But you know why we didn't get married."

"We could have gotten by. If we had shown more faith, the Lord would have helped us."

Hans hated this. They had repeated these same words to each other many times. He wasn't going to go over the numbers again: the failure of their combined incomes to measure up against the costs of merely renting and eating. So he said, "I can't do this to you any longer, Elli. I spoke to my boss this week, and he told me what I've known all along. He has an order to keep me at the lowest pay scale. He told me that Herr Feist, the *Stasi* agent, has been specific about those instructions. Nothing is going to change."

"But why?"

"You know why."

"Rainer has been saying things about you."

Since Rainer had entered prison, Hans had only had two letters from him. Both were brief and almost without content. They seemed a way of saying that he wanted to retain a friendship, but Hans didn't know what else to read into them. They could be invitations for Hans to write—and to make a mistake by saying something Feist could use, or they could be subtle warnings: *Don't say anything and I won't either.* Hans had written to Rainer several times, however, and had spoken openly about his life. He had nothing to hide and nothing to gain, really. He was weary of the games the *Stasi* played, and he wasn't about to calculate his words for the sake of some censor who might report him to Feist.

"Elli, it probably doesn't matter what Rainer says about me," Hans said. "If Feist wants me in prison, he could put me there any time he likes. I suspect Feist knows that he's hurting me most by allowing me to do worthwhile work—at least work that needs to be done—and paying me almost nothing for it. He knows I want to marry. This is his way of making it impossible. He probably hopes that I'll try to escape the country so he can put me away forever."

"It's what we should do. I've thought a lot about that lately. No one should have to live here. The Lord would help us get away if we tried."

"That's what I thought once—and it's led to all the problems I have now."

She had been sitting stiff, not touching him, but she turned now and took hold of his hand. "Hans, you keep saying that things can't get any worse. So why don't we take a chance? Maybe we *could* escape, and we could go to Salt Lake City, where your aunt is."

"No, Elli. I can deal with prison, but I would never forgive myself if *you* would end up there."

Elli let go of Hans's hand and crossed her arms. "I am in prison. What difference does it make?"

Birds in the courtyard were setting up an evening chant, and a remnant of light from the setting sun was glowing in the air, the clouds turning pink. But there was nothing growing in the flowerbeds, and the shrubs along the walkway had turned to skeletons. Nothing had been cared for, nothing watered. Hans watched Elli. Her skin was lovely in the radiant light, but her eyes were as dead as everything else out here. He had never heard such cynicism from her. "I know everything seems terrible right now, Elli, but that's only because you keep hoping that something can work out between the two of us. As soon as I release you from your promise, you can let others know that you're willing to start a new friendship.

There must be twenty young men in the GDR who are good Mormons
and who would be eager to marry you."

"So it's that easy for you to take back a promise, is it?"

"You know it isn't easy for me, Elli. It feels almost impossible, but I've
dragged everything out much too long. I've been telling you this whole
last year that we had to stop fooling ourselves."

"I won't take back my promise. I refuse to let you set me aside that
way. We could get married tomorrow if you loved me enough. We would
find a way to manage."

Hans had never been angry with Elli, but he was close to it now. It
was one thing to be hopeful, but Elli was acting like a child. A couple
couldn't "manage" without enough food to eat. They could perhaps move
into his tiny apartment, and perhaps get by for a time. But how could they
start a family? In all likelihood, Feist would continue to do everything he
could to make things miserable for the two of them. Elli's income was a
little higher than Hans's, and she could make a similar amount in Leipzig,
but Feist could certainly see to it that she never made any more.

"Elli, this is pointless. I'm going to catch the late train back to Leipzig.
I've never wanted to hurt you, but I don't know any other way to do this.
Someday, when you have a good husband and a nice family, you'll thank
me."

"No, I won't. I won't marry. I've not only promised you; I've promised
the Lord. In my mind we're married. If we'll do our best, things will get
better."

Hans stood. "This is nonsense, and you know it, Elli. I'm leaving, and
you won't be hearing from me again."

He kept watching her, but she wouldn't look at him. So he got up and
walked to the gate by the side of the building before he looked back. He
stood there for a time, aching, wishing that he didn't have to hurt her so
much, but then he said, "I'm sorry, Elli. This is terrible for me, too. But it
has to be this way. Good-bye."

She didn't look up. She didn't move. She didn't cry.

Hans walked away. His train ride back to Leipzig late that night was unthinkably miserable, but he was relieved. At least he no longer had to blame himself for ruining Elli's life. She would be crushed for a time, and maybe angry, but she would finally decide that Hans was right. Hans could go about his quiet life without the encumbrance of all the worry he had known these past few years. He had hit bottom. Feist could throw him into prison, but that mattered little at this point.

On Sunday Hans told President Schräder that he had broken his engagement with Elli, that there was no chance for the two to marry. "I know your patience has worn thin," President Schräder told him, but I wouldn't give up just yet. I still believe the Lord has great things in store for you. He wants you to marry and raise a family; he'll open a way."

Hans found this kind of logic maddening. It was what Hans heard from his parents, from Elli, even from Elli's parents. Certainly it did seem that the Lord would want the two of them together, but that was like saying that the Lord wanted missionaries to bring new members to the Church; that didn't mean that people would choose to come. In the GDR very few dared to be baptized even if they came to believe in the Church. Surely the Lord wanted his kingdom to move forward in this part of the world, so it was only logical that the Lord would want a different kind of government to take hold. That made sense, too. But it wasn't happening, and there was no indication that it ever would. The Lord had his own timetable, and Hans could accept that, but he didn't want to hear from everyone that he ought to ignore reality and make decisions based on their notions of what the Lord supposedly wanted.

On Monday Hans went back to work, and he put in a dismal but simple week. He thought of little else but Elli's unhappiness and how much he had hurt her, but he still preferred to think that he had finally done what he should have done long ago. He prayed a great deal that week, but never for things to change. He had asked for that too many times and nothing had happened. He only prayed now that he could accept his life the way it was and that Elli could be happy, in time. But he felt the loss of her. She had been part of him for a long time now, even though they had rarely been able to see each other. He was relieved that she didn't write to him, and at the same time, he was devastated each night when he came home to find no letter in his mailbox.

On Thursday, at work, when he came back from his lunch break, a note was sitting on his desk. It was written in his boss's familiar handwriting: "Herr Feist wishes you to visit him at 15:00 in his office at *Stasi* headquarters."

Hans was terrified of hope right now. The thought occurred to him that the Lord had seen his trials and was about to change something, open that door that Elli always talked about. But he knew better. People were not called to the "*Runde Ecke*," the *Stasi* headquarters, in order to receive good news. The great white building known as the "rounded corner" was one that East Germans were reluctant to approach. When an agent wanted to frighten and intimidate a citizen, he demanded that the person step into the atmosphere of all that power and authority.

So Hans steeled himself. He assumed the worst and also assumed that he could and would handle it. Back in his prison days, when Hans had thought he had reached bottom, something would happen and he would discover that there were new levels of hell in the GDR, and each time he had had to reassess his own strength. But it was hard to think that Feist had anything worse than prison in store for him now. What was worse?

So Hans worked for an hour and then checked out of his office and took the *Strassenbahn* to *Dittrichring*, a street in the center of the city near the famous old church, the *Thomaskirche*. He walked up the heavy stone steps and faced a guard with a machine gun and a fierce-looking German shepherd leashed nearby. The guard checked Hans's papers and allowed him to step inside, where he faced a long counter and three sullen bureaucrats who sat behind separate desks. "I'm to see Herr Feist at three o'clock," he told an older man who glanced up at him.

The man at the desk twisted to look at a plain, round clock on the wall. Hans was six minutes early. "Sit there," the man said, and nothing more.

So Hans sat in one of several chairs lined up against the wall. They were straight chairs, hard and stiff, certainly chosen for a purpose. Hans was left there to wait and think for nearly half an hour. He was more frightened than he wanted to be, and he hated that. It meant that Feist was winning. Finally the man Hans had spoken to before got up and came to the counter. "Herr Feist will see you now," he said. "Wait until his assistant comes for you."

Hans stood and waited, and in a minute or two a young man, sleek as a race dog, walked down the hall. "Stoltz?" he asked, and Hans nodded.

The young man merely turned and walked away. Hans followed down a narrow hallway, past lots of doors. He saw into a number of small offices with desks and lots of file cabinets in each. Feist's office, as it turned out, was only slightly larger, but equally cramped. He looked up from some paperwork on his desk and said, "*Ach*, Stoltz. Yes. Step in. Have a seat." But he didn't get up and didn't offer to shake hands. He returned to the papers in front of him and read for some time.

"I have a report here, from the prison," he finally said. He continued to look at the papers, not at Hans. "It concerns you."

Hans nodded.

Feist looked up. He pushed a lock of hair off his forehead. "It appears very bad for you, actually. Rainer Kuntze has decided to tell what he knows. He tells us now that you were in league with him. Both of you were planning to attempt an escape, and you were trying to obtain false identification papers. That's why he came to see you here in Leipzig. He's been telling us a little more about you from time to time—but he finally broke down and told the whole truth."

Hans merely stared at Feist. Rainer might have made claims of that kind. Hans didn't know. But this was likely another game. Otherwise, why hadn't Feist sent someone to his home or his office to arrest him? Why had he merely called him here?

"So what do you say for yourself?"

"I say it's not true, of course. But what difference does it make what I say? You will surely believe what you choose."

"This is the wrong approach, Stoltz. I've seen too much of this from you."

Hans stared at the man defiantly. He had been through these things too many times.

"Are you saying that Kuntze has lied about you?"

"That's one possibility. I only know that I did not seek false papers and I had no plans to escape the GDR."

"And I should accept that, merely on your word?" He had a way of expanding his chest and raising his chin when he spoke, his arrogance showing itself as much in his posture as in the condescending tone of his voice. But that voice was not as strong as usual today, and Hans wondered why. He sounded almost weary, and the stacks of files on his desk might have been the reason.

"Herr Feist, I had a chance to leave this country legally and I turned it down," Hans said. "You know that. Why would I, after that, put my life in danger to attempt an escape?"

"I've asked this question myself. I suspect that you came to regret your decision. People do change their minds."

"If that's what you think, why do you bother to call me here? You could have arrested me, if you had chosen, but I think you know very well that I'm not a problem for our government."

Feist's neck arched backward again. With greater force, he said, "Stoltz, do not attempt to tell me what I know. I deal with liars every day. You are no better, no worse, than most of them."

Suddenly Hans had had enough. "Herr Feist, put me in prison if that's what you want. I can live with that again if I have to. But don't call me a liar, and don't ask me questions if you won't listen to my answers."

"Be careful, young man. You are on the very doorstep of that prison, and another statement like that will put you inside."

"You've kept me at that doorstep since the day I got out. I've done nothing but good work for this country, and I've never caused anyone a moment's trouble. But you won't settle for that. You take too much pleasure in harassing me."

Surprisingly, Herr Feist laughed. "Is that what you think, Herr Stoltz? That I have time to worry about someone as insignificant as you? My government provides me with a list of suspicious people in our district—'Negative Hostile Elements' we call them—and I must account for them continually. It's not a pleasure for me to deal with your type—the ones who hate socialism and will do nothing to support the purposes of our government."

Hans didn't respond. He did indeed hate what socialism had done to the GDR, but Feist knew very well he was no danger to the government.

"You don't deny this, do you—that you hate our democratic socialist government?"

Hans was beyond calculating what he should or shouldn't say. "This is what I hate," he said. "A system that only stays in power by instilling fear in its people. I could make a fine argument for socialism. I've learned all about that in school. It's intended to raise up working people and end class systems. I can admire the optimism and goodwill of a philosophy of that kind. But in practice our government creates its own caste system. It walls in its people, denies us a voice, and then uses people like you to watch everything we do. There's no reason for me to be on your list of—"

"Stoltz, you must know this is very unwise, what you are saying to me. Every word will go in your record."

Hans heard something like concern, and he almost believed it, but he didn't care. He was tired of saying what people wanted him to say. "I'm on your list of possible troublemakers, and so you have to keep me on edge, worry me constantly, and hang threats over my head. What kind of motivation is that for me to love our system? The GDR is a nation of frightened people, willing to go along because they dare do nothing else, but it's not a nation of people devoted to the socialist cause, and it never will be so long as people like you keep everyone in fear."

"You are a traitor, Stoltz. I see it in everything you do and say."

"Of course you do. That's because individual thought is not allowed here. But that's exactly why this nation will never grow stronger. Not many dare say it, but no one is really happy here. The truth is, you aren't either. You know what you do is wrong."

Feist smiled, looked superior. "Stoltz, you're making this far too easy for me. You've not only dug your grave, you've jumped in and handed me a shovel to cover you with."

Hans didn't respond for the moment. He felt free, and he let his own chest expand, but behind his confidence was a recognition that Feist was right. He could end up in prison the rest of his life—in miserable work camps or in solitary confinement. Some of his initial fire was dwindling. Still, inertia carried him forward, or maybe it was the assumption that his fate was already set. "Now I've committed the ultimate crime. I've told you what I actually think. You can't allow that."

Feist broke into a bigger smile. "Not at all. Tell me anything you like. I've asked you to tell me the truth for many months now, and you only tell lies. I would say your government has been patient with you, allowing you to walk our streets with so much stored-up hatred waiting to break out."

Hans ran his hand up his forearm until he gripped his elbow, and then he pulled his arms in close. He sat that way for some time, and he told himself not to say anything more. But he was too tired, and his hope was gone. He had lied about his feelings before, and he didn't want to do that again. He wanted, just once in his life, to speak the whole truth to a man like this. "Herr Feist," he said, "I roomed with Rainer at the university, and we became friends. I knew he believed in our government, but I trusted him and told him I had been followed by a *Stasi* agent, and then I told him why—that I had tried to help a friend escape through a tunnel under the wall in Berlin. I told him the truth, that my friend had been killed. It was a relief to talk about that with Rainer, just to be honest with one person. We vowed to trust each other and not say anything to anyone else. But that was a terrible mistake for both of us. Our system depends on individuals never showing loyalty to each other, but only to the state itself."

"Loyalty to the state *is* loyalty to all. When all of us work for the common good, only then can we all prosper. This misplaced loyalty to Kuntze was the beginning of rebellion, and look where it has brought you."

"You say the words, Herr Feist, as though they're memorized from a textbook, but I think you know they're absurd. This country will explode someday, and it's because we're all tired of that kind of rhetoric. I don't believe it and you don't believe it. Do you really think anyone does?"

"Now you've made a threat, Stoltz—to blow up this country. You can prepare yourself for a life in prison, not a short sentence this time."

"Tell me what I've done wrong. I tried to help my friend escape, and I knew I was acting against the law. But I was caught, and I paid for what I did. I spent my time in prison. Since then I've been a perfect citizen. Why can't you be satisfied with that? Do you have to prove your theory—that I'm still dangerous to the state? You spend all your time doing nothing but breaking people's spirits. Explain to me how we can ever become a great nation with that kind of repression."

"What do you want? The kind of free will we see in America, where there's so much crime and racial hatred? This government asks something more of its people."

"You asked me to be a good draftsman, and I've done that. You won't allow me to continue my education, and I've accepted that. I've gone to work every day, not loving our system, but willing to do my job to the best of my ability. Each of my supervisors has praised my work. In fact, I think those men have kept me from prison—because my work is needed and I do it well. You've done everything you can, even tried to use Rainer to trap me into saying the wrong things. It's all because you fear I'm not quite subservient to your power. I'm sick of all that. Put me in prison and lose a productive worker if that's what you want, but you'll never control my mind."

Hans was surprised to see the look that had come over Feist. It was the first time Hans had ever seen a crack in his exterior, as though Hans's words had struck too close to home.

So Hans decided to say one more thing before he was taken off to prison. "Someday the wall will come down, Herr Feist—the wall and all the fences. And then you'll have no protection. I'm sure you hate what you do, but how will you explain it then? Can you even imagine how much you'll be hated by the people you've made so miserable? I'd much rather live with myself and the mistakes I've made than to live with *your* conscience."

Feist raised his chin, tried to get back that arrogant manner, but it wasn't there. He smiled a little and mumbled, "You must see yourself as much more important than you truly are. I haven't worried about you. You've done your work like a good boy. It was only Rainer who decided he had had enough. He broke, as you must have known he would. He told his interrogators that you and he had planned a major escape, and you were the mastermind behind the plan."

Hans didn't understand what Feist was trying to say. "But you know he's lying, don't you? Either that, or you're lying, and he never said such a thing. I *did not* try to obtain false papers. What I want to do is stay in this country. I want to get married, but I can't, because I can't afford to. I don't like the way this country operates, but it has no reason to fear me. I'll do

----- *294* -----

my work if I'm allowed to do it, and I'll never try to escape—or help any-one else to escape."

Feist was looking nervous, fidgeting, his eyes no longer locked on Hans the way they had been. "I've heard enough. I'll do you a favor and not ask you any more questions. I will report what you have said to my superiors, and they will decide what to do."

"What I said just now—or everything we've talked about?"

"They will have a full report, I assure you." But he still wasn't looking Hans straight on. "Leave now, Herr Stoltz. You will hear from us soon."

"Leave?"

"Yes. You heard me."

At least Hans would be allowed to go outside one more time. So he got up and walked out into the air, and he walked all the way home. When he got there, he thought of writing to his parents and to Elli, to tell them he loved them and might not be able to write to them for some time again, but he wasn't sure of anything right now. He had seen Feist lose his confidence, but a man like that might respond with furor, once his pride returned. So Hans didn't write to anyone. Instead, he picked up his Book of Mormon and read the story of Ammon, who had been thrown into prison and used his time well.

When morning came, nothing happened. Hans thought of walking all day, of enjoying one more day outside, but his instinct told him that he should go to work and not give anyone a reason to accuse him of slack-ing off. So he left early, and he walked to his office, and he put in more than an hour before Herr Meier arrived. Not long after entering his office, Herr Meier stepped back out. "Hans," he said, "I don't know when our government officials will make up their minds. I received a telephone call just now. You're to return to the office where you were working before you were sent back here. I hate to see you go, but it's good for you. You'll go back to the salary you were receiving there."

This could be another game. Hans didn't want to trust this. But then he felt something in his chest, warm and engulfing, confirming. He gathered up his things, and he took a streetcar to his other place of work, and along the way, the feeling kept enlarging itself, filling him up. Before he went to the office, he stopped and sent a telegram to Elli. "You were right. A door appears to be opening after all. I love you. I will write soon."

It was a very strange day. Hans wanted more than anything to catch a train to Magdeburg, but he couldn't do it. He had no time he could take off, not after his last trip there, and he had no money until he actually saw that his salary had increased. But he walked home that night, wrote to Elli, told her what all this could mean, and then he worked another day and did his best to concentrate. Three days later, on Saturday, when he returned to his apartment, Elli was waiting outside his building. "We need to talk," she said, smiling and crying. "I wanted to see you, and I didn't know when you could come to me."

He took her in his arms. "I think things are going to be better now," he told her. "My boss has made new promises to me. He feels confident about it."

"Let's get married now."

"Not quite yet. We need to make some arrangements."

"No. Let's just get married. We can live in your little apartment until we can get something else."

"But there's hardly room."

"Then we'll have to squeeze together, very close," she said, and she tightened her grip on him.

CHAPTER 20

G
ene was sitting in the Old Senate Building, Room 318, where the televised Watergate hearings were about to start for the day. He had been writing about the hearings almost daily since they had started on May 17, first for the *Daily Utah Chronicle*, the student newspaper at the university, and then, by invitation, for *The Salt Lake Tribune*. Gene knew that the *Trib* was trading on his connection to Washington, through his father, or he would never have been offered the opportunity, but he had written strong articles and was already becoming respected for his research and balanced analysis. It was true that Alex had been able to use his influence as a Congressman to get Gene a press pass for a couple of days, but Gene felt he had earned that right by having gotten out in front of the story, informing his readers how important the Watergate scandal was long before other writers in Utah had taken much interest.

This was an opportunity of a lifetime, but right now it meant nothing to Gene. He was going through the motions, trying to continue with his life, but for almost a month he had been living alone in his parents' big house. He talked to Emily on the telephone once in a while, and he kept telling her that he was doing better, that her leaving had opened his eyes, but Emily was dubious. She had told him recently that she hadn't known how on-edge she had been until she had spent this time away from him. She loved him, but she couldn't take the strain of worrying every minute that he was about to lose his temper again. Danny, she said, asked about his daddy all the time, but he also seemed more at ease now that he was with his grandparents, who showed him so much love. What could

Gene say? If he argued, he proved she was right, and if he accepted that she and Danny really were better off, he was giving away everything that mattered to him. And so he was trying to go on with his life, prove that he was making headway, but the fact was, he was not doing well at all. Nights alone were terrifying to him, and his busy but empty days were only driving him deeper into depression. But worst was the rage that sometimes welled up in him when he thought of the young man he had been, and what the war had taken from him.

It was Monday, June 25, 1973, and the big news was that John Dean, who had served as presidential counsel before Nixon had fired him, was finally testifying. Dean was a bright and able young man, but he had clearly been instrumental in the Watergate cover-up. Early on, Howard Baker, one of the senators on the Select Committee, had asked the question everyone now wanted answered: "What did the president know, and when did he know it?" Rumor was, Dean knew the answer and was ready to spill everything. The buzz in the room was that the "smoking gun" everyone was looking for would be revealed today.

The hearing room was spacious and had once been grand, with high ceilings and marble-lined walls, but Gene was surprised by the chipping paint and worn-out draperies. Even more, he was disappointed by the seating arrangement. Well over three hundred people, most of them reporters and photographers, were packed into the room, the reporters seated at long, narrow tables, in rows. All of them were behind the table where John Dean and his lawyer would sit. Gene, who was seated well toward the back, realized that his seat at home in front of the TV, with the camera close up on witnesses' faces, actually gave him a better view. Still, the atmosphere was interesting to experience. Most of the reporters were jaded old pros whose manner and talk rang with cockiness and hard-shelled skepticism. He wondered whether he would become like them. If he couldn't get his life back together, he feared he might be worse.

At the front, seated at a long table, covered in green, sat the row of

seven senators, some of whom had already become well known: Sam
Ervin, the folksy chairman, seventy-six years old, a Democrat from North
Carolina; Lowell Weicker, the lanky, bulldoggish Republican from
Connecticut; Daniel Inouye, Democrat and Japanese-American war hero
from Hawaii; Howard Baker, from Tennessee, the seemingly sincere
Republican who kept telling the world he wanted nothing but the truth.
Television cameras, with bright lights, were directed toward the witness
chair, but they also obscured the view for the reporters.

Gene watched as John Dean entered the room with his pretty, blonde
wife. Dean was trim and sharp in his tan suit, and he seemed even
younger than Gene had pictured him. He looked collegiate, intelligent,
with his horn-rimmed glasses and neatly combed hair. Senator Ervin
opened the day with a few remarks in a style that the whole nation knew
by now: halting, unvarnished, deeply southern, and yet eloquent, at least
in content. From the beginning he had set the bar high. This was more
than a legal matter, he had argued; the future of democracy was at stake.
Trust in the integrity of government had to be reestablished for the
American people. Then Ervin, after discussing a few procedural matters,
announced that John W. Dean III had a statement to read. Dean, in an
unassuming voice but in precise language, began reading his testimony,
and he continued all morning. After lunch, he kept reading for most of
the rest of the day, for a total of six hours.

Many of Dean's accusations had been leaked ahead of time, so much
of what he said was no longer shocking, but he portrayed Richard Nixon
as a man who never seemed to ask what was right or wrong, only what
was expedient. He cared about his image, about political advantage, about
winning elections, but in private he was ruthless, profane, even hateful.
Nixon, according to Dean, had assembled an "enemies list" and saw himself as under siege from the people named on it. He had hired assistants
and advisors with the same bunker mentality. A group called "The
Plumbers," under the direction of Charles Colson, special counsel to the

president, had been assigned to hunt down and stop any news leaks coming from the administration and to track people on the list. G. Gordon Liddy, James W. McCord, and E. Howard Hunt, three of the arrested Watergate burglars, had been Plumbers. Dean claimed that the Watergate break-in had been only one of several illegal acts by the group. Liddy and Hunt, in 1971, had broken into the Beverly Hills office of Daniel Ellsberg's psychiatrist. Ellsberg had released the Pentagon Papers to the news media, papers that revealed the behind-the-scenes decisions that led to many government misjudgments and lies about Vietnam. Liddy and Hunt had been looking for information to discredit Ellsberg.

The Watergate break-in had, according to Dean, been part of an "excessive concern" by Nixon and his advisors, which had manifested itself in a series of "dirty tricks" against Democratic candidates, along with wiretaps and other illegal surveillance of Nixon's perceived enemies. Donald Segretti led a team that had forged letters, leaked false information to newspapers, and, in the case of Edmund Muskie, had issued materials under Muskie's name that they had actually written themselves.

As Gene heard all of this, he felt justified in what he had been writing in his column. He wanted the truth to come out, whatever it was, but it was hard not to hope that Nixon would finally be shown for what Gene believed he was. Still, when Dean told about the president agreeing to pay "hush money" to the Watergate burglars, Gene found himself feeling sick. Dean had told President Nixon that the burglars were demanding money, and the president had merely asked how much they wanted. When Dean had responded that it might cost a million dollars to satisfy them, Nixon had told Dean that the figure was "not a problem." McCord had previously revealed that he had been paid to keep quiet, so in one sense Dean's revelation was nothing new, but it was disheartening to think of the president of the United States, sitting in his office, agreeing to commit a crime.

Gene knew he should be writing everything down, and he heard pens and pencils scratching all around him, but Dean's matter-of-fact account of the conversation about hush money had stopped him. He looked around the room. He didn't sense any great shock, but he had the feeling that the world had just changed. Nixon could deny all this, and surely would, and maybe it would always be Dean's word against Nixon's, but there was something in Dean's confidence, his detail, his specific quotes, that was hard to imagine as perjury. This wasn't the "smoking gun"; it was testimony that couldn't be proved. But Gene had sensed a change across the country lately. People were giving up on their president. Worse, there was a cynicism spreading that Gene had never felt before, as though no one trusted anyone anymore. All those lofty speeches that politicians made, that Nixon had made, now seemed empty lies.

The gap between the public and private Nixon struck with full irony when Dean reminded the audience that on August 29, 1972, the president had announced to the country that Dean himself had done careful research and reported that no one in the White House had been involved in the break-in. But Dean said the statement had been a lie, a complete fabrication. Dean had actually done no such research and filed no such report. The truth, Dean said, was that Nixon had begun to discuss ways to contain the scandal caused by Watergate within a few days after the burglars had been arrested. Nixon's claim, announced again recently, was that he had known nothing of a cover-up until March of 1973, but according to Dean, that was another lie. Nixon had actually done everything he could to avoid revealing information that could hurt his administration, including asking the CIA to help subvert the investigation being done by the FBI. Gene kept thinking of all those times President Nixon had appeared on television and told the nation he was doing everything he could to get to the bottom of the scandal and purge anyone who had been involved. All those statements had been lies.

Gene felt sure that most people would believe Dean's testimony. It simply rang true. Nixon had been digging his own grave and couldn't seem to see it, but it was hard to believe, now, that he could continue as president.

At the end of the day, after the hearings were adjourned, Gene noticed a number of reporters circled around a man he recognized from pictures: Bob Woodward, from the *Washington Post*. Gene worked his way toward the group and listened. "Is this the end for Nixon?" one of the reporters asked.

Gene had imagined that Woodward might be a flamboyant young man, thirty years old and already becoming famous. But he was wearing a tie and looked rather clean-cut. He spoke quietly. "I don't think so," he said. "He's tough. He'll hang on if he can."

"Thanks for what you've done," Gene said, and he reached out his hand. Woodward nodded, shook Gene's hand, and then began his retreat from the little crowd. Grandpa had told Gene over and over that Woodward and Bernstein were a couple of young reporters trying to make a big name for themselves, but Gene didn't see that in the way Woodward had behaved. He could have hung around and acted important, but he hadn't.

Gene worked his way through the crowd and then decided to walk over to his father's office. Alex, as it turned out, was in a meeting, but Gene waited, chatting with some of his father's staff about the day's events, and then finally was able to see his dad. "Come in, Gene," Alex said. "I didn't hear much of what went on today. Tell me about it." He sat down behind his desk.

"You almost had to be there to understand what happened," Gene said. He pulled a chair close to his dad's desk and sat down across from him. "John Dean just sat there and read his 250-page account of everything he knew about Watergate. There was no emotion; no loaded language; he just read in this straightforward, almost casual voice. But he laid everything out, in detail, and I think most people believed him. I know I did."

"Why? What makes you so sure he was telling the truth?"

"He gives all the details—dates, times, specific quotes. And he turned over a bunch of memos that backed up a lot of his claims. Besides, what does he have to gain by lying? He's making a case against himself as much as he is against Nixon, and yet the committee refused to give him immunity. He'll go to jail for what he said today."

Alex nodded. "But remember," he said, "Dean has every reason to put the blame on the President and on Erhlichman and Haldeman. Maybe he doesn't have immunity, but he's a young guy, and he wants to come out of this with some kind of reputation—and a future. He might have been playing down his own role in the whole thing."

"It sounds like that's what you've come to expect from everyone back here, Dad," Gene said.

Alex leaned back in his chair. Gene had noticed on this trip that his father seemed tired—looked tired. He was wearing reading glasses, which he put on much more often these days. They made him look older. There were also crow's feet at the corners of his eyes. Gene realized that the wrinkles must have been there for a time, but they were distinct now, and his eyes were noticeably red. Gene thought he was seeing what he had long feared: his dad was wearing down. Watergate had stopped everything in Washington, was tying up almost all legislation. Alex had complained the night before that there were things he wanted to accomplish, things that weren't likely to happen now. "I do get so I don't know what to believe, Gene. Everyone's trying to drop all the blame on Nixon and then get as far away from the man as possible. It wouldn't surprise me to find out someday that most of what happened came from some of his arrogant advisors—Mitchell, Erlichman, Haldeman, and even Dean himself. Nixon may have only gotten himself caught in the middle of the whole mess. I don't doubt that he tried to do damage control, but I'd be very surprised if he knew about the break-in before it happened."

"Damage control? Dad, he went on TV over and over and told bald-faced lies. That's become obvious now."

"Yeah, I think you're probably right about that. But there's a lot of that stuff going on around here."

Gene stared at his father. He could hardly believe the cynicism he was hearing. "Dad, we're not talking about putting a good face on things. The guy is a *liar*. That's what I'm calling him whether people back in Utah want to hear it or not. And when he gets himself impeached and tossed out of office, I'll be one guy who can say, 'I saw Nixon for what he was a long time ago.'"

"And then what will you be mad about?"

"What?"

"It's not Nixon you care about, Gene. It's still those holes in your gut. You can spend the rest of your life angry, or you can find peace within yourself, but right now Nixon is just your latest excuse to hate—and to do it openly. What's going to be next?"

Gene was staring again. He tried to think whether his dad was right.

"Is it worth losing Emily and Danny? It's one thing to write about some of these things, but you go around angry all the time, and you end up taking it out on your family."

"You've been talking to Emily, haven't you?"

"Of course I've been talking to her. I love that girl. And I love my grandson. It breaks my heart to think that you're letting them get away from you. And from *us* too—your mom and me."

Gene leaned back and let his eyes drift toward the ceiling. There was so much to say and nothing to say. Dad was right, of course, and Gene knew it. But he had tried for so many months to do better, and then, just when things had been looking up, he had let his temper slip again—and Emily had walked out. Why couldn't she understand—and why couldn't *Dad* understand—that he really was trying? Now his father seemed to be saying that even Gene's efforts to get his life going were somehow more evidence that he was still messed up. "I don't buy what you're telling me, Dad," he said, as calmly as he could. He stood up. He was getting ready to leave. "My whole life you've been teaching me to be idealistic, to stand up for the things I believe in, and now I do that and you tell me I'm even getting *that* wrong. I never have been able to satisfy you."

"Gene, that's not true." Alex got up and walked around his desk. He reached for Gene's shoulder, but Gene stepped away from him. "I'm *not* disappointed in you. I never have been. I think you're going to be a good reporter. There's nothing wrong with what you're writing. I told you that before. But you don't just report and analyze the news; everything you write seems an act of revenge. Those bullets wounded your soul as much as your body, and you want *someone* to answer for it."

"Maybe that's true; I don't know. But it's not like I'm *trying* to be angry. I'm fighting it all the time. No one seems to understand that."

"That's not true, Gene. Some of us do understand. Your uncles and I have tried to talk to you. We've been in battle, the same as you, and we had to get better. We know something about all that. But you don't want to talk to us. Emily said you went to the sessions at the Vet hospital, but you didn't really participate. So I have a little trouble believing you when you tell me how hard you're trying."

Gene put his hands on his hips. He looked past his father at the American flag posted behind his desk. It was such a confused symbol to him now. Nothing looked the same to him as it once had. He wanted to be himself, have his old responses return, but he simply didn't know how to make that happen. "Well, Dad, it's the same old thing," he finally said. "You came home with troubles, but you overcame them. You got it right. I never can live up to your standard. It's the story of my life."

"Gene, I don't want to hear that. I never put big demands on you."

"Maybe *you* didn't. But they were there. I never played a ball game without wondering whether I was playing as well—or as *hard*—as you would have. Grandpa—everyone I knew—told me all your stories, all the things you accomplished. I had to be student-body president because that's what you had done. And I knew from the time I was a kid that I had to go to war someday. That was how a man became a man. That was how my dad became a hero. I didn't have to go into the Lurps, but I did. And I gave myself all kinds of reasons for staying with those guys. What I knew, though, was that I had to find out whether I could measure up to my famous father."

"Gene, I talked to you about that. I told you I *wasn't* a hero and that you shouldn't try to be. You know that's what I told you."

"It didn't matter, did it? Because in my mind that was like saying, 'Don't try to be a great man like me.'"

Alex sat down on the edge of his desk. He looked at the floor for a long time. When he finally looked up, he had tears in his eyes. "So it isn't really Johnson or Nixon you're mad at? It's me?"

It wasn't a new thought for Gene. Emily had said things like that, and sometimes Gene had struggled to keep down a resentment that he had hated to admit to himself. But it wasn't in Gene to hurt his father, not when he could see what the man was obviously feeling. "Dad, I didn't say anything about being mad at you. I'm just saying people always expected me to be like you. It didn't matter whether *you* expected it or not. But somewhere along the line, I got tired of it. I don't want to live my life always worrying about whether I'm doing what you would have done."

"Gene, you're kidding yourself." Alex slipped off his desk and stepped closer. He looked into Gene's face until Gene finally looked back at him. "You've got to start looking inside yourself for the answers to *your* problems. You can project your anger at Nixon or anyone else, including me, but sooner or later you've got to deal with the anger itself, and you're not doing that. That buddy of yours is still out there on the ground, dead, and you still want to kill someone. You want some payback."

It was true—so powerfully true it was obvious, and yet, in some ways, new to Gene. It was good to see it clearly, to know it in words, to recognize what he had almost understood for such a long time. But it didn't help. Dearden was dead, and still on the ground, no matter what he tried to tell himself about that. "Dad, I feel like the bullets went through my heart," he said, and he began to cry. "I want to come back to life, but I can never quite do it." When his father touched his shoulder this time, Gene didn't back away. But he didn't want to be held like a little boy, so he kept his distance and merely let the tears roll down his face.

"I don't know how to stop this for you, Gene," Alex said. "But I know what I did. I talked things out with Wally and Richard, and that helped me understand what I was feeling. Then I tried to—"

"Don't, Dad. Please don't."

"Don't what?"

"Don't ask me to do it your way. It's just the same old thing. I'm not you. That's what I keep trying to tell you."

"That's not what I'm saying. It's what anyone has to do."

"No. Just because we talk about Dearden doesn't mean I won't dream about him tonight. It doesn't do any good. I've got to stop *thinking* about him. I've got to stop *seeing* him in my head."

Alex took hold of Gene's other shoulder and actually gave him a little shake. "Gene, think about it. You keep saying you have to do it your own way, but by now you ought to be able to admit, it's just not working. You're losing *everything*. You've got to look after your own son. You can't sacrifice that little boy to your own stubbornness. You've got to accept some help."

"That's not it, Dad. I'm not being stubborn. I've fought and fought against the things going through my head. I'm not clinging to them."

"I know that. But you can't just will them away; it doesn't work that way."

Dad tried to pull Gene closer, but he stepped back. He felt as though his flesh was melting, as though his mind was turning to vapor. If he gave way and fell into his father's arms, he had the feeling he would slip into insanity. He had to keep control. The real Dearden was dead, but the one in his head was trying to stay alive, and Gene couldn't let him consume his consciousness. Why couldn't anyone understand that?

Gene wanted Emily back. He wanted his son back. He wanted to be a man, a father, a good son, but first he had to keep from going crazy. Those men at the hospital, the ones who wanted to talk about everything, they were all nuts, babbling about their pain and feeling sorry for themselves. They weren't getting on with their lives, doing better, the way Dad said they should be doing; they were sitting around talking, complaining, getting crazier. Gene wasn't going to do that.

So Gene left. And he flew back to Salt Lake—back to the big, empty house. He called Emily every few days, and he tried to sound normal, upbeat, okay. If he kept doing that, he told himself, she would come back to him one of these days. And then he would treat her well, and be a great father. But he stayed up late every night, waiting for exhaustion, and afraid to get in bed. And the dreams kept coming.

CHAPTER 21

Two months after Hans returned to his higher-paying job, he and Elli were married. The official wedding took place in a government office and was handled with as much ceremony as one might expect in applying for a driver's license. But afterward, Hans and Elli returned with their families to the branch building in Magdeburg so President Neumeyer could perform a little church ceremony. Hans didn't know what temple marriages were like, but he knew that a couple was sealed there for eternity. He also knew that when he looked at Elli in her simple white dress, he wanted to be with her forever.

Hans and Elli stood at the front of the little chapel, and President Neumeyer stood before them. Many of the branch members were seated close around them, along with the Stoltzes and the Dürdens. President Neumeyer told Hans and Elli that they were beautiful young people who loved goodness and had allowed themselves to be guided by the Spirit. He asked them to remember this moment and how they felt about each other. "Could you speak harshly to each other right now?" he asked them. "Could you say anything hurtful? Could you put yourself first or be concerned about winning an argument? No. Of course not. You're overpowered by love for each other, by our Father's Spirit, and by your gratefulness that this moment has finally come. But on some other day, when the challenges of life enter in, you will find yourself tempted to say an unkind word, to accuse, or to argue. At times like that, hold this picture in your mind." He paused and gestured toward Elli. "Hans, look at Elli and think of all that you love about her. Now, remember that image forever."

President Neumeyer gave Hans a moment to look at Elli, and Hans looked carefully. As he did, tears spilled onto his cheeks. She was perfect in Hans's eyes. She was smiling a little, and her dimples were hints in her soft cheeks. He thought he saw in her eyes, ethereal at the moment, her own love for him. He couldn't imagine shouting at that face or wanting to hurt that spirit. Hans's father and mother had grown a little impatient with each other at times, but they had never sounded hateful, even when they argued. Hans knew he was blessed in that regard. He was well aware that many other marriages were not so happy.

"Elli, look at Hans. You know how good he is, how devoted to the Lord. And in case you haven't noticed, he's a handsome young man. Look into his eyes now and let his image sink all the way into your heart. Remember him forever the way you see him now. Someday, when he irritates you, or does something you don't understand, or even hurts your feelings, try to think of him then the way you are thinking of him now."

Hans saw Elli nod with the slightest of motions. The two had waited for each other longer than most couples ever had to, and Hans was overwhelmed at the thought of it, that she had fallen in love with him when she was still fifteen and had never wavered about that for these seven years.

President Neumeyer was chuckling now, and Hans looked his way, curious to know what was funny. "I was just thinking," the president said, "that I'm making this all sound just a little too easy. The fact is you're human, and days will come when you'll prove that to each other. If you're like most of us, you'll face some times when you'll hardly want to look at one another. All I can tell you is that you must try to make those times as short as possible—minutes, not hours. Compete to be the first to say you're sorry and to make things right. You can do that, but you have to put your marriage ahead of yourself, and that's a struggle for all of us."

All of that was hard for Hans to imagine. He had grown impatient with Elli at times, and he supposed he would get upset with her sooner or later, but he had almost lost her, and now he had her back. It didn't seem possible that he could be truly angry with her.

When President Neumeyer finally pronounced their vows, Elli said yes—"Ja"—with such simplicity and confidence, Hans cried again—or was still crying—so that it was difficult to pronounce his own answer. And then, at the invitation of President Neumeyer, Hans kissed Elli and held her in his arms. There had been many times in his life when he had given up on ever experiencing this joy. He hardly wanted to let her out of his arms.

"Let me speak of one more thing," President Neumeyer said. "When two people marry in one of our temples, they look into the mirrors in front and behind them, and they see a reflection that springs back and forth forever, fading into smaller and smaller images. A couple is told to see eternity represented in the reflections of the mirrors, and to think of their marriage the same way. This, of course, isn't the temple. I'm certain that every one of us has thought about that today—that this marriage, however wonderful, is just a little disappointing. You couldn't travel to a temple, and we have no temple here in the GDR. But the Lord is just. The day will come, perhaps in your lifetime—or perhaps later—but it will come, when you will be sealed to each other for time and all eternity. So think of your marriage as eternal. Never imagine it any other way. There is no death to marriage when it's sanctioned by the Lord. Know that this marriage is recorded in heaven this day, and that the temple ceremony will come to you in its own due time."

President Neumeyer then invited the families to come forward to congratulate the newlyweds. All the Dürdens hugged and kissed Hans and Elli, and then Hans's parents, with Inga, did the same. "I'm so happy for you," Inga told Hans.

"What's this I hear about a certain young man who's writing to you?" Hans asked.

"He's just a friend," Inga said. "I met him at Youth Conference." But she was blushing.

"Mama told me that he writes *often*, and he's coming to see you."

"I know. But I'm only nineteen, and he's only twenty. It's too soon to be serious." Those were her words, but her blush was deepening, and Hans thought he saw what she was really feeling.

"Is he a good young man?"

"Better than that. But he's not as good as you, Hans. No one is."

"Don't say that. You've always thought I was better than I am. But if he's good, and you like him, hold onto him. It's not easy to find someone in the Church."

"I know. And he's very nice to hold."

Hans hugged Inga again. He was happy for her. He only hoped the two could work things out financially. Mama had told Hans that the boy was smart, and he was learning to be an electrician. He could do well with that in time, but the next few years would be difficult. The story was the same for every young couple in the GDR.

The other members lined up and congratulated Hans and Elli, and then everyone moved to the biggest room in the building, outside the chapel, the one where the Relief Society sisters held their work meetings. Sisters in the branch had put together a little meal. Hans sat down at the table and looked around at the people he loved so much. When he had first left home and had come to Magdeburg to attend the university, these were the people who had welcomed him. He had good memories from that time when he had taught the young people in Sunday School, had gained a stronger testimony, and had still imagined a bright future. Since those days, little had gone right in his life, but suddenly he was basking in that same good friendship he remembered, and a decent future had reappeared. Everything seemed frighteningly too good to be true.

The members all told Hans it was what he deserved, to be so happy, but it was always hard for him to believe that. He so easily could have given all this up and gone to America when he had had his chance, and many times since then he had wondered why he hadn't done that. But now, it seemed to him, he had faced his challenge and received his reward. It appeared that the Lord wanted him to work in the Church, here, with all his heart, and he had been given a mate who would not only stand by him but raise him to new levels. He told Sister Neumeyer, "I hope that I can grow enough in this life to be worthy of Elli. She's a better person than I am—better than almost anyone I know. When the Lord speaks to her, she knows his voice—and listens. Lots of times in my life I haven't done that."

Sister Neumeyer laughed and then patted Hans's cheek. "You're probably right," she said. "You men are usually not worthy of the wives you get, but I must say, Elli could have searched all the GDR and found no better young man than you are."

Hans didn't bring it up, but what crossed his mind was that only a few months before he had almost given up on God. That was something Elli would never do. He was going to need her for that very reason. He was much quicker to doubt. He would always need Elli's faith.

After the little dinner, Elli left the room. When she returned, she had changed her clothes. She was wearing a pretty dress—not fancy, but blue like her eyes, and somehow she had been able to find some white gloves to go with a little white purse she was carrying. He knew that this was her traveling outfit. He wished he had a car so the two could drive away on their marriage trip, but at least his father had bought them train tickets to the Baltic Sea. Peter had also paid for three night's stay in a resort near Rostock. Hans had worried since the day he had officially proposed about bringing Elli back to his little apartment, but Papa's gift gave them a few days together and a chance to relish their happiness before hard realities set in. They would, after all, have to live with a tight budget, and it could be months before they found better housing. Hans had applied for an apartment, and he was on a waiting list, but he had no special influence with government officials, so he would simply have to work his way up that list as an ordinary citizen. Everyone knew that favors were often given to those in influence, and this meant the rest had to take the leftovers.

As Hans and Elli were saying good-bye to everyone, about to splurge and take a taxi to the train station, Elli's father came to them and said, "Hans, you and Elli didn't give me much time to save for this, but I wanted to make you a little gift. It might help you enjoy your marriage trip a little more—if that's possible." He laughed. "And maybe it will help you fix up your apartment just a little, until you can find something better." He handed Hans an envelope.

Hans knew that the Dürdens didn't have a lot, so the gift meant all the more. "You didn't have to do this," he said.

"Yes, of course I did. Hans, in this country, from the minute a baby is born, parents in the Church begin to worry whether their children will be able to find a worthy partner to marry. We have always hoped for someone who will pass the gospel to our grandchildren. Elli has been a special child, gifted with so much joy and faith, and I've feared that she would find no one worthy of her."

"She didn't," Hans said, laughing.

"Don't say that. You're everything we've hoped for."

"I've made so many mistakes in my life. Things look better right now, but I'll always be limited by the choices I made as a young man. I wish I could give Elli more than I'll be able to."

"We don't look at it that way," Brother Dürden said. "You tried to help a friend, and in this country that can be seen as wrong. But you committed no sin, and the important thing is that you used your time in prison to grow. All this is part of living where we do—and keeping the Church alive under such hardships."

Hans was not sure of that. Rarely did he get through a day without thinking of Berndt and wishing he could take back his decision. But he said, "I promise you this, Brother Dürden: I'll always treat her well. You'll never have to worry about that."

"I know that without your saying it. And you'll be a leader to your generation. You'll teach my grandchildren to be like you and Elli."

Hans hoped so. But already he had some concerns. Today was a day to hope for the best, for everyone to imagine good days ahead, but these last two months Hans had had plenty of time to think about realities. Elli kept saying that she wanted as many children as possible, but Hans worried about providing for them, and he worried about having a child right away, when they barely had enough to get by. He also thought of what those children would have to deal with. Educated in a school system that made belief so hard, they would surely be doubters, as Hans had once been. What problems would *they* have finding members to marry? Across the country, belief was dying out, and it was sometimes hard to imagine that the Church could survive, generation after generation.

But Hans's mother made him feel better. She hugged Hans and Elli, and she told Elli, "I was thinking how much alike we are. I was never as pretty as you, and never so spiritual. I didn't have the Church when I was a girl. But I knew the man I was supposed to marry when I met him—even though I was also very young. When he was gone to America and seemed unlikely to return, I kept loving him. I've never been sorry for that. Peter has been a blessing to me every day of my life. I know Hans will treat you the way he's seen his father treat me. You couldn't ask for anything more."

Hans promised himself that would be true.

Peter hugged Hans and Elli too, and as he held Hans in his arms, he said, "I knew this would happen. I knew the Lord would bring this about. I worried and fretted, and I got impatient with the Lord, but I always knew it would happen in time."

"I wasn't nearly so sure," Hans said. "I should have trusted what you told me in my blessings."

⌁

Hans and Elli took an afternoon train to Rostock and arrived there late in the evening. They then took a bus to the resort where they had reservations, and by then it was after midnight. Hans had gradually gotten nervous, the closer they had come to the resort. Elli, even though she had slept at times against Hans's shoulder, seemed wide awake by then—and also a little nervous, Hans thought.

On the following morning, they slept rather late, but Elli awakened Hans and said, "Let's go out and look at the ocean." She had only seen the ocean once before, so Hans understood her interest, but he was a little disappointed that that was what she thought of doing first.

Outside, what they discovered was that the air was heavy, the sky low and gray. The ocean moved under all that gray light, sloshing, weighty, muffled. "It's not so pretty as I remembered," Elli said. "It's sort of scary."

"It's still foggy, that's all. It's that way almost every day, in the morning. When the sun comes out, you'll see how pretty it is."

"How many times have you been here, Hans? Did you come often when you were a boy?"

"No. Just a few times. But I've never told you about one of the times I was here."

"What do you mean?" Elli stopped and turned toward him.

Hans had made the decision that he wanted no secrets from Elli. But he had never told her about his attempted escape, just a few miles from this place, so long ago. He hadn't wanted to tell her things that she would have to deny, if ever interrogated by the *Stasi*. But now they were married, and she needed to understand certain things about him. So he told her—told her about Berndt and him out on the water in the night on air mattresses, trying to make it to a passing ship, and then almost being drowned by a government boat. He told her how exhausted he had become, trying to get back to shore, and how close he had come to dying.

Elli was clearly surprised by all of this. "Did it mean so much to you, even that young, to go to America?"

"I don't know. Berndt made everything sound wonderful. I didn't know much about America, and I don't think I understood enough about life here in our country to make a good decision. You know how it is, at that age. Things seem simple and clear sometimes, when in reality they aren't. It wasn't until later that I realized what it would have meant to me to give up my family for my whole life. I've always been thankful I didn't make it, but you might as well know, it wasn't the only time I tried."

Elli was still facing him, but she was shivering. She stepped closer to him, and he took her in his arms. "You weren't going with Berndt that night when he was shot, were you?" she asked.

"No. But my family tried to leave once, before all that. We took a train into Poland, and we tried to leave on a ship, from Gdansk."

"Your parents? Your whole family?"

"It was at a time when my father's future looked impossible, and he thought of what he could give his children if he could get to Salt Lake City. His parents and his sister were there, and they were doing so well. It seemed worth the gamble to him."

"But what happened?"

Hans told her the story—again how the escape had gone wrong, and how close they had come to being caught. "It was the most disappointing moment of my life," he told her, "when we had to turn back and go on with life as always. We had imagined such wonderful days ahead, and we seemed ready to have them, and then everything was taken back." He stopped. "No, that's not true. It was the worst moment until then, but in June, when I thought I had to give you up—that was the worst."

"For me too, Hans." She nestled closer against him.

"It's all clear to me now, though," Hans said. "I pleaded with the Lord to let me have my way—to give me what I wanted—so I thought he wasn't listening. But look what he had in mind for us instead."

"Is it like that, Hans? Does the Lord know what he wants for us, and then make it happen?"

It was not a question Hans dealt with lightly. He had thought so much about these very kinds of things. "I don't know for sure. He doesn't *make* things happen for us. But if we listen, he helps us get to a good place. And when we ask for the wrong things, he knows enough to guide us away."

"Is he thinking about all of us—all at the same time?"

"When I was sixteen I had my mind made up that an idea like that was ludicrous. But now, after everything that's happened, I feel that it has to be that way. I was about to leave this country, after all those years of wanting to get out, and a voice—an actual voice in my head—told me I should stay. And now I have this moment, here with you. Maybe it's childish to explain all that as coming from God, but it just seems to me that this day was supposed to come." He held her, still warm against him, a lovely contrast to the cool air, and then he added, "But you're the one who knows how to believe. You shouldn't ask me."

"I do believe, but I don't know how to explain things the way you do. I merely trust."

"That's what I want to do more of from now on. I try too hard to explain things, and there's so much we'll never really understand in this life."

She pulled her head back so she could look at him. "I know you're worried about having enough money. But we'll be all right. I knew that when you didn't."

He leaned forward and put his cheek against her head, but he didn't tell her what he was thinking. There were things people had to work out for themselves. They had to be wise, and he and Elli had to be careful with the money they would have.

"You worry when I say I want lots of babies. I see it in your eyes every time I say it."

"No one has lots of babies in this country, Elli. You know all the problems."

"I know. And I don't know how many we should have. But I know for sure I want to have a baby soon."

"We'll be in that little apartment for quite a while, Elli. If the baby came before—"

"Hans, let's trust."

"It's not that simple, Elli." He pulled back. "The Lord expects us to use our heads. We have to consider our situation."

Hans saw immediately the hurt in her eyes. "Yesterday you *promised* you wouldn't talk to me that way, Hans."

"Oh." He pulled her back. "I'm sorry. Did I sound angry? I'm not angry."

"No. Not angry. But you make me feel stupid sometimes—like you think I'm still a little girl."

Hans could hardly believe this. Were they having a quarrel already, after the promises he had made? "I didn't mean it that way. I was just saying what I thought. I . . ." But he knew he did talk to her that way sometimes. Her simplicity was charming, at best, but she could also be annoyingly naïve. Almost everything in life seemed more complicated to him than it did to her. He realized he would have to be careful not to sound condescending. "I'm sorry," he said.

"It's all right. I do need to learn from you. I don't think enough about things."

"And I think too much."

"We'll either be good for each other or we'll make each other crazy."

She turned as though she wanted to walk again. But Hans held her back. "No. We can't do that. I don't want to argue about things. I want to discuss everything, so we don't feel as though we're working against each other."

"But I don't talk as well."

Hans was surprised by the idea. He had been in love with Elli for a long time, but they had never really spent much time together. Would he try to talk her into too many things, or try to change her mind, just because he held such strong opinions? Would their marriage always be a kind of balancing act? Why hadn't he thought about that danger before? "You'll always have to tell me when I push my own opinion too hard."

"I know."

"You knew that already?"

"Of course. I've been thinking about us together since I was fifteen. I've always worried that you would think I was ridiculous, once we were married."

Hans was amazed that she had seen this. He knew he had been impatient with her at times, but he hadn't thought nearly enough about putting his rational approach up against her instincts. The idea was almost frightening. His own faith had grown a dozen times over in the past few years, but still, he always had to think his ideas out, turn his faith into theology—an explanation of some sort—and then he had to find a way to turn his thinking into an actual decision. She would find him tiresome if he wasn't careful. Why hadn't he known that before now? "Elli, I'll learn to listen to you better. When the Lord tells you things, always tell me. I'll think about things too long. You might get the answer long before I do."

"That won't work. We'll both have to do things our own way, then find a way to make decisions together. But we have to remember to make each other happy. A lot of decisions don't really matter that much."

This was astounding. "You've known all along that would be our challenge?"

"Haven't you? You're the one who thinks so much."

Now she did take a step and start him walking, but she held her arms around his middle and clung to him. "I've only known how happy I was when I was with you," Hans said, "and I thought about *whether* we would ever have the money to marry. I don't think I quite realized how different we are."

"It'll be all right."

"We'll make sure it is. We'll work at it."

Elli laughed. She stopped again and made him look at her. "You think I'm pretty, don't you?"

"I think you're beautiful."

"I know you do. I see it in your eyes every time you look at me. I saw it even before you knew you liked me."

"Maybe so. But being pretty is not the most important thing."

"It might be more important than you think."

Was that true? Was love that dumb? How did Elli know such things?

"Do you think we did things right last night?"

Hans had no idea what she was talking about. "Did what right?"

"You know what I mean. After we got here."

"Oh . . . yes." But Hans felt his ears begin to burn. He wasn't sure he could talk about this. "I thought . . . I suppose . . . for the first time . . ."

"I thought it would last longer."

"Oh." Hans hardly knew what was happening. He had never talked to *anyone* about things like this—let alone to this beautiful girl smiling into his face. "I think . . . I mean . . . I'm not sure . . . but I think maybe I was too . . . uh . . ."

"Excited?"

"Yes. I think so."

"Mom told me that happens at first."

"She did?"

"I think what we need to do is practice a lot."

He was staring at her now. He had wanted to say something like that this morning, when she had wanted to come out here, but he never would have dared. "I think so too," he said quite seriously.

"You're blushing," Elli said. "I've embarrassed you."

"No, not at all. I think you're exactly right."

"Maybe, then, we should go back to our room."

"Yes. That's a good idea."

"See. It *is* a good thing that you think I'm pretty."

Hans was nodding again, and trying desperately not to seem embarrassed. But suddenly he was wondering who was smarter. He thought maybe he would have to work to keep up with Elli. But he did want to go back to the room. No question, it was a good thing that he was attracted to her. He was also thinking how much he liked her honesty. This was going to be a whole new life for him, no longer alone, no longer left to his thoughts so much. He wanted to know everything that was in Elli's head, and tell her all his own thoughts. He could hardly believe how exciting that idea sounded to him. But it was no more exciting than the thought of going back to their room together.

CHAPTER 22

When class ended, Kathy tucked her notebook into her book bag and worked her way up the aisle toward the door. She had finally started back to college that fall, having registered for a master's program in social work. But so far she had not been as excited as she wanted to be about her classes.

"So you were in the Peace Corps?" a young woman asked from behind her.

Kathy had finally made a comment that day about how things really worked, in the field, as opposed to some of the theory she was hearing in class all the time. "Yes. In the Philippines," she said, glancing over her shoulder.

"Was that just a fantastic experience?"

Kathy stopped and turned around. "Overall, it was a good experience. I learned a lot, and I loved the people. But it was frustrating, too."

"I'm sure it is, at times. By the way, my name's Tammy Ebbert." Some other students were trying to pass by in the aisle, so Kathy and Tammy stepped into one of the rows of chairs.

Kathy thought the girl looked about eighteen, but she had to be twenty-two or so, since she was in the graduate program. Kathy had noticed when Tammy had walked in, before class, that she was wearing jeans that were ripped at the knees and a sweatshirt with the sleeves cut out. She had long hair that was fine and light, with big, dangling earrings. The whole image seemed a sort of joke to Kathy. It was as though the hippie styles, which had died out everywhere else, had finally reached Utah.

"The way I look at it," Tammy said, "no matter how frustrating social work is, if you can change even a few lives, it's worth it. Most kinds of jobs don't really make any difference. It's all about marketing some product that people don't really need. When you change someone's heart, you've accomplished something."

"Well . . . yeah."

"Don't you feel that way?" Tammy rested her book bag on the seat of one of the desk chairs, as though she wanted to talk for a while, but Kathy wondered whether she really wanted to have this conversation.

"Sure I do. But it's not like you can go out and just take it upon yourself to change people. They have to want to change. You also have to start with the assumption that they *need* to change, and that's not always true."

"Right on. I agree with that. I don't think we have to make people, you know . . . more like us. But if you can give someone hope, or direction, so they can fill their own potential, that's what it's all about."

Kathy nodded. She edged back into the aisle, and Tammy followed her.

"I know what you're thinking," Tammy said. "That I'm really idealistic and naïve. And I'm sure I am. But I think things have started to change in this country—even in Utah—and it's going to take a lot of idealism to keep the revolution going. Too many people are giving up."

Kathy didn't want to laugh at the girl, but she thought of her days in the "movement," when she and her friends from Smith and Amherst had thought they could end the war and bring about a whole new era of peace, racial harmony, and equality of the sexes. Kathy had always been a little more skeptical than most, not really convinced that masses of people could change so fundamentally, but she really had believed that her generation was going to make the world a better place. And maybe a few things were better. But human nature didn't seem to change, and Kathy was disappointed with so much of what she saw going on in the world now. The war in Vietnam had slowly ended, but what remained was the deep scar left over from all the division the war had brought to the country. Now the Watergate mess had only deepened the cynicism in the United States. It wasn't surprising that a lot of trust in government had been lost, but Kathy felt more than that. It was as though Americans had lost belief in themselves. They had grown up with the idea that America was better than other countries, with superior morals and higher ideals. But that was being called a myth by a lot of people now, and some Americans were defensive about that, but the doubt had been planted, and Kathy suspected that the nation would never be quite the same again.

"So what do you think needs to be changed?" Kathy asked.

"Are you kidding?"

"No. I'm curious. If you want to continue the revolution, as you put it, what things are you fighting for?"

"Hey, I don't know about you, but I grew up a Mormon, and I'm sick of all that. People are great about delivering a casserole if someone gets sick, but they're judgmental and hypocritical. They compete like there's some prize for the one who collects the most toys. Everybody has to have a bigger house than their neighbor, drive a bigger car, brag about their latest trip to Europe. If we're ever going to have true equality, we have to drop our sick, materialistic value system. When it comes to loving and accepting people—the way Jesus talked about—that's like way down the list on anyone's priorities."

"So less materialism? What else?" Kathy stepped out the door.

"What is this, a quiz?"

Kathy was starting to move down the hall now, but Tammy had stopped. Kathy turned back toward her. "I'm just wondering," Kathy said. "I was in the middle of the anti-war movement, back east. I was in Mississippi during Freedom Summer. And I stood up for equal rights for women. But I think maybe I'm getting a little behind the times. Are there some new slogans?"

Tammy was staring at Kathy now, clearly confused. Kathy had put her credentials out before the girl, but then had asked the wrong question. "So don't you believe in any of those things anymore?" Tammy asked.

"I believe in civil rights. I still think the war in Vietnam was wrong. And I think women ought to get equal pay for equal work. But I spent a lot of years with the counterculture, and it was obvious to me that they hadn't overcome human weaknesses any more than anyone else. They could be just as petty and competitive as you claim Mormons are, and deep down, just as materialistic. Most of the people I knew who were trying to solve the world's problems couldn't even solve their own—no more than I could."

"You're a Mormon, aren't you? And I've made you mad."

"I am a Mormon. But I went a long way away before I came back. And I'll tell you something: When it comes to a society that cares about one another, and does its best to stay in touch with what really counts, we do as well as anyone I've met."

"Yeah, well, my dad's a bishop, and I think he cares more about going to meetings than he does about his own family."

Kathy looked at Tammy for a time. She didn't want to argue with the girl, but she wished she could save her from some of the stuff she would be going through for the next few years. "Tammy," she finally said, "all I can tell you is that we *all* ought to be a lot better than we are—and be more like Christ. That's the change the world needs to make. If I were you, I'd think about being a little easier on your dad; that would be a good start."

Tammy stared back. "I hope I never wear out," she said. "It sounds like you joined the fight for a while, but then you gave up and ran home to Mommy and Daddy—where it's safe."

"I guess it looks that way to you."

But Tammy was walking away.

Kathy felt bad about the conversation. She hoped that maybe she and Tammy could talk again sometime, but she did think about the things

Tammy had said—thought all afternoon. She tried to ask herself exactly where she stood now. She did believe that minorities, whatever gains had been made, still weren't treated fairly in America. She also believed that the war had been a tragic mistake, although she knew she and her friends had been much too harsh in putting blame on the soldiers themselves. And she believed that women should be equal partners with their husbands. What she suspected, however, was that all those situations were complex and would take time to correct. Change had to happen in people's hearts, one heart at a time.

And yet, Kathy had to admit to herself, Tammy probably had a point. Kathy *had* worn out in some ways. She liked directing the choir, but she wasn't sure she made much difference to anyone in her ward—not the way she had in the Philippines. And for all her idealism about serving in the community, she was doing almost nothing. Now that she was back in school and also working part-time, she used the excuse that she was too busy, that she would do more than her share when she finished her degree. But she also knew what social work would mean, and she found herself depressed at times, just thinking about pushing a big rock uphill all her life. She wanted to be enthusiastic about her future, but she just wasn't feeling much of that. She wondered how she could accomplish anything if she couldn't get off to a running start.

❧

A couple of days later, on a Wednesday evening, Kathy was studying for a test at the kitchen table, alone in her apartment, when the phone rang. She grabbed the phone and said, rather absently, "Hello?"

"Kathy?" someone said. A man.

"Yes."

"It's Marshall."

Kathy had realized that by then, and she was surprised. She had long since given up hope on the guy. After their picnic she had expected a call within a few days, and then nothing had happened. Eventually Kathy had heard that Marshall was going forward with his wedding plans. She had taken the news as her affirmation that the guy was still a flake, and she had told herself many times that she was lucky to be rid of him. But she had also been depressed, and her return to school had been, at least in part, an attempt to overcome that.

Still, Kathy sat upright, enlivened more than she wanted to be. "Oh, hi. How are you?"

"Well, I'm—what should I say?—kind of struggling to figure my life out, and I wondered if we could maybe get together and talk."

"Uh, sure. We could . . . hey, you're making fun of me, aren't you?"

"What do you mean?"

"That's sort of what I said when I called you that time."

"Oh, really? I didn't remember that." He sounded serious, but she wasn't sure. Maybe this was all tongue-in-cheek. "I wondered if we could maybe meet this weekend," he said. "Maybe Friday evening."

She decided she'd better keep this light. She really did suspect that he was playing around. "Let me see. Just a moment while I review my many commitments for this weekend." She paused, but he didn't laugh. "Well, I do have a date that afternoon, and a midnight rendezvous later on, but something in the early evening might work. My Saturday, of course, is entirely booked."

"Wow. You lead an exciting life."

There was no question now, this was a put-on, but she had no idea what he was up to. She sat back in her chair. "Okay, let's drop all this," she said. "Did you actually want to get together and talk, or is this another one of your jokes?"

"Kathy, you're acting strange tonight. I'm not sure why. You know how confused I've been, and I really need some guidance."

She finally laughed. "That's good. Because I'm certainly the person with all the answers."

"Oh, thank you for saying that. I was hoping you'd be able to help me. Could I pick you up as early as six—before the evening gets too cold?"

"Why? Where are we going?"

"Well, we usually go to the park on occasions like this."

Kathy was shaking her head. She wasn't sure what he had in mind, but she realized, in spite of herself, that she did want to see him. There was something oddly romantic in his wanting to take her back to the park—even in October. "Okay. Six. And I'll try to help you all I can."

"Thanks. I was hoping you would say that. Could you wear a flower in your hair—so I'll recognize you when I see you?"

"You mean, when you ring my doorbell?"

"Don't make this trivial, Kathy. It's very important to me."

"Yeah. Right. See ya' on Friday. You are serious about that part, aren't you?"

"Yes, yes. Of course."

Kathy put the phone down and tried to think what this meant. Was this the sequel to their conversation last spring—when he had promised to call her back once he decided what he was going to do about Lisa? Her guess was that he just wanted to have one last chat before his wedding. And that was okay; she did like to talk to him. But she was already hating herself for the hopeful thoughts that were jumping into her brain. She just couldn't do that to herself again. Yet, when she tried to go back to the textbook she had been reading, she found she couldn't concentrate. She told herself she wouldn't make the same stupid mistake this time; she wouldn't overdress, wouldn't try to "act" any particular way, wouldn't make a big deal of this.

But as she tried to read, questions did come to mind: What *should* she wear? What would they actually talk about? How could she keep him from knowing how bad she had felt when he had never called again after their picnic?

Kathy didn't tell her mom about the phone call, and she certainly didn't call Diane. She just waited the time out, studied way too little, and actually did go buy a new pair of slacks that were casual but pretty and went with a top she liked—one that brought out the color of her eyes, she thought.

By the time six o'clock came, she was stupidly nervous—and disgusted with herself. How could she let this guy wait months between phone calls and then respond like she was sixteen and he was the cute boy in her algebra class?

He arrived exactly on time, and she watched from her living-room window as he parked his car. It was only as he got out and walked around the car that she realized he was wearing a tuxedo. She laughed, but she hardly knew what to do. Did she actually need to change her clothes?

She hurried to her bedroom, let the doorbell ring, and then walked slowly back to the living room, just so he wouldn't know she had been watching him. She wanted to act surprised about the tuxedo, but when she opened the door, she was already laughing. "Is this what you're wearing to the park?" she asked.

He looked down, surveying himself, as though surprised at her question. "Oh, this old thing?" he said. "It's just something I threw on."

"How do you throw on a cummerbund?"

"What's a cummerbund?"

"Just answer me this: Do I need to change?"

"Kathy, never change. I like you just the way you are." He wasn't smiling, wasn't even looking sly.

"We're still going to the park, right?"

"That's right. Although we may want to fly off to Rio in my jet at some point, just to pick up a little something to eat. Still, I'll have you back for your late date."

"Thanks so much." She stepped over to the couch to grab a jacket she had planned to wear. The truth was, she was hoping he would drop this whole thing soon; she really did want to talk to him. But all the way to the park—only a few blocks away—he talked about his joy in seeing her, his struggle with his own confused life, and his hope that he hadn't dressed inappropriately. Then, at the park, he took her to the table where they had sat before. What he didn't have with him was a picnic basket. He made a point of leading her to the side of the table where he had sat last time. She wasn't sure what that meant until he sat down across from her and said, "Kathy, I have some big questions about my life, and I'm willing to do whatever you think is best, because I trust so much in your judgment." Then he reached across the table and touched her arm.

"Okay, okay," Kathy said. "You've made your point. I acted stupid the last time we were here, but I don't know why you waited all summer and now want to go to this much trouble to make fun of me."

He finally smiled—and looked very good. Something in the smile seemed to say, *Don't worry, we're going to have a great time together.* He dropped the tone he had been using and said, "Well, I'm just trying to learn from you. When you wanted to see me, you called and said you wanted to talk about your troubles. I figured that must be a good approach."

"As I recall, my approach—overdressing and touching your arm every chance I got— didn't work out that well."

"That's where you're wrong."

"Okay. Explain that one to me."

He leaned forward and put his elbows on the table. Kathy worried what he might do to the tux, although she had noticed that it was rather old. She had a feeling it belonged to his dad. "I have a problem," he said, and he seemed to mean it. "You may not have noticed, but I sometimes struggle to make up my mind."

"Actually, I have had that impression."

"Yeah, well, so has everyone else. But that night we sat here and talked, I had some pretty strong feelings about you. I really did want to spend more time with you and just see what might come of it."

"The idea must have slipped your mind later on."

Marshall grinned, but he didn't respond. He plowed straight ahead. "I've always remembered those few weeks when we went together and how I felt about you then. I've never really been quite that excited about anyone else, but I figured that was just because we were so young, and that first time I kissed you was more or less the first for both of us."

"Not 'more or less' for me. It *was* my first kiss, and I've experienced painfully few since then." She had no idea why she kept admitting things like that to him.

"Well . . . anyway . . . last spring I was *more or less* engaged, and Lisa and I had been looking at rings and checking out wedding catalogs—the whole thing. When I left you that night, I was thinking I was going to call things off with her. I really was. But I lost my nerve. Both families were completely into the thing, and my mom told me I was just having last-minute jitters, like a lot of guys. I started to think maybe she was right." Marshall reached across the table with exaggerated stiffness and touched Kathy's arm. They both laughed. "This story really is going somewhere," he said.

"Good." But her breath was holding. She thought she saw where it was going, but she didn't want to hope—wasn't even sure it was the right direction for her anyway.

"The thing is, I've never quite gotten over what you did to me when you came home from Smith that first time. I was really bonkers over you, and you treated me like I was some sort of reactionary numbskull. You were just so superior and so *right*."

"So *left*, actually."

"Well, yeah. And I'll admit, I knew next to nothing about Vietnam and still tried to talk about it."

"Actually, you knew quite a bit, but I couldn't stand to hear any opinion other than my own back then."

Marshall tugged at his collar. "This thing's too tight," he said. He pulled on one end of the bow tie and undid the knot. As he unbuttoned his collar, he said, "You *were* right, though. You were way ahead of me in figuring certain things out. After you went back to school, you hardly wrote at all, and I knew what you thought of me. Since then, whenever I've seen you, I've loved the way you look, and I've loved my memories of the way I felt about you back in the beginning, but I've always assumed you still thought I was stupid. And since I *am* fairly stupid, it's always seemed better to stay away from someone who had that figured out."

"I think I'll skip the discussion about who is actually stupid. Your little parody just demonstrated that."

"No, no. That was actually an amazing evening for me. We both knew it wasn't really you, but it bowled me over to think you would try that hard."

"I think all the rule books say it's better not to be quite so *obvious*."

"But 'obvious' was flattering, Kathy. You're so beautiful and brilliant and everything, and here you were showing that you were still interested in me. And I loved what we talked about that night. You understand this whole thing I've been mulling over—you know, about setting up a cabinet shop and all that."

"That's what brought the whole thing on. It's how I got the nerve to call you. That night at the ballet, when you talked about the life you wanted, it fit exactly with what I'd been thinking."

"I could tell that. After I talked to you that night, I couldn't stop thinking about you. You've always scared me because you're more intense about things than I am. But I like what you bring out in me."

Kathy still didn't know where this was supposed to go now, but she touched his arm, batted her eyelashes, and said, "Well, then, Marshall, where have you *been* all summer?"

"Uhhh—that is the question, isn't it? I spent my time stalling, mostly. Every time Lisa would put the pressure on, I'd start talking about my career in carpentry, and we'd have a fight. I was committed to wedding dates three times this summer—and really, it was Lisa who backed out each time, although I knew the trigger that would bring it on."

"So now what?"

"Well, we finally broke up. For good." He smiled.

"Really?" Kathy told herself not to sound too excited. She added, as casually as she could, "You do have problems, my son. We do need to talk."

"What happened was, I started graduate school—business school, actually—and satisfied her requirement and the wishes of my parents, her parents, and everyone else I know. And then, this week, I dropped out. I just couldn't face it. I can maybe build cabinets—and sell them—and in that sense become a businessman. But I hated every minute of business school. I couldn't even study that stuff, it was so baffling and uninteresting to me. I was getting lousy grades, too. So I dropped out, told Lisa, and she drop-kicked me right out of her life. But I walked away grinning."

"So are you going to stick with the carpentry?"

Marshall grimaced. "I think so," he said. "I really do need to talk to you about that. I love history, and sometimes I still wonder whether I want to be a history teacher. But I do want to live in a small town."

"Do you still like working with wood as much, or—"

"I don't want to talk about that right now, okay?"

"Oh. Okay. I thought that's what we were doing tonight."

He touched her arm, and it didn't feel like a joke. "I want to talk about us."

"Us?" she said, trying to breathe normally.

"Kathy, I've been in love with you since I was eighteen years old. Even all those years I didn't like you, I would think about the way we had talked. Remember that night up at Alta when we looked at the stars and talked about so many things?"

"It was the loveliest night of my life, Marshall—and still is."

"Really?"

"Well . . . actually, maybe not." She laughed, and then she said, "There was also that night I was getting ready to leave, and you finally kissed me—after I dropped about a thousand hints. I've relived that moment *thousands* of times in my life."

"Wow. Me too. Were we just really young or was that a *great* kiss?" He was leaning forward, smiling, but he seemed to mean the question.

To Kathy's surprise—and embarrassment—tears were filling her eyes, but she smiled and said, "Maybe we should try again—just to find out."

"Yeah. I think we should. Definitely."

They kept looking at each other, smiling and waiting, as if to say, *So who's going to make the move?*

But finally Marshall got up and walked around the table. Kathy stood at the same time and stepped behind the bench. She turned toward him as he stopped, close to her. He stood for a moment, and then she felt him touch her waist with one hand. He pulled her forward, very slowly, and then she felt his other hand touch her back. He continued to draw her toward him as though he wanted to enjoy every second, not rush anything. But when their lips were almost together, he stopped, and he whispered, "I sure hope I do this right. I may only have one shot."

Kathy broke up laughing and pulled back, and he laughed too, but then he began the approach again, not so slowly. This time their lips touched, softly. He didn't hold her long, just let the gentle touch of their lips spread vibrations through her. Then he pulled back a little and said, "I think we're onto something."

"I think so, too. Let's test out our theory one more time."

He laughed, but this time he kissed her with a little more energy, then held her in his arms. "Kathy," he said, "I'm sorry I waited so long."

"I am too."

"I do need to talk to you. I really do need to decide what to do with my life."

"Okay."

"Do you want to kiss one more time before we talk?"

"Maybe twice more," Kathy said. "We seem to be getting better each time."

It crossed her mind that maybe he still was a flake, and she shouldn't be doing this. But it didn't stay in her mind very long—not even as long as the second kiss.

CHAPTER 23

G ene was enrolled at the University of Utah again in the fall, but he was also writing a regular column for *The Salt Lake Tribune*. He had a desk he could use there, and he often did. He was crowded into a corner of a big room where lots of other reporters worked, but Gene preferred being there. No one paid much attention to him, but he felt part of the business. He still wrote for the student paper, and he took a few more chances in what he wrote there, but student writing seemed pretend work, and what he did for the *Trib* felt like the real thing. Gene was a little more hopeful, too. He had talked to Emily several times on the telephone lately, and she really did want to come back to him. He continued to reassure her that he was doing better, but most important, he felt it. Since he had talked to his father, he had tried more than ever to let certain things go. Mainly, he felt better about his father, but he had slept better too, and that was restoring.

Emily was not happy being separated, and Danny, she said, talked constantly about "Daddy." But she didn't want to come back only to have things get bad again. She thought that would be traumatic for Danny, who had seemed more relaxed and stable, away from the arguing and the anger. Gene kept telling Emily that his anger was diminishing. For one thing, he had sent another article to *Atlantic Monthly,* and it was a much gentler piece, about the nobility of some of the soldiers he had known in Vietnam. Gene had found it healing to think about some of the heroic, decent acts he had witnessed during the war. Still, Emily was not quite ready to take a chance yet, and that was frustrating to Gene—especially since he had to be so careful not to express his actual feelings about that and seem angry. Still, Emily's tone had softened, and Gene hoped she would come home to him before Christmas. She had hinted at that possibility.

Gene had continued to write about Watergate, and the scandal had expanded in lots of new directions. Members of the Senate Select Committee had been pressuring President Nixon to give them access to certain of his recorded White House conversations. The president had refused, so far, on grounds of executive privilege. At the same time, through the Justice Department, the Nixon administration had been conducting its own inquiry, and Archibald Cox had been appointed as the special prosecutor to lead the investigation. Cox, however, had also begun to press Nixon to turn over the tapes. In October, Nixon had proposed a compromise. He would have a synopsis of the tapes prepared and would be willing to release those. When Archibald Cox refused to accept the summaries as a replacement for the tapes, Nixon had made a stunning decision. He ordered his attorney general, Elliot Richardson, to fire Cox. Richardson refused to carry out the order and instead resigned his position, so Nixon pressed Richardson's assistant, William Ruckelshaus, to do the job. Ruckelshaus had also resigned. Finally, Robert Bork, the solicitor general and next in line of authority, agreed to release Cox, but when the news hit the nation, the decision blew up in Nixon's face. The purge was soon being called the "Saturday night massacre," and Nixon's prestige in the country had taken a further dive.

In the middle of all this, Nixon's vice president, Spiro Agnew, had been accused of taking kickbacks for favors to contractors in Maryland during the time he was governor and even after becoming vice president. He had pleaded "no contest" to accusations of income tax evasion and then, without much warning, had resigned. Nixon had announced that Gerald Ford, speaker of the house, would be appointed to replace Agnew, but the administration was humiliated again by further scandal. Agnew had long been the president's attack dog in denouncing war protesters and speaking up for the so-called "silent majority." No one had spoken with more self-righteousness about old-fashioned American values, and now he was admitting to old-fashioned American corruption. At the same time, Gulf and Ashland oil had pled guilty to making illegal political contributions to the Nixon campaign, and Maurice Stans, administration fundraiser, now secretary of commerce, had admitted that such contributions had been common and "expected" of corporations across the country.

War had also broken out in the Middle East in October. Egyptian troops had invaded the Sinai Peninsula during the Holy Days of Yom Kippur. The Israelis responded forcefully, and after two weeks a cease-fire had been agreed upon, but in the meantime, Arab countries had announced an embargo on oil exports to the United States. There were fears of an energy crisis, and many were questioning America's commitment to Israel. Nixon had already tried price controls to stem runaway inflation, but Americans were getting very nervous about both the economy and the possibility of an energy shortage.

It was the middle of November now, and today Gene was writing about the sentencing of the Watergate burglars. G. Gordon Liddy had received a twenty-year sentence, mostly because he had refused to cooperate, but the others had also gone to jail. Gene wrote that the front-line soldiers had been punished, and yet the "brass"—the leaders who had sent them to do the dirty work—had not been dealt with. He used that concept as a comparison to the Vietnam war, where committed young men had fought for things they assumed were right, only to be hated and punished for their acts.

Gene was typing at his corner desk when he saw a man walking his way. He was a stocky fellow, maybe fifty or so, wearing an aviator-style leather jacket. His eyes were locked on Gene. As he came closer, Gene saw the rage in his face. He was carrying a section of newspaper, rolled up. "Are you Alex Thomas's kid?" he asked from some distance.

Gene stood up. "I'm Gene Thomas," he said, as the man approached.

He was a short man with a head like a bulldog and a "white sidewalls" haircut.

"You ought to be shot as a traitor—and your old man along with you. He must agree with you or he would have shut you up a long time ago."

Gene found the man's accusations funny, actually, and he smiled. "You must not like my column," he said.

"My son died in Vietnam, and you dishonor his name every time you write. Now you're out to destroy the name of our president." He stopped next to Gene's desk and held out the paper, still in a roll. "Richard Nixon is a great man. He's had to make some hard decisions, but he's done it, and now you people in the press won't leave him alone. You take the side of the Communists every time."

"Communists?"

"Congress has no business nosing around, forcing its way into his private conversations."

Gene thought of asking the man to leave, even of calling a security man to take him out, but he decided to see if he couldn't calm him down. "I understand that argument. And I certainly think that you and I can disagree without getting mad at each other. But the *majority* of Americans actually agree with me. If President Nixon made those tapes for history, as he claims he did, they feel like he shouldn't be afraid to let us hear what's on them. To a lot of people, it sounds like he's got something to hide."

Before Gene could finish what he was saying, the man was shouting at him: "If that's what people think, it's because of the way you liberal reporters twist the truth."

Gene felt his patience wearing thin. He didn't have to waste his time talking to this guy. He glanced around the room to see that everyone was looking his way. A friend of his, Lew Daniels, had gotten up from his chair, not far away. He held both hands up, as if to say, *Don't let this happen, Gene. Don't argue with him.*

As calmly as he could, Gene said, "All I'm saying is, if he's not ashamed of his own behavior, why not release the tapes? Then we'll all know the truth—and we won't have to speculate."

"You're the one who ought to be ashamed. A man of honor doesn't bad-mouth his fellow soldiers."

"I've *never* done that. If you actually read my column, you ought to know that." Gene's voice had suddenly jumped in volume. He knew he had to stop now. The easiest thing was to walk away from the guy.

Gene took a couple of steps away, heading down the aisle between two rows of desks, but the guy yelled at his back, "Go ahead and run from me, you coward. You don't dare look me in the face and claim you fought with a recon team, because I know you didn't."

Gene stopped and looked back at the guy.

"That's right," the man said. "You're making up your own record, the same as you make up all this trash you write. You brag about your medals, but—"

"I've never said a word about any medals!" Gene shouted at the man. He took a step back toward him, but then stopped himself.

"I've read it all over the place: 'Gene Thomas, decorated Vietnam vet.'" The man walked closer, stood face to face with Gene. Lew was coming toward them, down the aisle, and Gene could hear someone else, coming from behind him.

Gene took a breath and then said, "It didn't come from me."

But the man slashed the rolled-up newspaper close to Gene's face. "Of course it didn't come from you. You know what a coward you are. You wouldn't—"

Gene's hands shot up, struck the man in the chest, and sent him stumbling up the aisle. The man caught his balance and then charged back, swinging with his fist. But Gene's reactions took over. He caught the man's arm and flipped him over, slamming him onto his back. His legs struck a desk, shoving it sideways. But Gene could only see the guy's ugly round head, could feel nothing but rage. He dropped onto the man and was about to drive the heel of his hand into his face when someone grabbed his arm. Gene jerked his arm loose and took another shot at the man, but by then someone had grabbed him around the neck and was pulling him backward. And someone else had hold of his right arm again. Gene knew it was Lew, but he tried to fight him, tried to hit him. He felt himself land on his back, and then Lew's face was in his, yelling, "It's all right!" Other people were grabbing him now, holding his arms and legs, but Gene felt crazy. He was struggling, kicking, trying to swing, and it took all the men to hold him down.

"It's okay. That's enough," people were yelling, but Gene jerked a leg free and fired his foot into one man's chest. He knew, and yet didn't know, that the man was a friend, a fellow reporter, Roger Crump. Roger got hold of Gene's leg again, this time held it down, and Gene gave up the fight for the moment, but he knew that he still wanted to break loose, and he wanted to kill that little man with the rolled-up newspaper. Kill him. Not argue with him. Just break his neck.

"That's enough, Gene. It doesn't matter," Lew was still saying.

Gene tried one more violent effort, arching his back and pulling with both arms, but the men held, and he knew he had no chance against them. So he screamed, "I'll kill him next time!"

"No, no, no. Don't say that. Don't say anything. Just breathe."

Gene did breathe, but he didn't care what the others thought. He could kill the man, would if he got the chance.

He lay quietly for a time, breathing, breathing, and then he heard sirens outside.

∞

It was dark when Gene woke up, and he didn't know where he was. He tried to move but felt the restraints on his arms and legs. "Gene, it's okay," he heard Emily say, but he couldn't see her at first. He didn't want to have her here, wherever it was. Why had she left him so long and then come to see him now? He was remembering the man with the newspaper and the things the guy had said. He remembered pushing the man, but he wasn't sure what had happened after that. Suddenly, he was afraid. He knew that he had done something, and he hoped it wasn't serious. He hoped he hadn't hurt anyone.

"Just rest for now, Gene." He felt her step close to him. She put her hand on his shoulder. "They gave you a shot, and you slept for a long time. Now you need to shut your eyes and relax."

"Did I hurt that man?"

"No. Not really."

"Did I try?"

"Yes. But Lew and some of the other reporters stopped you. It was all they could do to hold you, Gene, but you didn't hurt the man seriously. He actually told Lew he was sorry he had gotten so carried away. So sleep some more. You're going to be all right."

"When he came in there saying all that stuff, I just laughed at him at first. I was calm."

"I know. But he said some terrible things, and you lost your temper. Don't you remember that?"

"No." But Gene was starting to remember. He knew a bunch of guys had held him down, and he knew that he had yelled he would kill the man. Emily would have no way to understand that. She knew nothing about killing. She needed to talk to someone who had been in the war. Those guys knew. It wasn't just losing his temper; there was sense in it. If a man attacked you, you killed him. It was wrong to kill back here; he knew that. But there was still some sense in it; he had felt it at the time.

"Just sleep."

Gene didn't want to sleep, and he didn't realize that he had slept until he awoke again. He sensed that it was deep in the night by then. He thought he heard Emily breathing somewhere, the way she had when they had been together, taking long, smooth breaths. He loved Emily, and he knew she was upset with him. He told himself he shouldn't have tried to kill that guy.

The next time he woke up there was some light in the room from somewhere, maybe a window behind him. And when his eyes adjusted and he turned his head, he could see Emily in a chair not far away. "Can I go home now?" he asked.

Emily stirred and sat up straight. She looked bad—worse than he had ever seen her. Tired. Unhappy. Her eyes were squinting, and her hair was messy. "No," she said. "Not yet."

"When?"

"The doctor wants you to stay for a while."

"I won't hurt anyone."

"You don't know that, Gene. I thought I understood about your anger, but this goes deeper than I imagined. I'm worried about you. Everyone is."

"Who is?"

"Your mom and dad. Grandma."

"Does Grandpa know?"

"No. He's too sick. Grandma didn't want to worry him."

"But I'm okay now. There for a few seconds I wanted to hurt him, but I won't do it again."

"Gene, you fought six men. It was all they could do to hold you. You cursed and screamed. Everyone at the *Trib* is worried about you."

"It was just that second or two, and then I was all right."

"No. It went on for a long time. They finally had to give you a shot."

He remembered that. The men from the ambulance had pulled down his pants and given him a shot. That was true. But the whole thing wasn't as bad as it seemed. After a while he knew he was back in the States and shouldn't kill the guy. If people had given him a little more time, he would have been fine.

Emily came to his bed, but he couldn't reach for her. He was strapped down. The doctor must have thought he would try to hurt someone again.

It was such a stupid idea. He knew where he was now. He wasn't in Vietnam.

"If I can go home, I'll be fine. I need to get to school, and I need to finish my column."

"Not yet, Gene. You might have to stay here for a while. This time, you have to get better."

Gene tried to think about that. He knew he couldn't argue. Then she would think he was angry again. He decided he would never let himself get angry again. He would be very nice to everyone so they could see he was all right. But he needed to do all that as fast as possible, so he could get back to class and back to his work. "When's the doctor coming in?"

"I don't know. He said he would see you today. At first, you're supposed to rest."

"I feel fine. I can see him now. Could you try to find him?"

"Not yet. It's still very early."

"Is this the vet hospital?"

"Yes."

"Is it the psych ward?" Gene could smell all the things he hated— antiseptics, and just beneath them, vomit, or something sour and rank.

"Yes."

"Do they think I'm crazy?"

"They think the war had an effect on you, Gene. They think you had some terrible experiences there, and now—sometimes—the fear and the anger flash back. It happens to soldiers sometimes. Lots of them have problems like this, but the doctor told me you can get better."

"I'm better already. It was only those few seconds. Over there, it's what you do. If some guy comes at you, you have to—you know—stop him. I mean, like an enemy. Do you know what I'm saying? I think they gave me medicine. I'm not talking quite right. But the thing is, when he came at me, it seemed like I was back in the jungle. But I know where I am now. It was only for those few seconds that I thought I was back there."

"Gene, it's not good for us to talk about it. You're getting excited, and you really need to rest. Let's let the doctor—"

"I can talk about it. I'm not excited at all. I'm okay."

"But you don't know that, Gene."

"You told me I was my old self. Remember when you said that? If that guy hadn't yelled at me—and then charged at me like that—I'd be fine."

"Gene, I did think you were getting better. But you're still angry, and that's why I had to leave. There were times when I was afraid you would hurt me. Or maybe hurt Danny. I think you came pretty close a few times." Gene heard her voice break, and he turned his head to see that tears had begun running down her face. "But we're not supposed to talk about that. I don't want to get you upset."

"I'm not upset." But he was upset. He hated Emily when she talked like that. She had no idea how patient he had been with her. What if he *had* wanted to hurt her at times? He hadn't done it. The army had taught him how to kill, and no one had blamed him back in the jungle for doing it. They'd given him medals for it.

"Gene, let's have a prayer together. You need the Lord's help, or I don't know what's going to happen to you."

"No. I'm all right. I sort of lost track of everything for a few seconds, or maybe a couple of minutes, but everything's straight in my head again now."

"Why don't you want to pray, Gene?"

"I didn't mean that. I'll pray with you. You say it."

"No. You say it, Gene. You need to be the one."

"Okay. I will. But call the doctor after I do, okay? I need to explain to him. I'm sure I can go home now and be fine. If you could come with me, and bring Danny home, that would help me. Then I'd be all right. Maybe you could tell the doctor that. He needs to talk to me, and not make up his mind from what everyone else told him. And I don't want any more medicine. I know I'm talking all wrong. Just tell him you're taking me home, and coming home with me. Then everything will be all right. I know it will."

"The doctor said he would come by sometime this morning."

"Emily, don't do this." He heard his voice turn angry, as though it were outside him, coming from someone else. He didn't know why it had done that. He wouldn't do it again.

"Honey, you're struggling with things. I understand that. You can't help it. But you need to turn to the Lord."

"I go to church, Emily. You wanted me to go, so I'm going again."

"I know. But you don't pray the way you used to."

"I prayed in Vietnam, Emily. I prayed all the time."

"And you made it home."

"No, I didn't." And now he heard the bitterness in his own voice.

"Gene, you did make it home. It's just that—"

"Dearden didn't. He wanted to come home too. All of us did. But everyone died. Everyone got shot up. Whiley got messed up bad, and J. D. got his head blown off. His brains exploded. I know he was a jerk, but he didn't deserve that. He was just trying to help Whiley. All that stuff happened, Emily, just kept happening and happening, and no one stopped it. And then everyone says I'm angry. Do you know what I'm saying? I pound it down, but it all comes back, and there's Dearden with his blood running onto the ground, and he was just this good guy. He wanted to make it home. That's all we wanted. Any of us. I'm not angry. I'm just . . . I don't know . . . I don't know. I'll be all right. Just take me home, Em. Please take me home. Stay with me. Please stay with me." Gene hadn't meant to cry. She would tell the doctor he had cried. Everyone always made too much of everything. He just wanted to explain a little, and then he wanted to go home. The medicine was making things bad in his head. It wasn't good to take that stuff.

"Oh, Gene. I don't think I've had any idea what you've been going through. You need to tell me. You need to get all this out."

Gene twisted his head to see her again. He watched her use her fingers to wipe the tears off her cheeks, but more tears kept flowing. It hurt him to see that. He had made life so hard for her, he knew. But he didn't want to. "I'll pray," he said. "Hold my hand."

She came to him and took hold of his hand, and then he said, "I'm sorry, Lord. I'm really sorry. I've made things so bad for my wife and my son. I've been so angry. But I don't want to be that way. Please help us. Please help *me*. I don't want to be angry." Then he closed in the name of the Lord.

"That's a good thing," Emily said. "I feel better. It's what we need to keep doing."

Gene was remembering the man now—stumbling backward after Gene had pushed him. Gene seemed to be waking up, more all the time, and he could see the reality: he really could have done it. He could have killed that man.

"Gene, there's something you need to know."

"What?" Something in Emily's voice frightened Gene.

"When I left you, I thought maybe I was pregnant, but I wasn't sure. When I found out I was, I didn't tell you because I didn't know what was going to happen between us. But can you see me now? Can you see how big I am? The baby's due in two months."

Gene stared at her. "That's a good thing, Emily. We'll be a family again. You'll come home and we'll have two kids. I'll be a good dad. Honest. Maybe we'll have a little girl, like you always wanted. That'll be perfect. I'll treat her really nice." He tried to think whether he meant it, whether he could do it.

"Gene, you have to get better. Danny needs you to love him. He loves you, but you scare him. I asked him if he wanted to go back to our house and be with Daddy for Christmas. He said he did, but then he said, 'Does

Daddy like me? Does he want me to come home?' I think, in his little mind, we left home because you didn't love him."

"Oh, man. That's not it at all. You know that, don't you?"

"Of course. But think how he feels when you lose your temper with him all the time."

"I won't ever do that again. I'm going to try harder than ever."

"It's not that you aren't trying, Gene. You are. But you can't do it alone. You always think you can, but it hasn't worked. You've never admitted to yourself how serious your problems are. Maybe now, you can see what I've been afraid of, and maybe, if you talk to the doctor, and get to the bottom of things, you can do more than control yourself. You can actually get better, so you're not fighting yourself so hard."

Gene did have a problem; he had known that for a long time. He just didn't think talking would help. But he did need to get better for Danny. For the baby. And for Emily—especially for Emily. He tried to reach for her and then remembered the restraints on his arm again. But he saw that Emily had noticed what he wanted. She bent and kissed him. The kiss was so soft that it hurt. He had missed her so much, all this time.

Emily reached out and touched his cheeks. She wiped the tears away. He could see how hard it was for her to bend. He could see her bulging middle, his baby. He did have to get better. "I'll talk to the doctor. I'll tell him everything, okay? I thought that wouldn't work, but maybe it will. I'll try. I'll try anything. I don't want to kill anyone. I don't want to hurt Danny. I don't want to hurt you."

"Thank you, Gene. I think we'll be okay if you do that." She took his hand, held it tight, and she cried. Gene was glad he had said what he had; it meant so much to her. But he was terrified. Talking about it was like going back to see it all, and he had been trying for all these years to forget.

CHAPTER 24

It was Christmas, and Grandma Bea was sitting at the head of the table this year. Grandpa Thomas was home again after another brief stay at LDS hospital, but he was in bed, upstairs. Some of the family had gone up to pay him a visit, but he had had little to say, and those who had talked to him came back saying it might be better to let him rest. "He's such a grouch right now," Grandma said. "But he's not good at being sick. He's never taken time to learn. Nothing makes him so mad as to have to stay in bed."

The house was filled to overflowing, as it always was on Christmas. At the long main table in the dining room, along with Grandma, were four of her five children and their spouses. Beverly and Roger were with Roger's family and would be over later. Grandma had invited Diane to sit next to her "to even out the numbers." What Diane knew was that she was the one grandchild in the family who didn't exactly fit with any of the groupings. She was glad Jenny had fallen asleep in the car just before they had arrived at Grandma's house. She was upstairs having a good long nap after all the excitement of Christmas morning. Gene and Emily hadn't been so lucky with Danny, but his great-grandma had him next to her, on a chair stacked high with encyclopedias, and she was making sure he got more food than he wanted.

For John Burbridge, LaRue's new husband, this was his first Thomas family Christmas dinner. He and LaRue said they had to get back to John's children that evening. Diane noticed that John seemed perfectly willing to let LaRue be the one to shine, but he was congenial, and Diane liked him. At first she hadn't been sure what LaRue had seen in him. He had seemed too reserved and not as attractive as LaRue had made him sound. But Diane had warmed to him. He was not only smart but also thoughtful, and he talked to women easily, with a candor that seemed natural to him. He reminded Diane, in some ways, of her own father, and she noticed that Dad and John were quickly becoming friends.

Wayne and Joey, with their wives, were sitting at a card table. Wayne's wife, Dixie, had little Robert Walter on her lap. He was a year old now, walking, and squirming now to break loose. Cynthia Leigh, Joey and Janette's daughter, fifteen months old, was sitting in a high chair, making a mess on her face with candied yams.

Sharon and Joel were sitting with Kurt and Maggie, cousins who had never had much in common but who had always liked each other. Sharon was eight months pregnant and was looking flushed and uncomfortable. Joel was a strange young man, brilliant academically from all reports, but rather out of touch at social gatherings. Sharon seemed happy though, and Diane was glad about that. She and Sharon had grown up together, had always been very different, but they were finding things to talk about lately.

The high school group was small this year without Beverly's kids, but Glenda and Shauna, Kenny and Pam, were seated with Douglas and Ricky. There had never been anyone close to Ricky's age in the family, but he had always been a favorite with all the cousins. Diane noticed that he was talking more than anyone else at that table and was keeping the teenagers laughing. Douglas adored Ricky and laughed with the others as he always did, whether he actually understood the jokes or not.

"If Dad doesn't want to be in bed," Bobbi said, "let's have him come down and do the dishes."

"No. Not the dishes," Grandma said. "That's *women's work* to him. But ask him to shovel the walks and he'll be up in two seconds, looking for his coat and galoshes."

Wally was sitting at the opposite end of the table from Grandma. He called to her, "You didn't train him right, did you, Mom? Your sons' wives have done a better job getting their husbands in line. So have your daughters."

"All right, then, let's see you prove it," Grandma said. "I've been cooking since early this morning, and I'm not really all that excited about spending the rest of the day doing the dishes. This year, why don't you men clean up and we women will be the ones to sit and talk."

"Good idea," LaRue said. "John is wonderful in the kitchen. He cooks a lot just so we'll have something decent to eat." Diane watched how LaRue kept touching John's hand or leaning against his shoulder. She had always been an upbeat person, even during some hard years, but she had never seemed so happy as she was now, or so at ease.

"All right, then," Alex said. "We'll do the dishes. As the eldest brother, I'll supervise."

"You politicians are all alike," Wally told him. "You can't do an honest day's work."

But Alex had already stood up. He stacked Anna's plate on his own and then placed the utensils on top. Diane wasn't surprised when all the other men got busy bussing the dishes to the kitchen. Her dad always did that at home, and she had seen Wally and Alex do the same thing in their own homes. She was impressed, however, that the younger men got involved too. Gene carried some dishes into the kitchen and then came back wearing a frilly apron, which got a big laugh. He had been quiet today, but Diane could feel that something had changed in him since he had come home from the hospital. Diane had talked with him for a time, and he had told her about his plans to keep working as a reporter, but he hadn't bothered to get into any of his political opinions the way he had so much this past year. Diane had also watched him hold Emily, with his arm around her very thick waist, seeming to indicate that they were doing better. She was back with him now, and Diane, along with everyone else in the family, was hoping things would be all right between them.

Diane noticed Kathy's new fiancé, Marshall Childs, get up and start gathering plates and water glasses, and she could tell it was nothing new to him. He seemed comfortable around the family, and funny, and he treated Kathy as though he was thrilled just to be near her. Diane remembered the way Greg had been able to do that, but she had always known there was a level of performance in the way he treated her around other people, and she didn't pick up on any of that in Marshall. What she did notice was that he let Kathy be herself, talk to her cousins, express opinions, and he didn't try to influence what she said. Greg had always been embarrassed if Diane had said too much or said something he considered silly or stupid. On the way home, after, he would tell her the things she shouldn't have said. But Greg was married to another woman now, and Diane knew it was best not to think about him. She had been hired as a full-time teacher at Lewis School, where she had done her student teaching, and she was working very hard.

The dishes disappeared fast with so many men moving back and forth. Grandma was laughing by then. "I didn't think they would really do it," she said. "This is great."

Joey and Kurt returned about then. Joey said, "Dad told us to put away the extra tables and chairs." Kurt was wearing his hair almost down to his shoulders these days. Diane thought it was probably just as well that Grandpa hadn't seen him. What worried her, though, was that Kurt looked thin and pale, and he had had very little to say all day.

The women got up and moved out of the way. They gathered, as much as possible, in the living room. The younger cousins waited until the tables were gone and then took up residence in the dining area. Diane hardly knew where she belonged, but Grandma and the aunts, and some of the older cousins, were together, so Diane joined them. She sat down on the living-room floor since the chairs and couches were filled. Aunt LaRue always seemed the center of any gathering of this sort. "Kathy," she said, "Marshall is *impressive*. When you used to tell me about him, I got the idea that he was kind of flaky. But he seems smart, and he's *so* cute."

"I didn't want you to know," Kathy said. "You were still on the prowl, looking for a man of your own."

"That's right. I wish I'd seen Marshall first. I had to settle for that *old guy* you've seen around the house today." But she was beaming. "He's not too bad, though, is he?"

All the women had good things to say about both men. "John's distinguished looking," Grandma said. "He's so respectful to me that I want to say, 'Hey, I'm not so old as all that. You don't have to *venerate* me.'"

"That's how he is," LaRue said. "He treats his own mother the same way. But I've already learned how to shock him into reality. When he claims I've cooked a good dinner, I tell him he's going to go to hell for lying. He gets really red in the face. And I want you to know, I keep his face red a whole lot of other ways. I don't think his first wife was as forward as I am."

Lorraine, who was sitting on the couch with Anna and Bobbi, said, "I've had a crush on Marshall since Kathy brought him over the first time—which was about ten years ago. I didn't think Kathy was ever going to realize what she had."

"I didn't *have*. That was the problem."

"Well, you've *got*," LaRue said. "What's he decided to do?"

"He's negotiating to buy a cabinet shop up in Heber City. A man's willing to let him take it over without a down payment. Marshall wants to do it, but he's not sure he's ready to go out on his own. I keep telling him that's the best way to learn. But then, I want to live up there. That valley is so beautiful."

"That sounds good, Kathy," Diane said. "I envy you."

But that brought quiet to the room, and Diane was sorry she had said anything. Sharon had just arrived in the room carrying a chair from the dining-room table. She sat down awkwardly and took a big breath, as though breathing was work for her right now. She looked at Diane and said, "But I hear *you* have a boyfriend, Diane."

"Not really," Diane said. "There's a guy who . . . I don't know . . ."

"Who would give *anything* to marry her," Bobbi said.

"But it's not going to happen," Diane said. "I just don't feel that way about him." But she didn't want to be the object of pity and concern, so she changed the subject. "I hear you and Joel are going east for graduate school."

"Probably. Joel has applied to some really good programs, and it's almost certain he'll get in."

For a time the talk turned to what all the young couples were planning to do. Emily, who had been in the dining room talking to some of the younger cousins, finally walked into the living room. She appeared ready to sit on the floor, but with her baby due so soon, almost everyone in the room jumped up to offer her a seat. It was LaRue who won out. She slipped onto the floor and sat with her legs crossed under her, next to Diane, and Emily took the chair. "Emily," Kathy said, "I've been happy every time I've looked at you today. We all missed you so much these last few months."

"No more than I missed all of you. I feel home again."

"Gene seems so much better," Grandma said.

"I know. I guess everyone knows he ended up in the hospital a few weeks ago." She looked around, and so did Diane; everyone was nodding. "Well, that turned out to be good for him. He seemed to accept the idea, finally, that he was in trouble. He spent some time with a therapist and got some things off his chest. After that he finally opened up with his veterans' group. He's also told me a lot of things he had never said before."

Anna said, "Gene and Alex have been talking constantly since we got home from Washington. I have a feeling that's helping Gene, too."

"Actually, that's helped more than anything so far," Emily said. "Those two have spent *hours* together. Uncle Richard and Uncle Wally have both come over, too, and Gene's talked with both of them. Really talked. The truth is, he's still struggling. He's really nervous sometimes. But he's working hard to get things straight in his head."

"And he's doing it this time," Anna said. "The last time we were home, he couldn't control himself. Everything made him mad."

"I think he *is* quite a bit better," Emily said. "And a lot of it is just sheer effort. He wants so much to be a better daddy. He's been wonderful with Danny lately, and Danny is just *blossoming* under his dad's attention." Diane saw Emily's eyes fill with tears. She patted her middle. "He wants to do well with our little new one, too."

"Maybe his war is finally over," Grandma said.

"I don't think so. Not yet. But he's praying with me, and he accepted a call to the Young Men's presidency. That just happened this last Sunday. The week before that, he went to the bishop and told him he was ready for a calling. Always before, he'd claimed he couldn't handle anything like that. But he's still doing everything consciously—you know, on purpose. When he gets upset, I watch him fight for control. I don't know how long it will take until he doesn't have to try so hard."

Bobbi spoke quietly. "It took Richard *years* to get on top of things, and he was never exactly the same guy he'd been before. But it deepened him. He was a nice man before he shipped out. He was a *caring* man when it was all over. There's still a sense I have that he has this well of wisdom and knows how to reach it. He's not an impulsive person. He goes to that well before he acts. Just the opposite of me."

Lorraine took hold of Bobbi's hand and pulled it onto her lap. "It's as though they've known sorrow in a way the rest of us never will," Lorraine said. "There's no suffering that Wally can't imagine. What he tells me is that he saw so much death—and came so close to dying himself—that his whole life, since the war, has seemed a gift. He's got some of his dad in him, the way he sees right and wrong as pretty much clear cut, but at the same time, compassion is a natural response in him."

"He doesn't like weakness, though," Kathy said.

"That's true. He knows what humans can do when they have to, and he doesn't tolerate a lot of self-indulgence. Still, when I get really upset with people, he's the one who teaches me to be more accepting."

"I see things like that in Alex, too," Anna said. "He works so hard at his job, and he strains to get everything right, but sometimes I watch him sit and think, and I wonder where his mind is. It's as though he knows something I never will, and when he's tested, he goes back to it for strength."

"Gene has so much respect for his dad and his uncles," Emily said. "That's one of the changes I see. He told me yesterday that he never could have made it through this last month if they hadn't helped him. The more he's talked to them, the more he understands that they faced as much as he did—maybe more. That makes him feel that he can make it, too."

Diane watched Grandma, who had pulled out a handkerchief she kept tucked into the belt on her dress. She wound it around her bent fingers and dabbed at her eyes. Gradually, everyone noticed her, and quiet fell over the room. "You younger girls," she said, "it's hard for you to imagine what we all went through back then. Vietnam has been horrible, but it didn't change our lives at home very much. *Everyone* was part of World War II. All three of my boys went to war, and so did Bobbi, and it was such an awful worry."

Diane knew what Grandma was thinking. One of those boys had been killed, and on a day like this, she was surely feeling that loss all over again. Diane could see that LaRue was remembering too, and so were Anna and Bobbi and Lorraine.

Diane watched Grandma reach over and touch Emily's hair, then run her hand down to her shoulder. "But we didn't feel alone during that war. You and Gene haven't had the support we had, Emily. Maybe that's harder."

"We've had all of you, and that *has* made a difference. And he's still a Thomas. As mad as he gets at Grandpa for reminding him of the 'family heritage,' it's still who he is, and that's going to get him through." Emily looked at Anna. "He loves his mom, too. Lately, he's told me things about you and what you went through during the war. He told me that he gets ashamed that he's pitied himself so much when he thinks what your family had to face. The women in this family are just as strong as the men."

Grandma smiled. "Maybe stronger," she said. But she was still wiping away her tears.

Diane thought how thankful she was for these women she loved. She was going to survive too, she told herself. She certainly wasn't the first in the family to go through a hard time—and sometimes she let herself forget that.

❧

In the kitchen there were too many hands. Alex was elbow deep in water and suds, and he was passing dishes and pots and pans on to everyone else. Gene dried dishes for a time, but too many had wanted to help, so he had slipped over to the kitchen table and was listening to the men talk. Most of the discussion was about the oil embargo and the energy problems that had resulted. "I waited in line the better part of an hour to get gas this week," Richard said. "I had to keep starting and stopping my car, and my gauge was right on empty."

"It's bad here, but it's a lot worse on the east coast," Alex said. "You can pay over a dollar a gallon back there."

"I think Nixon was right to approve the Alaskan pipeline," Wally said. "We need to start producing more of our own oil."

Gene was not so sure about the pipeline. He wondered what effect the big pipe would have on wildlife. But he didn't say that. He knew that Uncle Wally still wanted to believe in President Nixon, in spite of everything.

Wally praised him for anything he could, but he also admitted that he didn't like what he was hearing about the Watergate mess.

"Alex," Marshall said, "what did you think about the Supreme Court ruling against the death penalty?"

"It was a surprise to me. And this is the same court that said abortion was okay. How do you put those two decisions together?"

Most of the men were standing, collected around Alex, moving in at times to get another plate or pan to dry, and all were facing away from Gene. Still, he knew they were waiting for him to react. He had created his own reputation this last year as the one with an opinion about everything. But Gene said nothing, and when no one else spoke, he asked, "Who's going to win the Super Bowl this year?"

Alex, as he handed a plate to Joey, said, "I don't see anyone stopping the Dolphins. They just run the ball down everyone's throat, with Csonka inside and Morris outside."

"I think you're right," Gene said. There were lots of nods and mumbled agreements, but no one had another opinion, and that conversation didn't go anywhere.

"Uncle Alex, what's going to happen to Nixon?" Wayne asked.

Alex glanced toward Gene before he said, "I don't know, Wayne. Things aren't going to get any easier for him."

"Do you think he should give up his tapes?"

Wally had finished drying a handful of utensils and was placing them, one at a time, in a cabinet drawer. "What bothers me about that," he said, "is that a lot of presidents have kept recordings. Johnson had them, and no one made him turn them over for the whole world to hear. How would you like to have all your personal conversations open for the public to listen in on?"

"It wouldn't bother me," Wayne said. "I don't have anything to hide. If Nixon is telling the truth, you'd think he'd be glad to turn them over and prove he's honest."

"That's the way I feel, too," Joel said, quietly but firmly.

Gene knew that all the men in the room were waiting for him to make his argument. He had made some promises to himself, however. He was going to listen more. A good reporter shouldn't be talking all the time; he should be learning from what others were saying.

Gene watched Alex reach around in the water and pull up a last few utensils. "He'll have to give up the tapes, sooner or later," Alex said. "I'm pretty sure about that. But it's going to take a long time for this country to heal, no matter what happens now."

"We've all become cynical," John said. Gene had almost forgotten that he was in the room. He glanced around to see that John was behind him, by the door, standing with his hands in his pockets. "We assume politicians lie, so we're not really that surprised when they admit it."

"I've been thinking about that lately," Gene said. "We talk about the underlying morality in our national character, but where are the people who won't sell themselves? Men with influence and money can manipulate the system and get what they want. The idea that the ultimate power resides in the common people may actually be a myth."

Alex walked over and sat down across from Gene. "When I first got elected, there was a kind of art to campaigning. People wanted to get to know you and get a feel for who you were. If they felt good about you, they'd vote for you. But now, campaigning is becoming a science. The honchos who run the campaigns know how to sell a candidate as a product. They tell you to wave the flag and spout a lot of platitudes when you speak for yourself, and hang a negative image on your opponent. Democracy has turned into a marketing strategy. Maybe it always has been, but marketers know more now, and they run this nation."

"So why do you keep running?" Marshall asked.

"I ask myself that question every two years. But I fear what sort of person some marketer can sell to my constituency. I'm not all I ought to be, but some of the alternatives scare me."

Gene glanced up. He saw that all the men were watching, listening, looking solemn. He didn't want the conversation to end the way it had been going, but he said, "I fear that the day is coming when all thought will be gone from our system. To admit that things are complex is like an invitation to vote for the guy who says that everything's simple. People actually don't like a candidate if he seems too intelligent. Stupidity has actually become an advantage. If a guy doesn't understand the issues, it's easier for him to repeat what his handlers tell him to say. He just smiles, stares glassy-eyed into the television camera, and stays on message."

Alex leaned toward Gene. "I think we stand at a crossroads," he said. "We're making this all about Nixon, but it isn't. It's about us. If we don't ask people to think, what is democracy?"

"But people *are* tired of the lies," Gene said. "And some *little* people did expose Nixon's lies. Maybe that's brought some of the power back to the grassroots."

"It's nice to think so," Alex said. "But remember, reporters can have undue power themselves. They can spread false information as effectively as anyone. What we need, more than anything, are honorable people who hold themselves to a higher standard."

Gene nodded. He told himself that's what he wanted to be. He had spent too much time with a point to make. He wanted to help people understand the issues, not push propaganda for his own position.

✎

Kathy and Marshall had promised to drive a couple of blocks over to the Childses' house for dessert. Kathy was starting to feel that she'd better go look for Marshall. But she was having fun with the women. They had often had talks like this while they had done the dishes on Christmas day, but it was better to sit back and relax together. She not only loved the closeness to her grandma, aunts, and cousins; she also liked hearing the muffled sounds of the men's talk in the kitchen and the laughter of the teenagers close by. She really wanted to stay at Grandma's house all evening.

The women had been talking—and laughing—about the challenges of raising kids, and teasing Sharon and Emily about wishing that their babies would come. "We all know the feeling," Bobbi told Sharon. "But rest well in the hospital. Once you get home, you won't get another good night's sleep for a long time."

"We don't *all* know the feeling," LaRue said. She looked up at Bobbi, seeming rather annoyed, and Kathy felt the awkwardness.

"Oh . . ." Bobbi said. "I'm sorry. I wasn't thinking. I just—"

"That's all right. I'm okay. Sure, you made me feel bad, but I can take it." LaRue was smiling a little by then—and looking rather sly.

Kathy had a sudden suspicion, but it didn't seem likely, so she didn't ask. But LaRue was smiling ever more brightly, looking around from one woman to the next. "What are you up to?" Grandma finally asked.

"Well . . ." LaRue lowered her voice. "It's still really early, so I'm not supposed to say anything yet, and I told John I wouldn't . . ."

Kathy thought her heart would stop. It was too much to believe.

"It looks like I'm going to have a baby. Can you believe that? I'm so old, and poor John has grandkids, but . . . what can I say?"

Five seconds must have gone by, and no one moved, no one said a word. It was as though no one could quite accept the idea. And then there was a burst of joy—a kind of whoop, like a victory celebration. Kathy dove for LaRue first, grabbed her in her arms, and then everyone rushed in after her.

❧

In the kitchen, the men were still talking rather solemnly when a scream erupted in the next room. Gene thought for a moment that something terrible had happened. But then he heard laughter, even joyful whoops. All the men stopped and looked at the door. Gene was about to head out to see what was happening when John said, "I knew LaRue couldn't get through the day without telling them."

"*What?*" Alex said, obviously guessing what John meant, and by now Gene was starting to realize.

John was smiling. He said, rather quietly, "I've been standing here thinking that I hope this country isn't in *too* much of a mess. I want our baby to grow up in the kind of nation we grew up in."

"Really? LaRue's pregnant?" Wally asked.

John was nodding. "I guess we're not as old as we thought we were."

The men put out something of a shout themselves. Alex was the first through the kitchen door, followed closely by Wally. Gene knew what this meant to the family. Even the younger guys knew. Everyone followed the uncles out and got in line. By then, the word had spread to the teenagers, too, and they had become part of the mob scene in the living room. The men held back and waited their turn. But Gene was standing close by when Alex came to John and put his arm around his shoulder. "America's going to be a good place for a long time, John," he said. "I really believe that. We have our problems, but we deal with them. Sometimes we're slow, and we're never quite what we ought to be, but I do think we keep working to get things right."

"That's what I've been thinking," John said. "There are so many scary things going on that it worries me to have a baby now, but I do think America has a good heart. And we've got two powerful families for our child to learn from."

Gene was waiting to tell John that he thought so too, and then he wanted to have his chance to talk to Aunt LaRue, who was still being hugged by all the females in the family. But Gene noticed Kurt, who had been standing in front of John and Alex and had certainly heard what they said. Kurt stood for a time, watched all the excitement, and then turned and slowly edged his way out of the group toward the entrance area of the house. He waited, maybe to see if anyone was watching him, and then walked to the front door, opened it, and slipped out.

Gene hurried after him. He had been wanting to talk to Kurt all day, and he hadn't had a good chance. Gene stepped outside, jumped off the porch, and then called, "Wait, Kurt."

Kurt turned around, close to his car, and Gene walked toward him. "I was hoping we could get some time to talk today," Gene said. "I haven't seen you for a long time."

"Yeah, I know. We'll have to get together. But I've got to go now."

"Could you maybe come by sometime this week?"

"Uh . . . I don't know. What for?"

"We need to spend more time together. We're brothers."

"Really? I don't see the resemblance." He shook his head, his long hair shimmering.

"I've been AWOL for a long time, Kurt—too wrapped up in my own problems. But I'm trying to come back."

"Don't worry. You'll be on top again. That's where you always feel at home." Kurt walked around his car and opened the driver's side door. Gene followed and caught up as Kurt sat down in his car. Gene grabbed the door so Kurt couldn't shut it.

"I love you, Kurt."

"Yes. You've told me that before."

"We need to talk."

"Gene, you heard what Dad and John just said. The baby is going to be fine. After all, he'll have *Thomas blood* running in his veins. But I have to wonder, What happened to me? Nixon isn't the symbol of what's wrong with America. I am. I stand for nothing at all, and I didn't even bother to vote."

"Kurt, you always say things like that. But I'm the one who's been a mess. I'm just trying to keep my head above water. Maybe if we talked, we could help each other."

"I've heard what you have to say to me: I ought to go to church, lay off the drugs, and be an upstanding citizen. If it's okay with you, I don't want to hear that speech again. I don't know why I even come to these family things; they make me feel like a freak."

"Kurt, I've been struggling to figure out what I believe and don't. But certain things are coming back to me now. We do have things we could say to each other. Why don't you come over tomorrow and—"

"I'll tell you what let's do. I'll promise to come, and you say, 'Great,' and then I won't show up. The nice thing about that approach is, you'll feel so good about yourself. I'm the family tragedy. But at least you can feel self-satisfaction when you offer to help me."

"Come on, Kurt. I'm being straight with you. Let me tell you what's gone on in my head lately. It's helped me to open up to people. Maybe it would help you if you could just talk out some of your feelings."

"Sorry, brother. You sound just a little too much like 'Tricky Dick.' Next you'll be asking me to trust you."

"Kurt, this family will always be on your side. We'll do anything we can to help you. I'm your brother, and I care what happens to you. You and I have both struggled to live up to Dad's image, and we've let it bother us way too much."

"You may be carrying Dad around on your back, but I've got *you* on top of me too. I don't think you'll ever understand that." Kurt jerked the door hard, pulling it out of Gene's hands. He started the engine and popped the clutch, screeching his tires as he accelerated away.

Gene stood and watched him go. He could smell the burnt rubber. He needed to go back and talk to Aunt LaRue, but he wished that, somehow, everyone he loved could be happy at the same time. It never seemed possible.

❧

On the following evening Gene turned on the ten o'clock news and learned that President Harold B. Lee had died. He was the president everyone had expected to lead the Church for many years to come. He had seemed in perfect health, and he had served only about a year and a half. Spencer W. Kimball was only a few years older, but he had not been in good health. Gene wondered how long he would be able to serve. Gene had been growing increasingly aware of the unpredictability of life; this sudden change only deepened the feeling.

CHAPTER 25

Hans and Elli were sitting in President Schräder's office. He had asked them before sacrament meeting if they could come in afterward. The little office was like a symbol of their branch—or the Church in the GDR, for that matter. The cubicle was hardly more than a closet, with plain walls, and little to make it fancy. But President Schräder made the place feel warm and comfortable. "So how is life now for our new married couple?" he asked. He smiled at them. Hans had once considered President Schräder a formal man, but the two had become close over time, and Hans knew that he could laugh, even tease, but he was more likely to laugh at himself.

"We're an *old* married couple now," Hans said. "We've been married over half a year."

"Oh yes, you're very experienced now. You've learned everything."

"The new apartment has made life easier. At first, we hardly had room to turn around without bumping into each other."

"*Ach,* that's something newlyweds don't mind so much." President Schräder laughed.

"We managed," Elli said, but Hans noticed that she was blushing.

"And I understand you have a baby coming. That's wonderful news. Have you felt all right, Elli?"

"Mostly. I have to go to work every morning, so I don't have a choice."

For the first time, President Schräder seemed almost solemn. He nodded. "Yes. That's how life is in our country. When I was a boy, hardly any women worked away from home. Everything's very different now."

"Even if it weren't expected," Hans said, "we couldn't afford to live without Elli working. We wish she could be home with our baby, but it's not a possibility."

"Life is not easy for the two of you, is it?"

"No, but it's wonderful, President," Elli said. "Hans is good, and he's smart, and he's very kind to me. What more could I want?"

"It's all true, *Schwester* Stoltz." President Schräder smiled. "But what if I ask you to do more work? Will you still be so happy?"

"Maybe not," Elli said, and laughed. "What do you have in mind?"

Hans, of course, knew what the president was talking about. Elli had been approved for a new calling in branch presidency meeting. Hans had told President Schräder it would be all right to ask her, but now he was wondering if it was really something she could handle. The problem was, he was sure she wouldn't turn it down, and he wondered whether he shouldn't have protected her from taking on more, with the baby coming.

"Sister Mehler has been called to be our new Relief Society president," President Schräder said. "She's asked for you to serve as her counselor."

"*Relief Society?*"

"Yes."

"I thought you might say MIA."

"I know. But Sister Mehler believes you would be good for Relief Society. Some of the younger women feel they're too busy to come to the meetings. She thinks you can be a good influence on them."

Hans knew that Elli sometimes felt out of place in Relief Society. Most of the women were much older than she, and they talked about so many things that were still ahead of her. She loved the women, but she didn't feel very close to many of them, even after being in the branch all fall and winter.

"Elli, in our country, if our young people are going to understand the gospel and grow in it, we have to pass along what we know from one generation to the next. We don't have Church leaders to teach us, the way they do in America. Experienced men must teach the young men and the boys coming up. For women, it's Relief Society we depend on. Young women need someone in Relief Society they can feel close to. Sister Mehler believes you could make contact with the younger ones who are drifting away from us and bring them back."

"I would try, President," Elli said, but Hans could see how overwhelmed she was. "It's just that I feel so young myself."

"Yes. But you've been raised by a family true to the Church, and you know what it means to live the principles you've learned in your own home."

Elli nodded. "I would do my best. It only seems that someone else could do better."

"Possibly. It's hard to say. But someone could be a better branch president than I—and yet, I'm called. We all serve as we're called, and we do our best. I wouldn't ask you if I didn't think you could do a wonderful job. Hans has told me this won't be easy for you, not with work and with a baby on the way—but you won't be expected to work every night at this calling. If you can give it a few hours a week, you can accomplish a great deal."

"It's good, President. I'll try to do it. God blessed me to have Hans; I won't ever say no to the Lord."

"That's the spirit I want you to show to the younger women in our branch. Hans can go with you at times and help you find them. Sister Mehler will help you too. Invite them back, and then show them what it means to be part of a sisterhood."

"I'll try, President. My mother was Relief Society president for a long time in Magdeburg. She was very close to the women. I watched how she did things."

"You'll learn it firsthand now, Elli. You're one of the brightest lights among our young people. The day is coming when you'll be a Church leader in the GDR. You'll help the next generation understand what you learn now."

"I need to grow so much," Elli said, and tears came into her eyes. "So many responsibilities are coming to me all at once."

The baby wasn't due until fall, but Hans had seen what the pregnancy had done to Elli. She had become more serious lately. She had read the scriptures with him from the beginning of their marriage, but she had asked more questions lately, deeper ones, and had plenty of insights of her own. Hans knew she wanted to be ready to be a mother. And now this.

When Hans and Elli left the office, Sister Mehler was waiting. She looked a little anxious as she watched President Schräder. "Yes, she accepted," the president said.

Sister Mehler hurried to Elli and took her in her arms. "You're so good," she said. "So lovely, and such an example of what our younger women need to be. You'll be perfect."

"You'll have to help me."

"I will; don't worry. But I don't know everything myself. We can help each other."

"Are you sure I'm ready?"

"I prayed so much about this, Elli. I asked and asked, and your name kept coming to me. At first I said, 'No, she's too young.' But the Lord kept saying your name. I would see you so clearly, every time I asked. So I told President Schräder, and he prayed too, and then he said, 'Sister Mehler, I'm going to call her.' So I feel certain it's the right thing."

Hans could see that Elli was moved by this. She was glowing when she stepped away from Sister Mehler, and tears were on her cheeks. Hans was impressed again, as he often was, at the idea that God cared about such things—that he knew Elli's name, that he listened to Sister Mehler's questions and answered them. The Lord could create a universe, but he could also guide a little branch, even listen to the question of *one* of his children. There had been a time when such ideas had been absurd to

Hans and proof that God was a myth, as his teachers at school had claimed. But he had experienced too much now. He had asked and God had answered. In prison, God had been there with him, lifting him, and when he had been about to return to prison, God had said, "Let my child go," and it had happened. All that still sounded like myth to Hans, and it would have been hard for him to make a logical argument to anyone that it could be so, but it was simply true for him. It was his experience. He could now live with truth that came directly, whether his rational mind could explain it or not.

Hans and Elli walked to the streetcar stop, and then they decided to walk all the way home, since the weather was nice on this March afternoon, and they had much to talk about. "Do you ever think we're too young to be doing all this?" Elli asked Hans.

They were near the main train station downtown, and lots of people were on the streets, even on a Sunday. Hans knew that most of them hadn't been in church that day, that the day was a holiday for most, their one day away from work. How different it was to know the meaning of the Sabbath in a nation that was clearing away all such ideas. "I knew this would happen; I didn't know it would happen so soon."

"How long have you known I would be called?"

"Only for a few days. But that's not what I mean. When I had a chance to leave this country, the Lord told me I needed to stay. It made sense to me then that he would need me to keep the Church alive in a land that doesn't believe in religion. But I had no idea I would be called to lead so quickly. And I didn't know you would be asked to do so much so soon."

"I was a child when you met me, Hans. I almost wish you hadn't known me then. I was so silly back then."

"I'm glad I did. I've watched you become who you are."

"I want to marry you in the temple, Hans. President Schräder told us we would have that chance, somehow, sooner or later. But with the baby coming, I wish it could be now. That's the one thing missing in our lives."

"No. It isn't missing. We're promised to each other for eternity. And the Lord will see to it that we're sealed. He wouldn't have asked me to stay here without planning to open up a way for us."

"You have so much faith, Hans."

Hans laughed. "No. I have so little. You're the one with real faith. But I can't deny what's happened to me. What I have is trust—based on all that's happened to us so far."

"Do you ever worry that the *Stasi* will think of some reason to come after you again?"

"Only every day."

"Do you really think of it that much?"

"How can I not?"

"Do you blame everything on Rainer?"

"No. If he did say those things about me, I understand the pressure they put on him. But I don't think he did. I think they were testing me— just to see how I would react."

"It's what you want to believe about Rainer."

"Yes, it is. And I want to think that *Herr* Feist has lost interest in me. The GDR is better off letting me design buildings than keeping me in prison. But it's hard to say. Something could happen again, and if it does, we'll have to be strong."

"I don't think I'm strong enough to let them take you away from me. But I don't think the Lord would ever let that happen."

Hans thought of telling her that the Lord let lots of things happen in this world, and Hans could be dragged away again. But he decided to rely on Elli's faith. His own faith was never on a steady plane very long. He was a born doubter, and doubts would come again. He wondered what tests might be in store for him and Elli. But he did believe the Wall would fall someday, and all the wire fences and guard towers would come down.

Maybe it wouldn't happen in his own lifetime, but if not, somehow the Lord would open the way and let his people reach the temple. Since the time of the children of Israel, the Lord had always parted seas for his children, and he would look out for them now. Hans and Elli simply needed to stay worthy.

∽◦∽

The end of the school year was not so far off anymore, and Diane was looking forward to some months off and some full days with Jenny. Jenny would be five next fall and not quite old enough to start kindergarten until the following year, but she would go to preschool, and she was already looking forward to that. She was such a mature little girl, and she had learned so much from Grandma. Bobbi had been wonderful with her, and Diane was pleased that Jenny wasn't rejecting the things that Diane had rejected. She loved books, and she was reading a good deal already. Bobbi had worked with her on her letters, and so had Diane. Jenny had made the connection of letters and sounds without the slightest difficulty. But beyond that, she liked the stories, liked to ask questions about the characters. Diane loved her curiosity.

Diane picked up Jenny after school on a Friday in April and arrived home to a house that needed some serious cleaning. But she wasn't going to start now; she would do that Saturday morning. She started dinner instead. Jenny loved spaghetti, so that's what Diane was boiling when the doorbell rang. Diane knew who it was, of course, and she wished it wasn't, but she walked to the door and opened it. "Hi, Lloyd," she said. "Do you want to eat spaghetti with us?"

"I stopped by to see if I could take the two of you out for hamburgers."

"Too late. Dinner's almost on. Come on in—and eat *my* spaghetti. I've been putting on weight this spring."

"If you ask me, you look great."

She saw him look her over, and she sensed his longing for her. It was amazing how little affection she ever gave him and how eager he was to accept whatever she granted. Greg would have written her off in a minute had she treated him the same way, back when they first dated.

Lloyd stayed for dinner. He teased Jenny about sucking her spaghetti into her mouth, "like worms," and Jenny laughed at him. Then after, he helped pick up all the dishes, rinsed them, and put them in the dishwasher. Jenny walked into the living room and turned on the TV. "Turn it down," Diane told her. "There's nothing on but the news." But she glanced to see that Jenny had found something to watch on educational TV.

"I've been thinking," Lloyd said. "I'd like to go on a real vacation this summer. I haven't done that for a while."

Diane was wiping off the table where Jenny had scattered plenty of her spaghetti. "Why don't you go to Europe?" Diane said. "You can afford it."

"Not really. I'm saving, and I might do that someday, but not yet."

Diane watched him. She knew he had something in mind that would involve her and Jenny. He was smiling a little, for no reason. He never could hide what he was feeling. He had a childish look about him with his carefully combed hair and his little boy's teeth that had never been corrected, as needed, by braces. "You spend too much money on Jenny and me. You could save a lot more if you quit doing that."

Lloyd closed the dishwasher and turned around. "No. That's not true. I'd have no life at all if I didn't do a few things for you two."

That, Diane thought, was sadly true. He worked, and he carried out his Church assignments, but his social life was mostly wrapped up in Diane and Jenny.

"What I was thinking is that maybe I could drive you two down to Disneyland. We could let Jenny ride on the tea cups and all those things. And we could stay at a place with a swimming pool. Jenny hasn't even seen the ocean."

Diane was rinsing out the dishcloth. She turned toward Lloyd and put her finger to her lips. "Don't let her hear you. She really wants to go there, and my parents have talked about taking us down. But I don't want her to know until it's really going to happen."

"Let's make it happen, then. We could go right after school is out in June—before the biggest crowds hit the place."

"No, Lloyd. I can't let you do that."

"Why not? I want to. My happiest times are when I'm with the two of you. I could go somewhere with one of my friends, but that's not the same. I don't want to travel just to be traveling. I want to be with people I . . . you know . . . care about."

"Lloyd, that's just the problem," Diane whispered. "Greg comes up to see Jenny less all the time. Jenny hardly knows she has a father. I don't want her to be confused by this situation. You're our friend, but I think she wants you to be more than that."

Lloyd stood for a long time, facing Diane, watching her. "So do I," he finally said. "You know I do."

It was the closest he had ever come to admitting what he actually felt for her. He had always been careful, and Diane knew why. He knew very well that if he asked for her love, he wouldn't get the answer he wanted.

"Sit down," Diane said. She motioned to the kitchen table, and the two sat down across from each other. "Lloyd, I don't think this situation is healthy for any of us. You're a good friend, and you've helped me get through a hard time, but I can't picture us ever getting married, so all we're doing is making things awkward for each other."

Lloyd wouldn't look into her eyes now, but he asked in a quiet voice, "Why couldn't we ever be married?"

"Lloyd, I'm not in love with you."

"And you don't think you could ever feel that way?"

"No, Lloyd, I don't. We're just too different. I appreciate you, but I'm not going to marry someone because he's been a good friend. Once you've been through a bad marriage, you don't want anything resembling it again."

"I'm nothing like Greg."

"I know that. But how could I be married to someone I don't feel that kind of attachment to? Marriage is a friendship, but it's a lot more than that."

"I think it can start with friendship and build." He finally looked at her. "It might be better if it does start with friendship. I know I'm not a good-looking guy, and I don't—"

"This has nothing to do with looks, Lloyd. You look fine. It's just that sometimes a person becomes your friend, not someone you want to give your whole self to, forever. You know how that is."

Lloyd looked at the table again. "Diane, maybe I have enough love for both of us. I love everything about you. I'm only happy when I'm here."

Diane hated this—hated what she was doing to him.

"I love Jenny, too," he said. "I could give her what she needs, and I'd make my whole life a mission to give you what you need—to make you happy."

Diane knew how it felt to be in love, and she knew what it was like to be rejected. She ached for Lloyd. She had seen this moment coming for such a long time and had always known how much it would hurt both of them. "Lloyd, we're not on the same wavelength. We have nothing to talk to each other about. We talk about Jenny and a few things in general, but you don't ask the same questions I do. I'm trying to figure this world out right now, but when I ask you what you think, you tell me you don't worry about those things. There's nothing wrong with that; a person can be happy without struggling with all that stuff. But I need someone who's as curious as I am, and someone who challenges me to think and feel. This is something I've grown into in the last few years, and I don't want to change back to the person I was before."

"I know all that. I've been reading the paper more lately. I'm starting to change, I think."

Diane was stunned by the words. "Oh, Lloyd, no. That's what Greg did to me. He said I wasn't adequate. I didn't know anything. I couldn't talk to him about the things he was interested in. So I tried everything to be what he wanted me to be—and I couldn't do it. I would never do that to you. There was nothing wrong with me, and there's nothing wrong with you. We're just different. Remember when we went to see *The Great Gatsby*, and it just blew me away? You were bored to death. That's okay. All I'm saying is, I wanted to talk to you about it that night, and you said you didn't see the point of the movie. Do you see what I'm saying? We're just too different."

"You could tell me why you like it, and what's good about it and everything, and I could try to see what you mean. I mean, it's just a movie."

"No. It's not the movie. It's the way we feel inside. It's how we react to things. It comes down to who we are."

"Look, I know I should read more. I should pay more attention to the news and stuff. I know it bothers you that I don't keep up with things better. But I know you'd change me after a while."

"You can't try to change yourself just to satisfy me—not without lots of pain and unhappiness."

"Diane, I don't know about that. I don't know if talking about things is the main thing in a marriage. My parents hardly did any of that at all. What I know is that I could provide for you and take care of you, and I could try to give you the life you want and need. I would always treat you like a queen."

"I know. I see that every day, Lloyd. But I don't want to be a queen. I want a partner. And I need to start my day thinking how lucky I am to be married to someone I love. It's not something I can force."

Lloyd nodded. He sat back for a time. "Listen," he said, "I didn't mean to get into all this right now. We don't need to go to Disneyland. I just want to help you any way I can."

"Lloyd, no. This isn't fair. I think it's time we stop seeing each other. I'll miss you, and Jenny will miss you, but it's what we need to do. I've been putting this off way too long. Neither one of us is going to find anyone if you're always coming here. You need to find someone else, and I need to start thinking about ways to meet more men. I do want Jenny to have a daddy someday."

Lloyd stared at her for a long time. "No one will ever love her more than I do," he finally said.

Diane began to cry. She reached for Lloyd's hand, and he gave it to her. "I know, Lloyd. I wish I could fall in love with you. I really do. But it isn't going to happen. I'm sorry."

"I've been thinking, lately, it's time for me to move," Lloyd said. "I need to buy a house so I can build some equity, and I need to start over with my life. I'm going nowhere right now."

"I know. I've told you all those things before."

"That's true. You have." He sat again for a time, and then he finally slid his chair back and stood. "Well, I'd better go now. I might see you at church, but I won't come over. I'll get the elder's quorum president to assign you a new home teacher."

Diane stood too, and she walked around the table. She kissed Lloyd on the cheek. "I'm so, so sorry," she said.

"I know." He took a couple of steps away, and then he looked back. "I'll always love you. You've made me happy these last two years. You know—even though it's been frustrating, too."

"I've been unfair to you—because I needed your help."

"Well then, I guess it was good I was here at the time."

"Someone's going to love you, Lloyd. It's what you deserve."

"Sorry if I don't believe that. But thanks for saying so." He stepped into the living room and said, "Good-bye, Jenny. I love you."

She was watching TV and hardly looked up. "Bye," she said. He walked out and shut the door carefully behind him.

Diane had never felt so ugly in her life, so cruel. If she had done this a month after he had first come into her life, that would have been all right. But she had taken and taken from this man and then finally sent him on his way. She sat at the table again and hated herself, and then she got up and called her mother. "Mom, I just broke it off with Lloyd." The words made her cry again. She leaned her forehead against the cabinets by the wall phone.

"You broke his heart, didn't you?"

"Yes, I did. I don't know what's wrong with me."

"Diane, you always knew that you weren't interested in him. He knew it, too. It was his choice to keep coming back. He must have been expecting this for a long time."

"Does it matter if he doesn't like the things I like? Can a marriage work all right with two people having their own separate ways of thinking about life?"

"I don't know, Di. I don't think it's so much about likes and dislikes. But there has to be an attraction, and who knows what causes that? There are times when I look at your dad and still feel all tingly. We're part of each other. Maybe a couple can work at that, but a certain amount of it has to be there to start with."

"I'm afraid to be married, Mom. Greg made me feel I was bad at all the intimate stuff, so I'm afraid to go back to that. Maybe I kept Lloyd away because I knew I would end up married again—and I'm still afraid of how I would handle that part."

"No. Some man is going to make your knees weak. And then you won't be afraid at all."

"I don't think so, Mom. I think I'm going to raise Jenny, and then she'll find a man she loves, and I'll be alone after that—forever." The tears came hard now, and she pushed her forehead against the cabinets.

"There's something in me that doesn't work right. Greg saw it, and now I can see it in myself."

"Don't tell me that. You're a pearl of great price, girl. Greg tried to teach you that you weren't, but get him out of your head. I know you better than he ever did."

"I don't want to be alone. And now Lloyd won't even be stopping by to visit. I'm back where I started."

"No. You're not. You're not even the same person you were when you left Greg. You're turning into the person you were always meant to be. You're smart and strong, and you know what you care about. Greg didn't let you have any of that. And you know as well as I do, Lloyd would never make you happy. The fact is, in the long run he wouldn't have been happy with you either. He doesn't think so now, but he would have found out over the years."

"I can't make all my plans in life based on whether I find a husband or not."

"No, you can't. You're a wonderful teacher and a wonderful mother. Do those things, and then see what else happens."

"Those are all the things I tell myself. But sometimes I'm just so lonely."

"Oh, Di. I wish I could make things different. I wish I could fix everything for you."

"You do plenty for me, Mom. I've just got to grow up. I've got a little girl looking up at me right now, wondering why I'm crying, and I've got to think about her."

"Okay. Do that. Call me again, later tonight."

"Okay. But I'll be over this by then. I'm not going to feel sorry for myself."

Diane hung up the phone, and then she reached down and picked up Jenny. "Don't cry," Jenny said.

"I won't. I'm sorry. Should we drive down to Farr's and get some ice cream?"

"Okay. Is Lloyd going?"

"No. Lloyd is going to move away. We probably won't see him too much."

"I want to see him."

"I know. But we have lots of friends."

"No, we don't."

"Well—we'll get some more. Right now, we need some ice cream. What kind do you want?"

"White."

"Vanilla?"

"Yeah."

"Aw, let's think up something better than that. Let's get fudge ripple or burnt almond fudge."

"I don't like those."

"Okay. That's all right. You choose whatever you want. You don't have to like what I like."

CHAPTER 26

Kathy and Marshall had moved to Heber Valley. A couple of months before their wedding they had not only bought a business, but they had also bought an old house, and Marshall had been putting in his evenings fixing it up. In June they spent their honeymoon at Banff and Lake Louise, in Alberta, Canada, and then returned for their first night in their Heber City home. It was still very much a work in progress, but Marshall did have their bedroom looking nice. He had torn out some of the old plaster that was crumbling, patched it with plasterboard, and painted the walls a soft beige color. He had also sanded the hardwood floor, then stained and finished it. With an antique brass bed and a patchwork quilt for a bedspread, area rugs on the floor and a tall floor lamp, the room looked quaint and old-fashioned. Kathy loved it. The only problem was, most of the house was still in shambles.

Marshall had lots more wall repair to do, and he wanted to remove the paint from all the old woodwork, including a pretty banister on the steps that led to the second floor. Eventually, he was going to tear out the cabinets, too, and modernize everything in the kitchen, but they couldn't afford that yet, so they were going to get by for now with worn linoleum and cabinets painted a dull shade of green.

It would be a beautiful house, in time—bigger than they needed, really—and Kathy wasn't discouraged by the work that lay ahead. It actually sounded exciting. The trouble was, for now, she was staying in college, and that meant driving all the way to Salt Lake most days—almost an hour's drive each way. Life was going to be challenging with Marshall starting his business, a good deal of work already lined up, the house to do, and Kathy gone so much. But Kathy wanted to finish her degree while she could, and the house had come very cheap because it needed so much work. For newlyweds, they had taken on a lot of debt with the house and the business, but they were both convinced they would come out fine. Marshall would have to work very hard for now, and Kathy would try to get some work once she finished school—unless, of course, a baby came along, and they didn't really want to wait very long for that. They were older than a lot of newlyweds, and they wanted several children.

But none of this worried Kathy. She had never been so happy in her life. The days in the Canadian Rockies had been a dream to her. Marshall loved to be outdoors, and even though Kathy had never been much of one to go camping, she did love to hike and, more than anything, sit where she could look out across mountains and lakes as they had done so often during their honeymoon. She liked the new intimacy—all of it. She loved long, long talks with Marshall about things that had always been hard for her to admit to anyone: her inner struggles over the years with her faith, with accepting others' opinions, with recognizing what was actually important to her. She loved to have him near her night and day, their skin touching, the little signs of affection. She hadn't known how alone she had been until she had experienced this constant contact.

"Hey, this is good," Marshall said. They were sitting at a card table in the kitchen—the only table they had for now.

Kathy had cooked one of her mother's favorite dishes. It was called a "skillet dinner" and was made with hamburger and tomatoes and noodles. Kathy had cooked a fair amount in her life, having been on her own a good deal, but she usually did things simply. She didn't consider herself a real cook. But during the spring, while they had been engaged, she had gone through her mother's recipe box, picking out things that would work well for two, and she had tried them out, practicing at her own apartment. Her mom had always liked to cook, and Kathy had been happy to let her do it. She had paid little attention as a teenager, but now she wanted to learn.

What Kathy really wanted was to be good at things that were basic, that built a family. She wanted to quilt and bottle fruit, and she wanted to learn to sew, which she had hardly done at all. It all had to do with the life she and Marshall had chosen. She liked to imagine herself as carrying on the tradition of the Mormon pioneers. She wanted to learn from the women in Relief Society, keep a good supply of food storage, teach her children to appreciate a solid, down-to-earth life. At the same time, she wanted to take them to Salt Lake to hear the Utah Symphony, to visit the Museum of Natural History at the University, and to wander through the zoo. She wanted life to be rich and interesting—full of good books, wholesome food, outdoor fun, and all the variety possible. It was all a vision to her, and if she was being overly idealistic, she didn't care. Marshall wanted the same things, but he laughed at Kathy sometimes, told her that real life was never quite so rapturous as she wanted it to be. But she was enraptured with him, and she refused to believe that their honeymoon ever had to end.

"Of course it's good," Kathy told Marshall. "I know how to cook."

"I'm not surprised you can cook. I just didn't expect this stuff to be quite so tasty. It looks sort of evil."

"One of these days I'm going to start baking bread. How will that be?"

"Do you know how?"

"No. But I'm going to learn."

"I think your hippie heritage is coming back to you."

"Hey, this is my pioneer heritage. I want to be one of those grim, overworked mothers you see in those old photographs—wearing an apron and a kid clinging to each leg."

"Sounds like a good plan. I need some bib overalls. In a few years we'll look like the old couple in the American Gothic painting."

"That's our future."

"I thought you were Miss Urban all these years—the Smith College girl who liked to go to New York for little vacations."

"I only did that two or three times, and New York made me nervous. But there was a time I thought I could only live in a big city. What I like here is that we're close enough to Salt Lake, but we can have all the small-town advantages." Kathy smiled to herself. They had been married nine days, and already they were starting to repeat conversations. Her parents had always done that, and she had thought they were strange. "It's going to be so good for our kids."

"Kids? Do we have kids?"

"Not yet. I'll have to ask my mother what we have to do to get some."

"Why don't you call her right now. I'll wait and be ready to do whatever I have to."

Kathy was thinking she would like to drag him off right then and take him up on his offer. But Marshall had been saying he was going to work in the living room after dinner. He had hung some plastic to keep the dust out of the kitchen, which he wanted to get finished next.

"If you don't mind, I think I'll get in there and start on those walls," he said. "We'll have good light for quite a while yet. It helps when I can see with natural light."

"So that's it? I cook and I wash the dishes, too?"

"No, I didn't mean that. I'll help you first."

"No. You go ahead. You have a lot to do—and I don't want you to work too late, if you catch my drift." She stacked her utensils onto her plate and was about to get up from the table, but he was smiling at her, and suddenly she wanted to forget the dishes and the walls and anything else they thought they had to do that night.

"Are you sure?" Marshall asked. "I'll help with the dishes. It'll just take a minute."

"No, that's okay. But I do think we always have to be fair in the way we divide up our jobs. Dad was always gone so much with his work and church duties that Mom ended up doing almost everything around our house. Dad was always loving with us—and he helped around the house when he was there—but lots of times he seemed disconnected from our family."

"Really? Disconnected? You've never said that before." He got up, but he carried his plate and utensils to the sink.

"You know what I mean. I wouldn't even see him. He'd go straight from work to a church meeting and get home after I was in bed." She followed Marshall to the sink.

As Marshall was rinsing his plate, he said, "I know you were on the outs with your dad for a long time. He used to tell me about it when I would see him during those years you were away from Salt Lake."

"He never stopped loving me, though. I hope we can give our kids that kind of support. My parents lost patience with me sometimes, but they never gave up on me."

"I don't ever want to be gone from our kids that much. I know I'll get carried away if I'm not careful. It'll be easy to get on a job and think I have to put in a couple more hours to get it out the door on time."

"And sometimes you'll have to do that."

"I know. But maybe I can get up earlier, or not take on so much. I want to be part of raising my family. My dad was always involved in a thousand projects. He traveled a lot, and I can remember how much I missed him."

Marshall had gone back for their drinking glasses. He brought them to her, and she set them in the sink. As she started to run some hot water, he picked up the butter dish and the salt and pepper shakers. "Where are you going to put this stuff?" he asked.

"Just set them on the counter. I'm still trying to figure all that out." A lot of her dishes and kitchen implements were still packed. She and Marshall had had a huge reception, with more gifts than Kathy could believe. A lot of things had been duplicated, so she needed to drive back to Salt Lake and do some serious trading, but she knew she would never have room for everything in this little kitchen. Part of the plan was to move a wall, in time, and add lots more cabinet space.

"I guess we'll never do everything right," Marshall said. "Our kids will probably blame us for moving away from Salt Lake. They'll feel deprived when they talk to their cousins who go to the big Salt Lake high schools."

"Yeah, and I'll probably have a daughter who wants to go east to college."

"No. She'll be a right-winger and think you're a pinko Communist."

"Yeah. Her hero will be Richard Nixon—just from all the nice things she's read about him."

Things had gone from bad to worse with Nixon lately. He had finally been forced to release his tapes, and every day there were new revelations. Clearly, he had done everything possible to hinder the Watergate investigations. Impeachment proceedings were coming, almost certainly, and sometimes it seemed that the country was on the edge of collapse.

"Let's always be fair with our kids, okay?" Kathy said. "Let's hear them out. And let's talk things out when we have differences or the work seems out of balance. I think we can solve any problem if we just stay open and willing to listen to each other."

Marshall was smiling. "Okay. We'll be the perfect family—the first one ever." He tried to put his arms around her.

She gave him a playful little push away, with both hands on his chest. "Come on. Don't do that. We can do things right if we start out right and never let down. If you start staying too long at work, I need to be able to tell you that—without making you mad. And if I get going on my causes too hard, you need to be able to tell me. We can be the same way with our kids."

"It's a deal."

"You're laughing at me. You just want to get off to the living room so you can work and not have to listen to me anymore."

"No. I want to get to work so I can get finished and take you up on that early-to-bed idea."

She nestled against him, then kissed his ear. "Why not now?"

"Don't do that, Eve. I'm powerless against your charms. But I do have to get some work done."

"Fine. Go ahead. Miss your chance. I may be tired later."

"Are you serious?"

"No. Go ahead."

He smiled. "Okay, but I'll stop early."

He started away, but Kathy said, "I know we won't be perfect, Marshall. I've always been too idealistic. Our parents didn't get everything right, and we won't either. But they're good people—your parents and mine. And we always knew that. Even when I disagreed with my parents, I always knew how good they were. We can do that, can't we?"

"We can. And we can love each other. Kids need to know that their parents are in love."

"My parents were crazy about each other. I could always tell."

"Yeah. Mine, too."

"I'm crazy about you, Marshall. I hope you know that."

He came back and took her in his arms. He held her for a time, and then he kissed her. "Now or later?" he asked.

"Both."

"Okay."

"Now, that's what I call finding balance," Kathy said. She had started to untie her apron.

∽✧∾

On Sunday Kathy and Marshall went to church in their new ward. Kathy had expected everyone to greet them, but only a few did. Others seemed not to pay much attention. She noticed more than a few men in sport coats with cowboy yokes sewn into the shoulders, and she hadn't realized that bolo ties were considered Sunday attire. She told herself to stop thinking those things, immediately. These were going to be her people. She wanted to get to know every person in the ward—make them her new family.

She and Marshall sat down in a pew, and Kathy looked around. It was a fairly new building, more or less a replica of the newer ones in Salt Lake. The Church had started using similar plans on all the new buildings. Kathy leaned forward and tapped an older woman on the shoulder. "Hi. We're Kathy and Marshall Childs. We just moved into your ward."

The woman twisted in her seat, and so did her husband, who didn't twist very easily. The woman was hefty, white-haired, and had on a cotton dress with little pansy-looking flowers in the pattern. "It's nice to meet you," she said. "My name's Beula Furniss. And this is my husband, Will." He nodded. Brother Furniss had a red face and a white head, mostly bald. He seemed the sort of man Kathy had called a redneck during all her years in the "movement." She and her friends had blamed him for all the wrong attitudes about the war and for harboring wrong ideas about race and civil rights. But this was the kind of couple Kathy wanted to get to know now. She had to drop her assumptions; she needed to enter into a dialogue with people like that and find out what they were really all about. "What house are you living in?" Beula asked.

"It belonged to the Taylors, just around the corner from—"

"Oh, yes. I heard they finally got their house sold. It was awful run down, from what I heard."

"Yes. But my husband's a carpenter. He's fixing it up."

"Well, it's very nice to meet you," Beula said again. "You bought out George Hanson's cabinet shop, didn't you? I heard about that, too."

"I guess a person hears about everything in a little town like this."

"Not always. Sometimes you have to work at it. It's been harder since they did away with party lines on the telephones." Beula laughed, and her cheeks bounced, even the loose flesh on her arms.

Will was shaking his head. "She talks all day on the phone. Who needs a party line?"

"Oh, I don't either. It's just that Will won't ever answer the silly thing, so if our kids call, I'm the one who talks to them."

"Yes. And what about Muriel Pederson? You and her talk four or five times a day."

Beula twisted to look at Kathy again. "Muriel works down at the bank, half a day. She hears everything. But she don't really call that much. She just likes to talk a long time when she does. She gets going, and she can talk an hour without me saying a word."

Will grinned and shook his head. Kathy thought the man rather liked his wife, in spite of the disdain he had been expressing. "Oh, you like to hear what's going on, too," Beula told him. "Men say they don't gossip, but you oughta hear what he's got to tell when he comes back from the barber shop."

"That's the only excitement we get up here," Will said.

Kathy laughed at the two of them, but when she leaned back and took a few seconds to think, she wondered whether she liked what she had just heard. She hoped people weren't cruel in their gossip. She had thought so much about this move to Heber City. She wanted to live in a place where everyone knew one another—so they could all pull together and offer help when someone needed it. If a teenaged girl got pregnant, or a marriage was breaking up, she hoped that people were supportive, not judgmental. She was suddenly a little worried that Marshall was right—that she idealized things more than she should.

Sacrament meeting was about like the ones in Salt Lake—except that the youth speaker seemed especially shy and brief, and the main speaker, a high councilor named Brother Luke, was painfully inarticulate. He was a man with deep folds and creases in his face; it looked like something that had been left out in the weather too long. He talked about the need for everyone to gain a testimony, and he told a long story about how he had acquired his own. He had gotten lost as a Boy Scout, out in the mountains east of town, and he had wandered for quite some time before he had finally prayed. Then he had kept following a stream downhill, and he had finally found his way out of the mountains. Kathy could only think that he had done the logical thing and the prayer hadn't really mattered very much.

Maybe Brother Luke was saying that the prayer had given him strength, or that it had confirmed his decision, but he didn't say that. It was almost as though he were saying that he finally tried prayer, and after that he automatically had a testimony. Kathy heard nothing that implied a struggle, or that he had ever had to question again, once he had discovered prayer. Maybe that was simple and good, but the easy assumptions were a little annoying to her. Still, she told herself she wasn't going to do that anymore. She needed to listen to his spirit, hear his testimony—and accept his expression of faith. If she was going to sit in judgment of people's testimonies, she was no better than those who gossiped.

When the meeting was over, Kathy said, "Let's go up and introduce ourselves to the bishop."

"This is usually kind of a busy time for a bishop," Marshall said. "Maybe we can—"

"Let's just shake hands with him and tell him our names. That will only take a second." She tapped Beula on the shoulder again. "It was so nice to meet you two," she said.

"Yes. Where did you say you come from?"

"Salt Lake."

"Oh, I see." Kathy had the feeling that Beula was going to call Muriel that night to tell her who had moved into the Taylor house. Maybe she would say they were a couple of Salt Lake kids who seemed out of place in the ward. The idea made Kathy nervous. But she took Marshall's hand and led him to the front of the chapel, saying hello to everyone she passed but not stopping to talk. She wanted to reach the bishop, and he was working his way toward the side door.

"Bishop," she called from some distance, before he could get off to his office.

He stopped and turned around. He was a round-faced man with thick, gray eyebrows. He was small, older than most of the bishops Kathy had known, and seemingly, from the way he had run the meeting, a man of few words.

"Bishop, we're new in your ward. We just moved in."

He nodded and smiled. "I'm Bishop Lewis," he said. "Are you the ones who bought the Taylor place?"

"Yes. I'm Kathy Childs, and this is my husband, Marshall." She loved calling herself by her new name.

The bishop looked at Marshall. "I guess you're the one who's taking over George Hanson's business."

"Yes."

Bishop Lewis gave Marshall's hand a hard but quick pump, but he didn't seem prepared to shake hands with Kathy until she stuck her hand out.

"Well, it's nice to have you in the ward. Where is it you're moving from?"

"Salt Lake," Kathy said. "We just got married last week. We're still on our honeymoon, more or less. Can't you tell?"

The bishop's moon face reddened. "Well, no. I hadn't thought about that. But it's nice to have you in the ward." He seemed ready to turn away.

"We want to help in any way we can," Kathy said. "We want to be part of the ward. So the sooner we can get callings the better."

The bishop took a longer look at Kathy, seemed to size her up. Kathy thought he looked a little worried. "Well, I'll have to say, no one's ever told me that before. I like your attitude." But he glanced at Marshall, and

Kathy had the distinct feeling he was asking, with his eyes, *Does she do all the talking for your family?*

Marshall must have felt it too. "We do want to help," he said. "But there's no big hurry. We have a lot to do to get settled in."

"I'm sure you do. I noticed you've been working over there, getting things fixed up."

"There's a lot to do," Kathy said. "But we can start serving in the ward. We really want to. I have a music background, and we're both good teachers."

"That's good to know," Bishop Lewis said. "Don't worry, we'll be able to use you."

"I spent some time in the Philippines, and I directed a choir over there. I did that in my ward in Salt Lake too. I don't know whether you need any help with that—substituting or whatever—but I'd be glad to be involved."

The bishop was nodding again. "You *do* have a good attitude," he said.

Kathy was suddenly embarrassed. Marshall said, "Well, it's nice to meet you, Bishop. We'll—" but Kathy jumped back in. "I'm sorry, Bishop. I didn't mean to be so pushy. I'm not trying to tell you what to do. It's just that we're starting out our marriage, and we're starting a new home and business—and we're starting out in your ward, too. I want to get involved and get to know everyone as soon as we can."

"Well, that's good." He turned a little, as though ready to walk away. Kathy was humiliated. But then he turned back. "We don't actually have a choir right now. It sort of broke up when Sister Neilson had her last baby. I think maybe I'm getting inspired to call you to get that choir going again. Does that sound like something you would like to do?"

"Are you calling me?"

"Well, no. Not exactly. I need to talk to my counselors. But it sounds like you could do that, and you'd like it."

"I'd love it."

"Well, then, don't be surprised if we stop by to see you one of these nights and talk that over." He looked at Marshall. "Were you ever much of a Boy Scout?"

"Well, yes. I do have my Eagle."

"Well, then, inspiration is working again. We'll get back to you."

He walked out, and Kathy looked at Marshall. "Hey, that's great," she said.

But Marshall was looking astonished. "Kathy, I don't have time to be a Scoutmaster right now."

"He wouldn't call you directly to Scoutmaster. He'd call you as an assistant or something, don't you think?"

"I don't know. It depends on what you *inspire* him to do."

Kathy heard something more than humor in his voice. Marshall was clearly irritated with her, and she *was* wondering what had gotten into her to force the issue quite so hard. She remembered her early days in the Peace Corps when she had tried to tell the mayor what to do. She knew she was going to have to be careful—not only with the bishop but also with Marshall. "I'm sorry," she said. "You know me. I always get carried away."

"That's fine. Just don't try to carry me. I can walk without help."

"Oooh. You're mad at me, aren't you?"

"No. But I don't like to come on strong like that. So don't do it for me."

A family was approaching the door. A little blonde woman was carrying a young baby, and her husband had another child in his arms, a little girl who seemed younger than two. He also had a diaper bag over his shoulder. Two older boys, maybe five and four, or even younger, were alongside their dad. The woman said, "Hi, we're the Baxters. Beula Furniss just told me you're new in the ward. You bought Rex and Janet Taylor's house, I understand."

"Yes. We're the Childs."

"It's so nice to meet you." Sister Baxter only nodded, since she had both arms around the baby.

"I'm Randy," the husband said, and he shook hands with Marshall. "You're going to run the cabinet shop?"

"Yes. That's right."

"I'm in construction myself. I do tile work."

"Oh, okay, we'll be crossing paths then, I'm sure," Marshall said.

"My name's Candy," the woman said. "I know—it sounds silly, Randy and Candy. The first time he asked me out, I told him we could never get serious, but then, you know how things happen. What can I say? I could go by Candice, but I hate that name. So how long have you two been married?"

"Twelve days," Kathy said, and laughed.

"What did you do, go to college first?"

"Yes. And then the Peace Corps. My mother thought I was going to be an old maid."

"What's the Peace Corps?"

"Oh. It's . . . uh . . . a group that tries to help out third-world countries. I was in the Philippines."

"That sounds really hard. Did you like it?"

"Yeah. Mostly. But it *was* hard."

"You must be really smart."

"I don't know . . . not so it shows." She laughed.

Candy seemed confused by the response, but she asked, "Did you go to the Y? I thought about going down there, but then I met Randy, and I never made it."

"No. I didn't."

"Where did you go?"

"I went to a women's college in Massachusetts. It's called Smith College. I'm going to the U. now, working on a masters degree."

"Wow. You *are* smart—probably too smart for us."

"No, not at all. I just—"

But the baby had started to fuss, and Candy turned to Randy. "Do you have her pacifier?"

"I think you put it in the diaper bag." He swung the bag off his shoulder, but the baby was crying louder, and Candy finally said, "We'll talk to you again. We hope you like it here." She and her family moved on.

Kathy and Marshall walked on out to their car. All the way, Kathy was feeling more than thinking, and a developing fear was moving toward panic. When she and Marshall were both in the car, she asked without looking at him, "Is this going to work for us?"

"Kathy, I've been telling you for months, don't idealize this place. We want a simple life, but this idea you have about people in little towns is based mostly on stereotypes."

"Are we ever going to fit in?"

"Sure. If we don't run them over, right from the beginning."

"I shouldn't have said that about working on a master's degree."

"Kathy, life is always messier than you want it to be. We'll like it here, and after a while, they'll like us all right. But you need to take things one step at a time, not force the issue too much. Just let things happen."

"No matter how much I try to change, I'm still the same person."

Marshall laughed. He reached over and put his hand on her neck, then pulled her close enough to kiss the top of her head. "You're a good person. These people, in two years, are going to talk about the pre-Kathy period, before everything changed so much in their ward and in their neighborhood."

Kathy wondered. She wasn't exactly the Kathy who had gone off to college ready to solve the world's problems. But she knew she was a little too eager to remake Heber City, and she needed to start backing off, right now.

CHAPTER 27

Diane was on her knees scrubbing the kitchen floor on a hot August afternoon when the telephone rang. She considered letting it go, but it kept right on ringing. So she got up, dropped her scrub brush into the water, and walked through the wet area she had just scrubbed. She picked up the receiver with a soapy rubber glove. "Hello," she said. She really hoped this was something important.

"Diane, it's Mom."

"Hi."

"My mother just called. She said Grandpa has taken a turn for the worse, and he's refusing to go back to the hospital. She thinks he wants to die at home."

"Is he really that bad?"

"I think so. Grandma said if the family wants to see him while he can still carry on a conversation, they might want to come soon."

"You mean . . . today?"

"She's not saying he'll die that soon—just that he might go downhill pretty fast now. We're driving down as soon as Richard gets back from campus. Do you want to go with us?"

Diane thought for a moment. "I guess so. Do I have time to finish scrubbing my floor?"

"Sure. Your dad said he'd be half an hour or so. We'll come by and pick you up."

"All right. Are you okay, Mom?"

"I suppose. I haven't had time to think. But I feel sort of sick. I thought I was ready for this, but maybe I'm not. It doesn't seem possible there could be a world without my dad in it."

"Yeah. That's what I was just thinking."

Diane went back to her work, but she felt strange. She hadn't dealt much with death in her life, and she had always loved Grandpa Thomas. She couldn't imagine going to the house and not having him there. He was supposed to be with Grandma. Diane began to cry.

She finished her floor quickly, faster than she wanted to, considering how dirty it had gotten. Jenny had gone down for a nap, and that's why Diane had chosen this time to do the floor, but Jenny wouldn't mind getting up to go for a ride with Grandma and Grandpa Hammond. She had been down long enough anyway. The only thing was, Diane didn't know what to tell her. Jenny would be five in a couple of months. She understood a little about death—about going to Heavenly Father—and the truth was, she wasn't really all that close to Grandpa Thomas. Jenny had always been a little afraid of him, with his jolting voice. Diane got Jenny up and dressed her, but she didn't try to explain anything for now. Maybe Diane would wait until Grandpa was actually gone, or maybe she could get some help from her parents.

When Bobbi and Richard arrived, Diane could see that her mom had been crying. Diane had heard the stories about Mom battling Grandpa when she was young—how strong-willed they both were, and how they had clashed over Bobbi's studying English, and especially over her interest in a young English professor who hadn't been a member of the Church. The story was a kind of legend to Diane. The professor had ended up dying in the war, but Mom had already decided she couldn't marry someone who had so little faith in God. It was told as a cautionary tale, of sorts, but Diane had often tried to picture her mother back then, trying to make a decision about that. Bobbi just seemed the sort, now, who would never have considered marrying out of the Church. Diane knew that her mother was opinionated and a bit of a rebel, but Diane had never seen anything but affection between her and Grandpa. It was strange to think that Mom had once been young, had dealt with hard questions, had not always had her answers. She seemed so confident in them now.

When Diane and her parents reached Grandma's house in Sugar House, they found Beverly there with her daughters, Suzanne and Beatrice—who everyone called "Little Bea"—and with Michael, who was now almost four. "I just came over to be with Mom," Beverly said in her gentle voice. "She likes to have the kids around. It keeps her mind off everything."

"Where's Mom now?" Bobbi asked.

"I told her to lie down for a while. She was up most of the night. She and Michael are having a nap together."

"Should we go in and see Dad now?"

"Yes." But Beverly laughed. "Mom told him you were coming down, and he got mad. He said, 'I'm not dying yet. You don't need to gather all the mourners.'"

Bobbi laughed. "Sounds like him," she said.

"Mom didn't bat an eye. You know how she is. She asked him, 'Do you want them to wait until you can't talk and you've got drool running down your chin?'"

Bobbi cringed. "What did Dad say?"

"He laughed. Mom can always make him laugh. He told her, 'You're not supposed to say things like that to a dying man,' and she said, 'I never have said what I'm supposed to. You wouldn't want me to start now, would you?'"

Richard was smiling, holding Jenny, but he said, "All of us will have to stay close to Bea. She's going to be *very* lonely."

"That's true," Bobbi said, "but she won't feel sorry for herself. She doesn't know how to do that. She'll keep busy."

"She's hurting more than I expected," Beverly said. "She's so tough I always think nothing bothers her. But this morning, when I got here, she was kind of coming apart. She didn't break down and cry, but she was shaking and talking too fast, and worrying about calling everyone."

Diane could hardly imagine that. But she said to her parents, "Why don't you two go in and talk to Grandpa first. I'd like to have a minute with him alone—with just me and Jenny."

"That's a good idea," Beverly said. "I don't think Dad can handle too much fuss. One or two at a time is probably better."

So Bobbi and Richard walked upstairs, and Diane sat with Beverly. Suzie looked like her mom, but she wasn't as peaceful. "Are we going to be here *all day*?" she whispered to her mother. It was hard for Diane to remember that Suzie was a teenager now, but she certainly sounded like one.

"No," Aunt Bev said. "When Michael wakes up, we'll go. I think people are going to keep coming the rest of the day."

"Can I still go swimming? My friends will probably still be at the pool—for a little while anyway."

The temperature had to be close to one hundred, but the big old house, even without air-conditioning, was fairly comfortable. Little Bea was reading a book, seemingly unaware that anyone was in the room. Diane sat by her on the couch and put an arm around her. Bea leaned against Diane, but she didn't stop reading. She was seven, still a kid. Diane didn't want Jenny ever to be fourteen, like Suzie.

Since Bobbi had first called, Diane had found herself looking back, thinking about all the times she had been in this house, and all her memories of her grandpa. She kept thinking of a picnic in Ogden Canyon. Grandma and Grandpa had come from Salt Lake and had gone with Diane's family. They had cooked hot dogs and eaten watermelon—all the usual things—but Diane remembered going on a walk with Grandpa. She must have been ten or eleven, and he seemed very old to her then—actually older than he seemed now. He had seen trout swimming beneath the ripples of the Ogden River and he had pointed them out to her. At first, she hadn't been able to see them, and he had patiently helped her look in the right place. A fish had been drifting in the water, like a shadow, and Diane had been watching it, not sure what it was until it swam forward a little and then drifted back. "See, see!" Grandpa had said, just as Diane had seen it move. Diane had seen the glint of silver and the rainbow coloring along its side. She hadn't thought about that for years, but she remembered the feeling now, walking with him, watching the water, and the joy when she had finally seen what he wanted her to see—joy more for him than for herself, she thought.

What Diane wished now was that Grandpa could be healthy a while longer, that he could take Jenny for walks, that he could hold her little hand in his huge one just a time or two when she would be old enough to remember. Mortality seemed cruel to Diane right now. It passed more quickly than she had understood until lately. Jenny would always have Grandpa Hammond, and she loved him, and she did have some contact with Grandpa Lyman, but Grandpa Thomas, in Diane's mind, was the fountainhead in the family. He knew who he was and he knew what life was for. Diane wished that Jenny could learn that from him.

Before long Bobbi and Richard came down. "Was he grumpy?" Beverly asked.

"No. Not really. He said he wants to get to the other side so he can get a healthy body—and then get back to work. He hates being in bed all the time."

"That *will* be better for him," Bev said, and she said it with such trust that some of the mystery of death seemed to pass away for Diane. No question, Grandpa would get out of that tired old body, get his strength back, and serve whatever mission he was called to. That's the way he liked things.

Diane picked up Jenny and carried her up the stairs. "We're going to talk to Great-Grandpa, okay?"

"Where's Great-Grandma?"

"She's sleeping. She's having a nap, like you did today. But Great-Grandpa wants to see you. He loves you."

"I know."

Diane tapped on the door, and then she stepped in. Grandpa was propped up in the bed with some pillows under him, but his eyes were shut. He looked over, however, and he said, "Hey, Jenny girl, come and say hello to Great-Grandpa."

Diane carried her over to the bed and held her over Grandpa so she could kiss him on the cheek. Then she set Jenny on the edge of the bed, and Grandpa took hold of her hand. He didn't say it, but Diane had the feeling he would miss the little ones in the family the most.

Grandpa looked up at Diane. "I'd tell you that you look pretty, but I've learned not to do that."

Diane turned and sat on the bed, next to Jenny. She didn't like the smell of the room. There seemed to be medicine in the air, like a hospital. "You can tell me that any time you want, Grandpa," she said.

"I can? What happened? Did women's lib change the rules on me again?"

Good old Grandpa. Everything was an "issue" to him. "Any grandpa can tell his granddaughter she's pretty. That's *my* rule."

"Then it's a new one. I remember you roughing me up pretty bad for telling you that once." He smiled, but he was looking distant, weak, and he was breathing deeply.

"I've calmed down a little now. I was still pretty shook up back then."

"I'll tell you one thing. You're a whole lot stronger than I gave you credit for. I'm proud of you for the way you stood up to that *numbskull* you married. And I'm proud that you've gone back to school and done what you have to do. You're a good mother."

"Thanks, Grandpa."

"I just wish you'd never had to go through something like that." He took a big breath, and his face looked almost as white as the pillows. "But one day you're going to find yourself an eternal companion—one who'll love our little Jenny. When I get to the other side, I'll see if I've got some influence back here on earth. Maybe I can send someone your way."

"That would be nice, Grandpa. But don't worry about me; I'm doing all right."

Grandpa blinked, and tears came into his eyes. "In some ways, I hate to go. I worry so much about all of you, and I wish I could stay and help. But the truth is, I'm no help now—probably never was. I drive everyone crazy with all my advice."

"No, Grandpa. We all know how we're supposed to live. We just watch you and Grandma, and that teaches us. I only wish you could be with us longer—so Jenny could know you better."

"That's how it always is with the generations. But she has Richard to look to—and Richard is the kind of man I wish I'd been. He doesn't have to say a word to teach his posterity. I always talked too much."

"I don't think so, Grandpa. All us cousins used to joke about you telling us what a Thomas was supposed to be. But now we've started saying things like that to our own kids. I tell Jenny about the pioneers, and I tell her about her heritage. She doesn't understand much about that yet, but she will. We're all going to keep passing along what you've given us. I promise you that."

President Thomas's eyes went shut, and tears squeezed from the corners, slipped into the deep wrinkles. He let go of Jenny's hand and held his big hand out to Diane. "Those old pioneers had nothing on you, little girl. You're as tough as any of them, and I'm proud of you."

Diane talked to Grandpa for a while after that, but she knew those were the words she would always remember, after he was gone.

∽∾

Gene saw Diane coming down the stairs, carrying Jenny. He could see that she had been crying. She had always been one of the prettiest girls he had ever known, but lately she seemed beautiful to Gene. She was such a good mother, and she was working so hard to make things work in her life. The truth was, he had never expected her to become such an impressive woman.

Gene and Emily had been sitting in the living room talking to Aunt Bev, Aunt Bobbi, and Uncle Richard, but Gene had been struggling to concentrate on the conversation. He was still feeling dazed from the phone call he had received. He had known that Grandpa's health had been failing for a long time, but he hadn't suspected that his death was close. Since Emily had called him, after getting a call from Grandma Bea, Gene had been fighting not to cry. When he had heard Diane coming down, he had walked to the foot of the stairs. Now, looking at her, he found himself struggling harder than ever. "How is he?" he asked Diane.

"He looks weak, but he doesn't sound so bad. Except he talks in a softer voice." As she reached the bottom of the stairs, she set Jenny down. Gene bent low and gave Jenny a hug. Then he stood and hugged Diane. He wasn't always like that—hugging everyone—but he felt close to his family today. "Is he dying?"

"I don't know. It doesn't seem like it. But I can tell he's accepted the idea."

"Maybe that's the trouble. It doesn't seem like him to go down without a fight."

Uncle Richard had walked into the entrance area at the front of the house. He picked up Jenny. "What is there to fight for, Gene?" he asked. "He doesn't like feeling useless, and there's not a doubt in his mind that life keeps on going when his spirit leaves his body."

Gene was embarrassed. "I know. It's probably better for him. But you know—it's just hard for the rest of us." Gene knew what he really meant. He and Grandpa had fought too much these past couple of years. He wanted more time to patch that up.

"Go on up—you and Emily," Diane said. "He's awake now, and he knows people are coming. When I was leaving, just now, he asked me who else was leaning against the wailing wall downstairs."

Gene and Richard laughed. But Gene did feel nervous about that. He didn't want to say good-bye. He just wanted to have a good talk and not act like he was there because the end was near. "Should we leave Danny and the baby down here, or should we take them with us?"

"Why don't you talk to him for a few minutes, and then I'll bring them up. He'll want to see them."

That sounded right to Gene. He got Emily, and the two walked upstairs. When they stepped into the bedroom, Grandpa said, "Did Grandma tell you to get one last look while the old boy was still breathing?"

Gene hardly knew what to say, but Emily responded before he did. "No, Grandpa. Gene wants to argue politics with you."

"Ah, it's no fun to argue with some young buck who's always wrong," Grandpa said. "Maybe I need to stick around long enough to get him thinking right."

Gene grinned, and he walked to Grandpa's bed. The upstairs, especially here on the south end, was always warmer than downstairs, and Gene wondered whether it wasn't a little too warm, but at least the room was bright. "How are you feeling, Grandpa?" he asked.

"Not so bad. They make me take so many pills, I hardly know day from night or anything else. I tell my doc if he'd lay off all the medications I could live another ten years. But he's another young buck like you. He thinks he knows more than I do."

"I'm not quite so confident as I used to be, Grandpa. Nothing is looking quite so simple to me as it did a year or two ago."

"Well, you were right about one thing: Nixon *was* a crook. It turns out he was lying every time he opened his mouth. I'm glad he resigned so we didn't have to suffer through an impeachment. The only thing I feel good about is Gerald Ford. I think he's a decent man."

Gene got a chair for Emily and brought it close to the bed, and then he brought one for himself. He didn't want to talk about any of that. Grandpa's voice actually sounded stronger than Gene had expected, but Gene could see submission in his face. Something was gone from him. Gene realized it was time to say good-bye, whether he wanted to or not.

"Grandpa," Emily said, "you need to know, Gene has been doing well. You two really could talk politics now, and he wouldn't lose his temper." She reached over and took hold of Gene's hand, pulled it onto her lap.

"That's what I've been hearing," Grandpa said. "What's made the difference, Gene?"

"I don't know, Grandpa. I guess I've finally let go of some of the things that were bothering me."

"He finally admitted he had a problem," Emily said. "And he's been willing to accept some help—not just from people, but from the Lord."

"I'm glad to hear that," Grandpa said. He let his eyes go shut, and Gene thought he saw pain in his face, or maybe just weariness. "It's good you're figuring some things out now, and not letting all those feelings fester."

Grandpa took a deep breath, and his chest expanded under the sheet that was draped across him, but that got him started coughing in bursts and panting almost urgently between coughs. It took some time for him to calm down, and by then Gene was worried for him. "Grandpa, should I get something for you? Do you need a drink of water?"

"No, I'm all right now. I get going like this every now and again."

"Would it be better if we leave and let you rest?"

"No. Don't go yet." He lay quiet for a time, letting his breathing steady itself. "Bea's getting ready for me to die, so I know exactly what the doc is telling her—even if he won't say it to me. But that's all right; I'm ready. This is no way to live. I sleep half the time, and then I wake up and can't do anything, so I just lay here and think about my life. I think a lot about the things I didn't do right."

"You've lived a great life, Grandpa." And Gene meant it. He worried about things he had told Grandpa in the past couple of years—probably some of the things Grandpa was worrying about now.

"I'm not ashamed of my life. I was a workhorse. I served in every way I was ever called. But the world changed a lot in my years, and the changes made me nervous. I had trouble talking with my kids sometimes, and trouble with you grandkids. And always for the same reason." He took a long breath, waited a moment, and then took another. "I had my answer, and if it was good enough for me, I figured it was good enough for all of you. Bea has been telling me that for fifty years and more, and I always knew she was right. But I didn't change enough. I wish now—even when I was stake president—that I'd listened a little more and asked a few more questions before I started laying down the law."

"But Grandpa, the world wants everything to be gray now. And there *are* some black and whites. You haven't given us a lot of 'maybe this and maybe that' kind of talk. You've told us what the Lord expects of us."

"Well, sure. I've stayed with the Lord, and I have no shame in that. But sometimes I thought I knew a little more than he did—or at least more than he had told me."

Gene watched Grandpa for a time. It was hard to see him like this—his face puffy, his arms thin, his skin shading toward blue. "Grandpa," he said, "I always knew how much you believed in me."

"No. I don't think so. I didn't always come across that way. I was too quick to tell people what was wrong with them—and what they had to do to get straightened out. A father—as well as a church leader—has to be careful with that kind of stuff. He can break a young person's spirit. I need to talk to Kurt one more time before I'm gone—if he'll even talk to me. I chewed him out too many times. He's stopped talking to me."

"You haven't caused Kurt's problems. He's made his own choices."

"I know. But I didn't help much, and maybe I could have."

"Grandpa, you're selling yourself short. You always told me what I ought to do, but there was never any doubt in my mind why you did it. You cared about me. You loved me."

Grandpa turned his head so he was looking directly at Gene. He was still taking long, steady breaths. "Thank you, Gene," he said. "It's what I would like to believe."

Gene leaned forward. He wanted to take hold of Grandpa's hand, but he was afraid that would embarrass both of them. "Grandpa, I want you to know that I honor you. When I was a boy, you made me feel that I was going to do something great with my life. I lost my confidence for a while, but I'm feeling some of that again now."

Grandpa shut his eyes, and for a time Gene thought he was drifting off to sleep, but finally he said, "Be careful, though, Gene. Here's what I've been thinking lately." Again he breathed. "You don't have to run for office, the way I've always told you to do. Lately I've been wishing I hadn't pushed Alex so hard in that direction. I don't think he's been very happy with that life. Be a good man—a good father and a good husband—and if you get called to serve in the Church, serve with all your heart. But you know what? Be thankful if you don't end up a stake president or something of that sort. We make too much of all those things. I look back now, and I realize I'll be gone from this earth, and not much of what I've done matters very much. But my family does. That's what I leave here. I'd like to take a lot of credit for what a good family I have, but Bea deserves most of that. I was too busy to do some of the things I wish I'd done."

"No, Grandpa. Grandma loved us, and that was important, but so did you. And you were the one who told us what we stood for. We needed that, too. Never once in my life did I doubt that you lived the life you preached."

Grandpa's eyes shut for a long time, and when they came open, they focused on Gene's face. "Thank you," he said. "If I did anything right, you pass that along to your children."

"We want you to see our kids, Grandpa. Diane's going to—"

"I'm here," Diane said. Gene turned to see that she was standing in the door. Danny was standing next to Diane, looking wary. Gene suspected that Diane had warned him not to be noisy. Diane was holding the baby, who was asleep.

"Come in," Gene said.

Diane walked to Emily, who got up and took the baby. Danny walked to Gene, and Gene picked him up. As Diane was walking out, Gene said, "Grandpa, Danny is five now. He's starting kindergarten in a couple of weeks."

"I never did beat him in a race. But I might yet." Danny was staring at Grandpa, probably confused by his color and his bloated face. "I'd race you right now, but I don't have a nickel to pay you off if I lose. And I pay my debts."

Danny didn't know how to respond. Gene wondered what he was thinking, and what he would remember. Would he have any concept of the man his great-grandfather had been? Gene wanted something special to happen here today. "Grandpa," he said, "you couldn't be there when we blessed our baby. We wondered, could you give him your own blessing now? We think it would be nice for him to know someday that you did that."

Grandpa nodded, and his eyes filled with tears.

"I'm afraid he fell asleep on the way over here, Grandpa," Emily said.

"Let me look at him. He's grown a lot since the last time I saw him."

Emily bent and reached forward so the baby's face was in front of Grandpa. "He's almost seven months old now."

"He looks like you, Gene."

"But he's named after you and Dad."

President Thomas nodded. Tears were seeping from his eyes now. "I know," he said. He raised his arms, spread his big hands under little Alexander, and took his weight. He seemed stronger than Gene had expected. "Alexander Thomas," he said. "With the power of the holy

Melchizedek Priesthood, and as your grandfather, I bless you and your posterity. I bless you with the will and resolve to face an evil world. I bless you with the strength of your forefathers and of your good parents. I bless you with strength of conviction, and at the same time, with kindness and patience. Be better than I was, little Alexander. Love and be loved, and pass that love to my posterity. Tell them I wait for them and long for the day when we can all be united in God's kingdom." He hesitated for a time, got his breath again, and then added, "Trust in the atonement of Jesus Christ. Know that the Lord forgives us when we make an honest effort to be like him."

He closed in the name of Christ, and then he looked up at Emily, who was sobbing by then. She took the baby and said, "Thank you, Grandpa."

"Let me look at Danny," Grandpa said.

Gene set Danny on the bed. "Are you going to be a good boy, Danny?" Grandpa asked.

"Uh-huh," Danny said, nodding.

"Do you know who Nephi is?"

Danny glanced up at Gene. "You know Nephi, in your Book of Mormon storybook," he said.

"Uh-huh."

"I want you to be like Nephi—strong and true and good. Will you remember that?"

Danny was nodding again.

"Okay. You might not remember me, but your Mom and Dad will remind you what I said—to read about Nephi and always be like him. And you'll know how to do it. Because all you have to do is be like your dad. He's just like Nephi. He doesn't think so sometimes, but he is."

"Thank you, Grandpa," Gene said, but now he was crying too. He picked Danny up and held him tight. No one knew how hard Gene was still struggling, but this helped. Grandpa still believed in him. He would remember that, and he would make sure Danny remembered what

Grandpa had told him. And he would teach Danny and Alexander to understand what Grandpa had said: to trust in the atonement of Jesus Christ. It was what Gene prayed for every day of his life now—that trust.

"Love those two sons," Grandpa said. "But don't push them quite as hard as I pushed all of you."

❧

As Kathy and Marshall drove to Salt Lake, Kathy worried that they might be too late. Marshall had been in the middle of a job, and he broke away as soon as he could, but when Lorraine had called Kathy, she had seemed to be saying that Grandpa was almost gone. At the house, however, Grandma pulled the two inside, hugged them, and said, "Oh, no, he's not that close yet. I was just afraid that if he suddenly died one of these days, everyone would say, 'I wish I could have talked to him one more time.' Who knows? He might spring out of bed in the morning and we'll all feel silly. But the doctor says he's run out of things he can do for him, and his heart can't keep going much longer."

"Is Grandpa asleep now?" Kathy asked.

"No. But he's tired. Almost everyone in the family has been here today."

"So he knows what's up, I guess."

"He knows, all right. But he just told me, 'I'm going to live a couple more years just to prove you all wrong about me.' I told him, 'Good. You do that,' but he said, 'I'm tired, Bea.' He didn't elaborate on that, but I can tell he's getting ready. Doctor Patterson said he would have been dead a year ago if he were built out of ordinary stuff." She patted Marshall on the arm. "He was never quite as handsome as you, but he was built like you, and almost as tall. I wasn't the only girl around who thought I'd like to be hugged by a man with muscles like that."

Grandma's dimples appeared. She had aged a lot in the past year or two, her wrinkles finally deepening to the point that she actually looked old, but it crossed Kathy's mind that she never wanted to let Grandma go. When both were gone, Kathy suspected she would feel abandoned.

"Go up now. Just don't stay too long."

So Kathy and Marshall walked up to his room. "Are you tired of this parade coming through here, Grandpa?" Kathy asked as she walked into the bedroom.

"Yes. But you're the one I've been waiting for. I'm not sure I've got you straightened out yet, and I've got a suspicion the Lord won't let me go until I do."

"Well, then, stick around, because I'm still a project." She bent and kissed him on the cheek.

Grandpa looked at Marshall, who stepped up closer to the bed. "How is she doing?" he asked.

Marshall laughed. "She's taken Heber City by storm. She's already involved in everything that's going on in town."

"I'm not being pushy, though, Grandpa. I'm really not. I'm just trying to get involved." She sat down on one of the chairs that was close to the bed, and she picked up Grandpa's hand and touched it to her face. Grandpa smiled, but not with that big grin she wanted to see. He looked drained. "I'm directing the choir in church, and that's been great. We have some good singers and they've gotten really excited, so it's a fun job."

"You're the one who got them excited," Grandpa said. "I know that for sure."

"That's right," Marshall told him. He stood behind Kathy and rested his hands on her shoulders.

"But they're good," Kathy said, "and they just needed to practice on a regular basis. The bishop is really happy about what's happening with them."

"She's on a couple of committees in town too," Marshall said.

"I just meet people and they invite me to do things. But it's fun. I love

Heber. At first I wondered about the place. But the people are great, and I know so many already."

"Are you still in college?"

"Not this summer. I'm going back in the fall. But Grandpa, I've got some news." She waited until his eyes focused directly on her. "I'm going to have a baby. I just found that out. I haven't told anyone else yet—not even my parents—because I wanted you to know first."

A little more life came into his eyes. "That's good, Kathy. Really good. That's a baby I'd like to see." He let his eyes go shut, and then he smiled. "Maybe I can look him up—or her—on the other side, and just give the poor little spirit a warning about what it's getting into." He laughed.

Kathy didn't want to talk about that. It felt wrong to say that he was dying. So she said instead, "I think I'll go to school fall quarter and maybe winter, but I'm probably not going to finish my degree before the baby comes. Marshall's business is doing okay. We're poor, really, but we can get by, and for now, I don't want to work. I want to be a full-time mom."

Grandpa laughed, and that made him cough a little. But he said, "You and I had a big argument about that one time. You were telling me that women should work and husbands should tend babies—and all that other women's lib stuff."

"No, Grandpa. I didn't say that. That was *your* interpretation of what I said. But I did want to have a career at one time—and maybe that's something I'll get around to. For now, though, I want to raise a family, work in the Church, and do some community stuff. I'm really happy with that."

"I'm glad you came home to us, Kathy. And I'm glad you're in the Church."

Kathy leaned forward and touched her cheek to Grandpa Thomas's. "Grandpa, I was lost. You came looking for me, and you found me. That will always be a miracle to me. I'll never forget that, ever. You didn't give up on me."

"That's because you were one of my favorites."

"Me?" Kathy sat up straight. "Really?"

"Yes. You and LaRue. I've struggled with you two. But you always knew things. I couldn't just tell the two of you what was what. You read everything and always had statistics to quote, or something of that sort, and I'd have to go back and read some more just to keep up with you. I've never liked to change my mind, but you two women—along with your Grandma Bea—have changed me more than the rest of the family put together."

"But I was a big disappointment to you for such a long time."

"You certainly were that. But you and LaRue have always been the most like Bea. Plucky. Spirited. It was the first thing I liked in Bea when I met her."

"That floors me, Grandpa."

"But I'll tell you, little girl, I was scared for you for a long time. You got way out there before you turned around."

"Grandpa, I was looking over the edge, just ready to jump, when you came looking for me that day. You grabbed hold and pulled me back."

"Don't give me too much credit; God sent me to you that day."

"But you heard God. And when I knew that, I knew God still cared about me." She kissed Grandpa again. "We're going to miss you so much," she said, even though she hadn't intended to say anything of that sort.

"Life is shorter than you think, sweetheart," Grandpa said. He patted her face. "I'll be seeing you before long."

CHAPTER 28

G ene served as one of the pallbearers at his grandfather's funeral. Then he joined Emily and Danny and sat near the front of the old stake center in Sugar House. Emily's mom was taking care of Alexander. The Thomases filled up much of the center section, but the building was packed, some people even standing at the back. Gene took hold of Emily's hand and pulled Danny onto his lap. Danny was confused about death. Gene and Emily had explained to him about Great-Grandpa, that he had gone to be with Heavenly Father, and Danny seemed to comprehend that, but then he would say, "Won't he be at Great-Grandma's house anymore?"

"No. Just Great-Grandma will be there," Gene told him, and Danny seemed to accept that all right, but when he had seen Grandpa Thomas in his casket, and especially when he had watched his father cry when the casket was closed, he seemed troubled.

"Don't cry," he kept telling Gene, and he seemed more frightened than empathetic. Gene wondered what he actually understood.

But now he was tired from all that had happened the past couple of days, and he leaned back against Gene and seemed to be drifting toward sleep.

"Are you okay?" Emily asked Gene.

"Sure." But in a moment he added, "I just wish we'd had a few more chances to talk."

Bishop Swensen was conducting the meeting. Marion G. Romney, of the First Presidency, was presiding, and N. Eldon Tanner, president of the Quorum of the Twelve, was seated next to him. Both were longtime friends of President Thomas. Spencer W. Kimball, president of the

Church, had written a kindly letter to Grandma Bea and expressed his regret that he couldn't attend the funeral. But he spoke of President Thomas as one of the great stalwarts in the Church who had devoted his life to serving and blessing the lives of the people in his stake. He also praised Bea for the wonderful family she and Al had raised and the positive influence those children and grandchildren were continuing to have.

The letter made a deep impression on Gene. Grandpa had said that when he died, it was the family he was leaving behind that would matter. Gene thought now that he wanted to make Grandpa proud. He wanted to write what the Lord would have him write, and not let his ego get in the way of his work. He also wanted to be a good husband and father.

The meeting began with the congregation singing "Choose the Right." Grandma Bea had picked the hymn because she said it expressed Al's simple motto for life. Gene couldn't help smiling. He remembered Aunt LaRue teasing Grandpa one time that now and then it might be better to "choose the left," and Grandpa hadn't found that funny at all.

And yet, it was Aunt LaRue who walked to the podium and said the opening prayer. She was wearing a gray suit, not her usual flashy colors and hoop earrings, but her stride still revealed her self-assurance. She was looking heavier than she had all her life, however. She had given birth to a baby girl only three weeks before. Gene thought her prayer was said with a beautiful spirit. She thanked the Lord for the blessing President Thomas had been to the family—for his steadfastness, his powerful faith, and his love of his children. "He did what was right and let the consequences follow," she said.

Aunt Beverly read Grandpa's obituary and added a few details of his life, as a eulogy. She looked almost childlike—her skin pale, her nose and eyes red, and her honey-colored hair resting on the shoulders of a simple green dress, "I am his youngest daughter," she said at the end. "Most of the family speaks of Dad's firm hand on the iron rod, and I know that was true of him. But I was the last one home, and I remember his tenderness. He was certain that he was spoiling me, but I could usually get what I wanted from him. He was like a chocolate cherry that feels hard when you pick it up, but if you squeeze it, it breaks open and is all juicy and gooey inside."

Everyone laughed, especially the Thomases, and Gene nodded. He had always known that about his Grandpa too—except when he had forgotten it for a time.

Uncle Wally was the first speaker, but he didn't speak long. Everyone had been warned by Grandma Bea. Grandpa had told her that if the meeting lasted more than an hour, he was going to rise up from his coffin and close the meeting himself. Wally began, "At about age sixteen I decided my dad was a tyrant, and I fought him at every turn. I wasn't entirely wrong, either. Dad usually thought he could make my decisions a lot better than I could." Wally stopped and smiled, but Gene could see he was struggling to keep his emotions under control. "The fact is, if he had made my decisions, I really would have been better off, but I had to find that out for myself. And I did. When I passed through the darkest days of my life—times that seemed impossible to survive—I could almost see him standing over me saying, 'You can keep going. Don't give up.' Dad had always told us stories about our forebears, and according to him, they had been the strongest people who ever lived. In his eyes, we were a pretty sorry bunch, by comparison. But when I needed strength, I told myself I could be as tough as any of those old codgers who crossed the plains. And I think I was. I think this Thomas bunch, sitting here before me, could walk across the plains, turn around, and walk back. We might not sing as we walk, might even quarrel a little, but we would make it. And I know why: we'd want to prove to Dad that we could do it."

There was a good laugh, but Gene could see the tears in Uncle Wally's eyes. "In some ways, I've been the same kind of father. I've put some hard demands on my kids, and I hope I haven't been unreasonable. Fortunately, I married a great woman, the same as Dad did. Mom could deflate Dad when he got too puffed up, and she showed him, by example, what it meant to love. We've had our problems, we Thomases, and some of us rebelled against Dad's strictness, but we're all here today, feeling part of the family, all trying to move in the direction that Dad and Mom guided us. When we've been a little too much like Dad, we've been lucky enough to have our non-Thomas partners to rein us in."

"After all is said and done," Wally concluded, "what Grandpa knew was that the gospel was true. And it's what he passed along to us. Some of us have gone through tough trials to come to the same conclusion, but we've arrived there—and we've always had Dad's solid witness as an anchor to our faith. Plus, we've had Mom's Christ-like love to 'feel' when our brain wasn't ready to 'know.' It's what I hope we can continue to pass along now, one generation to the next."

Aunt Bobbi spoke next. She was crying when she got to the pulpit, and she had to stand and wait for a time. "This isn't like me, I hope you know," she said when she finally got her voice. "I don't cry about just anything, and I don't believe there's anything to cry about today, but I had an image come into my mind as Wally was speaking, and it touched me." She began to cry again.

Bobbi pushed a handkerchief under the reading glasses she was wearing and then dried her nose. "I thought of a Christmas morning back when Alex was on his mission and the rest of us were still home. Dad wanted to have one of his family 'meetings,' as he called them, and Wally, who was a teenager, was complaining. He wanted to go somewhere, and Dad wouldn't let him leave. Dad started to give his traditional Christmas talk, and Wally teased him—because Dad always said the same things. Christmas was too commercialized, he would tell us. People had turned it into a day for giving fancy gifts and forgetting about Christ. Finally Wally pushed a little too hard and Dad got upset. He raised his voice, and he was always loud enough without doing that. He told us that this valley is *Zion,* and people here should remember that. We needed to live up to our heritage. He sounded almost angry for a time, and we paid attention.

"All my life I've thought of his saying that. It wasn't good enough for us to be like everyone else. We needed to remember that we were 'the Children of the Promise,' that the Salt Lake Valley was surrounded by the mountains that Daniel the prophet spoke of. We had to draw strength from the hills around us, and we had to live by a higher standard. Then, after saying all that, he read the Christmas story in Luke. That loud voice of his got very tender, and it was like he wanted us to see the connection between the strength he expected of us and that gentle moment when Christ came to earth as a baby."

Bobbi had begun to cry again, and it took her a time to say, "But that's not what made me cry. What I thought of was that our brother Gene had been with us then. Dear Gene. He was almost too good for this planet. I can't remember anything bad about my little brother—the one who was killed in World War II. He was like a symbol of the Christ-child, so innocent, and he died trying to stop the evil that was spreading through the world. And he got the strength to do that from our parents. It's easy to say that the strength came from Dad and the love from Mom, but it wasn't entirely like that. They are both strong, and they both love.

"It's painful to think back on that time when I was gone from home, working as a nurse in Hawaii. Alex was in Germany, in great danger, and I worried every day of my life about him. Wally was a POW in Japan, but we didn't know that for sure. We didn't know whether he was alive or dead, and we didn't know whether he could hold up under such terrible conditions. My husband, Richard, spent much of that time in harm's way too, and in the middle of all that, we lost Gene. It was all so horrible, and yet we found so much strength. In some ways, we were as stalwart as Dad wanted us to be. I don't know that we're quite so committed now.

"What I fear is that the grandchildren and great-grandchildren will think of those stories about World War II the way we thought of Dad's stories about crossing the plains—just stories. The fact is, our generation became who we are now during that time. And yet, when I think about it,

I fear that we never faced anything as hard as you young people are facing now. I just hope you can draw strength from us the way we drew it from our parents. You, too, are 'Children of the Promise,' and you must continue to keep your covenants, perhaps with more resolution than ever."

Bobbi stopped. She blew her nose quietly, and then she smiled. "I forgot to give the talk I prepared. And now I don't have time. But maybe these were better things to say than what I had thought of before. I hope so." She closed and sat down.

Emily patted Gene's leg, and then she got up and walked to the stand. She and Kathy, Diane, and Sharon had been working on a number all week. They sang "There Is Beauty All Around," a song that Grandpa loved. Gene was still thinking about Bobbi's talk. All his life he had heard about his Uncle Gene, the one who died, and the man Gene was named for. Everyone spoke of his innocent goodness, his bravery, his sacrifice for his country. There seemed an irony in that to Gene. He had tried to do the same thing, really, without thinking so much of Uncle Gene as he had about his own father who had fought for America. Something he had known for a long time seemed to sink in: his purpose had been just as pure, and he had probably gone to war as innocent as his uncle. He wanted to return to that state of mind now. Few people seemed to accept his sacrifice as worthy—because of their feelings about the war—but that shouldn't affect how he felt about himself. He had done his best; he had believed he was doing right.

Gene put his arm around Emily as she returned to him and sat down. He tried to let her feel his love, and she seemed to notice. She leaned against him, and he pulled her even closer.

Uncle Alex was the final speaker from the family. "Dad was strong," he said at one point. "We've all mentioned that. But another word for Dad was 'stubborn.' And that's a trait that can be of great value in this life. It's also a family trait we have to handle with care. During these talks I've thought about my own parenting methods, and I've tried to compare them to Dad's. I think I've done things much the same as he did, but when some of our family members have wandered rather far afield, Dad never gave up on them. I wish I could say I've done as well at that as he did." Gene realized that Alex was looking at Kurt. "I want so badly to be an anchor to my own children, but I'm not sure they know how much I love them. One of the problems in this family is that we all feel we have something to live up to. When that goes well, we feel the satisfaction. But when we fear that we've fallen short, we begin to believe that the standard is too high, and then we doubt ourselves. The fact is, our standards may be high, but we're human—all too human. We have all the usual weaknesses and problems." He stopped, and he took a long look at Kurt. "I love all my children," he said. "I hope *all* of them know that."

Gene looked down the row to see Kurt bend forward, looking down. Grandma Bea had told Gene that Kurt had come to see Grandpa, as Grandpa had hoped he would. Kurt had come down from the bedroom crying, and he had told her, "I made some promises; I hope I can keep them." Gene hoped so too. Kurt hadn't come to see him yet; Gene resolved to find ways to spend more time with him.

Elder Tanner and Elder Romney each took a couple of minutes, and the meeting did go over an hour—but only a few minutes—and then the congregation sang "Firm as the Mountains Around Us." Gene, as the oldest grandchild, had been asked to say the closing prayer. He got up and walked forward as the hymn was ending. It was all he could do to get the words out, but he said, after addressing the Lord, "We wish to remember the way we feel this day. We wish to live as our grandfather lived. We wish to remember that we are the 'youth of the noble birthright' and to carry on what others have begun for us."

After the funeral, the family drove in a police-escorted procession to the Salt Lake Cemetery, all the cars with their headlights on. Uncle Richard had been asked to dedicate the grave, and he did it softly and articulately, as he did everything. Then everyone returned to Grandma's house, and the feeling was like so many gatherings before. Gene loved being there more than anyplace else in the world.

~~~

Kathy was happy to get back to Grandma's house. The funeral had touched her deeply, but she didn't want any more sadness today; she wanted to gather with all her cousins and uncles and aunts, and she wanted everyone to be happy, the way they had always been in this house. And she did feel the happiness immediately when she got there. People were laughing and talking and eating, and Grandma was in the middle of it all, looking herself, plump and pretty, and smiling as much as anyone.

Kathy got herself a plate of food in the kitchen and then slipped out to the porch. It was hot out there, so not a place many would be looking for, but she had a feeling she knew who would. After a time her hunch proved true. Gene showed up, saying, "I've been looking for you, Kathy." He sat down in the chair swing with her. And only a few minutes later, Diane appeared. "I thought I'd find you two out here," she said. She sat across from them in an old wicker chair.

Kathy loved these two cousins, and she hadn't seen them very often since she had moved to Heber City. It had always been their tradition at family gatherings to find each other and compare how things were going.

"When you come here," Kathy said, "do you always think about that time we talked on Christmas day about what we were going to do with our lives—or am I the only one who does that?"

"I think of it *very* often," Diane said, "and not just when I'm here."

"I remember what you told us, Diane," Gene said. "You wanted a good husband and a family, and what?—a nice house to live in?"

"That's right."

"I thought you were *so* incredibly shallow," Kathy said. "That sounded like the worst thing in the world, just to get married, have babies, and do nothing important. Now look at me."

She patted her middle, even though she wasn't showing yet. "If someone had told me I'd be living in a small town *in Utah*—and I wouldn't be out fighting to save the world—I would have been furious."

"Aren't you fighting for anything now?" Diane asked.

"Actually, I am. I've been involved in a bake sale for the Friends of the Library." She laughed, and so did Diane and Gene.

Diane had been chewing, and she actually choked a little, but when she stopped coughing, she said, "But that's great. What's more important?"

"Here's the thing," Kathy said. "We raised some money, and we turned the money over to the librarian. She's already ordered some books. So we changed the world. We did something, and it worked. All the years I was out there fighting for this and that, I was never sure we accomplished anything."

Gene was holding his plate, not eating at the moment, but he was keeping the swing moving a little, pushing forward and back. Kathy liked the motion. "I wouldn't say that," Gene said. "When students started protesting the war, I kept asking, 'Who cares what a bunch of students think? How's that going to change anything?' But look what happened. Students raised the questions and forced a lot of people to answer. It took a long time, but these last couple of years, almost everyone wanted the troops to come home."

"I know," Kathy said. "I think a lot about that. And we've seen some progress in civil rights. But sometimes I wonder whether our protests didn't slow things down. We did raise questions, but we also made people mad, and then they got defensive. I wonder now whether we couldn't have raised the questions without being so angry and accusing."

"I doubt it," Diane said. "People don't pay any attention until a problem gets shoved into their faces. I think most people were happy to let blacks sit in the back of the bus forever. When Rosa Parks said no, a lot of people had to ask themselves whether she was right or not. And there was no good answer. That's when things started to change."

Gene was laughing by then, and Kathy knew why. So Kathy said it. "Diane, I remember talking about Rosa Parks back when we were all still teenagers, and you didn't even know who she was."

"I know," Diane said, and she laughed at herself. "But that's my point. If the whole race question would have been left to me, I would have thought everything was fine. Sometimes it takes someone like her to get people's attention. And it took someone like you to tell me about her."

"So tell me this," Gene said. "How do we each feel about the way things have turned out for us so far?"

"I'm disappointed," Diane said. "I thought life was going to be a fairy tale. I was sure I'd know the right guy when I met him, and everything would be perfect from that point on. I didn't think I could marry a guy in the temple who would do the things Greg did to me."

"We were all pretty naïve," Gene said. "I didn't say so, but I always wanted to be a hero, like my dad. I don't think it ever sank in that if I went to war I could actually get shot."

"You were going to be president of the United States," Kathy said. "Remember that?"

"Sure. In those days, it seemed that anything I wanted would be mine. It always just happened that way for me. It was like I was walking six inches off the ground when everyone else had to trudge along in the dirt. I don't know why I felt that way, but it almost destroyed me when I lost all that."

"So now what? No politics?"

"I don't know; it's still possible. But Grandpa told me, there at the end, to worry about my family first and not to worry about a political career—just the opposite of what he told me for so many years."

"But do you still think about running for office?"

"Yeah, I think about it. I see what my dad has done, and I still think maybe I could run for something. I don't know enough yet, but I think I'll learn a lot from being a journalist. I'd just like to make a bit of a difference somewhere. Dad says to do it with my writing."

Now it was Kathy's turn to laugh. "Make a difference. That was what I was all about. Now, I want to make a difference in my family and my ward and maybe my town. The way I see it, all those little differences add up to the big ones anyway."

"Yeah. That rings true," Diane said. "But I'm just scraping to make a difference to my little daughter. I may never have time for anything else."

"That's the most important difference you can make," Gene said. "I've let Danny down. I've got to work the rest of my life to make sure he's okay. It's what everyone said at the funeral today. We have to take the good things we get from our parents and grandparents and make sure they get passed along to our children."

Kathy thought of the change in all of them. Back in 1961, when the three of them had looked ahead, life had had a certain look to it, a feel. And now, nothing looked quite the same. She didn't exactly regret where she had been—although she regretted some of her choices—but she found it almost alarming to think she had made so many decisions without knowing much about life. No wonder she had frightened her parents.

The three seemed to sink a little into themselves as they ate quietly for a time, their paper plates on their laps, but then the screen door opened and Grandma Bea came out. "I wondered where you three were," she said. "You're still good friends, aren't you?"

"Better than ever," Diane said.

"Well, the three of you have worried me to death. I hope you'll stop doing that now."

Kathy thought how true it was. Diane and her divorce. Gene and his terrible wounds. And Kathy herself wandering off, lost to the family for such a long time. But Kathy said, "I think we're okay now, Grandma. I don't see much to worry about."

"Oh, Kathy, there's always plenty to worry about," Grandma said, and she laughed. "That's my specialty." She sat down in the other wicker chair. "People never know what life is going to throw at them. But I do feel good about the three of you. I'll try to worry more about some of the others." She hesitated and then asked Gene, "Have you heard the news about your cousin Hans Stoltz, in East Germany?"

"Yes," Gene said. "Mom told me a while back, and I talked to our grandpa at the funeral today. He's really happy about Hans."

"Poor Heinrich. His health isn't good," Grandma said.

"So what's the news about Hans?" Kathy asked.

"His wife is going to have a baby this fall," Grandma said. "Horst is thrilled to death. He wants a heritage to continue in his homeland. He feels like the gospel is surviving behind the iron curtain—and Hans and his wife are playing a role in that."

"That's wonderful," Diane said.

"But what about you, Grandma?" Gene asked. "Are you going to be okay?"

"Why do you ask that? Do you think I can't manage by myself?"

"No. I know you can do that. But I think you're going to be lonely."

"I know. Just don't feel so sorry for me that you drop off your kids all the time to keep me company." She laughed in a burst. "No. Just kidding. But I think a little loneliness will be sort of interesting. I plan to learn something new from it. There's no end to what a person can experience in life, and every experience has its benefits."

"That's a good way to think about it," Diane said.

"You should know, honey," Grandma said. "You're alone so much. And you've sent your friend away. Is that going to be okay?"

"I needed someone like Lloyd for a while, just to look after me. But I guess I'll learn something about faucets and screen doors now."

"Don't you know a man who would be glad to fall in love with someone who's smart and good and lively and interesting—and beautiful besides?"

"No takers, so far," Diane said. "But you know what? If I'm single the rest of my life, I'll deal with it. I'm twenty times stronger than I was before I left Greg. And if that's all I get out of life—strength—that's not so bad. I was pitiful before. I could have gone back to the Lord, and he would have said, 'Didn't you learn *a thing* during your life?' And I don't know what I would have told him."

"I know. But you can learn from happiness, too. You need someone. You should be looking."

"I do look. I'm just not going to marry someone out of desperation. If I marry again, this time I want someone worth having."

"Well . . . that's right." Grandma looked at Kathy. "And who would have expected Kathy to be the little homemaker?"

"I'll never be little, Grandma."

"No, you won't. You're a giant—and I'm not talking about how tall you are. I'll bet the people in your ward love you."

"I love them. I hope they love me."

"And you're happy?"

"More than I ever thought I could be."

"You too, Gene?"

Gene looked away. He took his time before he said, "No. I'm not terribly happy, Grandma. I'm still working to be okay." He set his empty plate on the floor of the porch. "I can't seem to get the joy of life back. Every day is an effort, just to keep thinking right. But I'm a lot better with Emily and the kids. And I'm way ahead of where I was last year at this time. That's a good sign, I think."

"I hope I can say that in a year," Grandma said, "that I've moved ahead with my life."

"What are you going to do now, Grandma?"

"Oh, my. Everything. For one thing, I've got a stack of books I've meant to read. But you know me. I love to sew, and to put up fruit, and I think it will be fun to clean my house from top to bottom, like it's never been cleaned before. I'll tell you something else. Al, bless his heart, was kind of a stick-in-the-mud. I want to go up to the University and see some of the plays and get tickets to the Utah Symphony. I've got friends I can go with. I'm thinking about traveling a little, too. Australia and the Holy Land, and maybe India."

"India?"

"Maybe. I don't know if I really would ever go. But people say that once you go there, you're never the same again. I wouldn't mind seeing why."

Kathy loved Grandma. She wanted to be what she was. She had, as much as Grandpa, guided this family, and she had done it with the force of her good nature, her love of life, and her love of her children and grandchildren. She had gone through lots of pain in her life, and plenty of disappointment, but she looked into the future and accepted all the hard things along with the good. Kathy wanted to be like that.

Kathy looked up at the mountains, brown now and gray against a good blue sky. She thought about the baby inside her. She wondered what sort of little spirit would be coming. She hoped its mind—and heart—would turn toward the family. It was scary for Kathy to think that she might have a little girl or boy like herself—such a big worry—but she also hated to think that her children would accept everything she said and never think for themselves. The whole idea of it—another generation coming along—sounded exciting, but she knew she was idealizing again. Hard things would come with the good. Grief and worry would surely come to her and Marshall—and to Diane and Gene and their families. But if the next generation could struggle through as well as this one was doing, it wouldn't be perfect but it would be good. Kathy thought of the generations that would keep coming, and she hoped they could link their hands, one to the next, looking forward but remembering the past. There would be so much learning and growing to do. But that was all right. As Grandpa always said, that's what life was for.

AUTHOR'S NOTE

O nce before I said good-bye to the Thomases, and they came back to life almost immediately. I doubt that will happen again. Ten books is enough. And yet, it's strange for me to say that. It's 2005 as I write this, and I started researching for *Children of the Promise*, the first series about the Thomases, in early 1994. That means I've devoted eleven years of my life to the two series. I've gotten up with the Thomases almost every morning, revised each of the ten volumes six to ten times, and read hundreds of books to collect the information I've needed. The research and writing—and everything that went with it—have changed my life in all kinds of ways. Perhaps the best part of the experience is the relationship I've established with the many readers. More people have read these books than anything else I've written.

I feel a little as though I've grown old along with President Thomas. I was fifty when I started, and I'm nearing sixty-two now. But I haven't lost my love of writing. In fact, I have the same dream now I've always had. I want, sooner or later, to write a really fine book. I always think it will be the next one. So I'm going to continue to write. In fact, I'm already working on another book set during World War II. In my research, I found things I wanted to write about that didn't fit into the Thomas stories, so I'm going to probe some of those matters in a novel about new characters in a different setting. This time, though, I only plan a single novel and not a series. Kathy, my wife, serves in the General Presidency of the Relief Society. When the time for her release comes, we plan to serve a mission, so it's not the right time to start another series.

Let me leave you with one warning. I notice that a kind of myth has built up about my research for *Children of the Promise* and *Hearts of the Children*. It pleases me that reviewers have applied the word "meticulous" to my use of historical detail, and I have tried to be thorough and careful. But I've made many mistakes over the years. Each book has elicited letters correcting little things I've gotten wrong. That doesn't surprise me at all, and don't misunderstand; I appreciate the letters. I'm often able to correct my mistakes in second printings. My warning, however, is never to trust a historical novelist entirely. History is hard to pin down, and in trying to be specific sometimes I have to make guesses. My advice is to read historical fiction for what it is—a method of making an era or event "experiential"—but if you're going to choose between historical fiction and history, choose history. Still, let me say, as I've said before, I've tried very hard to get things right.

Incidentally, the first book I published with Deseret Book was called *Under the Same Stars*. It was Mormon historical fiction for children, set in Jackson County, Missouri. Three sequels followed. The first three of those books have now been reissued under the series title *The Adventures of Young Joseph Williams*. So I'm being recycled. But what I hope is that another generation of young people will gain an appreciation and understanding of the great people who established our church.

Most of the resource books I used for *So Much of Life Ahead* were ones I have already included in my suggested reading lists in previous volumes. In order to remember the details of the Watergate scandal, I did reread *All the President's Men*, by Carl Bernstein and Bob Woodward (Simon and Schuster, 1974), which remains a fascinating account. I also read *Watergate: The Presidential Scandal That Shook America*, by Keith W. Olson (University Press of Kansas, 2003). It's a thorough book on the subject, well worth reading.

So Much of Life Ahead is my thirty-second book with Deseret Book. I've spent some years of my life at universities, and I've published with several publishers in New York, but the only organization I have a sense of tenure with is Deseret Book. Over the quarter-century-plus I've worked with Deseret, the company has grown exponentially, and it is now as big as many of the great national publishers, but during all those years I've always been treated as an individual and, even more, as a friend. I have outlasted many of the editors and staff members, but as the personnel has changed, my connection to the people has never been lost. One person who has been with Deseret Book as long as I—or close to it—is Jack Lyon. Over the years he has edited many of my books, including the volumes of *Children of the Promise* and *Hearts of the Children*. He's done much of the copy editing and has saved me from many an embarrassment. Besides that, when a mistake does slip through, he's been someone I could blame. I've joked with him over the years that when I write a good sentence, it's my work; when I write a bad one, it's his fault for not fixing it. I'll just say, here, that he's fixed plenty. I dedicate this book to Jack as a way of thanking him for all the devoted work, and also, if he doesn't mind, I'll use him as a symbol of all the editors and employees at Deseret who have been involved in this huge project. I feel blessed to have worked with so many genuinely good people.

ABOUT THE AUTHOR

Dean Hughes has published more than ninety books and numerous stories and poems for all ages—children, young adults, and adults.

Dr. Hughes received his B.A. from Weber State University in Ogden, Utah, and his M.A. and Ph.D. from the University of Washington. He has attended post-doctoral seminars at Stanford and Yale Universities and has taught English at Central Missouri State University and Brigham Young University.

He has also served in many callings, including that of a bishop, in The Church of Jesus Christ of Latter-day Saints. He and his wife, Kathleen Hurst Hughes, who has served in the Relief Society general presidency, have three children and nine grandchildren. They live in Midway, Utah.

If you liked this book, you'll love the *Children of the Promise* series by Dean Hughes!

What was life like during World War II? How did the war affect the lives of those who fought and those who kept the home fires burning? Find out in *Children of the Promise*, the carefully researched and beautifully written story of a family living through those turbulent years from 1939 to 1947. Meet the characters readers have come to love: Alex, who served a mission to Germany and returned to fight those among whom he had preached; Bobbi, a Navy nurse with a divided heart; Wally, a young rebel who finds his true path in the trials of a prisoner-of-war camp; and many others. *Children of the Promise* will touch your heart in an unforgettable way!

Volume 1: *Rumors of War*

Volume 2: *Since You Went Away*

Volume 3: *Far from Home*

Volume 4: *When We Meet Again*

Volume 5: *As Long as I Have You*